Frozen

Music

Frozen Music

Michael J. Vaughn

Northwest Publishing, Inc.
Salt Lake City, Utah

Frozen Music

BK 7-28-94

Edited by: G.E. Bloomsburg
PRINTING HISTORY
First Printing 1995

ISBN: 1-56901-360-8

NPI books are published by Northwest Publishing, Incorporated,
6906 South 300 West, Salt Lake City, Utah 84047.
The name "NPI" and the "NPI" logo are trademarks belonging to
Northwest Publishing, Incorporated.

PRINTED IN THE UNITED STATES OF AMERICA.
10 9 8 7 6 5 4 3 2 1

To my mother,
Grace Maze Vaughn
(1937-1993)

"A stone is frozen music."

—*Pythagoras*

Chapter One

Sunday
Prelude, presto agitato

Sadness underpins everything, nudging at you, circling your eyes like a summer gnat. Waving at it does no good, because it is small and light and vents off along the wind created by your hand. Forget it. The end of the day brings a list of external positives—a pay raise, a wink from Susan in sales, a day with no discernible memories—but nothing alters the basic gloom. The gloom throws in odd chemicals with long, scientific names, turning things into things they are not, twisting your life around until defeats are tragedies and victories defeats, for the simple reason that they are victories over sadness.

Am I a lunch-bag lunatic, or is this what happens when you grow up? That is, after all, what I'm counting on—that this is a process, that these are just the hellfire steps on the way to adulthood.

Looking at it from the other side of the screen, my life back then had a great tragic focus. That one overpowering situation sucked in my small sadnesses like a planet drawing asteroids. All other things took on a patina of joy. If you want to know the truth, I might have preferred it that way. The main thing? I *wanted*. I wanted intensely, I wanted *her*, and I lived. Today, today I am a cow in a pasture. I do not smell or hear or taste the world; I just lower my head and graze.

My tragic opera has been sung. The double bass player is trundling his load stage left from the orchestra pit. I should be happy, but I long to be back on the risers, singing my damn heart out. At the least, did I learn to love? Did I learn that I *could* love? Dammit, it had to be for something.

I begin with a bit of prehistory. Before I made my entrance, an event I can only imagine made what was to be a large dent on my life. By now I have cut it apart, thrown in details that may have never existed, and inserted myself into all three roles just to try to understand why this clichéd bit of melodrama would have such an effect on me.

A California businesswoman attends a week-long series of meetings at corporate headquarters in New Jersey. By Friday noon the meetings are over, and, anxious to return home, she switches her next-morning tickets to an overnight red-eye and grabs a cab to Newark (or possibly LaGuardia).

She lands at San Francisco International at five in the morning, and by the time the airport shuttle delivers her home to Santa Cruz, the sun is lifting over the coastlands to the east (Watsonville, Monterey, the long low strip of Sunset Beach). She unlocks the door to her condo and stumbles in, throws her bag on the couch and heads upstairs to the bedroom.

Her live-in boyfriend is a dark, burly Italian guy who is always the hit at parties, beer in hand, arm around a buddy, East Coast born and bred like our heroine, pleasantly rough around the edges. Our heroine looks forward to noontime when she will talk with him and swap stories about the old home territory, but for now she is dead on her feet and wants only to hop in bed next to his big warm body and sleep.

Only—and this you could have expected, because why else would I set you up like this?—her place is taken by someone else. This stranger's name is Barbie or Debbie or something else with an "ie" on the end for bounce, and she is just some secretary or schoolteacher or waitress who wanted some sex for the weekend and she and the likable Italian guy met at a bar and things…just…happened.

Our heroine enters the bedroom quietly so as not to wake her beau, but as she is removing her second black pump she looks back and counts one, then two mounds under the sheets. The picture hits her straight in the diaphragm, and before she can stop herself she lets out a high-pitched gasp. The larger of the two mounds rolls over and peers at her.

At this point the average Hollywood hack would have the big galunk chasing her down the stairs in his briefs, saying something stupid and useless like, "Honey, it isn't what it looks like," and the comedy would be under way, but not here in the real world. Our heroine stares at him in shock; he stares back in shock and shame, his big dark eyes that once glinted with amiability now as empty as a dog's. For three and a half seconds the frame freezes, then quietly, quickly, she leaves her shoes where they are and escapes out the door.

The burly Italian guy stares at his face in the dresser mirror until he comes to complete consciousness and realizes that what has just happened *has just happened*. He nudges Kellie or Connie awake and tells her he's sorry, but something terrible has happened and she has to leave right now.

As for our heroine, as for Stacy (or Stace, as they call her in the office, because two syllables seem just too stuffy for this one), she is downstairs at the kitchen table, drinking a strong cup of coffee because she knows this day will not end soon; this day will last a long, long time.

They have been together seven years. They bought this condo together, and a sailboat, and her car and his truck and the timeshare up in Tahoe. They are not married, but these next few months will be as thorough and harrowing as a divorce. She will lose her security; she will lose sleep; she will lose weight. She will lose money and time during long afternoons in a therapist's office. And she will meet a gullible, insecure young man and change his life in dramatic fashion.

In the large view of things, it is alarming to think how different life would be if the burly Italian guy with the bad sense of timing would have refrained from his pleasure that Friday night. Don't drink that fifth beer, buddy. Don't ask Shellie or Terrie to dance. Pay no attention to the way she grinds her hip against your groin, the way her tongue licks across your lips when you kiss her. But forget it, it's too late. The puzzle pieces are all in place. Go ahead, lift that sucker up, thrust it to the wall and watch the cardboard scatter, but you are only kidding yourself. You've seen the big picture, buddy, and it will take more than a fit of anger to get it out of your head.

Tonight, done with my weekend rituals, I girdle myself in this hunk of old oak and varnish, sweating over the desktop, grinding out flashbacks to clear my mind. The process is tiresome, and the heat is not helping; the sun soaked into the ground all day and now the warmth is back up, tearing at my pores. I keep a towel draped over the corner of my desk and when the sweat starts dripping onto the page I take a swipe at my forehead.

But the heat is not the only problem; other elements are at work. Specifically, two tomcats staging a fierce tête-à-tête down in the echo-chamber concrete of the parking garage. The sounds they make land somewhere between the scrape of a fork against fine china and the screams of a woman (a lyric soprano, I think) being slowly tortured to death. This is not conducive to creative writing.

A half-hour ago I gave up and stormed outside, frustration prickling at my sides like the needles of a cypress bush. A double-helix lightning bolt—Satan's own glissando—rolled in from somewhere between parking spaces sixty-five and sixty-nine. I squatted down at the small rock garden between my studio and the courtyard lawn and picked up five or six good-sized projectiles.

The rest of this feels something like a scene from *High Noon*. The stranger steps sideways into the glare of the fluorescent lights, weapons at his side, squinting, anxious. A second man drops down from the stairs at the other end of the garage and takes a similar stance, his hands holding what look like two small pieces of firewood. The stranger recognizes the stickfighter; he has seen this man in the laundry room. He is good, he is quick; he uses the right detergent. They are comrades in arms, joined in a fight against the big loud cats. The stranger waves a rock-loaded hand in silent salute, and the stickman waves back. They pace forward, listening, quiet.

When they are thirty feet apart, they hear a sudden scuffling and spot their prey, faced off on the hood of a mint-condition red Porsche. They are stunned; the big loud cats are smarter than they thought. The men cannot risk the welfare of so prized a possession. They are frozen for a second, but then the stranger runs at the Porsche with sudden fury and yells.

"Hah! Get outta here!! Whattya think yer doin'?!"

Like if they knew what they were doing they were gonna tell *me*. My stick-wielding friend yelled similar inanities and between us we managed to get their attention. They jumped a ledge and skittered into the bushes—a black one with white spots, a white one with black spots, although I can't be sure if they started out that way. As soon as they cleared the Porsche I chucked a rock after them but missed by a foot. The other guy couldn't do a thing but watch them go, firewood being a less accurate force than rocks. When we were sure they were gone, I turned to him and tried to think of an appropriate thing to say.

"Well," I said. "Ah'd best check in mah weapons befo' de sheriff come to get me."

The other guy laughed and said better luck next time and headed back up the stairwell. Maybe I'll see him in the laundry room some time and we'll trade war stories.

Between the adrenaline of the hunt and my third cup of

coffee, I wasn't ready to so much as *think* about sleeping, so I just sat at my desk wiping sweat from my brow, trying to figure out where the hell things are going for me. For God's sake, someone get me a road map. Which way out of this big side-of-beef lonely? I walked over to the dresser, staring at myself in the mirror, thinking about picking up *A Tale of Two Cities* for the fiftieth time, hoping I didn't have to.

God hears even the prayers of agnostics, I suppose, because just then I heard footsteps on the porch. It was Brownie.

Brownie is my next-door neighbor. Brownie is an alluring young woman with a sweep of chestnut hair that bobs when she walks, and that is why I call her Brownie. I watch her every morning when she leaves for work. She must have a job where legs pay—receptionist, secretary, aerobics instructor—because she always wears miniskirts, and always wears them well. I've lived next door to her for three years but have never had the nerve to introduce myself.

So Brownie clicks across the porch and opens her door, an action which you can't miss because the stripping in this place makes a sound like a rubber suction dart being pulled from the side of a refrigerator. I lie sideways on my bed and hold my ear against the wall. The lock clicks as she shuts the door. Dishes in the sink, then the scraping of furniture against tile—a stool.

Then voices. One voice was Brownie's, the other belonged to a man, not an especially low voice but definitely male. I couldn't make it out exactly, but I figured it was that guy I see her with sometimes. I think they're engaged, they sort of act that way. You know, not hanging all over each or anything but sort of…comfortable, familiar. By now I was having a hard time keeping my ear to the wall; my neck was stiffening up.

Seems like Mr. Brownie was really in the mood because he was engaged in some heavy-duty smooth-talking. His sentences, the rhythm of his speech would dip around, then down, and then sort of flutter at the ends, a poetic roller coaster. This guy was an artist, a woo-pitcher first class. I wheeled my arm around to loosen up the works then reattached myself to the Sheetrock, pressing harder to see if I could make out actual words.

The next thing I know, Mr. Brownie turns on some music, an old swing jazz tune played from a scratchy, tinny-sounding record, and I couldn't be sure, but they sounded like they were dancing in the kitchen. Had to be. I'm almost sure Brownie's studio has the same layout as mine, carpeting everywhere but the kitchen, so where else could they be making these tapping, sliding, shuffling sounds? Lord knows how they were doing it in such a small space, but give them credit for trying. And they were good, too, every move right in the flow, occasional step on the syncopation for effect, once even a unison clap at the end of a phrase. All I could figure was they took lessons at Arthur Murray or something.

The music dropped off right away, midsong, and I heard Brownie give out a little giggle, followed by the sound of a hand patting Mr. Brownie's back. Then Mr. Brownie started talking again, only this time more serious—a softer tone, straighter, no dips. I couldn't hear Brownie at all.

By this time my left ear had gone numb, so I rolled over on the bed, trying not to bump the post against the wall, and this time I put up my right ear. The fresh ear gave me a different, clearer sound, not stronger but more treble, sharper. I could hear the consonants now, not just the vowels. If I tried real hard I could even make out some words, and it was then that I realized I'd heard Mr. Brownie's voice before.

Mr. Brownie was Fred Astaire. Brownie was Ginger Rogers. And Brownie's television set was right up against my wall.

Chapter Two

Monday
Andante

My name is Michael Moss, born September 29, 1964, named after the badass archangel who kicked the devils out of heaven. I grew up in Sunnyvale, which is a great place to hail from because the name is totally neutral. It sounds like the name some Hollywood executive might dream up for a sitcom. No one ever assumes anything when you tell them you're from Sunnyvale; your identity is safely your own. In fact it is a suburban city of 100,000 in the heart of Silicon Valley, but you don't really need to tell anyone that.

Three years out of college, I needed an outpost for the confirmation of my personal identity, so I loaded up my dad's pickup and jogged over the hill to Santa Cruz, a beachside resort town with dual cases of geocentricism and multiple personality disorder (a walk down the Pacific Garden Mall downtown reveals leftover hippies in beads and tie-dye, Young Republicans in dark blue business suits, and neo-punks in green hair and leather, all surprisingly at peace with one another). I was soon to learn the hard lesson of the Santa Cruz tradeoff: you live in beauteous surroundings, you lose your employment. I quit my clerical job in the valley with the notion of finding a position nearer my new home and found out there was no such animal. Thus began my first and only period of unemployment, and it wasn't a pretty sight.

In some ways, though, I was lucky. From my days as a journalism intern I had a position as a freelance theater critic at the *Coastal Times*, a local weekly, and the publisher was nice enough to give me an advance on my next thirty stories, paying my rent for a couple months. It was through the *Times* two years before that I had rediscovered a childhood passion: baseball, or, in this case, softball. The company team took part in a series of cartoon battles entitled the Santa Cruz Media Softball League, and I found myself an all-star, displaying a knack for fielding grounders and slamming extra-base hits that I had never possessed as a nervous second-string left fielder in high school.

Unfortunately for this team, the people who actually worked on the staff of the paper showed little aptitude or interest in the game. After a couple seasons in the Media League, we had garnered so many ringers we decided to drop out and join a city league under another name. At the conclusion of an early spring practice session (we liked to call them "rehearsals"), my teammates and I sat around under the trees, drinking numerous beers and brainstorming names for our foundling franchise.

Macho names came up: "Terrorizers," "Nuclear Bats," "Assassins." Animal names: "Sea Lions," "Banana Slugs" (the mascot of the local university). Then, of course, silly names: "Safe Sex," "Unruly Beachmongers," and my personal favorite, "One Bad Inning."

The unfortunate winner was "Catch This," which just goes

to prove you shouldn't make major decisions while drinking beer. Sure, I'm the one who came up with it, but I didn't think they'd actually take me seriously. It wasn't until after we printed up the T-shirts that we realized what a terrible mistake we had made.

And so I met Stacy Wilkes on a softball team with a tacky name. I really can't remember when she came; she was just there one day, and I wasn't terrifically drawn to her. She left a vague impression as a bright, attractive woman who drank a lot of beer, couldn't field a fly ball to save her life, and laughed in a cute, slightly nasal way. It's hard to trace the line of recruitment, but the final link was Kenny, our second baseman, who worked with her at a manufacturing plant on the west side of town. He was a marketing rep of some sort; she was higher up, somewhere in the finance department.

One Sunday afternoon we were all gathered around a picnic table after batting practice, drinking—yes, more beers— when, during an animated conversation about golf, Stacy's face and general personality flicked some switch in the back of my brain that said: "This, my son, could be the key to your personal salvation." She said she had just taken it up—golf, that is—and I said maybe we should go shoot a round sometime. Which we never did.

But I took her to the movies that weekend. And I kissed her good night afterwards. No big deal, but I'll always remember the details because she talked about it a lot afterwards. We strolled in a half-burnt evening light to her car, catercorner from the cafe where we had met three hours earlier. I told her I'd had a good time, and she said me too and smiled sweetly, standing next to the corner street lamp, lifting her head just so. I held my hands together behind my back and leaned into it— a shy soldier after his first USO dance, a high school dweeb after the junior prom. My awkward motion embodied a brand of sweetness she wasn't used to, and I guess that's why it had such a powerful effect.

Stacy's friend Kenny was in his middle thirties, balding, and possessed a general unhealthiness from too much booze and too much work. But he was a good friend; he'd stuck by her after the whole rotten thing with her future ex-boyfriend. Kenny knew Stacy better than anyone, and, apparently because he thought I'd be good for her, he helped me out. He pulled me aside after the next week's practice and gave me the rundown.

"She's not ready yet," he said. "If you go after her right now, she'll freak out and you'll lose her. She likes you a lot, so don't give up, but don't go becoming her friend. Just *be around*, and be pleasant, and in about a month go ahead and ask her out again. It'll work, I'm sure of it."

Kenny knew her better than anyone, and Kenny was right.

Time is out of whack, the world is out of whack. We have no time to think straight, and we all know it, but we all seem just as unwilling to do anything about it. Let me take this somewhere.

There are two theories of evolution. We all know Darwin's theory; the other is Lamarck's. To be exact: Jean Baptiste Pierre Antoine de Monet de Lamarck (1744-1829). Rather than spell the whole comparison out in twenty-five-dollar words, let me inscribe the explanation on the back of a giraffe's neck.

Picture this: there is a pre-evolutionary giraffe standing in a field. He is hot. He is hungry. The meteor just hit a couple years ago and wiped out all his dinosaur friends, and the giraffe is thinking he's going to be next because the only available food is up in those high tree branches and he has been cursed with a short, short neck.

Here's what Darwin says: Shortneck survives long enough to have little giraffettes. One of the little guys has a mutation —an unusually long neck. This causes all sorts of ribbing from his school chums until they realize that they can't reach the tree branches and their basketball player friend can. So they all die off except for Wilt; Wilt makes time with a long-necked female giraffe down the street, and...*voilà!* Weird-looking, well-adapted critters all over the place.

Here's what Lamarck says: Shortneck looks up at those luscious, green, vitamin-packed morsels and longs for them, aches for them, wishes like hell he had a big ladder or a long neck or opposing thumbs so he could *just get himself some grub, man!* This deep yearning is engraved onto his little giraffe brain cells; from there it travels downward and is cast onto his genetic equipment. If the poor guy manages to last out the winter and find enough strength to initiate a few little giraffelings, the wish is made material and...*voilà!* Weird-looking, well-adapted critters all over the place.

So here's what I say: The world is changing so fast that we must initiate evolution during our own lifetimes. Either we latch onto Lamarck's theory and yank ourselves off the freeway, or we become global roadkill.

And it all starts with religion. Traditional religion is based almost entirely on feelings of awe, and the last time you felt awe was when you were three years old, standing in the kitchen during a family reunion looking up, up, up at all those giant adults. Or at your mom and dad, who exhibited no discernible faults, possessed all answers necessary to your existence, and ruled over your life with complete authority. That's awe, baby.

These days, the world is too small; we know entirely too much. Awe is an endangered species. Marry this with the massive acceleration of time, and one revolutionary action becomes absolutely necessary: we must invent our own religions. Personal, customized religions, religions carried around in an attaché case with our monogram in gold letters underneath the handle. And with each religion come rituals, the small, regular actions that allow life to be sliced up like a salami into manageable, sandwich-sized pieces. Portioned out by these deeds, the willy-nilly circles of time may drop back from the red line and perhaps, just perhaps, stand still long enough so we can fire off some tranquilizer darts and put a tag in their ears for easy tracking. Let's hope so, anyway.

My Monday night ritual is a trip to the Sunnyvale Community Center, where a large man-made pond stands encircled by lush mounds of lawn. The pond is only three feet deep all the way around, but the dark bottom gives the illusion of lakedom. The whole package is marked off by a fountain shooting a jet of water ten feet high or more, stores of blue turned into foaming white. It's a beautiful place. They have weddings here on the weekends. Around the corner is an orchard of five or six acres, a relic from Sunnyvale's agricultural past.

These days of spring-becoming-summer I arrive at the pond about a half-hour before sunset and walk its perimeter, a wide strip of cobblestone, three times around before I settle down beneath the old, far-spreading oak on its west bank. Peering into its branches I can see wires and cables latched onto its limbs, holding the big tree together.

From my seat at the edge of the pond, I watch the Bachelor Ducks, six or seven mallards who have adopted this structure of concrete and water as their home. I am no expert on duck behavior, but it seems like they're here because all the female ducks have been taken for mating season—a men's club for ducks. They do everything together: wading around on top of the drain cover, billing their feathers, scooping up algae, muttering to themselves in that gravelly, duck-like way. They remind me of a bunch of pitiful single guys hanging out in a bar, and I can almost make out what they must be talking about...

"Ah, fuck women anyway."

"Duh, I'd like to, but I can't find none."

"Ahh, shaddup! You know what I mean. This big, beautiful pond, all the bread scraps you can scrounge, and not one lousy dame to share it with. What I wouldn't give for a little hennish companionship—a nice cozy nest out in the suburbs, two or three eggs to guard, basketball hoop in the driveway—something to live for! I don't know why I hang out with you webfeets, anyway."

"'Cause you ain't got nowheres else to go?"

"Ahh, who as't ya?!"

"Bill, Bill—here, have a shot a algae. On me. You'll feel better."

"Yeah, yeah. Maybe you're right. Fuck women anyway."

"Quack!"

If I had an English-to-Duck translator, I would tell Bill and his buds not to sweat it. Things don't always work out, and besides, the only real tough part of being alone is if you have something else around for comparison. Once you're settled in to this stuff, it can be downright liberating.

It was here at the pond that I discovered the Westfield Community College Choir. It was about a year after my Great Trauma, and I suppose I was looking for a breaking-out party. I was cycling around between the art building and the meeting center when a sky-blue flyer called to me from the community center bulletin board. SINGERS NEEDED, it said and went on to describe the usual crisis situation, a shortage of tenors and basses for the spring semester, a need for people "with some performance and sight-reading ability" to round out "one of Northern California's finest performing ensembles." I committed an act of vandalism by tearing the thing right off the bulletin board and got up the nerve to audition the next week. After so many years I was more than a little rusty, but Mr. Stutz was impressed by my college experience, so he signed me up. He was right, too. My voice toned right up and the music came back to me within a few weeks—you could say it was like riding a bicycle. I've been with them two years now, rehearsals every Tuesday and Thursday, concerts at the end of each semester.

The light of sunset was fading out and I was getting ready to go, when something burst forth from the water. I looked up to see the Bachelor Ducks shooting down the length of the pond together, off, off, barely over the trees with those ridiculous bodies of theirs. They flew a loose formation over the lights of the car dealerships and circled back around, meaty silhouettes against the blue. I swear, the way they go off like that, you'd think they had one brain among them.

Chapter Three

Tuesday
Tutti vivace

Good omens followed me on my drive to Westfield College. I pulled into the parking lot carrying exorbitant hopes of finding a space, cruising the front row nearest the campus. A gray-haired lady in a '65 Mustang took the opportunity to pull out of her spot directly in front of me. I was in shock, but not so frozen that I didn't pull in immediately, lest someone take this heavenly gift away from me. To a Californian, this was the front porch of paradise.

The walk to the Westfield music hall is framed by white stucco classrooms capped in the red clay tiles of Nueva España. It rises to a Great Plains of a courtyard, an acre of concrete centered by a fountain of mermaids and nymphs all gracefully spitting out water. When I arrived, the sun was a

notch up from the horizon; the shadow from the music hall cut
the fountain in two.

The hall stands three stories high, a 1950s modernist box
laced with medieval gargoyles (anachronism is alive and well
and living in academia). The facade is a noble one: three wide
steps with brick fringes flaring up to four arched doors of glass
and steel. The inside is pretty much what you'd expect: a
recital hall with porthole-windowed entry doors, lobby bulletin board sporting concert fliers and class announcements and
pictures of faculty twenty years back when they still had hair.
Around the corner, a hall lined with practice rooms casts out
the smell of piano dust, old scores, and aging linoleum. Swing
around the jazz workshop—bebop session in progress—
through the high-ceiling echo of the elevator lobby, pull a right
just before the back exit, and there she is. The choir room.

I was twenty minutes early, but half the choir was there
already; I guess after two months of rehearsal we're all pretty
hyped about the concert. The choir is a full hundred members,
but the choir room could handle fifty more, easy. The high
walls are covered with acoustic tiles, five-foot-wide saltines
all the way up to the ceiling. The seats semicircle down to the
pit, which holds a podium, two grand pianos, and a chalkboard
striped in musical staffs. The left-hand corner reads "Handel's
wife ran off with a tenor," which isn't all that funny, but it's
been there five years and no one wants to erase it.

I drifted down to my place in the second row and set my
music on the chair next to me. The sopranos to my right were
chatting up tornadoes; they like to come in early so they can
talk about all the people who aren't there yet. Their leader is
Jenny, whose wardrobe style tends toward the military. Last
Tuesday it was an olive-drab jumpsuit with red beret, last
Thursday a white sailor's suit with navy blue trim. Tonight she
wore a business suit, deep blue with black pinstripes. Secret
Service.

But then, for fashion no one matches Barbie, hiding off in
the far corner with her frumpy drape, run-scarred stockings,
and scuffed pumps. She wears her mascara in large moons

around her eyes, circles of rouge like a Raggedy Ann doll, and caked-on cherry-red lipstick. She's a halfway or something, but she must know how to sing because otherwise she wouldn't be here. We don't even know if Barbie's her real name.

Frederick and Frank had their two-man show going in the bass section for an audience of one—Chester, baritone, destroyer of stereotypes. Chester's the only black guy in choir, but he can't sing negro spirituals worth a damn. No rhythm. Frederick and Frank were holding silver dollars over their eyes and making like German counts.

"Who eez zis Brahms fellow, anyvay?"

"Ein meister composer, Herr Friedrich. Zee toazt uff Berlin, I khear."

"But zuch uh melankkholy basssturd, Herr Frawnk. Death und doom, doom und death. Who vantz to lizzen to zuch scheiz?"

"But, Herr Friedrich, I *like* death und doom. Und unrecvited luff ezz aboot mein fffavoritt sing."

Frederick peeked over his silver dollar and studied his Aryan companion. "*You* arrr ein deprezzink perrrzzon, Herrrrr Frawnk!"

Frederick Guttman is a large man with a larger soul. He severed the knuckles of his right hand in a high school shop accident; the missing digits just seem to make his handshake more open. He laughs when he tells the story. "Yeah, when I saw all these free-floating fingertips scattered around the deck of that band saw, I had a distinct feeling something was amiss."

Frank DeBucci is stout—a five-foot-five square. Frank's only handicap is a constantly churning mind and no discernible filter between mind and mouth. I'm surprised he holds it in long enough to sing, although when he does, it's the finest tenor in choir, a soaring, angelic thing. Between them, the two F's make a compelling display.

I was scanning my rehearsal notes when Alex came up and nudged me on the knee.

"'Scuse me, sir."

"Certainly." I pulled in my legs and let him pass. "How are you, sir?"

"Fine, thank you." He took my music from his chair and handed it to me.

"How's the wife and kids?" I asked.

"Wife's fine. No kids yet."

"Still practicing?"

"Have to get it…just…right," he said.

"Right."

It's Alex Blanche—as in *carte blanche*. He's thirty-two, last time I asked, married a couple years now. Wife Betty works evenings at a restaurant. Makes it hard for them to see each other, but he does better in his night classes that way. During the day he's in air conditioning. Alex is a real break from the ego battleground. We've been next-chair neighbors two years now, and we carry on conversations in a different time continuum, minutes between phrases.

"So. How are you?" he said. "Sir."

I picked up the Bernstein and flipped to the first movement.

"I think I'm doing pretty well. Work's rough. Sinuses cleared up, though."

"Good."

"Yes," I said. "Now that I can hear, maybe I'll stay on pitch."

"Good…Good."

He picked up the Bernstein, too, and held it between his knees as he pulled off his work jacket, one of those blue numbers with the name patch—"Al"—over the pocket in script lettering. He opened the score and tapped beats against the page, then stopped and clicked his tongue.

"Are you having as much fun with these weird meters as I am?"

"God, yes," I said. "I've been snoring in seven-four."

He ran over the measures and counted out loud: "One two three four five six seven *one* two three four five six seven *one* two—Oh God, eighth notes now."

"Think of it in duple."

"Duple?"

"Yeah. Like this: Onetwo onetwo onetwo *one*onetwo onetwo onetwo *one*onetwo onetwo onetwo *etc*e-ter a-ad Bernstein *um*."

"Okay." He thought it through again. "That's better."

"Then, once you get that you can just tie the duple notes together: one two three *and*one two three *and*one two three *and*one two three…"

"…*and*one two three *and*one two three…Mr. Moss, you're brilliant."

"Nosir justa drummer *sir*Mr. Alex Blanchuh *sir*."

"Blanch-*uh*?"

"Fit the meter."

"Right."

I went back to my notes. Alex took out a pencil and started scratching in his measure numbers.

"Sure, you've got the meter," he muttered. "Now just sing in Hebrew and on pitch. *Oy vey nakashima*."

I was about to make a comment when the room began to hum. The doors bolted open to reveal the choir president and the assistant conductor and between them Mr. Stutz, straps of plastic bullets across his chest, a huge mascara mustache and a three-foot-tall, rhinestone-studded sombrero. He drew two silver cap guns and fired them at the ceiling.

"Eeeee-*haaaah!* Basses?! We don't need no *stinking* basses!"

He stormed down the steps.

"¡*Amigos!*" he cried. "¡*Arribe! Tutti vivace!*"

That was our cue. We dropped our music and stood as one.

"It occurred to me last *noche, señors y señoritas,* that to catch on to thees *siete/cuatro* time theeng, *nosotros* must theenk *como flamenco* dancers." No one got it. He stomped the floor with his boots. "You know—*flamenco* dancers!"

We got it. Frank DeBucci started stomping along.

"¡*Si! ¡Que bueno!*" he shouted. "*Ahora*, let's try eet all together, *como Señor* Bernstein. ¡*Todos!* One two three *and*one two three *and*one two three *y*-uno dos tres *y*-uno dos tres…"

He clapped each beat and stomped the *and* with his foot. The choir joined in, and the room shook in seven-four. The secretary in the marching band office must have been under her desk by now.

Mr. Stutz stopped and flung his sombrero like a frisbee into the alto section. Everyone stopped except Frank DeBucci, off by the sousaphone lockers, oblivious. Frederick Guttman wrapped his arms around Frank's middle and picked him up, but he kept going, limbs moving up and down like a wind-up toy. Mr. Stutz stood waiting at the podium as Frederick escorted his partner back to his seat and pressed an invisible off button on his back. Frank froze in his place, wearing a stunned expression.

"Good!" said Mr. Stutz. "Okay, now that we're gringos again, let's do some warmups, then we'll sharpen our Hebrew diction. Everybody take a de-e-e-ep breath, and let it out on an *ess*. Hold the diaphragm tight; see how long you can last."

His arms went up, then down, holding the hiss in his fingers—

H-u-hhh, SSSsssssssss-s-s-s-s…

"Hah! The Kwy-ah Boys!"

The men of choir made like infantry across the courtyard, and Sam the Cat greeted us from behind his coffee cart. He stood at the library entrance with three of his colleagues: a slim Persian, a scraggly calico, and a fat mottle of rainy-day gray and yellow we call Largo (musical notation for "slow and broad"). Sam calls him Minestrone.

"Sam! How's the tabby trade? The kitten cartel? The feline franchise?"

Frederick Guttman and his long legs arrived first, and he slapped Sam on the shoulder. Sam flicked a thumb under his mustache and scratched his whiskers. You almost expected him to lick his paws.

"More'n ah kin handle, Freddie. More'n ah kin handle. You in for ya regulah?"

"But of course, Samuel. Coffee black. Cookie, chocolate chip. Gum, spearmint."

"That's ya regulah." Sam grinned and filled a styrofoam cup from his pot. "One hell of ah suppah, y'ask me. Yo momma know 'bout this?"

"Mother dear is in Michigan, Samuel. Remember?"

"Ooooh yeeaahh, I knew that. She call me 'bout yo' eatin' habits, tol' me tah keep a *eye* on you. Says you eats like a hog. I said yeah, thass what keeps me in business, Miz Guttman. Don't know what ah'd do without Freddie, he's a one-man *industry*."

Frederick laughed, handed Sam two dollars and waved him off when he offered the change.

"Ooooh yeeaahh, ah forgot that, too. Young Freddie don' take no change. Makes too much noise jinglin' in his pocket, scares off the ladies 'fore he can catch um."

"Thanks, Sammie. Pet Largo for me."

"Ah tol' you boys thass Minestrone!"

As for me, I bought a cup of coffee, no goodies. I told Sam the Cat thanks but he was already on the next Kwy-ah Boy. Funny how none of the women come out here, I thought. Could be they're tired of us.

By now the action was at a bench off the library lawn, where everyone had gathered for act two of the Frank and Frederick show. F & F were facing off for a round of Can You Top This?

"Tell me, Frank. Do you believe in casual sex?"

"No, Freddie, I like to get dressed up for it. But speaking of sex, you know it truly distresses me that the average American woman will never know the joy of pissing at dartboard urinal targets."

"Oh, Frankie, Frankie. How can I miss you if you won't go away?"

Frank ignored him and shot off another round.

"Did you know the word 'commode' originally referred to an ornate cap worn by women in the eighteenth century?"

"Don't be a shithead, Frank."

Frank steadied an invisible bazooka on his shoulder and fired: "Kazowie! Blam! Pow! Aaaaauuuuuueeeeooooaaagh!!!"

"Ah, sound effects," Frederick boomed. "The call to arms of male bonding."

Two minutes of F & F is enough for anybody. I escaped during a half-second pause and walked back to the bricks by the courtyard fountain. Sitting there I shook my coffee and waves of light sparked off the surface. It settled to a perfect circle, my own Java Moon.

"Hello. Mr. Moss, sir." Alex. "How's the coffee?"

"Fine. Monsieur Blanche, sir. Fine. Warm. Brown. Carcinogenic."

"Such is life."

"Yes," I said. "Where were you?"

"Calling the wife." Alex sat with me on the bricks. "I sort of miss her."

"I can imagine."

"Oh, and no kids yet."

I sort of chuckled. "That's good. Fewer distractions."

"I wouldn't mind. Someday. Hey, you mind if I get a sip of that? That high A tonight is a real strainer."

"Sure. Here." I handed him my cup. "In fact, have the rest. I didn't want a whole cup, anyway."

"Thank you, sir." Alex took a swallow and arched his neck to let it smooth down his throat.

We sat there and didn't say much, didn't need to say much. I could tell by the feel of his silence, he was thinking about her: To have that degree without staying away from her so much. To have those kids, to have the time to watch them grow, but the time wouldn't come for a while.

"Do you know loneliness?"

I'd almost forgotten he could speak.

"Pardon?"

"Do you *know* loneliness?" he said. "Is loneliness an acquaintance of yours? Have you…been to his house? Have you met his family?"

I reached back and dipped a hand into the fountain, the cool water running over my fingers. It took me a while to come up with an answer.

"I knew it," I said. "I don't know it anymore because I call it by another name."

"An alias."

"Sort of. Solitude. Aloneness."

"Hmm."

The wind blows every evening through the valley, and it dies down about an hour after dark. It stopped then, as Alex Blanche sat chewing on my ambiguities. Someone in a trench coat turned a lever somewhere and the trees stopped moving, the echoes deepened. It felt like loneliness. A bat flew over the music hall and let out a G-flat.

"I can't call it anything else." Alex took a last swallow of my coffee and set the empty cup on the bricks. "There's a woman I'm supposed to be with tonight, and I can't, because that was my choice. That was *her* choice. Even if I was with her I'd be lonely because we've put so much into our choices we can't be together without them. Can you understand that?"

"Yes," I said. "I knew that...loneliness."

"Good." He put his hand on my shoulder. "That's what I wanted to know."

I smiled. Alex looked at his watch.

"And now, Mr. Moss, we sing the *Vesperae solennes de confessore.*"

"The Solemn Vespers. Perfect."

We stood and stretched. The Kwy-ah Boys trooped near across the courtyard.

"You seem to lose...attention," Alex said. "During the Mozart."

"Attention? What do you mean?"

He jammed his hands into his pockets.

"When we're doing the Bernstein or the Dvořák you're all energy. You breathe through your eyes. You sit on the edge of your seat. You tap out rhythms while the other sections are running through things. During the Mozart...I don't know, you're just not all there."

I was lost already; the Strawberry Moon.

"I thought maybe because Amy..."

Stacy used to tease me about that when we were going well. Every full moon I'd say it, the folk name some cowboy, farmer, Indian, explorer had made up for that particular time of year. I had an almanac with all the names, and I kept track of them, and I recited them even when she ignored me. The Yule. The Harvest. The Rose. The Green Corn. The Crow. The Strawberry.

"Hey, Mossy!"

Frank DeBucci, leaning out the door.

"Stop playin' werewolf and get in here!"

I gave the Strawberry Moon a last glance and turned to go. I guess Alex had gone in already.

Thinking of the Mozart, I think of lips so smooth and strong they must be chiseled from pink marble.

Chapter Four

Wednesday
Rondo

I woke up earlier than usual this morning and decided to stop for some doughnuts before I went in to work. The nearest place is the Doughnut Drop, at the end of a strip mall catercorner from the community center, next to tacky old Barb's Boutique (offering not hairdos but "coiffures"—for an extra five bucks).

When I pulled up and parked, I noticed an elderly gentleman wandering around by the row of newspaper machines out front. He was wrapped in an overcoat and held his cane far out in front of him as he tottered back and forth. Living across the street from "retirement row," a series of convalescent homes and senior communities, I was used to such sights, but something about this particular old guy sparked my sympathy. He was apparently so bored by the routine of his home that he had struggled his way down here just to check out the day's headlines and stomp around the sidewalk. He'd even dressed in a suit and tie for the occasion.

I stopped off to pick up a paper and realized after a quick search through my pockets that this machine required two quarters and I had only dimes and nickels. I was ready to give up when the old man scooted up to my side.

"What's a matter, ain't got no change?" he asked. "Lemme see 'f I kin help yah out here."

His voice was as worn as an old tire. He braced himself on his cane, angled his back to the side and dug a bony-fingered hand into his front pocket.

"Well, if it's..." I started. "I can always get change inside."

But he was already into it. He pulled out a fistful of coins and held them flat on his palm, then flicked through them with his index finger, separating the wheat from the chaff.

"No really, I can..."

"No problem," he said, still sorting. "No problem a'tall."

Finally he squeezed two quarters together and held them up to me between finger and thumb. I put out my hand, and he planted them there like a seed. I started to pull out my nickels and dimes to pay him back, but he wouldn't have it.

"Never mind," he said, flashing a toothy grin. "Me, I got plenty. You have yourself a good one."

With that he struggled off the edge of the sidewalk and scuffled across the parking lot toward the community center. I watched him go, then spun his silver gifts into the slot, thinking what a dangerous thing it is to feel sorry for someone.

I saw a woman today. She was in the underground parking garage, sitting in her car, eating a sandwich. She didn't know I was there, back in the shadows of the stairwell. She stared at the pickup in front of her, like any second a message would flash out from its headlights. Lunch was just another slot in the daily schedule, another line to be checked off in red pencil.

That's how I feel about my work. My work has nothing to do with me; these petty efforts I make between the magic hours of eight and five just don't mean much when it comes to the sum definition of my life. I work at a car finance firm, National Auto Credit, in the accounting department. I send out titles for paid-in-full accounts. At the end of the day I work the mailroom. In any case, it's better than being in the credit department, playing the villain, squeezing money out of people. That's got to be tough. Sending out titles is a lot mellower. Sometimes I even get to send one out to someone I know: my editor, my old Little League coach, some long-lost schoolmate.

I'm something of an oddball around here because I occasionally use my brain. They're very dense people, really. Nice, but not very sharp. Who am I kidding? They're not very nice, either. And I'm not bitter about any of it. Really. I just know that my mission here is to make a paycheck and go home, so why make an emotional investment out of it?

My deskmate Naomi was her peculiar self this morning. She had on this hellacious red skirt, oil-slick satin, a big white bow on the back, at her waist. The senior prom all over again.

"Mike? Do you mind if I ask you a *very* personal question?"

First thing in the morning. Imagine. I wasn't sure what to say, but Naomi wasn't really waiting for an answer.

"Where'd you get that black jacket you were wearing yesterday? You know, the double-breasted one with the big buttons? I was thinking, you know, I might like to get one for my boyfriend."

I released a silent sigh and told her the store, the rack, the price. Then I went for more coffee. I think in Naomi's world, a question about clothing really *is* a terribly personal thing. Maybe all those years of trying to explain how she can afford such a wardrobe on her income.

"Michael, do you have any girlfriends?"

Naomi never asks permission for *really* personal questions, she just jumps right in. I set my coffee cup down and answered.

"No, Naomi. But I *am* working on it. Trust me." I laughed for show.

She took on a funny shyness like she was amazed she asked me the question in the first place. If Naomi wasn't black, I could swear she was blushing; she giggled a little and covered her mouth. I reached into my drawer and pulled out the tools of my trade, seven rubber stamps reading: date, National Auto Credit, received, repossession, rebate due, trade-in and…well, I forget the last one.

"Who is that on your wall, Michael? That cute one there."

"That…" I breathed in too hard and choked a little. "That's a reminder, Naomi."

"Did you…" shy again…"Did you like her?"

"No," I answered. "But I loved her." I'm still surprised I told her that.

She started shuffling papers needlessly around on her desktop, like a news anchor during the credits. "Well, I…shouldn't be…that's your business, not mine."

"It's okay," I said. "I don't mind."

I opened my red stamp pad and smoothed it over with an ink roller. This job is nasty with ink. I go home with red fingers, red forearms, red spots on my clothing. Plus I keep dragging my goddamn ties all over it.

"Good morning, Michael."

"Oh, good morning, Miz Cater."

Speak of the corporate devil. Ms. Roxy Cater, accounting department manager and enigma. She's fifty years old, I know that much. We did the whole birthday-in-black routine last month, tombstones on her desk, gifts of long underwear and prune juice, black streamers everywhere. Aren't officemates a blessing?

The rest of what I know is entirely dependent on company gossip, and around here that's none too reliable. What I hear is that she went straight from college to the convent. She was a nun for ten years, then just woke up one morning at thirty-two and quit. Naturally, the next step was accounting.

She's about as professional as they come—dark blue

power suits, spectacles, a stare that cuts glass, a firm-yet-flexible management style—yet she breaks it up with this odd streak of girlishness. Someone brings up good news in the middle of a serious-as-black-coffee department meeting and Roxy turns into a junior high cheerleader: "Oooh, yay! Way to go!"

Then she goes to these branch parties at Sneakers, the company hangout. Some guy's leaving the branch ("traded to Fresno for fifty crates of raisins"), so we all show up, get drunk, and try not to admit to the branch manager how many office supplies we've snitched that month. And there she is, Roxy Cater, all fifty years of her, doing the twist like she never passed an audit in her life. I danced with her once when she was doing intravenous Long Island ice teas, and I *swear* the woman was eyeing my crotch.

I'd like to be friends with Roxy, and I feel sorry for what I know about her—the bottle of whiskey in her filing cabinet, the afternoons she comes back from lunch barely able to walk—but she knows something about me no one else here has the brains to figure out: I don't belong here. She sees the intelligence in my eyes, she knows I can do better, and she hates me for not telling her why.

I came to the branch as a temp and was brought on board three months later. Roxy thought so much of me she spent five hundred bucks to buy out my contract from the agency. I needed a job—*any* job—and I was grateful to know someone wanted me around. I took her up on it, but I didn't lie to her. I told her I wanted no advancement, no travel, no transfers to other departments; I had no ambitions whatsoever. She just blinked at me and went on to the health coverage.

"Michael, could you come with me to the mailroom for a second?"

Surprise. Roxy was at my shoulder.

"Sure," I said. "Let me sign this one...title. There."

She marched off in front of me. I followed ten feet behind, trying to keep up. She waited for me at the mailroom door, and I pulled out my key to unlock it.

She flicked on the lights and closed the door behind us. "Pull up a stool," she said. I perched next to the sorting shelves; the lunchroom snack machines hummed through the walls.

Roxy paced back and forth, then tried to find a comfortable place against the counter. She straightened one leg and arched the other one alongside, sort of sexy, really, though I was trying not to notice.

"I'm sorry I...picked sort of an odd place for this, but the manager's office was taken already, and I didn't want to talk with everyone else around."

"Oh that...that's fine."

"I was speaking with Mr. DeMartini yesterday, and he mentioned you. He said you seemed very bright. He's seen those party invitations you write, and he was impressed with your written communications skills. Between all the bad puns, you have a very solid knowledge of English."

"Yes," I said.

Roxy switched her legs and reached up to put a strand of hair back in place.

"He said he'd like to have you in his department. You'd make a good account rep, with the right training. Now, I know you told me when you started that you weren't interested in advancement, but I thought I'd at least give you the option. It would mean longer hours, but a lot more money, and it would be much more challenging than what you're doing now."

I thought about it for a moment, studying the names of the dealerships on the mail slots. Johanssen Pontiac. Motor City Mitsubishi. Roxy found some credit receipts behind the postage meter and sorted through them while I mulled.

"No," I said. "No thanks. I'm happy where I am."

I've not often felt as uncomfortable as in that mailroom, while Roxy Cater chased my eyes, trying to plow through the lie I was telling. After a minute I had to look right at her and repeat my answer: "No thanks. Really."

"Okay," she said. She stacked the credit receipts on the counter. "Be sure and sort through the forms in the stockroom this week. I want to trash all the expired ones before we switch the departments around."

"Sure," I said.

I wish Roxy would believe me, but she won't. She's too smart. I wonder if she knows about my degree?

My Wednesday ritual is a swim in the pool at the other end of the apartments. After a dinner of buttered vermicelli and lima beans, I slip on my canary yellow swim trunks, toss a towel around my shoulders and walk out into the courtyard. I pass the ivy-covered fence of the tennis courts, then the path dips down to the pool, double-framed by a rectangle of concrete and black iron fencing. I slip through the gate and toss my keys and towel on a lounge chair.

It's not much of a pool, five feet at its deepest, but the water is a good day's-end therapy. I do a cycle of strokes, a pattern that has changed little in the last two years: two laps of sidestroke, then two freestyle, two side again, then cruise into an easy backstroke. On my second lap of the backstroke I watch the sky straight above me, a dull square of blue, as if the walls come up from the pool and frame it there.

A hummingbird shoots into my square, slowing, stopping dead center. He hovers there and eyes me, shaking his needle of a beak back and forth like a nervous smoker. I stop my stroke and can see through the hummingbird's eyes, over the blocky tops of apartment buildings to the fading line of the sun, then back down to the blue lights of the pool, the dim creature in canary yellow paddling its limbs over the water.

He backs off an inch and is gone, shooting off in a gray streak over the apartments. My portion of sky falls dark, and I dip my head under the water.

Chapter Five

Thursday
Allegro, poco a poco accelerando

There are two early scenes that would later serve as markers for me, and I recount them to you here in almost cinematic form because that's the way they play back in my head: visual, atmospheric, a careful collage of images from which I often try to pull some sense that I might have been able to head all this nonsense off. On this side of the screen, alas, the vision is much too clear.

The first image is a pickup truck backing up to the end of a dead-end road, loaded down with shipping flats from a local manufacturing plant, and ten or so well-tanned men tossing them down to a pile on the beach below. Two hours later the bonfire is hitting its prime, orange flames licking up from the sand and coloring a ring of party-minded people in hues of pleasure. Someone in the ring has a dragon kite. Lord knows why—the wind died off hours ago.

Perhaps the kite is a present because this is a birthday party, Stacy's thirtieth. My backstage pass is the result of my membership on the softball team and nothing more, but after three beers I have convinced myself otherwise. Rough-hewn tug-of-war ropes connect my movements with those of the guest of honor; after all, we have a future together. Only, I am not supposed to act like that. Kenny told me otherwise.

I am trying with all my energy not to seek out the guest of *dis*honor, the burly, likable Italian guy with a beer in his hand and an arm around his buddy. I have information from reliable sources that he is here, and I am wondering more and more if I should leave. I might just see the wrong things. I might just drown in anxieties. But Kenny told me otherwise; I have to at least *be around*. I am a soldier for Kenny's book of etiquette.

I would die for someone to needlessly chat with. For a minute or two, my right fielder Toby does the job reasonably well, talk so small and low the words fade into sing-song mush. But enough! I need a break.

I leave the ring of fire directly after the traditional off-key cantata of "Happy Birthday" and head out toward the waves, a dark, empty slate lying in wait for the chalk marks of a tolerant god. This is a good spot. If it weren't for the fantasy of the newborn thirty-year-old following me out here, asking me why I'm not there with the rest of them, I would find absolute comfort here. If I close my eyes I can hear the worried swell in her voice: "Are you all right, Michael?" And I will feign gloominess to keep her out here with me, bonfire or no bonfire.

But that is not my job. My job is to stand square with the Pacific Ocean and watch one star straight out, blinking on and off as it is buried and unburied by the passing waves. A chunk of black in the shape of a boat moves like a chess piece over the bay, peering ahead with one glowing red eye. My turn is coming. My turn is coming.

The second scene begins with a fade-in, so cameraman take note. The weary sojourner has come in off the highway, his eyes worn to shreds by a patient congregation of oncoming headlights, the back of his shirt crumpled by the ribs of the driver's seat. It is Monday night, the Monday of mistakes, and he must have a beer before he goes home to fight down his bed sheets.

The bar is called the Hind Quarter, and the bar is about as classy as it sounds: phony gas fireplace, varnish an inch thick on the tables, bevy of olding girls hiding behind blonde caps with arrow-straight hinges of dark roots. Tonight the pretzels are out by the bowlful, and the men lean T-shirted bellies against the wooden bar, dodging their neighbors' heads, keeping up with the Monday night football game in the corner.

Our heroine sits strangely alone in the center of the picture, placed there with all the artificiality of a Renaissance mural. She has been taken out of her usual frame, a wood-carving of friends drinking ales and stacking green bills like playing cards at the center of round tables. She is as weary as the sojourner, and her needs are more, because she is thinking of what she needs and what he can give her and the distinct possibility that these two forces may meet in just the right places. When he walks in, it is as if she had typed out a purchase order and some remarkable bureaucrat had flashed by two minutes later with three of everything. These things do not happen.

The sojourner is surprised, too. He really had not planned this, but this lone woman is a welcome sight. He is tired of the wait. He is ready to strap on the chute, set the stopwatch, and fly out under the wing. He greets her with a hug and they sit across from one another. His next excuse is provided by the football game floating along in the corner because his favorite team is playing her favorite team, and in order to see these two colored forces smacking each other across the green, he must orbit around to her side of the table and sit...close.

Our heroine's team comes back with a startling last-minute drive and beats the sojourner's team, but he is winning in spite of it because their closeness is not now measured in inches but in breaths, in nudges, in the high soft voice of fabric against fabric and, lastly, in one bold kiss. Right there in the middle of the Hind Quarter. They talk and laugh and whisper to each other about nothing in particular, except for one mutual idea that will draw them out of the bar and back to his bedroom.

His room is small. His bed is small. Headlights flash by across his drapes; his window is too close to the intersection. They pull off their clothes with urgent, clumsy fingers. They are unlettered freshmen in the art of each other, have no notion of how his body fits hers, but still it is the only thing to do. To leave now would be to forfeit everything.

The sojourner nestles himself into the body of our heroine, sketching out her shadow with the lines of his own. Though the feeling is as warm as the color of toasted bread, he knows at the mid-line of a second—they have made a mistake.

Ah, home. Tear off the tie, pull out the shirt, kick off my shoes, fall into my chair thinking, Thank God. I could've stayed pleasantly supine till my rehearsal, but there was my round orange friend, under the dresser, pleading: "Come on, please? Bounce? Bounce?" Poor little guy's so old he can't even hold air. Slick as a watermelon. My little brother stole him from a playground ten, fifteen years ago. I rolled him out and took a few swipes at him with my bicycle pump, then spun him up on my finger, reborn.

My Thursday ritual is a session of hoops at this Catholic school a few blocks down the road. Some Hungarian friend told me once that if a parish had to choose between renovating the altar or buying new backboards, he really couldn't say which would win. We were at a wedding reception at the time—retractable hoops at either end of the hall. I used to go to the city park, but my friend was right, Catholics know their priorities. These have strong wooden backboards, single-wide rims that help out sloppy shooters, and ripped nets replaced within a week.

The sun is out and I am the only soul on the asphalt. I'm even shooting well. My basketball ritual is a numbers game: x number of shots from all around, then, when I'm all warmed up, sink a good long one and off to the free throw line. Sink seven out of ten, and I'm on to the next step. I shoot the ball from the top of the key and let it bounce three times before nabbing it and shooting from the spot. Sink ten in a row and I'm done for the night.

My first round of free throws I get six out of ten, but I sink a long one from the out-of-bounds line and come back for a clean eight. My first attempt at the three-hop game ends at seven when the ball bounces behind the backboard (a tough shot in any book), but I have it the second time around and take my streak up to fourteen before missing a pitifully easy lay-up. You know, I might even get good enough to play in a game someday.

Don't get sucked in by all my mathematics. Basketball is like music: you can analyze it and toss the geometry around until you get nauseated, but you can't define the last leafy touch of the rhythm. The rhythm is a radical element that will not fit into the first six pages of a textbook. You hit a certain righteous flow, sometimes on a single shot. Hop out, ring up the ball, top of the key, slap it behind you, switch it around it falls in your hands just right, not so much *there* as on a string, gather the spring up from your toes, all the way up, limber, nudge it off the tips of your fingers. Curve high, arrow off the bow, no doubt, not a thing but net, and the strings let out a sigh: *Fwip! Aaaahh...* Some shots are not attempted but *imagined*.

So then here's where it gets interesting. I squatted down against an old backstop and opened a book while my round orange friend settled next to me, letting out air. The book was a collection of Shakespeare, and I was into Scene Two, *Henry IV, Part 1*: Prince Hal, Falstaff, stuffy old Henry with the marble spine and the tight ass.

> *Unless hours were cups of sack, and minutes*
> *capons, and clocks the tongues of bawds, and dials the*

signs of leaping-houses, and the blessed sun himself a
fair hot wench in flame-coloured taffeta, I see no
reason why thou shouldst be so superfluous to demand
the time of day.

Four guys drove right out onto the playground in one of
those space-age vans and parked between the tetherball poles.
They were a clean-cut bunch, a range of thirty-five to fifty,
professionals—doctors, maybe. I was back to King Henry
(*My blood hath been too cold and temperate...*) when one of
them was right on top of me. I hadn't seen him coming. This
guy won the clean-cut contest hands down: about thirty-five,
red T-shirt, insignia on the pocket, angel-white tennis shorts,
close-cropped hair. Dentist? Lawyer? Anchorman?

"Hi there!" He flashed a big summercamp grin. "My
friends and I were off to a meeting and we thought we'd stop
and play some two-on-two before it starts. Only we don't have
a ball, and we thought someone here might loan us one."

I sat there blinking like an idiot. What did this have to do
with me?

"Would it be okay if we used your ball for a while? Fifteen
minutes?"

I looked at the ball next to me as if someone else must have
left it there.

"Oh, uh. Yeah. Sure. It's kind of old."

"No problem," he grinned. "So are we."

I reached over and flipped it up to him. He trotted back to
his friends like he'd just won the nickel toss at the fair.

By the time I got to Act II, Scene Three (*There's no more
valour in that Poins than in a wild duck.*), they were still at it.
One more scene and I'd be late for choir. But they were having
so much fun. I mean it. A real blast. Guys must've played
together for years, you could see all the little rituals: tapping
the ball back before an in-bound, calling fouls without arguments, cussing at each other without getting mad.

They made a real group study, too—well-defined types.
The best shooter was the oldest, spunky little fifty-year-old,

overweight, red-face puffing, but a hell of a turn-around jumper. He swore the most, too, every other word. My friend Doctor Stud was just okay, too many muscles for his own good, good passer but no touch on his shot. His partner was a fortyish Irishman with a full head of gray, football-coach burly. Drove in with his height and got away with it. Spunky's partner was a computer programmer-type, probably the youngest, strap-on glasses, curly black hair, fair passer, decent shot. Playing with Spunky, he didn't have to do much but root.

One thing for sure, these guys were all in some kind of shape. Forty-five minutes and they were still going full-bore. I watched them out of the side of my eye, between lines of text, nudging my way into *Henry IV, Part II* (*Hence therefore, thou nice crutch! A scaly gauntlet now with joints of steel must glove this hand.*). It was late; I was cold. The sun fell behind the trees. Maybe five more minutes. Okay, just five more, that's all. The barks and grunts of middle-aged basketball filled up the schoolyard. I kept reading.

They played themselves out at the end of an hour: a point a shot, eleven points a game, four out of seven, Spunky and Curly over Coach and Doc on a final, awkward hook shot. Doc looked over, ran a hand through his hair, checked his watch, spoke to his buddies. At about twenty feet he stopped and rolled it over to me, like if he got any closer he'd disturb my reading.

"Hey thanks," he called. "Hope we didn't take too long. Thanks a lot!"

"No problem," I said.

He gave me a look like he didn't entirely believe me and started back with a wave. Having invested so much in their happiness, I resolved to stay put and act like I was going to read all night. They stood around the van another ten minutes, shooting the bull, tying their shoes, stretching, spitting. Finally they climbed in and circled the playground, waving through the windows. I waved back and waited till they were out of the gate, then tucked the ball under my arm and started the jog home. The sun was long gone; I had to hurry.

I got to the choir room door and checked my watch—8:15, break-time in fifteen minutes. I turned an ear to the crack and heard the *Magnificat* of the Mozart, Amy calling instructions: "You've got to float this one, tenors. If you can't hit it light, then just go into head voice. Carry the tone through with intensity, not bravado. It'll come through, don't worry."

The tenors muttered amongst themselves like—well, like ducks—then she started them through again. Our section sounds pretty damn fine on the high soft ones, even with one of their finest stranded outside.

I sure didn't want to cut into class now and get ninety pairs of eyes staring me down. I slipped out the back door instead and looked for Sam the Cat. The night was getting cold, and in my rush I'd grabbed my thinnest jacket. I needed coffee bad.

"Say-eeh," Sam called. "Ain't you one o' them Kwy-ah Boys? Where's yo' compan-ee-uns?"

"Uh, yeah, Sam," I returned. "I'm kinda runnin' late, y'might say. Ah'm afraid the resta them boys won' be outchere for a while."

I'm a terrible mimic. Sometimes I don't even know I'm doing it. Sam didn't seem to notice it.

"Well, what'd yuh want, uh…"

"Michael," I said.

"Mike. Okay. Whadjuh want there, Mike?"

"Just a coffee."

"Okay, Mike. Ah'll do that."

Sam poured the hot brown stuff into a styrofoam cup while I fished around for my wallet, which wasn't there.

"Oh, jeez."

"What? You foget yo' money?"

"I'm afraid so. I…"

"Hey! Foget it! This one's on the house, Mistuh Mike. I know how these things go."

"Well, thanks Sam. That's…that's great."

"Jus' tip me real heavy next time. I know you Kwy-ah Boys. You's good kids. Enjoy."

I took the coffee from his hands, and I noticed Largo next

to the cart, tonguing his fur like maybe he could get that gruesome color out of it.

"Pet Minestrone for me, Sam."

"Well, huh!" Sam laughed, rubbing his whiskers. "Thass the fust time one ah you Kwy-ah Boys evah got that cat's name right. I was losin' hope!"

"Startin' a new thing, Sam."

"Jus' for that, you don't have tuh tip me nothin' next time. Okay?"

"Maybe I will anyway, Sam."

"Shoh. See yuh, Mistuh Mike."

"Bye, Sam."

I headed for the fountain. Maybe Alex would come out after he'd called his wife. I sat down and sipped my coffee and got to thinkin' (thinkin' in Sam-talk), it's so easy to make people happy sometimes. The name of a cat. A basketball. My price for making five people a little happy. Plus, well, half a choir practice.

"How are you, Mr. Moss?"

I'd expected a tenor voice. This was an alto. This was Amy. Where was my tongue? Oh, there.

"I...hi, Amy. Fine...um...late, I guess."

"I noticed."

I set down my coffee and pocketed my hands to keep them somewhere where I could find them. What was she doing here?

"Um...I'd explain myself," I said. "But you'd never believe me."

"Try me," she said. She sat down next to me and reached back to dip her fingers in the fountain water.

"I had a basketball game, you might say."

"You did say."

"I did. Uh..." Why did she care? "Why do you care?" Did I say that?

Amy pocketed her own hands. Aviator jacket, mall-bought, not a second of flight time. Hazel eyes, islands of green opal in a light brown sea. She followed the choir men trooping across the courtyard, then came back to me.

"Why is it none of the women go over there?" she asked. She'd given up the subject. I was glad. "I always see the men, but never the women. Do you guys look at dirty magazines over there? Or smoke cigars?"

She smiled: no harm done, no explanations needed. Mozart, lips, olive skin. *Magnificat*. Come back, Michael.

"I don't know," I said. "I guess the guys were just there first. None of the girls want to break it up. They're probably sick of us anyway."

"That sounds about right," she said, distracted. Amy stretched and looked skyward, twin puffs of cloud billowing back the yellow suburban light. Her legs swung up and kicked back against the bricks.

"Michael." She placed a hand on my shoulder. "Look at me during the Mozart, okay? It distracts me when you don't."

"I…"

"Oh, I know. Choir veteran like you, old Mozart's a little boring. So logical, four/four, six/eight, la-dee-dah, no tempo changes, no Hebrew, no fireworks. But this is important to me, Michael. I need your eyes on me. Would you do that?"

"Sh-sure. Sure, Amy. I'll try."

"Thanks, Michael." She ruffled a hand over my hair, then stood up and smoothed down her pants.

"I better head back in and talk to Mr. Stutz," she said. "Postgame wrap-up, you know. Alex should be right out; he's calling his wife. See you later?"

I caught a breath. "Yes. You will."

She smiled at me. Mozart. Lips. Chestnut hair.

"Good." Amy headed back, hands in her pockets, walking fast and sure like a veteran aviator toward the music hall. Alex came out and met her at the door. They talked for a few seconds, then he let her through and came out to talk to me.

"Hello, Mr. Moss, sir."

"Hello, Alex. Sir."

"You look a little pale."

"It's…it's cold out here, Mr. Blanche." I reached back and dipped my fingers into the water, just the tips. "Like some coffee?"

Chapter Six

Friday
Valzer cantabile

I read a collection of Grimm's fairy tales last month, and their themes come back like heartbeats. The ugly villain does something to the beautiful victim—lays on a curse, puts her to sleep, occasionally even cuts off her head—and the hero must wander into a dark wood to do something about it: kill the monster, slay the witch, trick the ogre. The details stray all over the place, but one thing remains constant: you must always go into a dark place to save something beautiful.

A month and a half after our first date and four weeks after our Monday night mistake, Stacy and I were settling into a regular dating relationship. We were seeing each other about once every three nights, going to movies, touring wineries, building campfires on the beach, sleeping together on the weekends. Things were really starting to shape up. I had the feeling that the only thing we needed to kick this idea into full gear was a minor trauma, some obstacle to force us into a decision: just how much did we want to be with each other?

One particular Saturday night, sitting in the poolroom bar of the Catalyst in downtown Santa Cruz, I received a telegram informing me that my minor trauma was about to arrive. COD. You see, I had a generational battle on my hands. All our friends from the softball team were Stacy's age or older, resulting in a couple of important conflicts. The first conflict was a matter of possession. I wanted Stacy all to myself; the Love Generation wanted Stacy to play the devoted party girl and member of the gang. The second conflict was drugs. For them, it was an idea they had grown up with, something as informal as a Saturday afternoon barbecue. As for me, I had watched a friend come close to flushing it all down the toilet when he got involved with a small-time cocaine dealer who spent most of her time snorting the profits. In a matter of eight months he lost seven thousand bucks and whatever remained of his innocence. I borrowed a pickup truck and moved him out at two o'clock one morning, just before an anticipated police raid.

So, I'm in this smoky poolroom debating the merits of jazz fusion with Johnny, a former Catch This outfielder who was out for a year after knee surgery. Johnny was driving a tow truck for a living, and he had some pretty good stories, one of which was an emergency job he pulled last weekend with a former Tower of Power horn player. I was on my fourth beer and feeling downright jovial, but I started losing Johnny's story when I saw what my teammates were doing out of the corner of my eye.

"So the guy had a twenty-foot stretch limo, champagne all over the place, and when I was hitching the thing up they rolled down the window a crack and I see this nude woman in the back seat…"

They were gathered at the other end of the bar, a fair

imitation of a football huddle, and it looked like Stacy was the quarterback. They were trading directions and speaking in hushed tones. And giggling. Something was up, and I got the feeling it didn't involve me. A couple of the guys broke off the other direction to hit the restrooms with this weird-looking cat all in leather who I had never seen before, and Stacy came walking our way.

"…and after I dropped them off at the hotel I watched them in the rearview mirror. It wasn't just *one* woman, he had three in there, fer Chrissake! They all got out and…"

"Excuse me, Johnny," Stacy said, nudging Johnny on the shoulder. "Can I have my dance partner back? I think Steve back there wants a word with you."

"Oh…yeah, sure, Stace." Johnny grabbed his beer and wandered back to the bar, tripping over the corner of a table for effect.

What Stacy wanted to tell me was that she and her gang wanted to go somewhere and party, and she was thinking it might be best if I didn't come along. She didn't think I'd understand. What I found out later was that they'd gone off somewhere to snort, and no, in a way I didn't understand, I would never understand. But what could I tell her? I had no other particular reason than the affections of Stacy Wilkes to live for, and why would I want to risk that on some small matter of principle? She at least had the decency to give me an anxious look as she left the bar, but I wasn't sure if that was enough. I waved good-bye, hoping she didn't take it as a sign of approval.

And so I was left there with my half pint of ale, watching the colored balls click and fly across their formal lawns. My thoughts flew off so scattered and deep I could find no outward orbit on which to escape. One thing for sure; I had to go somewhere, do something. I wasn't going to go home and sleep, for God's sake.

Joe Fatazzio held the dual honors of manager of Catch This and owner of a video store downtown specializing in old sci-fi stuff. You know, *The Cat Ate My Brain, X-Men in their*

Underwear, stuff like that. To this he added a third title, that of singer/guitarist, and for ten years he had entertained an increasingly familial ring of fans in the lounge of the Grapesteak Restaurant in Capitola. I had yet to see one of his performances, but I remembered Stacy mentioning they were usually on Saturday nights. Stuck in my bog of pool balls and cigarette remains, this seemed as likable an option as any.

The coastline clouds of Monterey Bay had a habit of letting you know exactly how they felt. During July and August they would huddle up against the land and chill the hills with their cold, wispy limbs. Tonight, now that September had marched its way into the Santa Cruz schedule, the clouds were extroverts, cast out on an ocean cruise across Monterey Bay, leaving the drive south on Highway One a paring-knife slice through moonless night, stars bundled together in cellophane, headlights shooting in stark procession down the hill. This rich aero-clarity pulled the ribbons on my abandonment and made me feel not so bad, like these sudden tones of sadness could be useful things in the right composition, held together by proper thumbfuls of texture and tempo. I circled the offramp and was walking into the lounge of the Grapesteak before I knew it, sitting against the far wall, ordering a seven-and-seven.

Joe Fatazzio leaned to the folk-tinged easy listening matter of the sixties and early seventies: Gordon Lightfoot, Harry Chapin, Pete Seeger, Everly Brothers, that kind of stuff (though he would surprise you once each night with an acoustic-rocker version of "Love Potion Number Nine"). He sang with a soaring, barrel-chested voice that matched his appearance, rough baritone edges to go with his thick beard. I was suitably impressed when someone told me he played straight sets of four hours long, but sitting here in the corner of a Saturday night, I was beginning to get an idea how he did it. Joe's actual singing time was markedly discounted by his propensity for chatter, good-natured quibbling and music trivia.

"This thing, 'Red Rubber Ball,'" he said, setting down his

drink, running a hand over his beard. "Great melody, great hook. Some of the *stoop*idest damn lyrics you ever heard, but you know who wrote 'em?"

"Richard Nixon!" someone yelled.

"Wise ass," said Joe. "Just for that, I'm not gonna tell you. Nyaaah!" The audience groaned. Joe relented. "All right, but let me start from the beginning. These three guys get together at a college in Pennsylvania and form a band, and they get pretty good so they set out for Atlantic City, and this hotshot New York attorney sees 'em one night and likes 'em. This attorney happens to be buddy-buddy with Brian Epstein, the manager of the Beatles, and this new group of his is looking for a name, so mister hotshot lawyer is hanging out with Epstein and the boys one night, and he asks John Lennon what *he* thinks and Lennon says, 'Well, I've always thought a good name for a band would be the Cyrkle.' C-Y-R-K-L-E.

"All right, so the Beatles had a little trouble with their spelling. But here these guys are, barely into the biz, and already they've been christened by His Holiness, the great rock legend John Lennon. The next thing you know, they're hanging out in Greenwich Village, and they meet up with these guys Simon and Garfunkel. The bassist, guy named Tom Dawes, takes a month off from the band to go on tour with Artie and Paul, and Paul plays him this song, 'Red Rubber Ball.' Says he can have it if he wants it. Dawes asks Brian Epstein about it, and Epstein says, 'This song is great, you gotta record it.' So they do, and it's a huge smash, and this unknown band is suddenly at number two on the charts, right behind Frank Sinatra and 'Strangers in the Night.'

"*Then*, as if Epstein hasn't done enough for these schmucks yet, he says the Beatles are coming over for a tour—their *last* tour, as it turns out, in 1966—and he wants the Cyrkle to open for them. So now they've got a hit single, *and* they're playing for 70,000 screaming Beatles fans every night. And who says it doesn't pay to network?

"But here's the capper: Paul Simon offers the band another song, 'The 59th Street Bridge Song,' better known to you and me as 'Feelin' Groovy.' *And they turn it down*. They turn it down!" Joe was aghast at this point, slapping a big hand across his forehead. "The guy who wrote 'The Sound of Silence,' the guy who gave you your biggest hit, Paul Simon, in the flesh, offers you another song, and you say, 'Oh, no thanks, we've got enough songs for now. Really. Besides, you've done so much for us already.' DUH!

"Well, the gods of rock 'n' roll were quick to mete out punishment. By the end of the '60s the group was driven back into obscurity where they rightly belonged, and they broke up.

"Oh, and one more thing. This guy Tom Dawes went on to write commercial jingles. He's the guy who wrote that 'plop, plop, fizz, fizz' thing for Alka-Seltzer."

Joe followed up by playing "Those Were the Days, My Friend," and when he got to the *lah-lah-lah* chorus, he left the last six *lah*'s to the audience. A few of the regulars knew the rules and jumped right in, but most of us came in about two seconds too late, totally disrupting the song. Joe stopped playing and set himself in a look of exaggerated disgust, followed by a shout to the bartender. "Hey, Tommy, no more drinks for these people, okay?" The circle of regulars fell into titters, and some old surfer-looking dude in the corner almost fell off his chair laughing.

This was great medicine; I really owed Joe for this one, and I'd bet in ten years he held a few markers other than mine. Actually, I was feeling so good, I was thinking of calling it quits and heading home, right after this last drink, and just then they walked in.

I never figured out if she brought the party there because she thought I'd be there, or if this was just stoopid luck. Their entrance caused quite a stir, though; they were whispering and walking tippytoe, but in that sort of hyper-drunk attitude that always draws more attention than it diverts. I pretended not to see them, but then Stacy sat right behind me. I froze for a count of three, but then I figured what the hell, I may as well acknowledge them. I turned and found her made up in her bad-puppy face, the cute collie seeking forgiveness for spilling the water dish. What could I ever say to those big brown eyes but yes?

"Hi," she said sheepishly.

"Hi," I said, barely getting it out. She took my hand in both of hers and studied it, trailing a finger over the knuckles down to my wrist.

The custom at Joe's performances was to write your requests on cocktail napkins, then fold the napkin in two around a generous cash tip and pass it to the stage. Stacy wrote something down on hers and put in a five, then struggled up between the tables to hand it to Joe personally. Joe raised his eyebrows as he read it, then went on to the next song, "It's All Over Now." I didn't know it, but my turn was next.

"There's a guy here tonight," said Joe, "and this guy plays a hell of a mean shortstop on my softball team, and apparently he sings, too, because this here napkin says 'Sing with Michael,' and I don't know any song called 'Sing with Michael.' In any case, Michael, why don't you come up here and join me?"

I had heard that Joe invited friends up to sing with him. The last one was this annoying friend of ours who loved to tell us the story of how she sang "Summertime" with Dizzie Gillespie at her parents' house in St. Louis when she was eleven years old because her parents were jazz buffs "and just knew *everyone*." And then she was so drunk one night she got up the nerve to sing "Summertime" with Joe, and she got up there and forgot all the words and the whole thing was as pitiful and despicable as old dishwater.

Hmmm…This was not an encouraging line of thought.

So there I was, sitting at my table after five drinks, suddenly asked to perform, and I was stuck for a song. Competing oldies-but-goodies flew in at me like yellow jackets on the hunt. Being a voice minor, I wanted something challenging. Being a show-off, I wanted something with harmonies. Being a tenor, I wanted something high. And since Stacy was involved, it should logically be something romantic.

All these factors in the course of a ten-second panic

shuffled themselves down to one song and one song only: "If I Fell," by the Beatles. I would never guess at the ironic potential of its lyrics. This, after all, would be Our Song, and as Our Songs go it was filled with skepticism and vengeful- ness. She asked me once if we could change it to something more, you know, *optimistic*, but I said no. Our Songs can't be changed.

I boarded the small stage, and Joe gave me a stool and a microphone. I negotiated the music with him—"You know the low part? Okay, I'll sing the high part. Yeah, that's a good key, that's fine"—and we got down to business. The intro sounded terrible, like it always does because it's so hokey and flat and British Invasion, but once we hit the harmonies we were on it like a cat on new furniture. Joe liked it so much he slowed down the tempo by half just to enjoy the sound. Joe wouldn't think of me as just a shortstop anymore; by the end of the song I had a new audience and a new girlfriend.

Stacy wouldn't take me into her condo that night; she wanted to sit outside for a while. The stars were still up there, eddying through the Indian summer sky. We faced each other on a wooden bench off the courtyard lawn, holding our hands together, feeling warm. She looked at me and broke into an embarrassed smile.

"Michael, I really don't know how to say this, but you have just blown me away. I've never fallen this hard for anyone, and that's why I had to get away from you tonight. I'm scared."

"It's…"

"Hush-sh-sh. Michael, I'm…hold me."

I put my arms around her neck and pulled her close, looking past her at the lights of the buildings across the harbor. After a minute I loosened my grip, and I watched her face as she said it.

"The company wants me to go back to headquarters in New Jersey pretty soon. I…I'm not sure when it's going to happen just yet, but when it does…I was wondering if…if you'd like to go with me."

She started crying and I let myself into her, into it all.

"I love you, Michael. I really do."

I kissed this brand-new creature and inhaled the night air in a rush. The stars whirlpooled above us and I began to feel dizzy. It was just too much to take in—that someone would want to make me that much a part of her life. I waited, silent, so that my answer would be fresh.

"I love you, Stacy."

It was the first time I had ever said it. Somewhere in the chaos of teenhood I had made a vow to treat those words as precious things, things not to be said without deadly earnest. Here, tonight, I had just condemned myself to adulthood.

The scene is a New York theater. A freakishly amateurish troupe is staging a murder mystery, *The Real Inspector Hound*. Noisy recitation, gestures reminiscent of upright llamas, klutzed entrances are the fare of the day—great parody. But just when you get comfy with the cartoon atmosphere, the playwright pulls the rug sideways. The stage goes dark and the house spots hit two theater critics seated in the audience, clad in tuxedos, kvetching back and forth over diction and pacing and plot devices. They are reviewing the play, but for the moment, over here, they *are* the play, warming over some nasty pretensions, professional jealousies, and one or two backstage scandals.

So you ease into this unabridged version of play-watching, but then the stage lights come back up while the critics' spots stay on. Whom do you watch now?

Shakespeare and his morose Danish friend invented the play-within-a-play long ago, but Tom Stoppard plays frisbee with it. Levels within levels usually produce absolute shit, but pried loose with the can opener of humor, they are capable of working wonders. I can't wait to get to the *Eagle* and see what I can do with it. A simple summary is enough to spin the wheels: I am the theater critic critiquing the theater critics critiquing the play although they're really part of the play, aren't they. So if they're part of the play what does that make the theater critic and just whom is he really critiquing? Open up your mind and say *AAUUGH*!

Theater people have this foolish notion that a review should be entirely dependent on the play itself. What they don't see is that the critic has the same demand as the performer—to entertain—and therefore must make his article a thing *separate* from the play. You have your obligatory mentions of directors and sets and lead players and other such bullshit, but to grab your reader's attention you've really got to go further. The play is just a starting point.

Intermission:

The scene is a warm Friday evening in late May, a small community theater constructed of corrugated steel. A tool shed with a box office. The theater borders on a soccer field, bright yellow nets hooked over the goals for Saturday morning matches. A dark figure traces the chalked boundary lines, balancing a cup of coffee in one hand, a fudge brownie in the other. His demeanor spells out "pensive" in large block letters, bold font, and you'd wonder why anyone would tackle such a brick-wall adversary.

"Michael?"

"Hmm?"

"Michael? Is that you?"

"Yes, it's…me."

He can't see her face, but the silhouette works across his radar. She comes to him with arms spread, and he has no graceful way out. He embraces her.

"Michael! God! It's been so long!"

Three exclamation points in a row. It's *got* to be Suzanne.

"Suzanne." He tries it out to be sure. "Suzanne! How are you? What are you doing on this side of the hill?"

"I'm *from* this side of the hill. I've come back for good."

"Are you working over here?"

"Same place, actually—that insurance office with Cindy. Only I'm a rep now instead of a receptionist, and I'm making *twice* as much money!"

Her eyes scrunch upward, that smile she makes with her whole face, cat-like.

"Oh, Michael, it's so damn good to see you. You always were the best lay in the county."

She was a hobby actress, no big talent, just a fondness for lights and stage dust. He met her at a cast party, in the days when he retained that young man's knack for guiltless lovemaking. He followed her smiling eyes back to her room and found some throwaway line in his young man's inventory, a tactful way to say, "I'd like to screw the daylights out of you until daylight."

"Have you ever," quoth he, "have you ever just *slept* with someone? I mean, no lovemaking or anything, just…sharing the bed?"

She didn't buy a bit of it, but she was flattered. He had himself convinced he was actually going to give it a shot, but the warmth of her body and the sound of her breathing drove his hand to her breast within ten minutes. Six times that night —that's what he would remember most. Still a personal best. It wasn't until three sleepless weeks later that he realized he wasn't attracted to her at all, just overcome by hormones, and he was truthful when he told her. She was something special the way she took it, and that's how they became friends.

The last time he saw her, she called him up to invite him to a party. He came to her house early, and within the space of a bottle of wine they made an agreement: they would go to the party together, but they were free to look for other partners. If one of them found someone, they were free to leave with that someone. If neither of them found anyone, they would go back to her house and screw themselves silly. A guaranteed winner, and the most unique piece of sexual consent he'd ever fallen into, but he never got a chance to see it through. Ten o'clock found Suzanne skinny-dipping with a bearded Deadhead named Joey. Still, he was honestly happy for her, and grateful to know she *would have*.

Suzanne was just about to tell that story to the goal posts when the theater lights blinked on and off.

"Guess we'd better hit the trail," he said. He took a last slug from his coffee and jammed the brownie wrapper in his pocket. Suzanne stood in her spot, rubbing a hand down the side of her jeans.

"Listen, Michael, I'm here with some friends. But would you like to join us afterwards, go out for a few drinks?"

He folded his program in half and slapped it against his thigh.

"Yeah!" he said too loudly. "Yeah, that would be great! I'll meet you right here after the show."

"Okay." Her eyes smiled again, and she ruffled a hand over the top of his head.

"Walk you in?" he asked.

"Sure," she answered. He pivoted and offered his arm. They waded into the entrance, and she left him at his seat, throwing a glance over her shoulder just to make sure. He smiled.

The theater critic critiquing the theater critics critiquing the play within a play steals out the exit and across the soccer field while applause shakes the corrugated steel. Life on the edge of living makes an exhilarating picture, but he isn't ready yet for another victory. He backs up and kicks a pretend ball into the bright yellow net.

Chapter Seven

Saturday
Legatissimo

My pleasure now comes from painless, boring things. I revel in routine. Saturday morning reports dead on time for a dance of food and housework and television. I wake up and turn on the set—cartoons, sporting events, tire commercials—as I shuttle my dirty clothes, whites, permanent press, across the courtyard to the laundry room. Off to the shower, soap, rinse and shampoo, towel off, slap on my weekend sweats. Wash is done, shove them westward to the dryer, French toast for breakfast, cartoons for forty-five minutes, hang up the permanent press over the curtain rods, twenty minutes of baseball, then fetch the cottons and fold them in a ring around my easy chair. The weekly movers trudge by my window, clanking and stomping and giving instructions, "easy, back,

easy now," piling sofas, bookcases, dinettes, into their orange-
striped U-Hauls and Daddy's pickup truck. In fall, I shuffle
bacon-colored leaves along the walk, the steady song of
college football ("...fourth and ten, this could be the play of
the game, he's back, he's got time...") tucked away in my
ears.

The *Eagle* aims its slick anti-establishment journalism
dead at the new rich of the baby boom, filling in the back pages
with rock 'n' roll, movie trivia, and syndicated underground
comic strips. The Revolution is just another way to make a
buck.

"Hi, Michael!"

Sasha Novesceu, the arts editor. She published a book of
poetry in college because Mommy wrote children's books,
which pissed me off right away until I read the thing and
actually liked it. Strange thing is, there's but no poet to be
found in this woman. Talk show host, fashion model maybe,
but no poet.

"How was the play?" She set down a bundle of press
releases and sipped from a mug circled with little red hearts.

"Great! Tom Stoppard stuff, slightly absurdist. Pacing
could've been better, but they got through it pretty good."

"Did you remember what I said?"

"Yeah, yeah," I said. "Sell the story. Make people want to
read it. I know. Hi Mark. Enthusiasm."

Mark was the production manager, new wave stylish, odd
angles, radical type fonts, and an overuse of magenta (his hair,
that is). Typical *Eagle*. He slouched by through the ware-
house-gray walls looking hangover-damned.

"Hi Michael. What's hoppin'?"

It wasn't really a question so I didn't answer.

"Right!" said Sasha, ignoring everything. "Invest your
article with power. Give people a reason to read it."

I had my eyes on the movie poster over her desk, *Gigi*,
French girl, wild red hair. Movie star names hovering around
her like insects.

"Computer number two?" I asked.

"Yes," she said. "Soon as Terry's done with the jazz column. Grab a cup of coffee."

"I guess I will."

If I had any gumption, I'd take this job right away from this cheerleading poet, preaching power as she alphabetizes the movie listings. Right now, though, it's enough to belong here for two hours a week, to get those regular phone calls from people saying, we *need* you to do this, we *need* you to do that. We *need* you.

"Hi Terry."

"Mikey boy! Whatsa digs, kid?"

I'll never figure out how a twenty-five-year-old got to be such a hepcat. He scooted his wire-rim spectacles up on his nose and stared at the screen.

"The digs is ten minutes till that jazz computer becomes a theater computer," I said.

"Hey, no sweat Mikey babe! Gotcha comin' goin' and standin' still. Straight out on the wrap in a microsec."

He punched the keys in a Bo Diddley beat (no kidding— chum-a-chum chum, a *chum-chum*) and ripped into his story like ten minutes to the Apocalypse. Nice to know some people actually listen to me.

"Where *did* you learn to talk like that, Terry?"

"Learn, schmearn, kid, I was *born* talkin' like that. I shot out of the womb rappin' goo, babe, like ga ga, man. Cool. Doc slapped my little red butt and I screamed, '*Shit*, man! Ten seconds on this scene and they're on my case already!'"

I had to laugh. This cat could spew like no one. I wonder if he has a real personality locked up in a safety deposit box somewhere (Gerald, bank teller, decorates his living room with pictures of movie icons).

"Later, Terry. Time for java."

"Yeh, *boom*-yeh."

My story came out *smooth*, baby. The more complicated plays are a snap; a mind-fuck like *Inspector Hound* feels almost like cheating. So much material gives you a lot of room to move around. You can catch the flavor of the thing and throw in a twist or two of your own without giving away every little plot detail. I won't even read the crap in the local daily anymore; their constant summarizing destroys any reason to see anything. I think union wages cause brain damage.

I stopped off at Sasha's Sheetrock hovel and saluted.

"*Finis, mon capitain.*"

"Will I like it?"

"You had *better*," I said.

"Is that a threat or a guarantee?"

"A guarantee, mein edi-*tohr*. Threats are for telephone solicitors and family members. Call me Tuesday with my next mission?"

"Certainly. Thanks for getting it in today."

"No problem. See you later."

"Bye."

I walked out into the downtown streets, nightclub signs lined up like bottles behind the bar, checked the movies at the porn palace next door—*Carnal Craze, The Sins of Lady Y*—and walked around the corner to my car, five minutes left on the meter. Like clockwork, babe, like clockwork.

Chapter Eight

Sunday
Allegro, con brio

So let's clear this up right away. I told you the spur to my initial rush of love was Stacy's offer to take me to New Jersey with her once that promotion to corporate headquarters came through. Well, the promotion fell through, tabled by some anonymous tribe of dark blue suits in a walnut-paneled, wall-to-wall carpeted conference room on the fifteenth floor of some building you or I will never enter. We're putting off such changes for at least a year while the company goes through some planned cutbacks, they said. No—we'd like to make the change, but we have no one qualified to replace you at the Santa Cruz plant. No—we really need a Pisces for the job. And your shoe size is just not quite amenable to the position; we were really looking for something in a size 6. The reason is unimportant; what's important is that it didn't happen, and by my reasoning that was just fine. What made me love her was the fulsome granite heft of the offer itself, not the promised action. Besides, who the hell wants to live in New Jersey?

In any case, it was after this that the good times began. If I had to give you a picture of those times, it would look something like this:

We wake up in her condo, a sweet little slice of building just off the harbor. We make slow morning love upstairs as the sun cuts through the curtains, and as we build to orgasm, my Stacy faces a dilemma. You see, she rents the room down the hall to a couple of college kids, and feels bashful about making loud animal noises when they're around. During orgasm, then, she has two choices: if the kids are not home, she will scream to the end of the millennium; if they *are*, she will grip the back of my shoulders until she draws blood with her nails. I encourage her roomies to take long trips whenever possible.

I leave Stacy in mid-wakefulness and head for the bathroom, where I sit on the toilet and read from a book of American folk tales. I have a theory about this book. If I finish this book and we are still together, then she is mine. If not…well, that I haven't considered, but it follows a certain fabular logic. I take a hot shower, peering out the screen at the damp lot beyond the back fence.

After toweling off and pulling on my shorts I head downstairs to make strong coffee, pausing at the bedroom door to watch the way her body works as she walks to the bathroom. When the coffee is done, Stacy is done, also, and she comes downstairs to meet me with wet hair and a kiss. We lie side-by-side on the sofa, sipping coffee and being as lazy as possible as the tiny movements of football games flash by across the television screen.

We eventually prop up our hung-over bodies and suit up for softball practice, a short drive past the ocean and into the foothills to a little elementary school with a backstop of antique wire. After warm-up we head quickly into batting practice, where I take pleasure watching her beerball friends—

elders all—retreat further and further in pursuit of my drives. The ball hangs in the sky like a kite and drops in, three feet beyond their leather grasp.

Stacy's buddy Kenny plays second base and has his own brand of self-motivation. He places a cold can of beer directly behind his position and spends the afternoon protecting it, as a knight would protect the Holy Grail. Kid doesn't have much range, but hit something toward his beer can, and he'll stop the ball or die trying. The wonder twins Monty and Marty like to hang out in right field, taking turns shagging balls and bowling them back at Kenny's can. Kenny was a good guy. I must say that. By the end of practice, the booze and the running would have him all red-faced and run down, but he'd be okay once we got him to the Hind Quarter and strung him up to the taps.

After one practice, Stacy and I headed straight home and up to the bedroom, where she stripped off her shorts and demanded I make love to her immediately. We didn't even bother taking off our cleats. We staggered downstairs afterwards and ordered out for pizza, then collapsed on the sofa with her stereo tuned into some jazz station, saxophones burbling us to sleep over the hum of the aquarium.

I guess late September and all of October went that way, and I had never known life so focused. I was unemployed, I was in a place away from home, and I was terribly, intensely in love, with no plans for changing any of it. But then, I should have known it would change on its own.

It is Sunday, noon. The ritual begins.

The players pair off and toss balls at each other, filling the air with the pop of leather on leather, the groan of arm muscles lubing up after Saturday night and three months of play. Big bearded Italian video store owner Joe Fatazzio gathers us around after warm-up and delivers us to our positions. Myself, I go to shortstop, the only position that exists, because here you are never left out of anything.

Joe picks up bat and ball and dings grounders at us, chanting out the bases: "Go for one! Shoot for two, shoot for

two now! All right, third and one! Home and in, home and in!"
It's a marvel how the guy manages all this yelling, considering
his Saturday night marathons up and down the Top 40 list at
the Grapesteak.

Our practice field—William Frawley Memorial—is about
as smooth and well-kept as a war zone, but we're too emotionally attached to go elsewhere. In a way, it's good practice,
because once we get to the professionally tended fields of the
Capitola Parks and Rec. Department, we can handle *anything*.
Fortunately for me, the earth around shortstop is much smoother
than the gopher university between first and second. I have
seen many a fellow infielder go down here: two black eyes, a
broken nose, and a busted finger in the space of three seasons.

Joe calls in Toby from right field, and it's time to start
batting practice. Viewed in the proper context, this is magic
time. Hundreds of balls off hundreds of bats, so many chances
for something new to happen. The magic wells up from the
grass, from the dust around the bases and the dried mud of the
batter's box; all these earthy elements come together to make
this little white ball perform its tricks. Epiphanies come at you
in the time-freeze flatness of line drives, knocking you down
unless you knock them down first.

Today. Me at short, no one at second, no one at first; four
of our players are off to the beach, and the infield is mine. Guy
at bat hits a shallow fly into right field, where there is precisely
no one. I rocket out there, straight out, blind to the ball, and
when I think I'm somewhere under it I look back over my
shoulder and find nothing but sun. I'm lost, I'm dizzy, there
are gopher holes out here, that soccer goal post down the right
field line, where am I? I'm trying to keep my footing and pull
that puppy out of the light when, at the last possible second, an
arc of shadow spins away like a partial eclipse. I reach out at
contortionist angles, off from the path of my flight, and ball
hits leather—*puph!*—the sound of a marshmallow flaming up
over the campfire.

Perfect. Shouldn't have had a prayer. If that's not faith,
bring it to me in a box.

So, my teammates sit around and drink a couple of beers and bitch about the heat and occasionally discuss strategy (we have never won a championship, but that's hardly the point), and I take off down the road beeping and waving, off to the beach. Our beach.

"Beautiful tonight."

"Yes. You are."

"Hah! You never miss a chance, do you?"

"'Course not. Never. Why would I? See that boat out there? Red running lights?"

"Mmm...yeah, shu-wah."

"I love it when you talk like a New Yawkah."

"Can't help it. Can't lose it."

"Don't bother. It's you."

"I love you, Michael. You know that, don't you?"

"Shu-wah. Gimme a kiss."

"Mmmmm..."

"Race you to the rocks?"

"You're on. But give the old lady a head start."

"Okay, old lady. Five seconds. Ready, Se..."

"Seeyuh!"

"Hey! Ah...One! Two! Three! Four! Aaah shii-i-i-i-t!..."

The initiate carries his gray-blue gym bag to the public restroom, where he strips off his muddy, sweaty shorts and replaces them with canary yellow swim trunks. He trods around the lagoon and finds the fine, dry sand where he spreads out his gear: a basket of strawberries, a wind-worn dragon kite, and a paperback book. He dons dark glasses and reads a chapter—an emotionally deprived daughter growing up in sixties Massachusetts—then he naps for, oh, thirteen minutes. When the sun presses too heavily on his skin, he sits up, yawns, slips his keys into his pocket and trods down to the water. He stands square with the Pacific Ocean—chilly migrant water carried down from Alaska—and drinks in the sunlight flashing up from ripples of blue-green and foam.

He tests the coldness of the water and drifts in up to his

ankles. He takes a foot in his hand and stretches it up behind his back. He takes the other foot and repeats the motion. He starts in a jog up the beach, splashing through the shallows, dodging shell-seekers, wave-chasers, passing a narrow stretch near the rocks (their rocks) and going a half-mile on, past the private coves and lifeguard stations. As he passes the final station he breaks into a sprint, hands swinging in the air, legs pumping against the sand, slowing only to the end when he reaches home plate, a bluff of sandstone rising up to stop him. He touches the wall. He knows he doesn't have to, but he touches the wall, dug-in notches for climbing, corporate rows of barnacles in dark blue suits down where the waves hit.

As he jogs back, his legs curse him in their chemical language (L-A-C-T-I-C A-C-I-D! L-A-C-T-I-C A-C-I-D!), knowing he will ache tomorrow and regret. But now when the sun angles the waves in his direction he has no limbs to worry, he pads along on the wet sand, leaving his toesteps, tasting the sea air coursing his lungs, cleaning out his tanks. When he can look landward and spot his beach towel, weighted down by his gray-blue gym bag, he slows to a walk and strolls to the edge of the harbor, an armada of butterfly sailboards stacked on the sand in military formation. He touches the navy blue boulders of the breakwater. He knows he doesn't have to but he does, and he turns and walks back to his towel, eyes down for sand dollars.

The beach towel comes even with him, and he eyes the rocks (their rocks). He feels the wind blowing through him, and he envisions the moment two months past their parting when he first felt this, when he knew he would make it, he would be all right, he was whole, he was—can we say it?—he was born anew. And now the initiate brings it all to an end, sloshing into the water up to his knees, reaching down and scooping it in handfuls up over his head. The water runs down his spine, and he shivers with pleasure.

Chapter Nine

Monday
Arioso Mesto

On the rare occasions when I give someone a ride in my car, the question always comes up: Why no radio? It's a natural question. Most people know I'm a singer, and generally into music, so why wouldn't I have a radio in my car?

The initial answer was always that I bought the car straight off the lot, late in the model year, at a bargain price. I was midway through college and in need of something cheap and basic, so who cares about a radio? Just get me from point A to point B, from Albuquerque to Botswana. For that matter, the color wasn't right, either. "Hey," said the dealer, "you're not gonna see the *color* while you're driving, right?"

The installation of some kind of music-producing device remained on my to-do list for the next couple of years, but something happened along the way. I started singing to myself.

I've sung at weddings. I've sung in garage bands, at talent shows, and in choirs, and through the years I've had to learn a lot of songs. I found out the best place to learn them was in my car, nothing else to do but drive, and something interesting happened along the way: I grew attached to not only the practice but the feeling.

Let's take this somewhere else. When I was a junior in college, I took a road trip to the Shakespeare Festival in Ashland, Oregon, a folksy little town just over the California border. I had planned to go with a friend, but somehow it fell through, and I ended up saying the hell with it, I'm going by myself. This was a little strange for me, and a little intimidating, and more than a little exciting. Childhood and teenhood for me—no different than anybody else—was a long string of group activities: family dinners, high school cliques, choirs, baseball teams. Spending three or four days straight without a familiar social contact (*or* a radio) was really a jump off the cliff.

Surprise, surprise: it was a great trip. Even on a Fourth of July weekend I was able to get good seats right up to curtain time because I was a single. I saw *Cat On a Hot Tin Roof* in the indoor theater and *The Taming of the Shrew* in the outdoor theater. I spent the rest of my time going to restaurants by myself, checking into motels by myself, hiking through the park by myself. And something odd happened.

When you spend that much time by yourself, time itself begins to waver. And if you think about it, the major reason you keep track of time in the first place is to synchronize yourself to other people: dates, choir practice, work, games, parties. Here you are entirely self-timed, and a lot of the time you don't even have to know the time. You begin to think about daily life and wonder if, in some postapocalyptic wilderness, a pseudo-human life form will consider a long hike into the woods, glance automatically at his bare left wrist and exclaim:

Njorgegou! Au frianta elgran onk!?
Translation: "Why the hell do I always do that!?"
The other thing you discover is your own voice. Where
you usually use your voice constantly in the process of
communicating with others, here in the world of solitude you
don't have to use it at all for hours on end. I could order lunch
at one in the afternoon and not have to speak another word
until I got to the box office at six. Hours of complete muteness,
and the inner conversations bring you closer and closer to
yourself.

Back through the desert mountains of the Siskiyous, back
by the stark white temple of Mount Shasta and through the
long brown seas of the Central Valley grassland, I used my
voice for singing and singing only, old folk songs and new
rock songs, German lieders and however much of those Italian
masses I could remember. For myself. I sang only for myself.

I woke up this morning to the sound of goat's hooves
across my porch, *click-clack, click-clack.* Once I swept the
cobwebs from my head I realized it was Brownie, stepping off
toward the parking garage in her high heels. This was my
wake-up call. I stood and stretched and stumbled to the blinds
near my bed so I could check out Brownie's Monday attire.

She wore a black leather miniskirt with brass buttons
along both sides, topped by a fuzzy beige mock-turtle sweater.
I took faint rhythmic pleasure in the sway of her step and the
way her hair bobbed as she walked. She was nearing the corner
of the garage, and I was about to leave my duck blind to head
for the shower, when she snapped her fingers—universal code
for "Oops! I forgot something"—and turned, spinning smartly
in her spot like a Broadway dancer. The movement surprised
me. In my rush to close the blind, I managed to get it stuck
open, and I was positive she caught me watching.

Oh shit. I tried to gather a casual frame of mind, oh, just
checking the weather outside before I dressed. Oh, was that
you out there? I didn't even *know* you had to go to work so
early! God.

Then the doorbell rang.

Make that uppercase: OH SHIT. I panicked for a long second, wondering if I should just pretend I wasn't home. I covered my mouth to make my voice sound far away from the door and said "Just a second!" I slipped on my bathrobe and breathed once, twice for good measure, then unlocked the door and opened it.

"Oh, uh, hi," she stammered. "I'm Sheila, your next-door neighbor?"

She didn't seem angry, but she was reaching for her purse. Mace? Stun gun?

"Oh, uh, hi," I stammered back.

"Are you Michael?" she asked. *She knows my name*, I thought.

"Um...yes, I am," I answered.

She drew something from her purse. I thought for a moment of slamming the door, but decided to take my punishment like a man. I braced myself against the doorjamb. *Go ahead*, I thought, *I deserve whatever you want to do to me. I'm bad, I tell you! I'm bad!*

Brownie held out a small white envelope.

"They must have, um, switched these in our mail," she said. "I thought I should get it to you. Looks important."

At this point I was unable to start my sentences without first rehearsing the vowels.

"Oh, uh, ah, yeah," I said. "Thanks."

"Have a good one," she said, then spun on her taps and skipped down the porch. I stood there like a deep-frozen jerksicle, one hand white-knuckle on the doorjamb, one bobbing my insurance bill up and down between thumb and ring finger.

I closed the door and flipped the bill like a frisbee across the room. It smacked against the side of my desk and dropped smartly into the wastebasket below. I cursed and fished it out, then headed for the shower with the strange feeling I had forgotten something. I snapped my fingers—universal code for "Oh, yeah"—came back to the blinds, still open, and caught the last ten feet of Brownie's morning excursion. God, that girl's got talent.

Work. Everything seemed pretty normal today. For the first ten minutes. I gave Naomi (wardrobe report: a jungle land elf in zebra-stripe polyester) my usual morning howdy-do, toured the dining room for my premiere cup of coffee, found the usual leftover doughnuts, and smuggled a maple bar back to my desk.

Once in a great while I can actually get excited about my work, sort of dig into the accelerating chant-like rhythm of it all, and this morning was one of those times. Maybe my sunrise adventure with Brownie, er, Sheila, had knocked my adrenaline button to the high side. In any case, I looked to the top of my cubicle and studied those stacks of green contract cards with steely-eyed vengeance.

"Ah'm gonna get you suckahs," I said, cocking my Colt .45 rubber stamp in their mute little bureaucratic faces. *K-chung! K-chung!*

"Did you say something?" Naomi, pausing in her clerical-type motions.

Vowel rehearsal!

"Oh, uh, ah, no," I said. "Not at all." I reached into the file drawer next to me and began pulling out all my official stamps, then filled up my stapler like a good soldier loads his machine gun, and readied myself to send out car titles unto the far reaches of the globe.

Bring down the record sheet. *K-shaw!* Punch the record number into the computer. *K-shaw!* Early payoff? No. Late payments? Only one. Grab the pink title from the record sheet, sign it off, stamp company name across the signature, staple it to the pre-printed thank you note and original payment contract, fold the package into a window envelope, and stack it on the mail pile. Stamp "Paid in Full" and the date under "Title Sent" on the record sheet and stack that puppy up for filing. *K-shaw!*

One down. Three minutes. Zillions to go, but I'm ready,

dammit. Next patient, please. *Zrabowinskiev, Fyodor J.* Shew! That's not a name; that's an appellation. Ooh, late payments, too. Probably took him too long to sign the checks. Have to check with Doris in Credit Eight on the title.

"Michael?"

It was Naomi, leaning over the partition.

"Hmm?" I answered.

"Mr. Cunningham said he wants to see you in his office. Right away."

"Oh, uh, okay." I put my date stamp back down and brushed my sleeve against the stamp pad, putting a nice red swash across my nice white shirt. Mr. Cunningham, what does *he* want? And why did he call Naomi? Is she my secretary or something? Shee-yit. What kind of manager interrupts a guy when he actually wants to get some work done?

I dodged my co-workers, most of them walking around with their heads attached to their paperwork, and threaded a rat's maze of cubicles to the office of Michael Cunningham, vice president, operations. Nice guy, generally. Leaves his door open all the time, just to make sure we know exactly what his open-door policy signifies. Tries too hard, though, to be one of the guys. Thinks of himself as still a darn good softball player—even at his age—misses all the practices, plays in the games, and makes two or three errors, then sits out the rest of the season with that darned hamstring problem of his. Me, I wish he would just be a big shot and stop palling around with us.

He was on the phone when I entered.

"Yeah. Yeah, Doris, go ahead and send out the repo squad on that. We've been trackin' this lady much too long to give her another chance now. Okay. Good job, Doris, keep it up. Bye now."

He clicked down his phone, then pressed a special red button that would automatically forward his calls to his secretary, Stephanie.

"Michael, Michael, Michael, always good to have more Michaels in the office. Hey, grab a seat."

I pulled a chair next to his desk and let myself down, not entirely sure what to do with my limbs. I crossed one leg over the other and pulled my foot back toward me with both hands. That kept everybody busy.

"Naomi said you wanted to…?"

"Yes, yes. Sorry about that. I was talking to Naomi about something else and just figured I would…"

He paused, then picked up his paper clip holder and fondled it like some kind of small pet.

"Michael, do you have a college degree?"

I was stuck. I hadn't wanted them to know this, but he seemed to know anyway, so what good would it be to get caught in a lie?

"I, uh, yes," I answered. "Yes, I do."

"What in?" he asked. "If you don't mind telling me, that is."

"Journalism," I offered.

"Journalism! Very good degree to get. Useful in many fields."

I looked past Mr. Cunningham's head to a softball trophy on his shelf, trying to make out the year—'73 or '78, I couldn't tell.

"So why did you not pursue journalism?" he asked.

I was quiet for a second, studying the laces on my shoe, the one in my hands.

"I'm not sure," I said. I retreated from present, active thought to a set line I give people at parties: "I guess it took me four years of journalism school to find out I didn't want to be a journalist."

"Very good." He smiled. "I've always thought that's what bachelor's degrees are *for*, actually. My own major was psychology, believe it or not."

"I believe it," I said.

"It's been of great value for management work, working with employees, trying to get them to do their very best…"

He set down the paper clip holder and stood from his chair, pacing to the inside window, looking out on a field of cubicles.

"That's why I wanted to talk to you this morning, Michael. I've seen the fine things you've written around here, the invitations for office parties, the softball reports—oh, and that wonderful memo you composed for Roxy about our sick leave policies."

"Well, I…"

"And I've also seen your theater reviews in the *Eagle*. I do read the paper once in a while."

"Oh, that's just a hobby," I said. "Just keeping my hand in."

"No, no," he said. "The writing I saw was not that of a hobbyist. That review last week on that Chekhov play was a fine piece of work. But that's beside the point. I guess what I'm trying to figure out, Michael, is…why aren't you using these obvious skills of yours to get ahead?"

"I didn't think it appropriate to my talents…"

"Talents, shmalents," he said, raising his hand and waving it back down at me. "You've got a head on your shoulders, Michael. That and a Swiss Army knife is all you need in this life. Anyone who can graduate with a journalism degree can learn the credit department. It's a cinch. And who knows? In a couple of years you could work your way into management. We're talking long hours here, we're talking tough work, but the payoff is excellent. Look, you've got a girlfriend, right?"

He didn't give me a chance to answer.

"You've got plans, right? Maybe get married, maybe have some kids. Hell, maybe send *them* to college. You've gotta have money, Michael, you've gotta get out of this accounting department graveyard."

I was no longer listening, really. I stared at my shoe and pretended to find a smudge, wiping it off with my hands. Mr. Cunningham let my silence reel out for a while, then wrapped up his argument.

"Look, Michael, I'm not asking you for some immediate answer here. These are important, complicated things to consider. But think about it. I've got good jobs for college graduates here. There will always, at one time or another, be a spot open for you. Think about it."

"Thanks," I said. "I will."

"Now get out there and send out some titles," he laughed. "Roxy's probably pissed at me for slowing you down like this."

I spent the late afternoon and early evening flying a kite down at the community center. It was a dragon kite, a twenty-foot dragon kite. I bought it the week after my first break-up with Stacy. I flew it next to a sculpture there, this oddly attractive pretzel of rusted metal and geometric figures entitled *The Cosmos and Everything*. Once I got the kite up and flying steady, I looped the stick around the corner of the sculpture and sat myself down on the grass, watching it whip its tail in the wind like a cat ready to attack. Down by the pond, an old man shrinking into a tattered gray suit had set up an impromptu feeding station for the Bachelor Ducks. From his pathside bench, he reached into a loaf of day-old bread and threw bite-sized chunks into the flurry, delighted at all the fuss he was causing. After five minutes a young woman jogged by with a golden retriever who barked and sent the Ducks scattering back into the pond. The old man sighed and looked at his watch.

I didn't get much done today after my meeting with Michael Cunningham. A half-hour and eight contracts into the pile, I found a title with Stacy's name on it. I stared at it for a full minute, searching for instructions beneath the surface— treble clef, crescendo, fermata, anything. I signed it illegibly and threw it on the stack.

Chapter Ten

Tuesday
Allegro molto, stringendo

I discovered the Rose Man early one morning on the long
way over the hill, Highway Nine, threading through the Santa
Cruz Mountains. I was driving back from a friend's house in
the valley, trying to take as much time as possible to reach
Stacy's condo. You see, the night before she went out with her
old lover, the amiable Italian guy. I thought it might be over
now, I thought I'd find her gone. She asked me if it would be
all right if she slept with him. For old times' sake. It was the
first time I ever told her no.

When I showed up that morning she had a hangover, but
she could see something was bugging me, and she said,
"What's the matter?" When I told her, she said don't be silly,
I love you. Funny, I don't remember her ever telling me that
when she was sober.

I bought her roses that morning, but at the time I was in such a daze I really couldn't remember where I got them. It was the next week, when things were going well again, that I recognized the place: hand-painted sign reading Roses and Redwood Gifts tacked onto a tree at the side of the road. Kind of tacky, but hell, three ninety-nine a dozen is something to stop for. I checked my rearview mirror for tailgaters and pulled into the dirt lot. He was out the door before I could leave my car: chubby middle-aged guy, tangle of gray-brown hair, three-day beard, drab mountain clothes.

"Hi there!" He opened his arms to the sky. "How're ya doin'? Hot date this mornin'?"

He stood in front of me and placed his hands on his temples.

"Now, wait a minute. I...can...feel...her...name. I'm a whiz at this, y'know. Some of my friends think I'm psychic. Her name's Da...Do...Do-Do...hummmm...Dorothy!"

Auntie Em would've been closer. But the second guess he hit it right on. He took me into the shop, which was really the front room of their house, and he showed me a wedding picture over the sink.

"Can you believe that handsome young devil is *me*? Celebrated our twentieth anniversary last week. Most wonderful woman in the world."

"Great," I said.

The most wonderful woman in the world walked in just then with an Oh-my-God-he's-got-another-customer-by-the-throat look on her face. She asked me if I wanted a ribbon, and I said yes, please, white roses, lavender ribbon. Mr. Showbiz, meanwhile, told me all about the operation, how he gets all these slightly blemished roses from his cousin down in Castroville and that's how come he can sell them so cheap. I said hey, there's an art to imperfection, and for that he liked me even more. The wife took my money and handed me my roses. Then her husband tried to guess *my* name.

"Me-me-me...ma-ma...Matthew, right? Gotta be Matthew."

"Close," I said. "Michael."

"Michael. That's good. Archangel, you know. Real badass. Whipped all the devils in Revelations. You have a good time with Dorothy, Michael!"

I didn't bother correcting him. I must've bought about two hundred roses from the Rose Man, and all for her.

On Halloween we went to a costume ball sponsored by my sole employer, the *Coastal Times*. The *Times* is no gem of a paper, but it puts on one helluva party. Its annual Halloween Ball is helped in no small terms by the Santa Cruz citizenry, which considers the mad role-playing fandango of October 31 the event of the year, Christmas or no Christmas. The ball takes place at the Cocoanut Grove, a restored Roaring Twenties ballroom at the tail-end of the Santa Cruz Boardwalk.

Hundreds of them slink out of the woodwork, supposedly normal folk in outlandish and silly and incredible costumes. Two such men came as the Golden Gate Bridge, painted all in orange, twin towers with a full span of cables, lights, roadway, toy cars and people between them. One couple came as a ten-foot-tall pay phone. The girl, dressed as the phone, could actually hang herself up on her boyfriend, the receiver (no comment). One group came as the cast of *The Wizard of Oz,* including the tornado, a circular curtain of fabric adorned with miniature cows, fence posts, and farmhouses flying around on strings.

Stacy and I had a brilliant idea that transformed itself into two really stupid costumes. We put on our finest business suits, complete with power ties and briefcases, then splattered our faces with white pancake, scars and fake blood. Zombie Executives! Night of the Living Yuppies! Get it? Yeah, neither did anyone else.

We took ourselves and our pitiful outfits to Annamaria's Italian Restaurant for some pre-dance nutrition, and I think it was there that it all started. I was reading something different in this woman, something besides the funny makeup. She was annoyed. I could see it in her eyes and hear it in her voice: the way she wouldn't look straight at me, the sharpness of her tone when she spoke to the waitress, and a series of sawed-off, snippy answers to my casual questions. But of all things, annoyance? What had I done to inspire annoyance? I might have been able to handle any other emotion, but this one had me frozen.

And so I took my precautions that night. I tried to let it go. I tried to give her as little cause for annoyance as possible. After we got to the ball, Stacy headed directly to her friends at the back tables, and that's where I left her. I took the opportunity to wander out on the floor, checking out the costumes, listening to the band, seeking out friends from the paper, anything to save me from being cast as a cloying nuisance. These were small things, I thought, these were the basic symptoms of coexistence, stray pencil marks I could erase with doses of intentional absence.

But no, it didn't work. When we returned home the barriers were still there, and I knew I was on to something. She was getting away from me. I became nauseated that night and spent an hour and a half after midnight lying on the sofa downstairs, lights off, a bottle of stomach medicine next to me on the coffee table. You could say it was just the natural reaction to fettuccine Alfredo, too much beer, and hours of dancing and partying, but this was just the beginning. My stomach would grow weaker and weaker in the months to come.

The Sunday before Halloween we went to Bargetto's, a small winery in Soquel. Stacy was a member of their wine-of-the-month club, and while we were there picking up October's chardonnay we bellied up to the tasting counter to sample a few others. A quick run down the menu—reds, whites, dessert wines—had us ensconced in the yellow-feather walls of a Sunday afternoon buzz. I sat her down on a garden bench and asked if I could take her picture, right there in the middle of the courtyard with people standing all around. She smiled for me, but in a shy, endearing way, eyes halfway down, a face I had never seen before. I snapped the moment shut and afterwards, studying the print, was convinced I had captured her essence, that this photograph entitled me to a share of this woman's soul. I even wrote a poem about it.

The child of a human face sheds its contours
a not unfamiliar form
held within the arch of a friend's fingers in
brassy barroom light

She smiles sideways at me
trapped within her four-cornered frame
and taking her in my palm
I ask if the original could ever be mine

Though this smile I have shared in wrinkles of the night
and these eyes have danced with mine in waking quartets
Though my breath has fluttered the soft measures of her
hair

Probably it is only here, on a square of silver and paper
that I can have her

And perhaps, too, this is enough
as I slide her into the
pocket of my shirt
her face to my breast

The turn in the poem surprised me. I still don't know if I wrote it that way to satisfy the fashions of self-possession, or if, that early in our story, I already knew the ending.

"Michael, is that picture of that woman gone?"

"Geez, Naomi, don't I ever get a 'Good morning' first?"

"Good morning, Michael," she said, sweetly, *dolcissimo*. "So why's the picture gone?"

"I, uh, it was time, that's all. Just…time."

"Oh," said Naomi (dressed, by the way, in a cherry red suede jumpsuit).

Naomi began shuffling papers and looking like she was actually about to go to work. I was about to do the same when she started again.

"Michael, I have a friend I'd like you to meet. I think you two would make a sweet couple."

"Naomi, I think I'd…"

"Oh come on now, Michael, just *meet* her. I could bring her to the company party on Friday. She won't even know you're checking her out."

I stood from my desk.

"I think I forgot something in the mailroom yesterday."

I could feel Naomi's eyes glaring after me. I didn't care.

"Michael? Is everything all right?"

It was late afternoon. I was sorting the outgoing mail, and Roxy Cater leaned into the room, looking…*eager*, for God's sake.

"With? Oh, you mean…" I stammered. "I, uh, talked with Mr. Cunningham yesterday, and…"

"No, I didn't mean *that*," she said, ticking her tongue and smiling. "I mean just…anything. Is anything wrong?"

Concern from the boss. I was confused. What should I say? She interrupted my thoughts.

"Michael, just let me know if I can do anything. I'm here if you need me."

The words are not that odd, especially now that I have set them down on paper. It was what she did as she said it. Roxy Cater, former nun, current ice-queen accounting department manager, stared into my eyes, placed a hand behind my neck and slid it slowly, enticingly, back along my hairline.

"Jeannie, Jeannie, Jeannie…"

Despite a specific note from Leonard Bernstein instructing otherwise, Mr. Stutz had assigned the second movement male-alto solo of the *Chichester Psalms* to a very female Jeannie Pletman. Bernstein's ghost was punishing Mr. Stutz for this infraction by causing Jeannie's vibrato to swell to the size of a 300-pound mezzo soprano.

Tonight was our first rehearsal with the Westfield Community College Orchestra. We were in the concert hall, instrument-toting dweebs caged up in the pit, extrovert singers on stage in chairs (risers would come later), and a thousand upholstered seats stretched out before us like a fabric desert.

"Jeannie, you *have* to suppress that urge for warmth! I want you to sing *flat*. I want you to sing like the tenor section when they haven't warmed up! You are an eight-year-old boy in your first Sunday mass, and when you hit that D—'Ado*nai* ro-i'—you have to somehow get up there without your vibrato. Forget everything we've taught you. It's worthless!"

The rest of the choir snickered along during this speech, and we felt a little guilty, of course, because Jeannie was up against it, trying to unlearn vibrato. It reminded me of the time I joined a coed softball league where you scored by running past a line to the side of home plate (thereby avoiding collisions and lawsuits). "Not touch home plate!" I screamed. "You might as well tell me not to breathe!"

But Jeannie, a thin, petite sophomore who seemed built for boys' solos, was ready to try again. She closed her eyes in a concentrated effort to cast out those devil vibratos, then got the tone so right and so flat that she proceeded to lose the tempo, the rhythm, and the words.

"Yi!" Mr. Stutz squeaked. "All right, all right. You've got the tone. Now let's just put...it...all...together. Orchestra? Watch me close on the 2/4. I'm separating the quarter notes for the soloist. Remember, you don't move."

(Meanwhile, Bernstein writes: "...the long male-alto solo in the second movement must not be sung by a woman, but either by a boy or a counter-tenor.")

Jeannie took three deep breaths, closed her eyes for a second or two then nodded at Mr. Stutz. Six beats at 3/4 and she entered, a voice stolen from an English chorus, purposely flat but beautiful in its own wobbly, eccentric fashion. She took the high D with only a hint of vibrato, then followed three measures on with the purest of E's, ranging out over three beats, then one beat of a 2/4 measure, and down into the quicker, tougher rhythms, *Bin'ot deshe yarbitseini* ("He maketh me to lie down in green pastures"), eighth notes weaving their way into multiple meters.

The men had no part in this—we had four pages to rest—but we watched Jeannie in earnest, urging her on with our eyes and our stomachs. By the time she neared the entrance of the women's chorus she had it free and loose, dangling the triplet like a jewel between two *Adonai roi*'s and eyeing Mr. Stutz for the *poco ritard* leading into the chorus.

But Mr. Stutz was no longer conducting. Jeannie slowed for a split second then went on by herself, holding the final note out for six long beats even though no women's chorus had followed her. She stopped finally and looked at her conductor in a mix of curiosity and anxiety.

Mr. Stutz said nothing. He folded his arms together and studied her. He held out his baton, pointing it up and then across in the air. He stepped to his music stand and set the baton down. He lifted his hands up in the air, and clapped them together once...then again...then faster. He broke out in an elfin grin and shouted to the choir, "A round of applause for our boy alto!"

The choir stood and applauded for a long minute as Jeannie Pletman demonstrated the full range of the color red: strawberry, burgundy, scarlet, vermilion. The basses began chanting in guttural tones: "Jean-nie! Jean-nie! Jean-nie! Jean-nie!"

"Okay, okay, okay!" Mr. Stutz called out. "Now that we've embarrassed our soloist out of her gourd, let's take a break already. It's, let me see, seven forty-five now—how 'bout everyone be back at eight o'clock, ready to sing Mozart."

Shuffling out of the tenor section, I could hear Frank DeBucci yodeling in falsetto, "I bet *I* could sing boy alto." And then, like clockwork, Frederick Guttman right behind, "I bet you could, Frankie boy. And I bet I could help you out. Wham!"

"Ouch!" Frank yipped.

So I was watching the F&F show and *not* watching where

I was going, because I turned left at the door at the same time someone else was turning right. *Wham!* My shoulder went right into her. I grabbed her by the waist just in time to keep her from falling. After I regained my feet I found out it was Amy.

"God, Amy…I'm sorry, I…"

Amy put on her best Mae West. "Ooh! I do like a man who's *rough!*"

"Are you all right?" I asked.

"Yeh, I'm fine." She smiled. "I used to play a lot of tackle football as a kid."

I steadied her one more time, squaring up her shoulders with my hands, and tried not to look at her eyes.

"Sorry…again," I mumbled, then walked off down the hallway, lost.

I wandered around for a few minutes, past a music room where a guy was practicing jazz drum, brushes on a snare, tossed-salad flutter, and at the lobby I ran into Alex.

"Mr. Blanche, sir," I said.

"Mr. Moss," he said.

"Calling the Missus?" I asked.

"Just finished, Mr. Moss."

"How are things?"

"Fine, sir. *Muchos grandiosos.* Two more weeks of classes, a gallon of hell-week finals, and I get my love back."

"Hey! I'm glad for you. Really. That's great. Care to chat by the fountain a while?"

"To tell you the truth, I have to zip by my locker, pick up some notes for a friend of mine."

"Can I ask you something, Alex?"

Whatever it was I had found him for had suddenly become urgent. I must've sounded like some kind of outlaw, desperate for answers, worried over roadblocks. Alex jammed his hands in his pockets and studied me for a second.

"Sure," he said. "What do you need?"

"Do you know anything…about Amy?" I asked.

"Umm…you mean conductor Amy?"

"Yeah, Amy. Amy Fine."

"What do you want to know?"

"Anything," I blurted out. "I just need to know anything. Do you know anything?"

Alex started fidgeting, like a kid asked to give an answer in class.

"Well, I heard she was an orphan. I heard her parents died in a bus crash in the mountains when she was in high school."

"Oh," I said, staring at the baseboards, wondering if this held any significance. "You know anything else?"

"Anything else? Um…no. That's it."

"Okay. Thanks," I said. We broke off in opposite directions; me for the water fountain, Alex for his locker. I wandered by the Help Wanted board—"Bassist needed for R&B group, must have own amp," "Need second violinist for string 4tet. Prof. ambition only. Weddings, some recitals"—wondering, what the hell am I doing this for?

The members of choir drifted onto the concert hall stage for the second half of rehearsal at about five after eight—five minutes late being the international standard for choir tardiness. Jenny was standing up in the front row of the soprano section, leading the windstorm of chatter like a majorette, arms flaring left and right. Would I ever marry a soprano? I doubt it. Jenny was pretty typical of the basic soprano attitude, a blatant denial of the glut of high-voiced females in the world of music. Every move seems to say *I am so special, I can hit a high B*. Give me a whiskey-voiced alto any day. In any case, the soprano section settled down finally when assistant conductor Amy took the podium, spreading her score in front of her like a picnic blanket. She raised her baton for attention, waited for absolute silence, then put it back down and began to speak.

"Thank you. What I'd like to do tonight is run through the entire Mozart, and *then*, if we have time, go back through and hit all the trouble spots—especially the entrances. Now I know you've heard choir directors say this before, but I *swear* to you, even if every single person in this room loses their place, I will keep conducting. Even if *I* lose my place, I will keep conducting. Even if an eight-point-oh earthquake knocks the ceiling down on our heads, I will keep conducting. They will have to pry the baton from my cold, dead fingers..."

She smiled to herself, realizing she had stretched the point a little further than needed, and fought back a laugh.

"All right, all right. Straight from the top: *Dixit*. Oh, and could everybody stand? Just for the run-through. I'll let you sit for the second part. Thanks."

Amy gave the upbeat, a little stiffer, a little more precise than Mr. Stutz would have—she would gain looseness with experience—and choir and orchestra came together:

Dixit
Dominus
Domino meo:
sede, sede, a dextris meis
donec ponam inimicos tuos scabellum pedum tuorum

Mozart seemed ultimately logical by this time—the thunder you expect to hear after the lightning strikes—especially after riding the uncertain trolleys of Dvorák and Bernstein. The basses scamper up the scale on rational eighth notes into a long whole, whereupon the tenors take the baton and run higher, beginning the fugue, and the sopranos and altos offer up their parts like sections of a paint-by-number until the last *tutti* unison where you place the final piece of sky there above the steeple with a grand *maestoso* homophonic *Amen*.

And I guess that's why I thought I could get away with not looking at the conductor. That and the privacy of my position—four rows back on a flat stage, my eyes sandwiched between the heads of Frank DeBucci and Carl Lapone (who could see beyond Carl, two inches taller than me with a full head of dazzling silver hair?). She would have to lose her beat to even notice. To compensate for the lack of visual signals, I anticipated the orchestra by a microbeat, which kept me well in sync for the whole work: the lively 3/4 stroll of the *Dixit*, a

tennis match between the choir and a solo quartet in the
Confitebor and *Beatus vir*, the somber fugue of *Laudate pueri*,
the beautiful, soaring soprano solo of *Laudate Dominum*
(what this guy could do with 6/8 Andante!), and, finally, the
Magnificat, starting in princely Adagio and chasing its way
into Allegro full of tricky tied notes and off-beats.

Take the top of page 66, for instance, nineteen stinking
measures from the final cutoff. There's a trick entrance in the
tenor line there, right after the solo quartet winds up a brief
passage, then a quarter rest, a lightning-fast eighth rest, then
a quarter note on the upbeat, completely exposed, on a high
G—which just happens to be the breaking point of Michael
Moss's singing voice.

So I'm not paying much attention, gearing into the full
cruise of the Mozart Expressway, and I turn the page and
there's the note, right on the off-beat. Like a driver slipping to
the side of the road, I overcompensate, jumping in a full
quarter beat early, all alone and half a step sharp from the
adrenaline, sounding like the horn of an adenoidal taxicab lost
in the fog. Amy nearly breaks her promise and stops, because
the choir is snickering and losing it now, and I'm turning as red
as Jeannie only for all the wrong reasons, but somehow we
hold it together and pull into the final "Amen."

Amy cuts off the orchestra on the dotted eighth/sixteenth/
quarter note combo that makes up Mozart's final punch, then
turns to us, waiting while the nervous energy of the choir
settles in around her. At this point, a hundred sight lines
jabbing at my ribs, I could've handled a grand whimsical
statement, the kind Mr. Stutz would have rolled off, but Amy
had other feelings about it. She threw me a look of simmering
disgust as she spoke her judgment low and flat.

"Well, if you're going to screw up, screw up loud."

What I needed was a fortissimo burst of laughter, descending *poco a poco* over six measures, staggered breathing, some
device to turn my blatant screw-up into a harmless entertainment—a *divertimento*, if you will. I needed ribbing, a few
hearty backslaps from my fellow tenors. What I got instead

were nervous titters, sheltered whispers, the sounds of shame. Amy held up her baton again and waited for silence.

"First, let's go to page seven, middle score. Basses, you're missing the dotted quarter there. Let's run through it alone..."

I was about ready to call it a night.

With Dvořák's great curtains of brass and timpani still ringing in my ears, I wandered off the concert hall stage, a lost man. I heard Alex tell me good night, and I muttered something similar in return, then marched up the aisle, through the lobby, and into uncertain night.

From the long low steps outside the music hall I could see across to the library entrance and the shaggy silhouette of Sam the Cat, there with two of his feline kin. I followed my steps across the courtyard, pausing to dip my fingers in the fountain, and found Sam rummaging busily around his cart, muttering to himself as he worked.

"Hi, Sam!"

"Sorry, Mistah," he said. "I'se closin' time. Gotta git home. Gotta git up early t'marrah."

He said this looking into the belly of his cart, stashing away potato chip bags, re-stacking styrofoam cups. When he finally looked up, he squinted at me and smiled.

"Hey, it's one o' you Kwy-ah Boys, huh? Wha's yo' name again?"

"Michael," I answered. "Michael Moss. Tenor."

"Well, well," he said, wiping his arm over his mouth. "High-voiced critter, huh? Ah *am* impressed. Whatchoo be wantin' here? You wants some coffee?"

He spoke the word coffee in a snort, as if it only had one syllable.

"If you got it," I said.

"Yessuh, I got some left, ah think. Lessee here—yeh, here's a cupful. Help yo' self."

He handed me a small cup with coffee black as oil— bottom of the barrel. But it was warm; that's all I wanted.

"He'e ya go," I said, the mimic kicking in again. God, I

wish I could stop that. I handed him a dollar.

"Oh no," he said. "I ain't gonna be chargin' foh no dregs. Be wasted anyhows if you hadn' a come along."

"Ah owe it to you from befo'," I answered. "Y'borrowed me one las' week." God, this was getting bad.

Sam squinted at me again, pushing his cart back and forth on a wheel. "Okay. Ah'll take that fo' a ansah." He took the bill from me and folded it into his back pocket, then leaned against the low wall of the library entrance, peering at me from the shadow of his eyebrows, snapping his fingers to a song in his head. I sipped from my coffee and winced at the taste.

"You remin' me o' someone," he said, running the back of his hand against his whiskers. "Got that partikler look on yo' face. A seeker. Yeh, that's it, you lookin' foh somethin', ain'tcha?"

"Yeah, I am," I said, then laughed, a single staccato note. "Wish I knew what it was."

Sam reached down and picked up the Persian, a stocky-looking veteran with ragged ears, clear yellow night-eyes and fur of chocolate brown and white. He held him in one arm while with the other he scratched him just behind the ears. The Persian took on that deceptive feline face, a forehead-crunching squint that looks like annoyance but actually signals great pleasure.

"Ah, there's a life there. Don' have no partikler thoughts 'cept findin' the next meal and waitin' foh someone like ol' Sam to come along and scratch yo' ears. We all—you an' me an' the rest o' the human spee-cees—we jes' mess it all up by thinkin' too damn much. Thinkin' jes' lead to wantin', and wantin' mean you gotta take it from somebody else."

I walked over to reach under the Persian's chin, and after he came to accept my presence his squint grew deeper and he started purring, toy lawn mower humming away in his chest. Kitty heaven.

"You lookin' fo' a ansah, there's *one* fo' yah. I dunno if it's the one you lookin' foh, but it's one a my favorites—anytime you lost or in trouble or jes' plain messed up, go back to the basics, go back to yo'self, yo' instincts."

I gave a last smooth pat to the Persian's neck, and he gave me a playful jab with his claw, not wanting me to leave. But I had to. I reached down to pick up my music and turned to go.

"Thanks, Sam. I don't know what for yet, but thanks."

"Y'welcome, Michael Moss. Hey! You gotta holiday in yo' name, you know that? Michaelmoss. Thas' a good one."

I took off one way and heard Sam pushing his cart the other. I wasn't ready to go home yet, so I took my prescription-strength coffee out to the Westfield football field and climbed to the top of the new bleachers. They put them in just a year ago, rising stripes of aluminum still shining like the sides of a great spacecraft. Two or three diehard runners paced around the six red ovals of the track, and at one end through the goal posts like a good kick the electronic scoreboard flashed Day Planner entries into the night:

MEN'S BASEBALL...VS. TRAMMELDON...1 PM SAT MAY 29...DAPPER FIELD

JOIN ASU NOW!!!...*Memberships still available for summer...*

SUMMER REGISTRATION...JUNE 6...GET YOUR CLASS SCHEDULE IN THE WESTFIELD BOOKSTORE...

This is worth a photograph, I thought, steam wafting out of my coffee cup over a dormant football field. *This is as much worth a photograph as anything else.* I took a deep, bitter swallow of my warm mud and chewed a few grounds through my teeth, taking a quick breath—shee-ooh!—to steal away the acridness.

You can think of photography and music as diametric opposites. Photography depends entirely on the stoppage of time, whereas music depends entirely on its passage. Between the two, you'd have to call music the more natural, the more reflective of the actual operation of life. You can't hold on to that note, that chord, forever. The fermata will end, the conductor will kick you back in to the flow, and like everything else the chord will pass on, first into overtones, then into sonic dust, then into nothing. Give it up. Let it go.

After ten minutes the scoreboard ran back around to MEN'S BASEBALL. I clanked down the shiny aluminum strips, drifted out through the outdoor weightlifting area, rusty barbells clamped into iron yokes, and tossed my empty cup into a dumpster before entering the low yellow lights of the parking lot.

Where I found Amy. She was out in the center of the lot, tunneling through the back of her orange hatchback like a badger on speed, throwing out books and tennis racquets and God knows what else, mumbling to herself in not very pretty language.

"Son of a bitch thing, can't find the fuckin'...God why does this happen to me anyway, why can't you pick on someone else for a change—OH!!"

She noted my presence.

"Oh God, Michael, you scared the shit out of me!"

"What are you looking for?" I asked.

She sat down on the bumper of her car and gritted her teeth.

"Ooh...I've got a flat, and I can't find my lug wrench."

"Oh," I said. "Umm, mind if I look?"

"Hah!" she chirped. "Go ahead, you'd have as much luck as I would in this garbage scow of a car. And please, don't tell *anyone* I'm this much of a slob. *Please*."

"Looks just like my apartment," I lied. "That old bachelor lifestyle."

I lifted the board supporting the floor of the hatchback and peered into the tire well, then reached in to check something.

"Uh-*huh*," I said.

"What? What?" Amy asked, about to jump out of her shoes with anxiety.

"The lug wrench is missing, and..."

"And?"

"And your spare tire is flat."

"Oh, jesus fucking christ," she said, then broke out in laughter and grabbed the shoulder of my jacket. "Oh God, I'm sorry. I'm a little foul-mouthed sometimes."

She straightened up and eyed the car like a sick patient.

"I'd better find a phone."

"No, no, don't," I said. "You have a thirteen-inch wheel, right?"

"Um, yeah, I think so," she said.

"Well, so do I. Listen. I'll drive my car over here, loan you my spare, and you can return it after you get your tire patched."

"Um, yeah. Sure," she said. "That is, if you don't mind?"

"Sure I don't! What am I gonna do, leave you stranded out here? I'll be right back."

I retrieved my car and parked it next to Amy's, pulled out my spare, and began the operation. Having just rotated my tires two weeks before, I almost looked like I knew what I was doing. I was wiping my hands on an old T-shirt I kept in my trunk when she came over next to me.

"Michael, you're wonderful. I don't know what I would've done if you hadn't come by. Listen…" Her voice decrescendoed (conductor's voices don't just *soften* like other people's). "I'm sorry I was so hard on you tonight, I…I guess I'm still mad at you for not watching me."

"I didn't think you…"

"Yes. I noticed. And I guess you can't tell me why, since it's obvious you know the music by now, and you look up during all the other pieces…"

"Well, why is it so important?" I blurted out. "Why do you care?"

Amy Fine trained deadly hazel eyes on me and crept up to kiss me on the cheek.

"Because I like you," she said. "And because I need to know you respect me."

"I…I do, I do." I was all out of thoughts, and breath. I looked at my left wrist, which had no watch because I'd taken it off to replace the tire. "Um, listen, I gotta go. I'll see you Thursday. Don't drive over fifty on that spare, okay? It's just one of those temporary things, it'll overheat if you drive too…um…well, seeyuh."

I jumped in my car, started it up, and took off out of the parking lot before Amy could say another word. I caught her in the rearview mirror, hands on hips, staring after me as I wheeled out the exit. *What she must think*, I thought. *What she must think.*

Chapter Eleven

Wednesday
Allargando

It was about a week after Halloween that Kenny had his accident. Catch This was headed for its usual mediocre finish in the fall league, winning about as many as we lost, and we figured if we won our last two games we would make the playoffs. Usually by this late in the year our bodies are all too stiff and crotchety for extra workouts, but we decided a midweek rehearsal (as we liked to call them) would up our intensity for Sunday's game.

We scattered ourselves about William Frawley Memorial Field like stray dogs and, after cramming through a quick infield drill, marched our batters up to the plate for ten swings apiece. By the time we'd worked through four outfielders, the catcher, and our first basewoman, the October sun was losing its patience with us. It was getting dark, and it looked like we might not make it through the whole lineup.

Kenny, a strict line-drive singles hitter, was displaying some pretty good cuts, sending the gophers ducking for cover with up-the-middle grass burners and frozen ropes between me at short and Cindy at third. Not that Cindy was actually going to get in the way of anything; her main objective, as always, was self-preservation.

Anyhow, at the end of each batter's quota of swings, he or she is generally expected to "run one out" to instill a hypodermic of reality into the situation and keep the rest of us alert. Kenny's philosophy on this matter—identical to my own—is to "run one out" until you *get* out. In other words, if you keep on running no matter what, you force the rest of the team into practicing such useful game-time paraphernalia as relay throws, cutoffs, sweep tags, and the occasional second-to-first-to-short-to-pitcher-to-left fielder rundown. The bonus, of course, is that you might also make them all look like idiots.

So Captain Joe Fatazzio dips the last arc of a pitch to Kenny at the plate, and he nails a solid drive to right field. Toby, the right fielder with sheep-like demeanor and a Howitzer for an arm, picks it up on a hop and blisters the ball to me at the second base bag, and we've got Kenny roped and branded. Except, of course, that Kenny is not about to stop. I'm holding the ball low, waiting for a slide, but all I see are Kenny's shoe tops as he hops over my tag, hits the base and speeds on through, headed for third.

I pivot quickly and shoot the ball to Joe, who has smartly taken over third from Cindy. But Kenny's not dead yet. Deciding his team needs a tasty game of pickle, he prepares to put a juke move on Joe before he spins and heads back toward second. And this is where everything comes back in slow motion: Kenny shakes back and forth like James Brown in sweats and plants his right leg to spin back toward me, only his knee decides to take a separate vacation. One second he's churning his arms in the gray evening hum, pulling up slide-show images of the major tease job he's about to perform on us, the next second he's in red-hot agony, falling to the grass with a thud and grabbing at his knee.

It's remarkable the way people react in a situation like this. My own immediate inclination—result of six whole months of Boy Scouts and a first aid merit badge—is to fight off any symptoms of shock by coming to Kenny's side and beginning with the questions: Where's the pain, Kenny? You think we need to get you an ambulance, Kenny? Tell us where you are, Kenny. All right, take it easy, you're gonna be fine. Let's get a jacket on him, huh? It's cold out here.

Everyone else's immediate reaction is to gather around their dear teammate, still writhing around on the ground like a run-down squirrel, and spend the next fifteen minutes sharing their own personal horror stories.

"Yeah, one time in fifth grade I fell off the roof and broke my leg in two places, and you could actually *see part of the bone sticking through the skin*. Geeawd, I get nauseous just thinking about it."

"I had somethin' like this last fall, you remember, Joe? Playin' tackle football. Re-e-eal stupid! Caught a ball up in the air and some guy lays me out—*Wham!*—then lands on my knee on the way down. I was laid up for three months."

"Hey, boy. I'll bet it hurts real bad, huh, Kenny? Yo, someone get this man a brew!"

We got our answers that Sunday when Kenny showed up to our game in a full-length cast. Without our usual second baseman, Catch This had no chance for the playoffs; the Bruins took us out in five innings, beating us by the ten-run "stomp" rule. I can't help but wonder if Kenny's injury was a turning point in other ways, too. Now when I don my perfecto-vision spectacles I can see that physical dependency holds hidden advantages, whereas emotional dependency can only be ugly, ugly, ugly.

Roxy walked back into work about a half-hour after lunch, and it must have been a real zonker. Roxy knows all the tricks, she does all the things you can possibly do to hide those liquid lunches—heavy on the makeup, pour down some mouthwash, grab the strong coffee—but you can always tell anyway. For one thing, she's always touching herself—adjusting the hem of her dress, putting that stray hair back in place, rubbing a finger under her lips. Another hint is her mood. She's always much cheerier than when she's sober (I mean, hell, at least Roxy's a pleasant drunk).

"Oh, Michael."

Speak of the corporate devil. She was at my cubicle, right behind me. I turned to see her leaning around the corner, playing peek-a-boo at the edge of my filing cabinet.

"Can you come over to my desk, Michael? I've got something I'd like to show you."

Boy, doesn't *that* sound provocative. I walked off behind her, watching the way her hips rolled as she went (not bad at all for a fifty-year-old). We got to her desk, which is really just a double-sized cubicle with a view out the windows, and she sat down, smoothing her skirt over her legs with a hundred little nervous touches.

"Here, come look at this," she said, beckoning me closer. "I'd like to take advantage of your clerical skills for the afternoon and have you type out this memo to the different dealerships. Use the memory typewriter in the workroom; you'll only have to type it through once, then just change the address each time after that. Could you do that for me?"

"Sure, Roxy, sure. No problem." I took the handwritten memo from her desk and turned to leave.

"Oh, and Michael…"

I looked back.

"Are you coming to the party on Friday? For Fred?"

"Um, uh, I wasn't really sure," I said.

"You really should come, you know." She threw me a pout with her lips. "You did such a wonderful job on the invitation. 'Traded to Fresno for a crate of raisins.' Ha! You *are* a kick, you know that, Michael?"

"Well, yeah, I guess I am," I said. "I'll try to be there."

"Oh, and, Michael, thanks for doing the typing. You're a sweetheart."

"Yeah," I said, waving the piece of paper over my shoulder. "No problem."

Sheesh.

I took Roxy's memo to the workroom and was halfway through the initial memory entry (which by the nature of the machine has to be performed perfectly), when in popped Naomi, today wearing a rather demure black pants-and-blouse affair (everything else must've been at the dry cleaner's).

"Hey cubicle-mate, you've got a call on line seven."

"Oh. Naomi. Okay, I'll be right there. Tell 'em two minutes."

"Yes *sir*," Naomi sniped.

"Thanks."

I was one stinking line from the end when I spelled Sincerely "Sincarely."

"Shit!" I shouted under my breath. I rapped the typewriter up the side of its little electronic head, ripped out the sheet and crumpled it into the wastebasket, then headed back to my desk.

"Michael Moss here. May I help you?"

"I just *love* it when you use that ultra-professional office voice."

"Sasha! Hey, well don't get used to it. Most of the time I just say, 'Yeh, whattin the fuck ya want?'"

"My, my. I'll look forward to it. Meanwhile, I know you're pressed for time this weekend with that concert thing of yours, but I've got this play that needs reviewing and I'm all out of writers and the director's been on my case all week."

"Sasha, I'm booked! I got a company party on Friday, a concert Saturday, and a dress rehearsal tomorrow. Do they have a Sunday matinee?"

"Wait a minute. Let me look." I could hear the sound of press releases being shuffled, then she came back on. "Uh, let me see, no Sunday matinee but...but...hey! We got a preview showing tonight. Can you see it?"

"You think they'll mind? I mean, they don't usually like me to see previews."

"Hey, these guys are desperate. They'd let you see the casting call if it would get them some press."

"Okay. Where do I go?"

"Just says Duncead Productions, above the Varsity on Tenth Street. Downtown."

"Oh yeah, I know where that is. Went to a gallery reception there once. Do I need to call them?"

"No," she said. "Why don't I set it up right now so I can get this guy off my back? He actually threatened to picket the paper if we didn't send a reviewer."

"Sounds like a real winner."

"Yeah. Catch this: 'A bold new rendition of Shakespeare's *Richard III*.' Anyway, the tickets'll be there in your name."

"Okay."

"And Michael—you're a sweetheart."

"So I've been told. See you probably on Sunday."

"Oh, Michael? Wait a sec. Terry's got something he wants to ask you. Here, let me transfer you."

I waited as the line clicked over.

"Mikey babes!"

"Terry babes!"

"Hear you scammin' a proscenium arch tonight, Mikesky. Mind if I trotsky alongsky?"

"Terry!" I laughed. "Your social life that bad?"

"Oh woe and no dough be to the lone jazzman, Horatio."

"Yeah, sure," I said. "I could use the company. Where do I pick you up?"

"How 'bout right here in the central spot-o-rama, Mikesky? I'll be tappin' the heavy rimshit all evening."

"Seven-thirty?"

"Got you comin' goin' and fryin' eggs, babe!"

"Ciao, Terry. Oh, and Terry?"

"Yeh, Mikesky?"

"Learn to speak English, wouldja?"

"Ha! No way, Manet."

When I got home, I found a nice little surprise in my mailbox. A shiny new absolutely virgin credit card, holographic eagle image, magic cash numbers and everything, credit limit a whopping twenty-five hundred smackers. This called for a celebration.

"*Eagle*. Terry Rabinowitz here."

"God, Terry. You sound so *normal*."

"Don't get used to it, babes. What's on the platter, Mad Hatter? What's the news on your blues?"

"Let me take you to dinner, Terry. I just got a brand spanking new slice-oh-plastic, and it's just beggin' for mercy." Uh-oh, here I go with the mimcry again.

"Ya know, Michaelheimer, I'd love like Thelonius to take you up on that, but I got too much rhythm and rhyme and not enough time. Got on that workin' fedora, and the fit is *tight*."

"Well, okay. Look, I'll see you at seven-thirty, okey-dokey, artichokey?"

"Till then, red hen."

I picked up Terry at the *Eagle* and we walked four blocks down to the Varsity. The Varsity is this classy old place that until recently was the site for hipsters and intelligentsia gathering to see the underground, the foreign, and the all-around eccentric film greats. The place was bought up two years ago by some son-of-a-CEO who wanted to renovate it and turn it over to showing classic films. They were currently in the middle of a week-long Henry Fonda festival, *Young Abe Lincoln* and *Grapes of Wrath* up on the marquee.

"You know," I said to Terry. "I'd almost rather see old Henry than this play. I've had enough Shakespeare lately to choke a horse."

"A horse, a horse! My kingdom for a…"

"Yeh yeh, I know."

We entered the lobby of the Varsity and found a table at the bottom of the stairs covered in blood red *Richard III* flyers, manned by two confused-looking female student-types. Theater critic's omen number one: if the box office folks look lost, the production itself is in deep doo-doo.

They got around to finding my tickets after thirty seconds of a Laurel and Hardy routine ("Do *you* know where they are?"

"I don't know. Do *you?*" "Shouldn't they say something like 'press' on them?"), then gestured us toward the stairs. Halfway up the flight we were greeted by a man with a flashlight, his face hidden in the shadow of a cloak. Ah, trolls for ushers! He led us into a small, stuffy room, completely dark. There were figures tumbling on the floor in front of us, groping the air like flipped-over cockroaches, moaning hideously. One woman to stage left was in a particularly desperate state.

"Oh terror! Auuuuieegh! Horror! Nooooooh, I can't bear any moooooorre!"

My sentiments exactly. Our usher the hobbit split us up, dispatching Terry to one side of the room while I was pointed in the opposite direction. We sat there looking curiously at each other across the way. Terry, poor guy, looked like he was on the verge of panic. A man down the row from me turned to whisper something to his seatmate, whereupon a misshapen figure positioned at center stage shot a piercing beam of light into his eyes.

"You! There!" he shouted. "Shut up! Shut...up! SHUT... UP!"

The man, trying not to laugh out loud, shut up. The misshapen figure kept the light on his prisoner's face ten seconds more before pulling it back.

Ah, I thought, confrontational theater. Alienate the audience. They're only, oh, thirty or so years off the curve here. Oh well, maybe it'll get better. I settled resignedly back into my hard wooden chair.

I was wrong. It didn't get better. I had never seen *Richard III* before, and I guess I still haven't. The actors were all dressed in black, head to toe, symbolic of great...blackness. The only lighting came from flashlights, carried by the actors and shone into each other's faces in some strange improvised Eveready choreography, while they recited lines in bad British television accents, heavy on the consonants, quadruple-rolled R's, K's tossed forth with great quantities of spit. And they drooled. OH, they drooled! I've never *seen* so much drooling.

An excruciating hour and a half later, I realized the Royal

Droolers' Company was forgoing an intermission (smart of them not to let their audience out of the room). After one particularly hydrothermal exchange ("Kkhum-muh, Kkhuzzin-nuh, kkhans-tuh thou Kkhwakke an-duh change thy kkhholour? Mmmurder thy brea-thuh in middle of a wor-duh?") I stood up and marched quietly out. I expected Terry to spot me and follow suit, but he didn't. I came back and peeked in through the curtained doorway, motioning to Terry with my finger. He didn't see me. Finally I walked back in, snuck down the aisle, and tapped him on the shoulder. Terry shot me a quizzical look—probably expecting one of our cloaked hoodlum usher monks—and finally got up and followed me out.

"You know," said Terry. "I thought if I watched for just a few more minutes, I would get it."

"Terry!" I laughed. "There's nothing to 'get.' It's called shitty acting."

"Is *that* it?" he said, slapping himself on the forehead. "I knew it was something."

I invited Terry out for a drink, but he couldn't make it. Had some business to take care of at home. This new God-given credit had to be put to some good use, so I drove south to Orchard Towers, an upscale shopping plaza nestled under the watchful eye of two ebony-plate high-rises, and took the elevator to the top of the big brother, up to a restaurant called Benjamin's. I toured along the semi-packed bar, lorded over by a trio of silk-tie Iranian businessmen, then found a smoke-glass table alone in a corner, next to a window. The waitress came over and sized me up.

"Are there more, or are you by yourself this evening?" she asked.

Ah, a daunting question, no? I chose as my defense the blunt reply.

"I'm by myself this evening. I'd like to start with a brandy. Straight up, please. And may I see a bar menu?"

Seventeen stories aloft in the Silicon Valley sky, I could see the whole sordid lightscape, inarticulate yellow dots branching out to the foothills in one huge electrical spider

web, and the cars on the freeway below, brake-light cor-
puscles over three-lane arteries. People. So many people.

"Yes. I'll have the beer-grilled oysters and a dinner salad
with the raspberry vinaigrette. Can I see your wine list?"

My phone rang when I got home tonight. Whoever it was
hung up.

Chapter Twelve

Thursday
Presto, con fuoco

Our life together began unraveling, small certain pieces at a time. Our meetings, our couplings, our quiet moments would cause her to glow, and tremble, but let them pass and the signs of annoyance would return—the dark sideward glance, the constant sense of distraction, the hurry to get somewhere other than here. Here, with me. Every piece gone left me smaller and smaller, unable to fish out any part of myself in the quickening stream.

In the cold mid-air rush of the falling I held onto words. Since Stacy was the first woman to whom I had ever uttered the words "I love you," I reasoned, she damn well owed me something in return. Those three fragile syllables became my lifeline. Or my lance. It all depended on how I used them, but they became the only way I could harm her in some substantial, rewarding sense. I shot them at her like darts, and she would react with an inner cringe, the look of someone struck with a stun gun. But no matter what, she would not fight with me, which, after all, must have been what I was looking for. Confrontation was too difficult; all she could offer me was the empty luggage of annoyance.

Jerry was an auditor. Sent out from Michigan by company headquarters in New Jersey. Sent out to go through the books and increase efficiency and check out the personnel department. Jerry possessed an easygoing style and a comforting appearance: pleasantly receding hairline, wire-rimmed spectacles, an easy smile that made him harmless and welcoming all in the same stroke. Throw in a carload of experiences and a well-honed touch with a story, and Jerry the auditor became an instant hit with the older brothers and sisters that made up the assembled family of our softball team. And one more time, just one more inning, there I was at shortstop, softball in hand, the only place among this crowd where I really belonged.

They went out bowling one night. Stacy escaped the unpleasant task of disinviting me; I had a play to review. Writing about plays was my only income, and my publisher's largess in granting me an unusual thirty-story advance demanded loyalty. I couldn't afford to miss one; she missed them all. I must have reviewed all thirty during our time together, and Stacy came to exactly one of them. Theater was just not her thing.

After the play—an East L.A. Bloods-and-Crips update of *West Side Story*—I dropped by the bowling alley, a small set of lanes down by the boardwalk. I walked through the glass doors of the entrance, past the cocktail lounge, and stopped at the corner. I could see them; they had not yet seen me. And the tape played back like this: laughter. Snippets of conversation. Jokes passed along with gestures, like a rag tossed across the score sheet. Here, dry your hands with this. Smiles, not broad ones but small ones verging on intimacy, swimming in the air between Stacy and Jerry the auditor. And the sudden uneasiness as they saw me coming, the downward glance and the overeasy attitude covering up the...annoyance. Jesus. My jealousy grew and festered, my breath shortened, my forehead filled with heat, but I would not have anything to do with this. To put at risk the solitary important thing in my life, that was a button I could not press. I said nothing out of the ordinary, then sidled down the racks to find a bowling ball.

She drove Jerry around the town, wearing her department captaincy as her cover: of course she had to show him around, it was part of her job, and she hoped I didn't mind, but the poor guy was away from his home territory and besides, he's such a kick! Lunch at the wharf, drinks at the harbor overlooking the wind surfers and sailboats and beachcombers, afterwards a stop for yogurt or coffee and I don't care to guess. I stayed buried at the condo till late in the evening, burning all her logs in the fireplace, calling friends from my previous life and asking what should I do? without quite telling them every-thing, like the visions I had, her and the team at the funeral, what would they think? Would they care? Would they stop their parties and their games and their jobs for one goddamn day to think of what I had brought them? Is the end of life a good test for loyalty? Five hold-your-breath moments after I'd given up on her, the gears of her garage door kicked in with their peculiar cat-like whine, and I dashed in to the bathroom so that *I* could make the entrance instead of her—nonchalance being the last phony weapon of the desperate and pitiful.

I asked her about Jerry.

"Jerry?" she said. "C'mon, he's a fun guy. Don't worry, Michael, I'm not fucking him or anything. But I'll tell you, it was fun to spend time with someone new, watching him take in everything around this bay of ours with those fresh Mid-western eyes. We really need to spend more time with other people, Michael, it's very...rejuvenating."

She was drunk, but just a little, and she was probably telling the truth, but I couldn't know. That night I targeted my deadly three syllables on her again, and this time I received a brand new response.

"Michael, look, I love you too, but I wish you wouldn't say it so much. I can't handle so much affection all the time. I'm just an old East Coast hard-ass, I'm sorry."

Another piece drifted away. I straddled a footbridge wet with moss and tried to stir it out with a paddle. Jerry went back to Michigan, his mission accomplished, his audits clear. Stacy said she was too exhausted to see me on weeknights. She encouraged me to spend more time and energy finding a job. She was too tired, she was too drunk to make love, or else she had to wake up early in the morning for work. Even the Thanksgiving trip, even that would have gone the way of excuses and alibis, but I wouldn't let her. She had promised me, and I insisted on going.

By Thanksgiving I had moved back to the valley in hopes of finding work. I rented a room from an old high school buddy who was buying a house with his fiancée. The rent was cheap, I had some decent assignments from a temp agency, and I was slowly catching up with my bills. Stacy drove up early Thanksgiving morning to pick me up, no look of annoyance but instead a kind of stoic acceptance. Very businesslike.

The day was perfect—beautiful, warm, sunny, clear; you name the adjective, it fit. We took the inland route straight down the middle of Western California, great oaks, branches over their eyes, scouting from the crests of brown-grass hills, the unnatural geometrics of farm plots triangling their fences to the flats of the Central Valley, finally the coast and an ocean shining with a million fish scales of sun. For the first time in the month of November, I thought I had a chance. The scenery called for nothing less. After a hundred miles of deliberation I reached over the stick shift and took her hand. I didn't say a word, but she knew what I wanted.

"We're just different, Michael. We come from different cultures." She looked at me once along the straightaway, when it was safe. "In seven years, Tony and I never *once* sat down to talk about our relationship."

"And look what happened," I said. I was into sudden-death overtime now; it was okay to piss her off.

"Yeah," she answered, tough girl again. "Maybe you're right." She dropped a hand to light a cigarette, then clicked the lighter back in the dash. "I come back from a business trip and the asshole's fucking some bimbette. In *our* bed, for Chrissake."

And look how much better you've got it with me, I told her with my hands. We plowed the same ground back and forth for the next hundred miles until the hard crust opened up and the soil sifted pleasantly through our hands. Stacy decided she was really horny and would I mind if she pulled over some secluded somewhere and fucked my brains out? No, I smiled, not at all.

Two hours later she changed her mind. If we didn't drive straight on to her brother's house we'd be late. Funny, I thought, two months ago the promises used to be enough. But then, the promises used to last a little longer.

We hit an off-ramp into a suburb just north of Santa Barbara, middle-income, palm trees along the curb. A short block off the freeway and there we were, traversing the lawn, surrounded by strange relatives who had spent the last seven Thanksgivings with Stacy and Tony, Stacy and Tony. East Coast hard-asses all, but also East Coast alcoholics, and by our fifth bottle of after-dinner wine I was wearing them down with my false laughter and the remarkably vivid remnants of my sense of humor. Her sister-in-law made an especially easy target, a long-married, pleasantly plump, fair-haired Southern girl who ate up my attention like slices of white meat. Female relatives were my specialty. Ask me to brown-nose with Dad over a few brewskis and I could manage, but with aunts, mothers and second cousins named Carla and Linda I was Clark Gable meets Bob Hope. Maybe this was my problem.

I thought my gallant performance might merit some sexual reward, but Stacy nixed that at my first foray. Not in her niece's bedroom, she said, not with the whole family in the house. This from the woman who six hours earlier had wanted to fuck me a few yards off the interstate. My body twitched all night, convulsions of alcohol and hormones. Stacy slept the sleep of angels across the room on a roll-away.

The next day, her brother Tom invited me out for a postbreakfast tennis match, and I acquitted myself rather well, dropping a close two-out-of-three in the final set. In the ordinary sense, it was beautifully orchestrated. This is the way you lose to your boss, close enough to earn his respect but letting him win to preserve his ego. But no, I wanted to beat the bastard silly, I wanted to wipe his little overcaffeinated East Coast hard-ass all over my precious California asphalt. I might have done it, too, with my own racquet, but I had to borrow big brother's number two.

Stacy and I may have said twenty words to each other all the way home, most of them dealing with the dry logistics of meals and rest stops. She passed along a compliment from her brother regarding my tennis ability, but it didn't really mean much. My athleticism was the one established thing between us, the only quadrant of my ego that didn't require massive replenishment.

She dropped me off at my new house. I gave her a good night kiss, told her to be careful driving over the hill. I knew she had to be very tired. I called her an hour later to make sure she got back all right. We made no plans for the coming week.

At some point during the trip, passing through Salinas, Stacy mentioned the changes in Kenny, how he was starting to push the boundaries of their platonic relationship. Kenny was a real picture of pity now, a middle-aged man with a disappearing hairline and a body that had failed him. She said he was starting to drink even more; he had so much time on his hands. She said she found the whole thing annoying. I didn't think much of it at all.

The parking attendant eyed me strangely, pocketing the pupil of one large brown eye toward his forehead. I ignored him and kept singing as I plucked the ticket from his hand and sank into the cement pillars and tight fluorescent spaces of the garage.

Te Deum
laudamus
te dominum
Confi-TE-bor...

Dvořák's motif carried such a strong melody I couldn't spring it from my head if I went cliff-diving at low tide. Catchy little sucker. I crammed my car into a tiny spot, sandwiched between two four-wheel-drive megatrucks in a section marked Compact Only, then tried to slink out my door without puncturing myself.

I dashed up the stairs and into the *maestoso* spaces of downtown. It wasn't like this ten years ago. Ten years ago the place resembled post-nuclear Hiroshima, but boy, spill in a few high-rises, redo the park, and tape it all together with a brand-new trolley system ("light rail," they call it) and the place developed a genuine urban attitude: a whole lot of people doing a whole lot of things in the space of one well-marked commercial playground. It was great to be back where the action was, if only for the evening. I skipped over the trolley rails and headed for the eye of the needle down the straight-arrow path of Diaz Park.

The park is a pure north-south oval of green, iced off with rows of fountains that spurt straight out of the courtyard, water-pipe ballets that inspire the summer-browned downtown munchkins into spontaneous sprinkler dashes. Me, I prefer the old Market Fountain at the north end, eerily reminiscent of my home fountain at Westfield College: same low circle of bricks, same metallic mermaids spitting H2O for the passersby. I surveyed the spot on these bricks that would match my spot on the Westfield bricks and settled down to go over my Mozart. I still had fifteen minutes till the start of our final rehearsal, and, especially after Tuesday's fiasco, I didn't want to miss a thing. I ran over my botched entrance a good seven times.

The last time through the finale I felt the presence of someone or thing and looked up from my score. An elderly Mexican man with a gnarled wooden cane out walking his German shepherd. No. A thirtyish businessman in dark blue suit and wrap-around shades pulling a silver BMW away from the parking meters. No. A covey of college-punk intellectuals, black leather and crayon hair colors wandering aimlessly toward the opera house. No. An orange hatchback slowing at the intersection and pulling into the parking garage from whence I had just come.

I leaned back and dipped my fingers in the cool fountain water, shaking them dry as I walked off toward the church.

St. Michael's was a flurry of activity, the floor in front of the altar a maze of chairs, music stands and open instrument cases, patches of silver, wood, and brass open to the light. Frank DeBucci and Frederick Guttman wheezed, grunted and cracked jokes as they assembled the risers.

"Ah! Ah!" Frank gasped. "Just a little more, Freddiehoney, I'm al...most...there." The riser support clicked into place with a sweet smack. "Oh, Freddy, you're sooooh gooooood!"

Frederick sneered. "That's the only riser you'll get from *me*, baby."

With the luxury of arriving early, I sat in a pew and took the time scanning the architecture. St. Michael's was a cathedral in the grand Italian sense, domes and vaults, chandeliers, icons everywhere. The diocese had just finished a six-year refurbishing job, and the interior was magnificent. The walls of the nave were marked off with large simple oils of Christ's journey to Cavalry: *Jesus Falls for the Second Time*, *Jesus Speaks to the Beggar Woman*, etc. Stained glass fell in twenty-foot ribbons down the far sides of the church, deep blues, reds, and purples of saints and heroes in positions of beatitude. Straight up from the altar was the grand cupola, frescoes of the four evangelists ringed by cherubim with scrolls—the Word descending on the congregation. Behind the chancel were the pipes of the newly installed organ, some a foot tall, some as high as trees.

In the ten-minute span of my architectural rapture the

choir trickled in, sopranos as giggly and nervous as Girl Scouts, basses somber and business-like (considering the great responsibility of being the foundation, after all, of the choral harmonic, rubbing their whiskers thoughtfully like old Jewish men as they filed down the pews). I eventually rose and joined them on the risers, watching the orchestra warm up, thinking how nice it was to be a chorister and not have to spend all that time and energy on technical matters like tuning, polishing, rosining, soaking, cleaning out spit valves. It's no wonder they're all so nerdish.

Mr. Stutz strolled in from the back room, stroking his beard, spreading books of music out on the clear Plexiglas conductor's stand, coughing nervously. He called us all to attention and handed down our marching orders.

"Okay, people. Tonight is it. I want you to think of tonight's rehearsal in terms of *performance*, because if we don't know these pieces well enough by now to *perform* them, we are not in a good place. We'll run through the pieces in the order we'll be presenting them, which, if you hadn't heard, is the Chichester first, Dvořák second and the Mozart as our finalé. If you *do* miss any spots tonight, I expect you to mark them down and work them out *yourselves* by Saturday."

Everyone has their quirky speech patterns, and Mr. Stutz's is this: pre-concert anxiety turns him into a veritable font of accents. Write up his dress-rehearsal speeches in musical notation and you'll find the little arrowheads of *accent* all over the place.

"*Tonight* we will take a small break between the Dvořák and the Mozart—just ten minutes or so. Please get yourself adjusted to your spot while the *orchestra* tunes up. And *please*—remember where you are. If we have any mixups while filing in Saturday, just *remember* that spot and go to it. Do *not* worry, the audience will *not* notice."

Due to the awkward configuration of the altar, some of us were not able to stand on the actual risers. Some of us meaning me. Being one of the taller tenors, I was squished onto a sideways-facing step ascending to the altar. This made my sight-line a difficult one. I would likely get a sore neck, not being able to shift my body the same direction I had to look. I had some good company, though. Alex was a step below me—and beside me—in a similar predicament.

"Shitty placement, Mr. Moss," he whispered.

"Break out the Ben-Gay, Mr. Blanche," I whispered back. "Yes sir, yes sir."

"Michael," he said. "I have something for you."

He slipped me a canary yellow envelope. I placed it atop my music folder and loosened the flap with my thumb, pulling out a piece of beige paper folded in two. I crunched the envelope into my pocket and unfolded the note.

I'm counting on you! it read, signed *A.F. the semi-conductor.*

Ah, Jeez, I thought. *That's all I need.* I rubbed my eyes.

"Orchestra! Choir! Are you ready? From the top, Chichester Psalms. Watch me all the way, especially entrances."

Mr. Stutz tapped his baton twice on the podium, cueing the orchestra up, bows lifted, mouths on reeds, the timpanist holding his skins mute.

Being the most exotic and challenging of the three pieces, the Chichester had drawn more of our energy during rehearsals. In other words, we had it down cold. We really didn't have any rough spots at all. The only slip was a 10/4 passage in the third movement. The conducting instructions for this passage are thus: *This 10/4 should be conducted in the shape of a divided 4 beat, adding an extra inner beat on 2 and 4 (1+2++, 3+4++).*

The choir had somehow adjusted to the pattern, but the orchestra, which learned the piece under its director, Madame Forgé, hadn't caught on and proved a little slipshod. What's worse, the movement later slips into a 5/2, then a 12/2. We had our theory on this: Bernstein wrote this particular movement during a 1964 vacation to Monte Carlo, where he borrowed his meters from winning numbers on the roulette wheels.

We got a real treat on the Dvořák. We'd been skipping over the bass solo in the second chorus for lack of a soloist, but tonight we were introduced to Thomas Chapman. He's a choir alumnus, a tall, distinguished-looking black guy with a huge mustache. Thomas sings like God would if He used steroids. Thunder, earthquake, horse's hooves, black of night, great horned owls, Orson Welles—you think of the metaphor, it works.

Tu rex gloriae, Christe!

The King of Glory. One or two of our sopranos almost swooned off the back of the risers.

The only comedy came in the third chorus, right after the men applied a coda to Thomas's solo. The strings lay out a track of galloping eighth notes over 3/4 measures, and the sections of the chorus pass a driving *vivace* vocal line from one to another in a relay race, alto bass soprano tenor, which finally drops into several more manageable phrases of unison. The first two words in the initial entrances are *aeterna fac*, but the rapid pace and the odd rhythmic accents (an abbreviated marcato at the end of the phrase) conspire to turn this into *aeterna* fuck—especially with our meek little altos, who seem to have a mental block about the whole thing.

After months of rehearsal we thought the thing was an old joke, but here in the rarefied air of St. Michael's Cathedral our papally endorsed obscenity took on new strength. Our somber, businesslike, beard-fondling basses just couldn't handle it and began tittering so uncontrollably they almost didn't make the re-entry on the unison section. Directly after the piece, and with many accent signs hanging over his words, Mr. Stutz chastised us, explaining how in *certain* languages, *certain* words may take on the *sound* of certain, shall we say, *unorthodox* words of our own language, and that we should, in a *word*—get past it! He let an appropriate test-silence sink in, then set down his baton and looked at his watch.

"It is now eight-ten," he announced. "I will expect *every-one* back in their places, ready to sing, at eight-*twenty*. Let's all be on time so we can get home at a decent hour."

Most of the choir wandered out the door to the front steps, congealing into the usual cliques about the steel rails and Samson-sized pillars of the church's facade. A trio of basses hip-hopped across Diaz Avenue to a fast-food place, hoping to score some ten-minute fries.

I felt like doing nothing. Or else I *didn't* feel like doing *anything*. The conjugation is entirely optional. The Solemn Vespers pulled at me like a huge weight tied to the laces of my shoes. I sat by myself on the bottom step, watching a traffic cop whiz by with his yellow passing light ablaze, following the triangles of high-rise rooflines as they cut into a deep purple afterglow, further south the long curve of the convention center with its warehouse roof. Looking up toward the rest of the choir, I considered the ease of hiding in a crowd. Hell, even Alex, up there swapping jokes with Marcia Balentine, he doesn't know I'm here. No one does. The only other lone figure I could pick out was Barbie, the halfway with the one-and-a-half makeup job, ten feet away hugging a parking meter. Pretty scary company, but then, maybe I'm just a halfway myself.

The end of ten minutes snuck up like Thomas Chapman's *basso profundo,* and I could not move, perched there on my stone step like a gargoyle, scaring off evil, keeping the rain off the sidewalk. That's it—I'm St. Michael, after all, I *own* the place. Don't tell *me* where to set my stone tennies. The choir drifted back in packs, tailed by the trio of french-fry basses still stuffing spuds in their mouths. Following a jetliner over the skyscrapers, I held my face to the evening breeze, blowing north-to-south through the wind tunnel of buildings, and suddenly it stopped, the only sound the stream of cars along Pearlman Street. It felt like loneliness. And glory.

I managed to rise and prod myself into the vestibule, stood there peeking in through the crack of the ever-so-slowly closing door, and there she was, Amy Fine, stepping up to the podium in charcoal wool pants and a deep blue sweater the color of saints and a blood red scarf the color of devils and lips of pink marble waiting to chew me apart...*da capo al fine*...from the beginning to the end...

No! They can't have me yet! I don't belong to them. I am St. Michael, after all, the badass archangel who kicked the devils out of heaven. I let the door slip shut and turned around, not quite knowing what to do. A directional sign in gold lettering called out "Choir Loft," answering my query with an arrow toward the south stairway. I creaked up two flights of narrow steps and found the door to the loft unlocked. *Deo Gratias!* The loft was dark and dusty, seven pews deep, hymnals and old church bulletins in wooden pockets over jade green kneeling pads. I crept along the shade of the wall and into the highest pew, any sound of my steps covered by the chatter of the choir and impromptu blats of horn players trying out their valves.

I set my music next to me—*Deo Gratias* I had brought it with me during the break—and retrieved the Mozart. This was my plan: I didn't want to skip out entirely, I would just follow along from a safe distance up here in this choral retreat and Saturday, yes Saturday! I would sing for everyone to see and hear. And then everything would be over and I could wake up in the morning and make some French toast and watch a couple of football games in peace. I could only hope Alex was covering my spot. I could only hope Amy didn't notice. She *had* to be too preoccupied to look for something as small as one solitary tenor. She *had* to.

From the top of the loft my compadres looked like a toy choir, something you might see on Christmas morning television but not really real. I was up among the cherubim now—how could I miss? Amy straightened up, hit a quick downbeat and pulled the choir in to her. On the waft of her four-pattern swing she extended her hand on a thread, serving out portions of air in two downward loops then pulling it back up for the fourth with the wrist-flick of a yo-yo master. I could watch her, at last, without watching her eyes.

The piece was over before I knew it. In my head, I sang it perfectly, hitting that last God-forsaken entrance dead on the mark. Mr. Stutz took Amy's place at the podium to hand out final instructions.

"Be here at six-thirty for run-through. We open the doors at seven-thirty and start the concert at eight o'clock *sharp*! Men, black bow ties, check with Gordon on extra tuxedo shirts. Women, no heavy jewelry or *perfume*. Oh, and remember, there's a party afterwards at Paula's house. See Paula for a map and instructions. I encourage you all to come. Believe me, after the *great* performance you are about to give, you will be *wired* and ready to party! Good night."

His final instruction was my cue. I galloped down the stairs and snuck out the front door before the rest of the choir could get to the vestibule. I jaywalked across Pearlman, just missing a pizza delivery truck ripping by, and headed for the park. I had to go to the fountain. I slowed as I hit the center path, catching my breath, feeling my heart beating *prestissimo*. Two Latino boys in L.A. Raiders jackets whizzed by on both sides, staring at me under low-brimmed baseball caps. I turned around to watch them go, then paced on, coming at long last to my altar of bricks and mermaids.

Perched on the wall, my hands soaking in the water, I thought, Ah, that was why. *Tu rex gloriae, Christe!* I closed my eyes to hear the small sounds of citydom: trolley bells, chatter from a hotel plaza, lead-pipe bass line from a nightclub on First Street, idle of cars stopped at the light on Park, footsteps up and down the sidewalks, slow scuffles and medium plods and one rapid set of taps, staccato beats growing and growing as they neared.

"Why Moss? Why!?" The beats erupted into Amy Fine's harried shout, over me and atop me and everywhere. I couldn't get away. I pulled my hands from the water, splashing her face, right up against mine. "Are you trying to make me feel like some kind of fucking idiot? I don't *need* this shit! I don't! I *saw* you up there in the loft, you chickenshit! Why are you hiding from me?!"

She got out of my face—*Deo Gratias*—and started pacing back and forth, a lion in a cage, smell of raw meat, feeding time, nostrils flaring, her breath getting shorter and shorter as she built up her rage. I tried to keep my balance. I was dizzy,

I couldn't sit right, watching her go back and forth.

"Oh no, oh no, *I* have to like the one guy in choir who won't even *look* at me, I have to have the hots for the American Psycho. How do you think that makes me feel, Moss?! I'm not a bad-looking woman, and I've heard that from some pretty good sources, too, and yet *you* can't even bear to be in the same fucking concert with me! Just for a blown entrance in some lousy…Mozart!"

She spit the word in my face like "Mozart" was the foulest of obscenities, then grabbed me by the shoulders and shook. Hard. (She was stronger than I thought.) I didn't know what to do. I thought next she would slap me, but instead she backed off and continued berating me with the relish and vigor of a drill sergeant.

"Have you got anything to say? Anything at all? Because if you don't, I don't care if I ever see you in this fucking *choir* again, or in this fucking *city*, or…or in this fucking *lifetime*!"

"I…"

That's all I could say. But I said it twice for good measure. "I…"

She looked away and snorted, grabbing at her hair like an operatic soprano doing a mad scene, then she turned back, eyes of pure venom.

"That's it? That's it!? That's all you've got to say?"

I was down to one vowel, one stinking vowel to save my life.

"I…"

She looked at me for one more long second, an expression of pure disgust, then huffed and turned to leave. But she fooled me. The dizziness took over. I closed my eyes; I was a ready target. She spun around with a siren scream, hit me with a body slam, and, before I knew it, the park was flipping around like a deconstructionist slide show and I was underwater, back into the fountain before I knew she was coming. For a second I didn't know if I was facing up or down, but I felt for the bottom with my hands and managed to prop myself to a kneeling position, hoisting myself up with what turned out to be a

mermaid's tail. Amy was gone; I heard her taps fading off
behind me. Water dripped from my hair, over my face. The
sensation was even morbidly pleasant—how much farther,
after all, could you go?—until I realized just how thoroughly
soaked I was. Not a square inch of dry clothing.

I crawled to the bricks and pulled myself over the edge like
a man getting out of a swimming pool, one foot over then
pulling up with my arms. Drunk with puzzlement, trying to
find a line on this situation, I could think only of how others
would see me, a lone man on a ring of bricks, large puddle
growing under his posterior, a line of water dripping down the
wall and making its way into the cracks of the sidewalk. The
lone man shivers, and, seeking some verbal salvation, mutters
the first odd phrase that comes into his head: *Saint Michael
Receives the Holy Baptism...*

I can't remember much after that, and I don't think you can
blame me. I wrung out my sweater and squeegeed my hands
down my jeans, then slopped over to the fast-food joint across
from the church and managed to sneak past the counter help
into the restroom. Twenty paper towels and ten minutes under
the hand dryer, I looked decent, but not very. I evaded the
inquisitive looks of three or four late-night customers and
crawled out the door onto Diaz Avenue, then plodded around
the bank building to the parking garage.

When I got to my car I started up the engine and sat there with
the heat full on and the vents all turned in my direction. After five
minutes of treatment I thought to look up, and spotted an alien
object through the windshield. There, placed square in the center
of my hood like an offering, was my spare tire.

Chapter Thirteen

Friday
Scherzo

There are Christmas lights strung around Stacy's tree, and strings of popcorn and cranberries, and underneath a gaggle of gifts from friends and far-off relatives, most of them in glossy aluminum wrap. It is Sunday evening, our favorite time of the week, and we are back from a movie, *Casablanca* on the big screen. She makes blackberry tea, steaming cups of melancholy whose sweetness would become my second addiction.

But it's the Christmas lights I will remember. Their insect spots of colors, just out of the plane as my eyes come in on her face, and her sweater, skin of soft white fuzz; she is the picture of an old-time movie, the ones where the men are always sharp and clear, the women always dipped in soft-focus gel, as if they could only be beautiful if they were slightly unseen.

And I knew what was coming. Buried in paper mountains of self-delusion, I could not prevent myself from picturing this scene ahead of time. It would not be all that bad, actually. It would in fact be a relief, because it would spell out every negative feeling I carried about our situation and about myself and would unstring all the terrible pounding anticipation of the bad things that were bound to come. It would also help my stomach.

"Michael, I need to tell you something, and it's not going to be easy...so I'd better just have out with it."

Oh God, here it comes. Hold your breath, hold your teacup.

"I need to stop seeing you so much. I need you to release me from this...arrangement we've got going. I love you, Michael, I really do, but the time just isn't right for us."

I could've said something hostile. I could've said something defensive. I could've broken down and not been able to say anything, but I knew what was coming all along, so I was ready. And strong. Stronger than I ever expected. I took a sip of blackberry tea, swallowed, and answered.

"So...you'd like for us to break up?"

Calm, like a lawyer in cross-examination.

"I still want to *see* you," she answered. "But I need to be my own woman. I don't want to feel like I'm...answerable to anyone."

Sometimes the only true moment you find in a romance is near its end, and sitting on this lovely woman's couch in a calm blue ocean of truth—truth, at last truth—how could I not honor such a reasonable request? She wants to be her own woman—is that so much? And really she didn't need to ask me for it, but she had done it to put me in this particular position, the position of an adult—serene, wise and rational, every child's magic-marker sketch of the God-like grownup—able to see someone else's life as equally as important as one's own.

"Okay," I said. "I think I understand."

"Oh, Michael," she said, kissing me, holding my head in

her hands. "I'm so glad, I was so scared of hurting you…"

Oh, you have, I thought, but it'll come later, later when I get home, and tomorrow at work, and tomorrow night, alone in my bed, searching the ceiling for little magic checkmarks. And every time I smell a cigarette on someone's breath.

I got a new temp assignment that week. I was very pleased about it because for this one they actually required an interview, and I had passed—they liked me! The job wasn't much—answering a telephone hotline for computer maintenance centers—but it was a nice place, and the pay was a couple more dollars than what I was getting the week before. I shared the line with this nice Mexican girl, Lenita, and when one of us took a break the other would cover the phones.

I took my breaks on the unreal perfect lawns of the company parking lot, the ones none of the permanent employees seemed to appreciate, armed with pen and paper, leaning back against a white maple dropping perfect yellow leaves at my feet. I wrote her a letter which grew to novella proportions; by the end of the week it had reached twenty-three pages.

"I'm doing okay," I wrote. "I miss you very much, but I think this separation may help us work out things in the end. Who knows? But I shouldn't be thinking so far ahead. I've got to stick to right here and now. Maybe the only way I can give you independence is to write you out of my future, to erase every single one of my expectations."

That's how it began, anyway, self-comforting lies cribbed from pop psychology. My true feelings came later, and five pages on I knew I could never send it to her.

"Why do you value love so little when I value it so much? Why do you only tell me you love me when you're drunk, or when you're hung over? Why do I feel like such an infant around your friends, so insignificant, so disposable? Why did you have to end it, dammit? Did you think you'd come home from a business trip to find me fucking some blue-eyed Darcie or Jackie? Don't you *know* me? Haven't you been paying attention?"

I saved the letter for two weeks, then one night I burned it.

Not wanting to soil my housemates' pristine fireplace (they refused to use it, an obnoxious California habit), I placed my pile of yellow notebook paper in the oven and set fire to it, watching it flame up through the tempered glass then spending the rest of the evening sponging out the ashes.

And then I met Nancy. Or *discovered* Nancy, because actually I'd met her long before. She was one of the production workers at the *Coastal Times*. I would see her on Monday nights when I came to punch my theater reviews into my editor's computer. She'd be in the next room pasting up advertisements, blaring the radio, singing along, laughing at someone's jokes, acting generally like a production person, and sparking only the faintest bit of interest from the theater critic in the next room. We had a passing acquaintance— literally. I'd pass her at company outings, I'd pass her at the water fountain, waiting for the office restroom, on the way out at night, down the elevator and don't forget to lock the fire exit door, everything just passing. But the light provided by an oven full of insecurities had forced me to toss aside my blinders, giving me an open view of the crowd, leading me to ask questions. Where was that smile, those green eyes, that silver satin jacket, that highly available look, two months ago? Not to mention—let's be honest—that great ass?

Well, the great ass had something to do with her aerobics class, but the rest had all the world to do with a recent separation from her husband. The only thing left was for me to ask her out. I was in bed with her by our second date, and believe me, this was no teenage waif; in fact, she was two years older than Stacy. But deprived with a capital D. She had married at eighteen and had not slept with anyone else her entire life. Now, after fourteen years with a man who came to their trailer every night and smoked pot until he passed out on the couch, she was finding out just how much time she had wasted, and, inversely, just how much time was still left.

Nancy and I became the only successful case of mutual use I have ever witnessed. I used her wonderful body and enthusiasm to drown my memories, and from me she desired only desire, company, pleasure, and the willingness to answer questions: How does that feel? Have you ever slept with two women? What does it feel like when you first enter me? Are you sensitive there? Where should I put my tongue?

We made love in my rented room, old jazz on the turntable, her taking me into her mouth as soon as I stood up to doff my pants, searching my eyes for signs of stimulation, testing, probing. We made love in the driver's seat of my car, parked in front of an elementary school near midnight, a security guard rapping on the window two minutes after I'd come inside her and we'd put our clothes back on. "Oh, don't worry," he smiled. "Happens all the time."

She played her favorite tape one night while we steamed up the windows, parked next to the beach, and one of the songs became so obviously ours: "I Didn't Mean to Turn You On." We drove all around the suburbs on Christmas Eve, seeking out home lighting displays, the best ones—the manger scenes, Santa and his reindeer strung out on the roof, white bulbs wrapped like star-powered snowflakes around the cypress bushes—always in the middle-class neighborhoods, rich enough to pay for the electricity, humble enough to appreciate holiday kitsch.

Then I drove her back to the house. It was all ours; my housemates were gone to the mountains for the week, visiting with her parents. Nancy microwaved some leftovers from a Christmas party, then after dinner I laid out a blanket under the Christmas tree and opened *her* for an early present. She wore a black and yellow striped sweater, her bee suit she called it, and she told a mutual friend, my editor in fact, that I had attacked her with my "stinger."

The list, like Santa's, goes on and on. Nancy gave me my first book of erotica, *Delta Venus* by Anaïs Nin. Nancy introduced me to the wonders of phone sex ("I'm open and waiting for you now, are you going to enter me? Oh, I can feel you sliding in..."). She sent me a card with a drawing of a female tongue about to enter a male ear, inscribed with the words "Thinking of you." She would even listen to me when

I spoke of Stacy, even went so far as to ask me what she was like in bed.

"You're so much better, Nancy," I said. "So much more eager, so much more attentive. But...I'm not in love with you. I was...am...in love with her, and love always gives sex a rare kind of intensity."

There came one weekend when I made love to both of them—Stacy on Saturday, Nancy on Sunday—and *told* Nancy about it! It was the first time I'd ever done that—two partners on one weekend—and once more Nancy was just...interested, and asked more questions. Apparently, I was her postgraduate course.

"Is it confusing that way?" she asked. "Does it make it more difficult to focus on the woman you're with? Do women feel *different* inside?"

What Nancy didn't know was, the night before I had taken a courageous action. Obviously, Stacy's Declaration of Independence had not stopped us from seeing each other and sleeping with each other, but, fueled by Nancy's lovemaking, I took the final step. I told Stacy I couldn't see her *at all*. A complete break, I said, was the only way I could possibly come up and fish for my soul again.

Stacy was taken completely by surprise. The news about Nancy, about Michael off bedding another woman so soon after our break (word travels quickly in a small, geocentric town) had her in a state of odd disappointment, seasoned with the uncommon spice of dumper's jealousy.

"I have to go back to myself," I told her, a half-hour after a home-cooked meal in my new valley residence. "I realize now that I can't do that and maintain contact with you. You...have too much of a pull over me. I find you too distracting. I have to get on with my own life."

"But can't we see each other at *all*?" she said. "Doesn't that seem kind of extreme?"

"If you love me, or if you ever have loved me...," I said, "do this for me. I need you to do this for me."

I wrote that night into a poem.

> *I retreated for a candle*
> *and found below the lip of a wax-strewn bottle*
> *a wick near death*
> *stale snub slipping its sheet*
> *ready to drop in level darkness*
>
> *I pulled out a box of pearlescent wands, primed for duty*
> *but stopped*
> *because something was right*
>
> *I came back and placed the orphan light before you*
> *told you I could love you as a memory but not a fragment*
> *The flame drowned in its oily waste*
> *and the light disappeared*
> *four damp eyes and scarred love*
> *tossed in strands of gray*
>
> *The performance was perfect*
> *but later on a bed of one last night*
> *you whispered to me in the morning sighs of a child*
> *of your dream*
> *two ends of a box that would not meet except in our kiss*

The poem devastated her, just a little. It was meant to. These were the days I could find revenge only in small, covert, emotion-filled packages wrapped all in glossy aluminum. We made desperate love that night, gripping each other as close to tragedy as we dared, hanging by our fingers from slick walls of granite.

The next night, Nancy took off both our clothes and straddled me on the sofa. A left-on television sent murmurs of light swimming across her smooth, ivory white hips, working up and down, enveloping my cock, just for that minute an organism completely removed from Nancy's body, or mine, or anything in the known world. And how odd, a minute later, that I would find myself watching the television screen instead.

I hate weeks like this. I've got too many things going on. I can't keep up. There are traps set up for me at every corner, sneaky little lion pits holding spiked poles with my name on them. I forget things. This morning I realized I possessed not one single clean sock. I had to wear the socks I wore last night. Of course, they were washed, in a way. Fountain-soaked, then draped over the heater during the night, baked up all nice and crispy like pork rinds.

Fountain-washed. I don't know what I'm going to do about this. The Mozart is maybe twenty minutes long, and there's no getting around it, I have to look at...at...that woman. My God, don't you see? I can't even write her name! But I have to watch her the whole time. I must. I may swim in the scummy shallows on other issues, but no veteran chorister could break a cardinal rule like keeping your eye on the conductor. My choir-mates would have every right to take me out to the middle of Diaz Avenue and stone me with pitch-pipes until I am groaning in twelve keys of agony.

Besides, if I don't watch her, she may *drown* me this time. But then again, if I *do* look at her, I hate to think what may happen. I'm not ready for this, I'm just not ready.

So I crunch in this morning on my french-toast hosiery and count the steps to my cubicle, flipping hi's and howareya's left and right to my fellow early-arrivers. When I get to my desk I am overtaken by the desire to stretch, a full-body yawn beginning in my toes and spreading upward. I lean forward with both hands on top of my filing shelf and let the thing draw me out stiff—uuunngh!—opening my eyes onto my Van Gogh calendar, *Room at Arles*, 1889, oil on canvas, 22 3/8" X 29". A look down and I find a photograph, placed square in the center of my desk like an offering.

She had that dark, exotic, Mideastern look, bronze skin and eyes big and black and deep, caverns of onyx drawing you in. Assyrian, maybe, or Indian. Hard for a dumb Yanqui like me to tell. A strong, thin face, prominent nose, hair thick and black, falling in soft curtains, stage dressing for a tense but pleasant smile, sure hint of shyness, that last second before the camera clicks, *Oh God I hope I look all right*, and the smile draws itself down, just a whisper, small turn of Mona Lisa smirk. She was in a garden somewhere, rose bushes deep green with sprays of yellow and white blossoms, sunny day toward evening, sunset light just a little orangish in the distance.

"What do you think?"

It was Naomi. She'd caught me in my study and was grinning Cheshire-like over the partition, almost drooling with expectation.

"Of what?" I answered, buying time.

"Of *her*, Michael! That's Joanna. That's my friend I want to introduce you to."

"Oh," I said. I flipped the picture back to her like a playing card. "Cute."

"Cute?!" said Naomi (Wardrobe Report: white lace dress, puffy shoulders, red velvet bow in her hair). "Michael Moss, you *know* better! I have *yet* to meet a person who doesn't take one look at this picture and say this woman is *gorgeous*. What *is* the matter with you, anyway?"

Just what I was afraid of—accent marks. Now Naomi was getting mad, and you can't have cubiclemates mad at you. Better to piss off your best friend.

"Okay, okay," I said. "She *is* pretty, I'll give her that much. She has beautiful…" I checked the photograph, still in Naomi's hands "…eyes. She has beautiful eyes."

"So would you like to meet her? Huh? Would you?"

I looked at the picture again, falling a little deeper. But no, I had enough lion pits already.

"Um, no, I'd rather not."

"Well! That's what I get for trying to help, huh?"

Oh, she was going to be miffed now.

"See if I try to improve *your* love life, Mr. M. Michael Moss. Bad enough you can't see *beauty* when it's right in *front* of you, but now you won't even *meet* her, I mean, my God, what kind of…"

"Naomi! Please, please…" Accent marks! Accent marks!

Let there be no more accent marks! "If I agree to meet her, will you stop this ranting?"

Naomi smiled like a Sunday school teacher. "Certainly."

"Okay, okay," I laughed. "I'll meet her, but not until next week, okay? I'm developing an ulcer here."

"Oh," she said. "Um…okay."

Naomi had something up her little white lace sleeve, but I wouldn't have time to investigate because Roxy and Maria (Roxy's sergeant-at-arms) were zipping up and down the rows like crop dusters, corralling accounting department types for our weekly meeting.

"Meeting!" Roxy called. "Everybody in the lunchroom! We've got doughnuts!"

Mm! 'Nuff said! I'd suffer the dullest of department meetings for a little lard and sugar right now. The lunchroom isn't too bad this time of day, either. The morning light comes slanting in through those east-facing windows and sets the place aglow like a commercial for dishwashing liquid. Roxy lays out two dozen of my favorite sugar bombs—french crullers, glazed old-fashioned, maple bars, chocolate-covered raised, even one or two apple fritters and a bear claw. Being the first one in, I manage to grab the bear claw before the rest of the gang hits the boxes. I retreat to a back table and place my prize square in the center of my napkin.

The accounting department is mostly female, especially toward the top, and with Mark and Vijay out sick this week, Larry Coulter and I are the only males to be found. Larry comes to sit with me—a survival instinct, no doubt—escorting a luscious piece of cherry cake doughnut.

"Ostentatious display of culinary finery," he said, pointing out my bear claw.

"Indubitably," I answered.

Larry and I have this running joke. He's about the only other specimen in this rat's maze of a moron shop who can match my vocabulary, so we spend our conversations bartering twenty-dollar words.

"Quite an awe-inspiring plurality of feminine representation this morning," I said, extracting one bear-toe and stuffing it in my mouth.

"Just on happenstance," he answered, "and on testimony of the present visual evidence, I would seem to have no alternative but to concur with you, lest my perceptual capabilities be drawn into censure."

"Mm-hmm," I mumbled around my mouthful. Larry sat back in his chair and rubbed his beard, content to watch me try to swallow too fast in order to answer him in suitable fashion. Instead I got a chunk of sugar glaze stuck in my trachea and started coughing. Larry reached over and pounded me on the back, perhaps too forcefully to achieve a simple clearance of my passageways. In other words, he was enjoying this.

"Michael? Are you all right?"

It was Roxy, perched up front, showing off her fifty-but-not-finished legs, short blue skirt, white lace stockings. If I wasn't dying I'd have been impressed.

"Yes! Hughch! Mm-HEM! Yeh, I'm okay."

"Well," she smiled. "You don't have to rush so, there are plenty of doughnuts left."

The female majority certainly enjoyed *that*. I'm apparently only here for their entertainment, anyway. Larry smiled some more, fully cognizant that he had instigated this minor affair. I sipped some coffee to calm my throat down, then Roxy proceeded.

"We have a company video this morning," she said. "Now, I know most of this is geared toward the sales department, but I *would* like you to pay attention. As employees, you should know what direction the company as a whole is headed. Lucille, could you push the play button, there? There on the right. No, above that. The red light. There you go. Thank you."

Maria flicked off the lights and pulled down the east-facing blinds, cutting out the glare on the television screen.

It always amazes me how our company refuses to hire professional speakers for their videos. Their little monthly faux newscasts begin with the same kind of slick computer-generated graphics you'd expect from national football broadcasts, letters

casting about the screen with the flair of F-18s, and yet these
same geniuses populate the heart of the program with vice-
presidential geekazoids, cheap suits and ten-dollar Nebraska
haircuts (or worse, ten-dollar hairpieces), reading out each
line of type as if it had nothing to do with the preceding or
following lines, eyes spasming back and forth across the
teleprompter. Of course, National Auto Credit *is* headquar-
tered in the great Midwest—that might explain something.
With film crews on every street corner, we Californians are
pretty stuffy about production values.

Larry leaned over and whispered, "Brazenly amateurish
hokum."

I readied a return salvo but caught Roxy's eyes across the
room. She wasn't watching the video; she was watching me.
No scolding or shushing sounds—no leveling of the eyes, no
index finger to the lips—just watching. It was so eery I had to
shudder.

Five minutes later some even more highly paid bozo came
on the screen, overweight, bald, huge, thick eyeglasses, company blazer, looking like a refugee from the corner hardware
store, but this guy was at least more natural in front of the
camera. He came across with a next-door-neighbor kind of
appeal, the guy who is always out front working on his car on
Sundays, the guy who offers to lend you his leaf-blower for the
afternoon. I checked out Roxy, who was finally watching the
screen, but a second later she looked back, and I looked away,
pretending to watch some blather about a quarterly sales
program—first-buyer incentives, college-graduate discounts,
teenage virgin rebates. She was still watching…Oh, the hell
with it. I leaned over to whisper to Larry.

"Mr. Amos's capacity for oratorical verisimilitude is
vastly superior to that of his colleagues."

"A detectable improvement," Larry concurred.

I looked back to Roxy. Still watching. Oh, Jesus Christ and
the Twelve Apostles. I stared right back at her and winked my
most gaudy wink. She smiled, almost imperceptibly, and
crossed her devil legs.

We watched cars drive off into the sunset, much faster and more steadily than those produced by our company, and the credits rolled on. Cameraman, producer, director, scriptwriter—these had to be pseudonyms, right? The picture cleared to FBI-warning blue and Maria lugged her two hundred pounds to the corner to hit the light switch. The accounting department lifted its hands as one to cover its eyeballs.

"Ummm, I don't actually have a lot of business this morning. Remember, we're changing to new credit slips next week. Be sure and throw out all those A-7's by tomorrow. Carolyn, did you have anything?"

Carolyn was the matron of the collections department: cookie-cutter born-again schoolmarm type—cotton print dresses with high collars, long straight hair in barrettes, plain white stockings, sensible shoes, pseudo-Midwestern when she spoke. Rumor had it she was actually only about a year older than me, but I'd want to see that birth certificate.

"Just come to me if you have any audit questions. Oh, and double-check on bankruptcies. We've had a few go through the cracks in section five this week."

Roxy waited to make sure Carolyn was done.

"Okay," she said. "One last thing. I *know* everyone's busy, and I don't want to cut into your social and/or family lives too much, but I would like *everyone* to come by Fred's farewell party at Sneakers tonight."

No one said anything, but a silent unison groan spread through the room like an oil spill.

"Now you know, Fred made a tough decision in transferring to Fresno. He's been at this branch almost twenty years, and this is quite a stressful time for him."

What she couldn't say was that Fred's wife ran off last year with her lesbian lover, an overnight flight to Denver while Fred was away at a car show in Reno. Not that Fred deserved better, anyway. You could find mitochondria with more highly developed social abilities. Something like Mr. Rogers as possessed by Satan.

"Anyway," said Roxy, "please come by, if only for a few

minutes, just to at least say good-bye. I would *personally* appreciate it very much."

Roxy targeted the word "personally" in my direction. Holy shit! I'm surrounded.

So here I am in the mailroom, sorting intercompany envelopes into a row of slots, one clear plastic sleeve for each dealer, all makes, all brands; they all use our credit, the row of spastic-light suburban showrooms near my apartment, the sleazy used car dealers downtown, Teddie Smith and his horse Smithie, bulleting their sick grins from the TV, white cowboy hat for each, squeezing the words "NOBODY beats Valley Ford!" through their narrow equine sinuses. Well, here's your mail, Smithie. Oh too bad, coupla repos today, no oats today, pal, cain't trust those late-night viewers, they're sleaze bags one and all, cain't barely pay the rent much less buy a four wheel drive from you and your saddle-pal.

I dreamt I peed my pants last night. Not that I was in *bed* peeing my pants. Oh no, that was much too private and easy. No, I think I was at a bar, or was it a public park, or was it a church, during a concert? *Deo Gratias* for black tuxedo pants. Only the bass to the right of me can hear the adagio drip-drip-drip onto the marble floor next to the risers, and this ain't holy water, ladies and gentiles, this is the real stuff, a little yellow puddle, then a miniature spillway, then a one-one hundredth scale model of the Grand Coulee Dam, apple cider river of urine spilling down the nave, through the narthex and down the steps to Diaz Avenue. My God, where's it all coming from? And there's Amy Fine, *da capo al fine*, out on that island out there, missing nary a beat behind the podium. How *does* she do it?

I run the last of the overdue payment envelopes through the postage meter, whip a rubber band round the whole ensemble, and pack it into the plastic postal service box. On the way out the front door I spy Roxy, walking away in her short blue skirt, five o'clock energy pushing her hips to and fro and fro some more because she is going to get some meat tonight, baby, she is headed for the land of long-necks and green olives and no excuses! She glances back, looking for the clock, catches me near the service counter and finally returns that wink.

One way or another, I am going to wind up wet tonight.

Sneakers.

No matter what happens at the Sunnyvale branch of National Auto Credit, when there is some reason to go out and drink and dance and carouse, Sneakers is the place. Sneakers is our night-care center.

The locale is perfect, a simple tenderfoot route down El Camino three lights, then right on Wolfe, four blocks and you're there. The distance is perfect, too, just close enough to get there before you start realizing how tired you are, just far enough so you can unshackle your office chrysalis and let loose that social butterfly.

Then there's the atmosphere. Plunked down in the middle of a corner shopping market, right next to a supermarket for God's sake, Sneakers nonetheless maintains a wholly separate identity once you step inside. The active current is a sports-bar *rowdismo* reminiscent of the average halftime beer commercial, only the people ain't so blame good-lookin'. It *is* dark enough, however, to make everyone look pretty attractive—indirect plastic surgery spots focused on the walls covered with sports memorabilia: dog-eared pennants, newspaper clippings, team photos, old baseball gloves and tennis racquets and wood-shafted golf clubs with rusty heads. And a sailboard lifted up across the ceiling, underbelly of Day-Glo green.

The furniture is comfortable faux-wood, chairs with nice big cushions and booths with red vinyl upholstery and tall round tables circled by tall round stools and brass railings, all around some rectangle of a pit they call the dance floor. Legendary sports figures romp across the walls in acrylic paint—footballers making fingertip nabs, baseball heroes winding themselves out of home run swings. When the music comes on—a bland, gorpish slab of Top 40 old and new—the folks dance while a screen flashes a full library of on-the-edge action sports: swimming pool skateboarders, cliff skiers, bungee-cord divers, and sundry other licensed suicide artists.

I went to the bar and ordered a long-neck, even though I knew they'd all be drinking from pitchers by now, managers and small-time execs throwing down twenties just to show how big and magnanimous they are. No, I bought my own bottle to preserve my own identity, to feel more secure knowing I possessed my very own individual consumer package of alcoholic beverage. That's how desperate I was getting.

The first person I encountered was Brad, a tall, wiry cuss from the wild Northwest who liked to chew tobacco and played a pretty decent brand of softball when he wasn't downing six-packs just before game time. Brad was one of our repo wizards and the best storyteller in the bunch; they could make a television series from the big shiny whoppers he laid out. As for me, I needed to take this socializing thing little tadpole steps at a time, and Brad's welcoming horse laugh seemed a good first boulder across the river. He was just finishing up a game of bar basketball, an ingenious quarter-sucking monstrosity with nets all around and a hoop in which you try to sink as many dwarf basketballs as possible by the end of the time limit. Five seconds left out of forty-five, Brad was up to fifty-four points, pretty remarkable for anyone.

"Shit!" he spit out, missing the last shot short off the rim. The timer clicked to goose eggs and gave him the equivalent of an electronic raspberry: HUUNNNN!

"Damn cocksucker piece a…oh hi Mikey! Hey you ever try this thing? Nifty little gadget here."

"Umno," I said. "But why're you so mad? Looks like a pretty good score to me."

"Oh uh, yeah, it is, but if I woulda sunk that last one I woulda got ten more bonus seconds."

"Oh, I get it. So, how's the party goin' here?"

"Here, go ahead, try it," said Brad, not the least fooled by my change of subject. "I got a coupla quarters right here."

He popped them in the slot and then reached for a large paper cup on the railing. I thought he was going to drink from it, but instead he meshed his jaws together and let out a stream of bubbly reddish brown ooze. I'd only ever seen this on baseball telecasts, and believe me, television does little justice to the genuine article.

I wasn't ready for competition this suddenly, but when Brad reached over and punched the flashing white square and four little orange spheres came at me like marauding huns, the adrenaline hit and I was right back out on the Catholic schoolyard. Brad shouted instructions as I went.

"No, not straight in, hit it off the backboard, yeah, like that, now try it one-handed, roll it off your fingers, yeah, you got it. Hot damn, Mikey, you're rollin'!"

I was. In one stretch I hit a dozen in a row, straight off the same spot on the backboard, an inch low from the center of its pumpkin orange square. I shot with my right hand, while with my left I searched for balls like a dishman feeling for plates in the sink water. I fetched them up one by one, transferred them over to my shooting hand and fired, never taking my eyes from that magic impact point. Just before zero I hit one last shot, around the rim and in, and reached the bonus score. Brad made up his own cheering squad.

"All right, Mikey, Do it, do it! You're a bonus baby, boy!"

The adrenaline surged, spilling over the rim of my tanks, too much. I overshot a couple from the excitement, then hesitated a split second, setting myself back in rhythm like a second hand. *Andante*, I thought, *andante espressivo*, baby boy, baroque pulse, Bach, think Bach! and sank the last five, swishing my final shot at the buzzer.

"Holy shit!" Brad shouted. "Seventy-six! You little hustler! Here, let's do another."

"No," I said. "No, I don't think I could, man, thanks anyway. Think I'll quit while I'm ahead."

"All right, Mikey! Hey, let me buy you a beer, though, and we'll go over and tell our lady friends all about your hidden talents. Shee! Score like that'll get you laid!"

Brad hopped off to the bar. I scooped up the remaining two balls and hook-shot them dead through the rim. This could be all right, I thought, this could turn into a decent night. In all the excitement, I forgot I still had two-thirds of my original beer left.

"Here you go, buddy," said Brad. "Let's take off."

We quick-stepped away, me with twin bottles, Brad with a bottle and a cup of red goo, up the ramp to corporate headquarters, the far corner over the dance pit. We liked to think of it as our own little office annex. I noted the circle worn into Brad's back pocket by various containers of chaw. This dude was serious.

He led us right up to the capital table, manned by Michael Cunningham, Fred Glynn, the guest-of-honor-headed-for-Fresno himself, and the femme fatale of accounting, Miz Roxanne Cater. Roxy was licking her lips already, first sign of impending drunkishness. She was taking scuba-diver sips from a hard drink, just guessing maybe a Manhattan (ever notice how all the nasty drinks are named after New York?). Mr. Cunningham and Fred were at the tail end of some glorious repo saga from days of yore when women were girls and men drove Buicks. Cunningham was talking.

"...and that ratty little sucker followed me for half a mile, *on foot*, screaming like a banshee the whole way. I had to run a red light to finally get away."

"Y'sure run into a whole lottasholes in repo, Cunningham," Fred tried to say, pointing a finger at some important spot in the ceiling. "I ssshure miss it."

Fred was plugged into intravenous margaritas, crystals of salt hanging from his mustache. *Fresno*. Poor guy.

"I'm gonna miss you, Fred. Hey! Look who's here, my young compadres Brad and Mikhail! How're you doing, fellas?"

I gripped both beers in one hand and shook Cunningham's big paw with the other. He gripped tight, almost squeezing my fingers out of alignment, but I was ready for him and had on my survival grip, palm deep into palm, keep those knuckles out of the vise, save yourself a little arthritis some day. These auto guys were dangerous with their handshakes.

"Mikey here just skunked me in bar-sketball," said Brad. "He's got hidden talents."

"I know, I know," said Cunningham. He turned to Fred finally, releasing me from his death grip. "I was trying to get young Mr. Moss for your department, Fred, but he had other items on his agenda, chasing all those tender young skirts in accounting."

"Issashame," Fred drooled. "Dirty shame. Coulda used ya."

Roxy gave me a look of pure candle glow, whether from alcohol or latent hormones I don't know. She didn't look anywhere near capable of speech, but she'd surprised me before. She licked her lips all the way around in a 360-degree curl before she uttered her testimony on my behalf.

"Mr. Michael Moss is a hundred-watt bulb in a room full of night lights," she said, then sighed—my God—sighed. "He is a bona...fide...sweet...heart."

"Oh-hoh!" said Cunningham, who, I'm sure, with his former-jock mentality had designs on taking Roxy to some discreet location after the party. "No *wonder* I can't pry you from Roxy's iron grip, eh? Can't say as I blame you."

Not that I'd give Brad this much credit for clever timing, but he immediately changed the subject. I secretly thanked him.

"Did I tell you about that full-gonzo psycho case last week, Freddy? Told the guy I was gonna come get his ol' heap, and then next morning found it in a parking lot around the corner from his apartment building, completely penned in by ten other cars! Like a goddamn wagon train, circling for the Indians!"

"Nooohh!" Fred blurted out. He picked up a napkin and wiped up the saliva he'd blurted out, too. "How dee doo it?"

Given Brad's flair for storytelling, you can always divide the numbers by five—this was probably a case of two cars, for instance—but that was beside the point.

"I dunno," he said. "I guess Mr. Asshole called all his friends over and had them pull in all around him—thought we'd give up or something."

Dramatic pause. *Tick Tick Tick*. Roxy took the bait, leaning forward on her stool.

"Well? What did you do?"

The finish welled up like magma in a volcano, and Brad had to let it out in a burst, slapping the palm of his hand against the table.

"Hah! Ah-ha-ha-ha-ha! We called the trucks in and towed them *all*!"

"Oh God!" Cunningham said, grinning. "*That* must have been a project!"

"Lov't'see th'look on…on the guy's face when gotbek," said Fred.

Brad smiled a leafy red smile and spit a wad of juice into his cup.

"I did," he said. "I went to a diner across the street and staked out the place till he came back."

"Oh Brad!" said Roxy. "You're *ee*-vill!"

Fred hiccuped and said, "Cunningham, we ought not…pay this man so much. He has too much fun on the job!"

All during Brad's story I had the faint feeling my name was being called, but attributed it to the crowd and the music blaring away over the pit. When the voice finally came through, it sounded like Betty Boop or Olive Oyl or some other squeaky cartoon character.

"*Yoo*-hoo! *Mi*-chael!"

Like Naomi. She was standing on top of her barstool, waving a napkin at me, and what she was wearing? Holy shit! Gold lamé blouse, white matador jacket studded with red and orange rhinestones, and a black leather mini with fishnet stockings. Nothing to be wearing when you're standing on top of a barstool waving a hanky.

I waved back, hoping she'd disappear. I turned back to the table and drank from one of my beers. Now she was yelling at me, a distressed mother calling her naughty boy in for dinner.

"Michael! Get over here!"

I really had to get to these things earlier, before everyone got quite so drunk.

"Sounds like you've got a fan, Mikey!" said Brad. "I'd get over there quick before she cools off. I told you, man— seventy-six points, man."

"I guess you're right," I said, then flashed my best phony smile to the Round Table. "Be seein' you folks."

"Save me a dance…Mikey," said Roxy, and smiled. Oh God.

I broke my way through the mob like a fullback on a goal-line run, throwing tacklers, picking up blockers, finally parting two linebackers from sales to find Naomi seated next to her friend with the deadly onyx eyes. Oh shit. No escape now.

"Michael, this is my friend Joanna. Joanna, this is Michael Moss. He's friendlier than he seems."

Not having any recourse, I faced the enemy, taking her fingers in my hand.

"Hi, Joanna."

Joanna's lips quivered up in that shy smile from her photograph—oh, why did she have to do that?—and she greeted me back.

"Naomi's told me a lot about you."

"Naomi…" I began in my lecturing voice. "I thought I…" Oh God, now she's brushing her hair back with her hands. "I…it's a pleasure meeting your friend, Naomi."

Somehow in the nonstop din of Sneakers, Joanna and I managed an awkward silence. Naomi, never one to tolerate a silence, broke between us like bologna in a sandwich.

"Let's all dance!" she announced. Who did she think she was, Dick Clark? Co-workers turned toward us en masse, little light bulbs dangling over their heads.

"Yeah!" said someone. Invitations passed from boy to girl to male to female, and the corner began to empty itself toward the pit, a migration of locusts.

"Dance with Joanna, Michael." Naomi smiled at me devilishly. "She's a great dancer!"

Joanna looked down just a tad and then came out from under those black-curtain bangs with a broad smile. I fell back, blinded. And those lips, reminiscent of…Mozart…

"Well," she laughed. "I *can* keep a beat."

Oh God, I thought, *What now? Where now?* Out of the corner of my eye, I caught a face falling into a Manhattan.

"I'm sorry, Joanna, but I promised to dance with Roxy. She's my boss—you understand."

"Umm, sure," she said, not too sure.

"I'll, umm, catch you later, okay?"

"Sure."

"Nice meeting you." I was already weaving back along the tables, approaching the Round Table, watching Joanna's onyx eyes fade over my shoulder.

Well, I had to do this now, I guess. I figured Roxy would be at the touching-herself phase now, harmless and drunk, and besides, I'd score some political points, never know when they'd come in handy…

"Roxanne," I said, out of breath. "Would you care to dance?"

Roxy set herself into the Oh-I'm-too-old-I-need-to-be-coaxed posture.

"Oh, I shouldn't, I really…"

"Nonsense, Cater!" Mr. Cunningham growled good-naturedly. "Get out there and show these young punks how it's done!"

"I really would appreciate it, Roxy," I said, smiling my best phony smile. "Come on, let's dance!"

"Oh…Okay," Roxy said. She hopped off her stool and grabbed me by the hand, dragging me down to the pit where most of the company's young tribe had set about jumping, whirling, twisting, mashing.

The song was some heavy funk tune, metal guitar solo, some pretty wicked downbeats—not anything Roxy was probably used to, but she surprised me. This fifty-year-old could really move. She ground her hips while drawing out a circle in the dance floor air, then moved up and ground her hips against *me*. Cunningham and Fred sat on the rail, cheering her on.

"Get him, girl! Yow!"

The next tune was some kind of retro rockabilly number, heavy two-beat on every other bar, taste of country chug-a-chug. I thought about bowing out now, but Roxy had herself a full head of steam, and besides, I could see Joanna watching intently from her seat, little pink ice cream shop number in her hands, waiting patiently. My only hope was that she'd get into a conversation with someone so I could sneak the hell out of there. I was brought out of my scheming by a hard slap on my rear.

"Come on, Mikey! Dance!"

Jesus. Well, okay. Actually, if she didn't get any worse here this wasn't so bad, I mean, I like dancing, and Roxy was quite the terpsichorean. It seemed likely she wouldn't remember any of this. She surprised me again by thrusting her pelvis forward, crossing one leg over the other and spinning twice, fast, finishing with a slide, hands stretched out like an umpire calling safe. She licked her lips and winked at me, then bounced forward, her blouse dangerously unbuttoned. She rubbed up against me and spoke in my ear.

"You know how to touch dance, Moss?"

"Umm, yeah, sure Rox."

"Then *spin* me."

I took Roxy's hand and motioned her around once, then she yelled for another. Okay, I thought. As long as I'm out here I might as well show off a little (*oh no*, the basketball game wasn't enough for me). I whirled her around and caught her by the waist, passed by her side and let go, sliding off a hand, then reaching behind my back to take the other, springing back, then one step toward each other, release, and let her slide into a spin, rolling along her arm till she was about to fall, then stopped her with a hand, worked her into a double pirouette, finishing her off by pulling her in close and walking us around in a tight, fast circle.

"Whew!" she exhaled, eyes lit up. "You're *good*, Michael.

Can you do that shoulder slide thing?"

"Sure," I said, not missing a beat. I let her back and then pulled forward, curling a hand over the back of her neck and sliding it along her arm, catching her hand at the very last second and spinning her back into me.

"Where *did* you learn all this?" she asked, still spinning.

"Mom and Pop," I answered. "Best damn swing dancers in Indiana."

"I like," she smiled.

The end of the tune was coming, so I spun her once more and leaned her into a full dip, touching her hair to the floor. The music ended. Our two-man peanut gallery went wild, Cunningham yelling "woo-woo-woo!" like a train whistle. Roxy covered her face in triumphant embarrassment. Then a slow tune started, some sexy Motown soul thing from the sixties. I searched for the Persian girl along the railing. She was gone.

"Well, thanks Roxy, I'd better..."

"Come on, Michael, let's slow dance. It's been so long..."

"No, I'd really...I have to..."

Roxy leaned to my ear and turned the request into a command.

"*Dance* with me, Michael." (CC: Board of Trustees, National Auto Credit.)

What could I say? Nothing, unless I wanted plenty of trouble later. I *did* need to pay the rent. I took hold of Roxy Cater, my boss, almost a quarter-century older than myself, around her sexy little former nun's waist and took one extended hand. Roxy closed her eyes and began to sway with the music, a slight gospel feel to it, nirvana in the amen corner. She swooned forward into me, close-close. Her legs were inside mine. She pushed her breasts against my rib cage and spoke in a trance.

"I used to dance to this song back in college...with my beau..." She giggled. "You don't call them that anymore, do you? He was a tall man, a little taller than you, Michael, and boy could he dance, could he...dance! You're like him,

Michael, you've got that blood flow, that sense for rhythm, so...*sensual*."

Now was the time for panic. *Tick tick tick...* Had I not been placed in enough terror-filled situations for one week? Were the gods not happy with my sacrifices? Had I cheated a little boy out of his place in line on the bumper car rides, some Sunday three years past, and was I paying for it now? Had I no control whatsoever over my own life, dammit!? In movement three of my solemn vespers, Roxy Cater cuddled up against me, craned her neck over my shoulder and inserted her tongue in my ear.

"How would you like a taste of something with a little...*vintage* tonight, huh, Michael?"

Holy shit! Was anyone watching us? Someone had to be watching us. Naomi, or her onyx-eyed friend, or Michael Cunningham, getting pissed because I was cutting in on his late-night rendezvous. I don't want her, Cunningham, she's all yours, call the tow trucks and repossess her right now! No one answered. There is no God. My life was over. I tried to keep dancing, maybe sway her back out of this and she'd forget the whole foolish idea, go back to her Long Island ice teas and drink till she started touching herself again. I felt the sweat beading up on my forehead.

"Now Roxy, I..."

Her next step was to take her hand off my shoulder and move it down to my crotch, where she began massaging me as she listed further opportunities.

"I know you're not ever going to give me your mind, Michael Moss, but can I at least have your cock?"

"Roxy, come on now, a joke's a joke, but come on, stop that now."

I tried to take her hand back, but she eluded my grasp and put it right back, finding my zipper and pulling it southward.

"Come on, Michael, I bet you'd be a great fuck."

Now I was pissed. If there was no God, if I had no way out, I would by damn take the worst way out. I grabbed her shoulders and pushed her off me, hard.

"Roxy, get your hands off my balls!"

Funny what adrenaline will do to your volume controls. I thought I was whispering. I wasn't. Every person in the Sneakers establishment at that moment did two things. Number one: sat frozen at their tables, a battalion of deaf-mutes turning to stare at Roxy and Michael on the dance floor. Then number two: realizing what they had just heard, began laughing. *Uproariously* laughing. In unison. *Tutti! Vivace! Espressivo! Fortissimo! Balls! Ah-ha-ha-ha-ha!*

Roxy flushed so badly I thought she was going to drop right there, but she recovered quickly, turning a bloody thermometer red from a combination of rage and embarrassment. She turned and stormed up the steps, followed by me, limping from the erection she had just given me with her talented fingers, blurting the beginnings of apologies.

"Roxy, I'm sorry, I...I didn't know, I...Please..."

It was then that time began to slow down again, and I knew I was in trouble. As Destiny with a capital D would have it, a cocktail waitress crossed our path at that very moment, the crosshatch of the double reverse, the wide receiver swinging back around to the halfback coming the other direction, holding aloft a pitcher of ice water. Cold, wet ice water. Roxy Cater, being an opportunistic businesswoman, who by reacting quickly in all situations, after all, had worked her way from the convent to the head of a sizable accounting department in the nation's second largest auto credit agency, commandeered the pitcher, pivoted with a litheness and smooth coordination that would have impressed Wilt Chamberlain, and deposited the ice water over my head.

I froze in midgesture, one index finger pointed skyward. I lost my erection. The coldness hit me like an explosion. I couldn't breathe. I thought my heart would stop. I shook my head—bladee bladee bla—chunks of ice clattering to the floor. I was snapped back by the roar of the crowd, thirty, forty, fifty what the hell the Roman Colosseum what did it matter co-workers standing and whooping and slapping their knees. Brad would tell the story and have Roxy dumping five pitchers of mai-tais over my head. *"And then she stuffed three jars of maraschino cherries down his pants!"*

It took me one long second to decide what to do. I surveyed a path between myself and the door, and I took it, quicker than a base runner breaking for second when he sees the high kick and knows the pitcher's throwing home. I didn't bother with the restroom and the hand dryer. I didn't bother with cleaning myself. I didn't bother with my coat still draped over my stool next to Naomi and the Persian lady. I sped forward, churning my legs, dodging tables, bursting out the doors into the night, narrowly missing three girls outside, then skidding around the corner of the sidewalk to my car. I thrust out my key, hopped in, and revved the engine, ready to go, when someone knocked on the window.

Cheese it! The cops! No, it was Larry, looking in at me, curious and a little set back. I cranked down the window.

"Michael! What the…"

"Larry!" I said, smiling in delirium. "It's been a pleasure working with you!"

I shook Larry's hand then burnt back out of my spot, taking that car for all it was worth across the lot and out onto Wolfe Road. I saw Larry in the rearview mirror, huge invisible question mark over his head.

A question for the nonexistent God: What is it about me that draws women and water? Am I the moon?

Chapter Fourteen

Saturday
Allegro moderato maestoso

It was the first week of the new year. Nancy and I were seated in the balcony of the Catalyst in Santa Cruz, taking in some crazy Tex-Mex band, David Lindley and El Rayo X. I didn't really feel like dancing; I didn't know why. Nancy was scratching a fingernail along my thigh and peering over the railing at something, completely distracted.

"What's the matter?" I said, taking her hand from my leg and wrapping it in my fingers. "See a ghost?"

Nancy didn't respond. She was focusing too intently to answer me. Then she stopped and held a hand over her eyes.

"Omigod," she said. "It's him. He's here."

No need to explain who *he* was; it was her husband. And I had carried around this thought for the whole month: *I am fooling around with another man's wife.*

"Where is he?" I asked. "Is he coming up here?"

She looked over the railing again, picking apart the crowd.

"No. I think he's just waiting. He looks like he knows where I am. He's just waiting."

From what I'd heard about hubby, this was typical. I almost wished he'd come on up, just for fun. Something about being the spoiler in the middle of a soap opera plotline appealed to me at this moment; there was *power* there. On the other hand, I knew it wasn't the way Nancy would want it, and the guy might just be lulu enough to pull something uncalled-for. Nancy took a sip from her Blue Hawaii margarita, considering her next step.

"I'll go down and talk to him," she said. "You stay here."

"Are you sure? Are you gonna be okay?"

"I'll be fine," she said, grabbing her purse, leaving her jacket. "Mark's a pussycat. A screwed-up, worthless pussycat, but a pussycat nonetheless."

I watched the band while she was gone. The guitarist was out on some heavy metal solo all of a sudden, kneeling at the front of the stage where women in bandanas and southwest colors reached up on tippytoes to lay on a hand. The time shouldn't have gone fast, but it did. Nancy returned and settled into her seat, visibly shaken.

"I'm so embarrassed, Michael." She laughed nervously, then put on a mock French accent: "She eez a wonton woo-mawn, out een zee cloobs with her jhee-goh-loh. Zen zee jealous huzzbawnd walks een. *Merde*! It eez zee beeg-time truh-buhl!"

"Hey, it's okay," I said, trying to keep from laughing. "What do you want to do?"

She let out a nervous sigh. "I want to wait fifteen minutes, then get the hell out of here. Then I want to go home. I...can't sleep with you tonight, Michael. It'd feel too weird right now."

"Yeah," I said. "I understand. I feel a little weird myself."

Back in the offices of National Auto Credit, back in the valley, I was interrupted in my filing work.

"Michael, can I see you a moment? Let's go into Mr. Cunningham's office. He's out sick today."

The lady was my boss, but I still had trouble remembering her name. Roseanne? Rochelle? I played it safe and called her Miz Cater, slurring the z because I also couldn't remember if she was married or not. I heard some rumor about a convent, but you really couldn't believe that kind of stuff, especially when you were just temping.

"Please sit down," she said, not an invitation but a request. From all indications, Miz Cater was an agreeable person to work for. I was just happy to be there; by this time I'd almost caught up with all my bills. She gathered herself on top of Mr. Cunningham's desk while I settled into a low chair, hands gripped along the metal arms for balance. I wasn't quite used to this office stuff yet, and any meeting with a superior was likely to set off my stomach.

"I've been pleased with your work this month, Michael. You show a high aptitude for the tasks we've given you. You've been especially helpful in cleaning out our filing system, and in doing so you've shown a great deal of initiative and perseverance. I know it's menial, hard labor, but believe me, it is just as essential to the operation of this office as all the other, more challenging work."

You could find no more revealing picture of my mental state that year than my reaction to this little official-sounding preamble. I kept waiting for Miz Cater, Roxy it was, I think— I kept waiting for her to say, "however" (or its blue-collar equivalent, "but"), followed by all the necessary niceties required to terminate my employment at this branch of NAC. Come on, everything else this year had fucked itself inside out, why not this? The whole pattern of Roxy's speech reminded me of how Stacy had gone about breaking up with me: "I love you, Michael, and you've shown a great deal of initiative and perseverance in cleaning out my filing system, but…"

"Well, anyway," said Roxy, "what I'm getting around to is—we'd like to hire you on permanently, full-time. We couldn't start you too high due to the inconsistencies in your recent work history, but the company health benefits would more than make up for it. Also, and this should give you a good indication of what we think of your work, I will be spending a goodly sum buying your contract away from the temp agency."

Roxy perched higher on Michael Cunningham's desk and crossed her legs. "So. What do you think? Will you stay on?"

Approval at last! Glory! Rapture! Shock! This was good news, and I had no memory of how to respond. She may as well have been speaking Swahili. I responded by gripping the arms of my chair so tightly I thought I might bend the metal in my bare hands.

"Umm...Ungghk!" (I had to clear my throat.) "Um, yes, I'd like to work here. It's...why, yes."

Roxy clasped her hands together and gave them a short now-we're-cookin' rub. "Great! I'll have the paperwork ready for you by the end of the week, and you can start officially next Wednesday. Oh, and I'll have some new responsibilities for you, too. I think you'll enjoy the challenge."

Roxy gave my shoulder a little rub as she walked out of the office, a motion of reassurance, but she had already done a better job of reassuring me than anyone or anything in a long time. Nothing speaks so clearly to the soul as cold, hard cash. Our little conference had lasted right up until closing time, so I went to my tiny corner desk to fetch my jacket and switch off my lights. I took the elevator to the ground floor, stepped out the front doors and breathed in the air with lungs more full and white than the day before.

I don't believe too much in dreams. I mean, I believe in *having* dreams, but I don't believe in making too much of them. It's all just excess energy shooting itself off in the night, unrelated reflections, tiny magneto-rays tapping along your synapses. But some of them are beautiful, and this one I had last night was pure. Pure is a rare quantity.

I was circling a pond in the high hills east of the valley, tall brown grass all around, almost desert country in the summer, dusty trails, chaparral full of manzanita and prickly scrub ready to take you down by your shoelaces. It was overcast, and I was traversing dry cracked lake bed turning slowly to mud, starting to envelop the bottoms of my shoes. I had a camera strung around my neck and was trying to position myself behind a submerged tree, slick white branches rising from the grey water like the ribs of a brontosaurus. Just a little further, just one foot further…I sunk in and stayed there, positioning the lens, then took two shots, a horizontal catching the breadth of the lake, a vertical leading the driftwood ribs skyward into chimney-smoke clouds. One of these would turn out, hope I had the f-stop right, had to crank down a little because I'm shooting into the sun.

And then it landed. A crane, soap bar white against the grey of the pond, the mute of the sky, the strips of brown shoreline in between. I had to get it. The crane settled onto a small island only a few feet off the far bank, folding in its long wings like Chinese drapery. I slopped through the mud all the way around, stepping carefully so I wouldn't make a sudden move and scare it off. A barbed wire fence blocked my way, but I slipped along over a ten-foot stretch of shallow next to it, hopping back onto muddy shore on the other side. The mud here was deeper yet, sucking away at my sneakers, flipping up onto my corduroys in odd impressionist brush strokes. Yeesh. But I was almost there.

I found a piling off the bank, almost as if someone used to tie a rowboat there. I lifted myself up and knew I had the shot; the crane was still, like it hadn't even seen me. I preset the f-stop and shutter speed, slipped off the lens cap, and held the viewfinder to my eye. Right there, right there…

And gone. The great bird scattered off before I could focus and landed on the other side of the pond, an indistinct spot of white. Nothing. Not worth it. But maybe if I headed back, what the hell, I had to head back anyway…

And on the other side, fifteen minutes later, the same thing: hold the camera up to your eye and just about to focus when the feathers stir upward, the legs lift up long and trailing, and he is gone for good, a streak of white signifying nothing. The crane circled the pond twice, looking for a third place to land, then changed his mind, shifted to a higher circuit, and drifted on over the hill, effortless, uncatchable. I slipped off my shoes and stepped barefoot into the water, feeling the earth take me down.

This morning, after the shower, I towel myself off and am completely dry, but I know it is not for long. Women will come and throw water at me until I drown or give up, or both. They are the enemy now, clear as Nazis. I must stay away from them. But that's what I've been trying to do all along and it's not working a hell of a lot of good, is it?

I may have lost my job last night. I suppose it depends on how drunk Roxy Cater really was, and, God, I hope she was truly skitzeroo. In any case, I am trying to cover these wounds with the adhesive strips of my Saturday morning ritual, trying to remember that I have an important night coming up; the choir is depending on me, Amy Fine is depending on me, and I know in front of an audience, behind a podium, the worst she can do is spit in my direction. That I can handle.

And so begins the ritual. I crack three eggs into the shell of a margarine bowl, whip up a fork from the silverware tray, and skip it into the yolks, taking their character, their little sunshine nodules and the clear noxious goo on the top, and turning it into a comfortable, nondescript yellow. You are ready for me now, I say, you are all mine, I have made mush of you! I pull out a loaf of whole wheat bread and take two slices to begin with, dipping them through the eggs back and forth, just enough for a solid coat, and splash them onto the skillet, the excess egg on the sides sizzling like mud flaps, little yellow tongues giving me the raspberries—pspspspspsps!

I've got a couple minutes, I know, the skillet isn't up to full heat yet, so I grab the remote and flip on the TV. Cartoons, no, farm report, no, documentary on marine life (education! are you kidding me?), ah, baseball, and my favorite announcer, who bindeth my wounds with familiar quotations of scripture:

a floater on the inside right past him, he got quite a jump on the kick home, McNally flashes the sign, looking for the forkball on this one, he got him! It's deep, that one is…wayback…wayback! wayback! YOU CAN TELL IT GOOD-BYE!!! Loopy Smith ties up the game with a MON-STER home run!…

So here's how I figure. I am incapable of having further bad luck this week. I have used up my allotment. Now, I know there is some variation here, I know some folks are delivered grams of misfortune whilst others receive megatons, but this I am sure of. I have no more cash and no more credit in the bank of bad dreams. Forget it. I am going to kick some holy butt tonight, because no one can hurt me. I've got this thing licked.

The next man up lifted a fly into shallow right, and the right fielder couldn't track it, the sun was right in his eyes. The second baseman flipped up his shades and tailed backward, but he couldn't see so he flipped them back down. You couldn't see his face, he was holding his glove up between himself and the ball and the sun which were now the same object. He kept wandering out, looking over his shoulder, until now he was headed back toward center, turned completely the wrong direction. At the last second he pulled that ball out of the sunlight and reached his glove around as he spun for it. *Pummph!* Quail in a basket.

"He shouldn't have had a prayer!" said the announcer. "Klatten just pulled that ball out of nowhere! Jim, if that isn't a miracle, bring it to me in a box…"

Pittsburgh went up by five runs in the sixth, so I decided to shun the laundry and wander out to the community center for a postbreakfast constitutional. It was warm outside, so I slipped on my bathing suit and T-shirt and scrambled out barefoot, loping up the sides of apartment house entranceways with their pool table grass still wet from the nighttime sprinklers. I crossed the street in front of an impatient-looking cab driver with an elderly passenger. I thought he was about to run me over, so I skipped across the asphalt without looking and landed on a nice bit of sharp gravel on the other side. I hopped over the sidewalk in pain and fell on the grass to reach down and dig it out of the thick skin on the bottom of my foot.

As soon as I recovered, I stood up and, avoiding the paths with their pebbly rock surfaces, limped up the hill and past my kite-flying sculpture to look out on…an empty pond.

What the hell was going on here? Water everywhere but here? It was gone—gone gone gone—nothing in the place of my lovely blue-surface illusion but an off-white plain of scummy concrete not more than three feet down from the rim. I strode down the hill to the edge and found my answer, a sign on top of the drain reading, THIS POND DRAINED TO FACILITATE SUMMER DROUGHT CONDITIONS. WE APOLOGIZE FOR THE INCONVENIENCE.

Inconvenience, hell! What I wanted was some water, goddammit! Not on my head, not in my socks, but just lying there, passive and pretty, doing its damnedest to improve the scenery and the lives of men. And where for God's sake were the Bachelor Ducks?

I sat down on the rim of the pond and gave the park a good scan. Buildings, elm trees, orchards back on the rear acres, check, group of little kids playing with a whiffle ball, check. Bachelor Ducks! Two o'clock! Confused as an elephant in a New York subway, but at least they were still here. At least something was normal in this godforsaken town. They were milling around under the large oak on the far side, quacking and squawking like some duck shriners' convention, trying to figure out what this sudden, unnatural change could mean.

Apparently it meant departure. The big ugly black one with the albino bill scouted out what used to be the edge of the water, took a final look around and, in a moment of admirable executive decision-making prowess, raised his wings and took off. The rest of them reared up their webbed feet behind him, and soon they were shooting off together over the algae-stained lake bed of their home. They circled once for good measure and took off over the auto dealerships, only this time they weren't coming back. I was on my own.

When I got back to my apartment, the Cubs had rallied in

the ninth to take the game 8-7. The Pittsburgh stopper came in with bases loaded and walked in the winning run. I decided I had better do my laundry and not count on anything.

I had no idea what fate St. Michael's held for me that night, the night of the concert. This could be the end of a part of my life. This could be the end of my life, period. Once Amy Fine trained those deadly hazel eyes on me and told me to sing, I would not be the same. With all its rhythms, its give and take, its dependence on motion and breathing and the diaphragm, and on sounds so close to the character of ecstatic moaning, choral singing is too much like sex. It should never be done in public.

"I want to be an organist tonight," said Mr. Stutz. "I want each of you to be a key, and I want to play you with my fingers." Organs. Playing people with your fingers. See what I mean?

"I'd like to warm you up tonight by running through the *entrances* to each *movement* of the works." Uh-oh. Accents again. "This is *not* to check parts, this is simply to get into the *flow* of things, to know where we are all *headed* together. I want you to sing only loudly enough that it's comfortable. These three works are very *hard* on the voice. I don't want you to strain yourself *now*. You can strain yourself *later*, when it counts."

"But *first*," he went on. "First, I want you to look around you, at your *choirmates*, at *me*, but mostly at this *incredible* piece of art and architecture. There are saints here on these walls, and angels, and people from long ago, and one *particular* individual"—he pointed to Christ on the crucifix of the far wall—"who has had quite a bearing on all of us. I want you to do this place *proud*. I want you to sing these pieces as beautifully, as *magnificently*, as you are capable. Don't let *anyone* who sits in this audience tonight forget it! Go ahead, look around, I'll shut my trap for a few moments..."

I waste no time on my choirmates, I know them well enough. My eyes fly directly to the ceilings and arches and stained glass and statuary. The thing you come to realize in a church, in a cathedral like this one, is that, even without a congregation, the place has hundreds of people in it. Between the evangelists on the corners of the cupola are other saints, performing various religious-looking, beatific acts: St. Lucas, St. Joan, St. Francis (with the requisite animal entourage), St. Ignatius. They are each attended by devout-looking young companions, holding the edges of their master's robes or assisting in prayer. Altars to Jesus and Mary stand at left and right, little Italian marbles bracketed by deep rectangles of stained glass.

Then I look behind, bracing myself so I don't knock my legs against the edge of the risers. King Jesus is perched thirty feet above us, sitting on a throne looking as happy and glorious as if he were heading up a meeting of the local Rotary, a parade of saints, popes, and bankers joining him on either side, looking straight ahead like John F. Kennedy into the debate cameras, lesser people, commoners, congressional pages, and children fading off behind, all centered on the grand throne and its inhabitant. I look down and discover yet more paintings chronicling the voyage to the cross: *Jesus is Taken From the Cross, Jesus is Laid in the Tomb, Jesus Falls for the Third Time, Jesus Stripped of His Garments.* Gollee, the Catholics had this thing covered better than the Super Bowl.

"A last word," Mr. Stutz broke in. We returned our eyes stage front. Mr. Stutz set his baton on the podium and flexed his fingertips together. This was his sign; this was important.

"You will spend very *little* of your time here on Earth listening to the sound of *applause*, and taken to its *basics*, it is a wondrously strange custom—whacking two parts of your body together to produce sound—very strange stuff when you think of it. But, taken past the oddness of the thing, applause is *affirmation*, a form of spontaneous percussion multiplied so many times it turns into an outright *stream* of praise. To you it should be the sound of *ecstasy*, and, since we don't have the resources or inclination to *pay* you for your performance tonight, you may also consider it your compensation. So eat it up, for God's sake! And *smile*, try to look like you're *enjoying* yourself! I have seen one too many stone-faced choirs in my life!"

He picked up his baton; important part over.

"Now, when we bow, I want you to follow my motion down into the bow, and when you reach bottom, I want you to say quietly, to yourself, the words *tutti vivace*, and then come immediately back up. The audience will be none the wiser, and we will look more coordinated than the USC Marching Band. Try it one time. Watch me."

Mr. Stutz cut us off as if we were at the end of a piece, then turned and bowed to the audience, a solo, conductor's, acknowledgement. Then he came back up, smiled in our direction, held out an arm and, in a grand sweep, invited us down to face the floor. You could hear the choir whisper as one—*tutti vivace* ("everybody, lively")—and we came back up as a single organism, lifting its petals to the sun. Mr. Stutz beamed at us.

"Great! *Now*, let's get down to our *entrances*. Bring out your *Chichester...*"

We had an hour between the warm-up and the concert, and I had to be as alone as possible. I descended the steps of St. Michael's and followed Diaz Avenue southward. I crossed the street at Pearlman and was headed around the corner when a neon sign caught my eye: Vendini's: Fine Italian Dining. Upstairs. Before singing—an Italian restaurant! What could make more sense? I entered the elevator next to the sign and pushed a button. It was a half-glass, half-metal job, and I could see out onto Pearlman, down the sidewalk a black man pushing a cart, stopping to rub his whiskers like a cat.

I stepped into the crisp, white-tiled lounge area and ordered a soda, asked the guy at the bar if I could sit out on the terrace, the most isolated space I could find. On the way through the tables I noticed a series of large framed photographs on the walls, bright color shots of Europe: old-town markets, boats in Venice, parks in Rome, places I'd never been, places that existed only in photographs, movies, late-night television reports.

The warmth of the day had stayed on through evening. I was surprised no one else had opted for the cool of the terrace, but the place had just opened for business and there weren't that many customers. I chose a spot right next to the railing, so I could watch the entrance of St. Michael's across the street. Concertgoers in suits and floral ties, evening gowns, sweater vests, sports jackets, pant suits, trickled in couple by couple, group by group, until the trickle became a crowd. It was going to be jam-packed, all right, as many people as possible in this little Christian arena so they can all gape when Michael Moss makes a fool of himself drooling all over Amy Fine the superconductor, mistress of the airwaves.

Odd, though. I got through the warm-up just fine. Amy must've been up there about ten minutes, and I looked straight at her the whole time and none of my internal organs blew up. I even sang well. Who knows, this could be a whole new thing, maybe I'll be all right. I checked my watch, and it said a half-hour before concert time. Time to get to the rehearsal hall and run over a few things. I slid twin quarters on the table for space rental and headed into and out of the restaurant. A photograph adjacent to the front door drew my attention, an ornate, decaying, German-looking cathedral. I leaned down and checked the artist's note: *St. Martin's Church, Salzburg, Austria (Birthplace of Mozart).*

To tell you the truth, I remember very little from the first half of the concert. I remember I got to play drum major by leading the choir into the church (no special honor, just a result of my odd placement off the end of the risers). The only problem I remember was the sustained notes in the third movement of the Bernstein. I mean, for God's sake, who writes in 10/4 anyway? I also remember when we let loose on the final *Allelujah!* in the *Te Deum* and cut off, left to stand there breathing hard like spent track stars while the orchestra put the cherry on the sundae, an eighth note/eighth note, full, hold it, bring it up, let it go, lift that bow, stop that valve, strike that timpani. And that tiny nickel of pureness in between when a thousand people, a choir, an orchestra and a dozen ushers wait in silence for the conductor to drop his baton and signal the rain of applause. That split second was so grand I almost resented the interruption of the clapping, but I took Mr. Stutz's instructions to heart and let the sound waves strike my exposed teeth; I smiled with my mouth wide open, wide enough to let the air back into my worked-over lungs. Mr. Stutz turned to us before he led us into the bow and gave us that peculiar, hands-clasped salute that all conductors give. They must learn that in a special class somewhere.

In any case, we filed off the stage and out the back of the church, me last, and headed for the rehearsal hall, a brand spanking new addition with wallpaper in the trendy colors and mod-looking chairs and a shiny stand-up piano. The Mozart soloists were already warming up, ringing out their superior voices against the high-ceiling echo chamber of the foyer while the rest of us gathered in our seats.

If you ever need a cheap evening of entertainment, I highly recommend halftime backstage at a choir concert. The singing and the applause and the knowing we're halfway done and god I can't wait till it's over so we can get to the party and relax only feeds on itself and creates new surges of artistic fission, prodding forth the budding ham in all of us. Postperformance energy is safely scattered throughout the city, but during intermission we can't go wandering out in public so here we are, amateur night at the rehearsal hall, no charge, nouveau vaudevillians on parade.

The rookie tenor with the Alfalfa haircut jumps into an impromptu duet of tap-dancing drills with the Debbie Reynolds soprano, a musical theater wannabe. The four or five hipster immigrants from the jazz department sit in a corner and work an a cappella chant, herding all species of vocalese beasts over the bass line, supplied by a prototypical tall coatrack of a guy named Charlie, boom-bah-booming like he could lay down the stripe all night. The soprano section is one big stock exchange of yammer and faux opera—LAAAAAAA!—did you hear this and did you see this and do you think we ought to this...And of course a couple of real pros—Frank and Frederick—behind the shiny new piano, playing the theme song to *All in the Family*, alternating the rasp of a castrated female goat and the distinct Irish-after-five-pints baritone.

"And you knew who you were THENNN!"

"Goils were goils and men were men..."

"Mister, we could use a man like Hoibert Hoover aga-ee-ain!"

I find only one non-performer, alone in the corner, a fellow tenor, his feet up on the chair in front of him, writing something on the copyright page of his Mozart score, deep in thought. Yet another reason Alex Blanche was the closest thing I had to a friend—he alone could produce calm in the face of hurricane-magnitude shtick.

"Hi Alex."

Alex finished a line of his writing then looked up.

"Mr. Moss. Sir."

"No 'Sir,' Alex. Please."

"Oh," he said. He returned to his score, eyeing the words scribbled there. "Something different?" he asked.

I had to think about it a second. "Yeah," I said. "Me."

"Nervous?"

"Yeah," I said, scratching the back of my head. "Nervous."

"About singing, or..."

"Amy," I said. I could finally say it. "About Amy."

Alex swiveled his feet down onto the ground and sat up straight. "You have to watch her, you know."

"Yeah," I said. "I know."

"It's blasphemy not to. You're a good singer that way. You've got your rules."

"Yeah. I just hope I'm all right."

"You will be," he said. He didn't say it in a rah-rah kind of way, just as a point of fact.

"Do you love her?"

His bluntness surprised me. I wasn't ready for that kind of

question. I tried to change the subject, and Alex didn't fight me.

"What're you writing?" I asked.

"Poem," he said.

"Your wife?"

"I should hope so," he said. "I have my rules, too."

"That's nice, Alex. That really is. Hey, let's knock 'em dead with this fucking Mozart, okay?"

"Yeah," said Alex. "Let's do that." He smiled, for him an unusual action. He looked good smiling.

By this time the intermission was over, and we were just waiting for the madrigal group to finish its fifteen-minute set starting off the second half. The choir was down to a dull roar now, after a stern warning from the choir president, Anne Marie Karringer. A few minutes later we filed up behind the sacristy and crept in the back door, the choir lined up behind us all the way across and into the rehearsal hall. The madrigals were finishing up a delicate Byrd motet, accompanied by hand chimes and a small drum, both instruments played by singers in the ensemble. A second past the final strike of the chime the applause swelled up to us, striking the back of the church and ricocheting into acoustic mush. I waited for the stage manager to signal me in. About half the madrigal group—those who also sang in the choir—stayed in their spots on the risers, and I had to circle around them to my place at stage left. As I waited for the rest of the choir to fill in, my eyes were drawn down to the brass section, specifically the odd stands they use for their instruments. Bathroom plungers in reverse, horns and trombones sheathed upside-down, the dome bracing the bell of the instrument and holding it straight up.

I'll be okay. I'll be okay.

I looked out on the audience, and they broke into cordial applause. That would be Amy, coming in with the soloists. Without turning my head I slanted my eyes to the right, picking up the singers in their concert finery, standing to the side of the podium where they would await their turns: short, stumpy tenor and tall, thin bass in white bow ties, perfect tuxedos with long tails and textured white vests. The soprano and alto were both in sequin affairs, gloriously low backs, the soprano royal blue, the alto blood red and dazzling. All four were masters candidates from the local university, and no one in the choir knew them all that well. Ray, David, Gina, and Inez, I think.

And then…Amy. She strode up the steps to the podium and bowed devotedly to the audience—*thank you, oh thank you, your gracious servant, I am sure.* She wore a graceful, conservative skirt of black velvet, but above, above—jumpin' jehesus jehoshaphat—a monarch butterfly, splashed across her blouse back and front in sequined rows of gold, black and crimson, battling for glory with the very saints above her, its wings extending out to her sleeves. It had to be such a wonder to watch this from the audience, for surely when Amy began to conduct the monarch would begin to fly.

She turned to greet us with a discreet for-the-choir bow, then snuck out from behind her conductor's mask to grin as she picked up her baton. She was one of us, it said. *Let's kick some ass!* it said.

From there it all began to happen. From there the steady crescendo of infatuation behind my loud public cries of *laudate* and *hominibus* could be measured by movements, moved by measures. Let me paint it for you.

Her hands are separate from her body. They are doves flying in loops to her sides, a dance that pulls the breath from our throats. The two creatures begin at the middle and split, one still portioning out the beat in half-moon vanilla scoops while the other opens and sculpts down the air, *softer, softer*, down to the grassland chirps of *piano.* Until the chord change, the minor third pulled from the air, teased forth from the strings like blown glass, and the singers with their look of surprise, as if they themselves didn't see it coming, such a change, such a change, who heard of such a change?

Her eyes brighten and flash as she leans across the chasm to coax us into a waltz. She rocks with it, strumming it from us; we are hers, ninety-six of us on the ends of her lute-strings.

She breaks into two on the *maestoso*, the pit for the pendulum, the fulcrum from the lever, the strength and power of her hands belying the calm of her face and posture. But when the time is right, oh when the time is right, her eyes will light fire at our feet, the opening strikes of a fugue that will breeze around the church and carry us off, higher, higher. And I will fly with her, climb the rails to the top of this burgundy tower of sound, carried off by Amy's hands into the grottos of Matthew, Mark, Luke, and John, pitching my song into the clouds of cherubim and back to the choir loft, droplets of wine poised at the ears of the congregation. Take, eat, listen, hear. And be full.

By the end of the piece I am near death of one sort or another. I close my eyes and let the applause settle me back down, then watch as Amy Fine follows a train of soloists up the steps for her curtain calls, for a bouquet of red carnations from the usher, for two bows more and another and then to sweep us down into our chant: *tutti vivace*.

Then she is gone. And they are gone. I stand in the square of lawn behind St. Michael's and stare up at the stars. Orion's belt. The Pleiades. God, what can I do after this? Anything more will surely kill me, will make my heart cave in on itself like an overinflated balloon. Then I feel a hand on my shoulder. It is Alex.

"Hi. You all right?"

"Yes, Alex. I'm fine. I'm incredibly all right. Would you believe that?"

"You know something now."

"I know something now."

He smiles. Twice in one night. He looks good smiling.

"Come on," he says. "We're going to a party."

The energy involved in a postconcert party is simply the energy of a rehearsal-hall intermission doubled and strung out over four to five hours. Bring survival gear. Paula Meyer's house was jam-packed that holy night with glowing, consuming, smiley-faced creatures from some annex of Mount

Olympus where the natives sport used tuxedos and black choir gowns. Frank and Frederick seemed almost normal in such circumstances. Frederick grabbed Frank by the neck and threatened to throw him in the fireplace.

"I'll be sendin' ya down to a fiery hell, I will. The river Styx, boy, whattya say? Ya gonna put that horz-dee-orves down or ya gonna roast for all eternity?"

"All right!" Frank screamed, flapping his arms like a trapped bird. "I'll put the damn pizza roll back!"

Well, almost normal.

The choir lecher, Steve Gilbert, had poor Rosy Oakland leaned up against a wall in the hallway. Rosy was barely out of high school and naíve even for her age. Steve gained a couple inches in proximity even as I passed, but Rosy was trying to be nice.

"The marines, huh? Wow, was that dangerous?"

A boy-girl-boy-girl quartet was strewn across the couch, playing some Babylonian mode of hand jive against their knees, fingers wagging together left and right, then slapping over against some other person's legs, then a series of moves that seemed to have no united choreography whatsoever leading to the inevitable burst of laughter and group collapse.

And the kitchen, the kitchen was one big roly-poly, a mob of people so tight you had to crowbar your way through shoulders, necks, and hairdos just to get to the sink or across to the dining room for the punch bowl. The punch bowl was what I wanted, the punch bowl was my promised land, what I had to have, and I hoped it was plenty spiked, too. I did an Australian crawl through the last three shoulders, said "excuse me" for some odd reason, and as I popped out of the undergrowth looked back just a flash to find Amy, in black pants now but still with the same sparkling butterfly top, holding out a carrot stick like a cigar, saying something witty. Tonight she is a celebrity, surrounded by well-wishers, people without faces.

I rushed to the punch bowl and ladled out a full cup, then chugged it down quickly before loading up another. I was gonna need this plenty. Familiar hands reached down around my face and fluttered over my chin like feathers, smell of wisteria, nails polished in satin white. I turned and she was there, and what could I do now? I stood stock-still, watching her hands, waiting for a downbeat.

"Hi," she said, pulling me into those hazel eyes like she'd been doing all night. She flicked a finger in a C motion across her bangs and over her lips. Pink marble. Chestnut hair. Mozart. Salzburg.

"Hi," I replied. I'd be happy to repeat whatever she said all night. I was, after all, on her string.

"You have beautiful blue eyes, Michael Moss. I'm glad you decided to use them tonight."

"Yes," I said. "I did look, didn't I?"

"I don't think you looked down once," she said. "You knew that piece almost by heart, all this time."

I stared into the pink soup of my punch—heavily spiked, by the way. *Deo Gratias. Agimus tibi, propter magnam gloriam.* The blood was rising to my face because suddenly I cared so much about what she thought, this woman with the magic fingers and the dancing eyes.

"I'm...I'm so sorry," I said. "If...I'd have known, maybe I...You were terrific. And that blouse..." I ran the back of my hand down her butterfly's wing, ticking my nail against the sequins. "It's spectacular."

She shuddered with my movement. Did I do that? To her? Now she folded her hands together, bringing in her wings— her turn now.

"I'm sorry, too. I really didn't need to give you such a dunking the other night. I hope it wasn't too bad..."

I extended my hand. "Saint Michael Receives the Holy Baptism."

She took my hand and laughed, then cupped my cheek with the other and nuzzled up for a kiss on the lips.

"You really are a honey, Michael Moss. And sometimes I'm just a little too...passionate."

Prestissimo accelerando a fine!

We were that close to whatever it was we were about to do

when Frederick and Frank began their expected riot up at the front of the living room.

"Ey! Tutti vivace! Ev-ah-ree-body!" Frank yelled, perched on Frederick's high shoulders, reciting Chico Marx. "We's a gonna have a game a tag inna da corn-a-field! Ev-ah-ree-body's it!"

Flashes of black and white began streaming out the front door, more tuxedos than gowns, more men than women. I looked to Amy, and her eyes grew wide with excitement.

"You want to?" she asked.

I chugged the last of my punch and felt the pleasant tingle of booze-burn, up from the stomach to the head, wasting cells all along the trail.

"You betcha," I said and took her hand.

A little explanation. Paula's house lay in the middle of built-in-the-sixties suburbia, subdivided now for three solid decades, but between her tract and the expressway stood the city's major anachronism, a five-acre square of cornfield. Developers had been bidding on the thing for ages, trying to turn it into condominiums, but the owners, an old Portuguese family, kept fighting them off, content to spend their summers at a roadside stand they called the Corn Palace.

The agreeable California weather allowed them to plant the corn in sections, some earlier than others, thus sustaining their harvest time over several months. For our purposes we headed for the tallest section, about six feet high, just enough to hide everybody but Frederick Guttmann. Amy and I started out next to the southwest corner and searched each other for a moment, a sudden mutual strike of shyness, wondering exactly how the rules worked in this little game.

"Let's break up!" she said. "I'll find you later."

"Okay…sure," I said, and she was gone. Little mosquitoes of doubt broke through the top of the church and jabbed at my skin. God, what am I getting into? Five minutes and she's already talking about breaking up.

"Bullshit!"

I thought I had said it myself, but it turned out to be Chester and Johnson, fighting over who was "it" in their particular regional playoff of tag. I ran up to where they were, Johnson squatting, catching his breath, and loosening his bowtie at the same time.

"Aw come on!" he cried. "Let's have some *rules* here, for Chrissake."

"Hey, don't swear," said Chester. "Julie's out here. You know how she gets when we swear."

"Hey guys, don't worry," I broke in. "New game. I'm it."

"Hey, you got it, baby!" shouted Chester. He turned on a heel and took off down the row, ducking under the larger ears. Johnson cut straight through the stalks and into the next row, almost crawling.

I let them get a head start then ran all the way down the row, thinking Chester would be the slower of the two. Through my own quickening breath I could hear the cries and taunts and laughter of the rest of the choir, somewhere out in that field, a whole crop of spring loonies just begging for trespassing citations. Fuck it, I thought. Fuck it all. This is fun. Isn't this fun?

I slowed up at the end of the row and snuck a look around, finding Chester, hands on knees, blowing out breath through pursed lips. I snuck in behind him like a Cherokee warrior, careful of my steps. Just touching him on the shoulder and yelling "You're it!" wasn't enough. Oh no, I was shooting for style points. I fell in behind a tall stalk, becoming one with the corn, then leapt out and slapped Chester full on his upturned butt.

"You're it, bay-bay!"

"Ah shit!" Chester wheezed. "I'm it."

I was gone, spinning my wheels in the loose dirt down the row, corn leaves slapping against my cheeks like the hands of fond Italian grandmothers. I found one-half of a moon above me and reared back to howl, not caring a damn where I was going, nearing the other end of the field at a full clip.

What hit me next, I thought, must have sixteen wheels and a driver named Rölf who coaches Olympic weight lifters, likes his ales dark and thick, and listens to heavy metal. It was all that shattering and all that sudden. The sound went something like: *Whack! Higigagiga thump! Roll roll roll hummmph! ooh!*

Something like a good James Brown tune. I could've sworn I blacked out, because the next sound I heard was not a sound you would expect after a near-fatal collision. Laughter. Squeaky and high and uncontrollable. Amy's laughter.

"Ah-hahahahahaha!" she howled. "Oh! Ay! Ah-hahahaha!"

She was rolling on the ground like a brown bear trying to rid himself of honeybees, grabbing her ribs either in pain or exultation. I don't even know if she knew it was me. She tumbled around in the corn leaves a couple more times, then finally lifted herself to a sitting position and pulled the hair back from her eyes to see who it was she had just steamrolled. The features of her face lifted bit by bit, a hair-trigger air pump of laughter exploding on the words: "Michael! Ah-haha! MichaelMichaelMichael! It was YOU! Oh! No! Ohgh! AH-HAHAHAHAHAHA! Michael Moss! It was Michael Moss! Ah-hahaha! Oooh!"

She rolled backwards again, completely delirious, a jumble of sequins and hair and skin over the dark ground. Through my pain I thought it was pretty fucking hilarious myself, but I had ideas other than joining in on her gigglefest. Truth was, I knew what I wanted now. I knew what I wanted for the first time in a century, and no amount of laughter would make me put it off any further. I grabbed the base of a cornstalk, rough and dry against my hand, and pulled myself up to my knees, crawling over and taking Amy by the shoulders. I turned her around to me and set my hands at the sides of her face to calm her down.

When she knew what I was doing a look of absolute wonderment passed over her, and I let it settle deep into those lightning-flash eyes before I brought my lips to hers. The shortness of our breathing, hers from laughter, mine from trauma, drove up the urgency, set our passion breaking over us in fever chills, and the smell of the earth and the cornstalks hovering over us like sentries, a new world, a world with one radical new equation: Michael Moss and someone else, too.

I pulled back for air. I had to set a duck on my trail, something to get me back home.

"You're magic, Amy Fine, and you have music in those fingers of yours. I want in. I want in on all of it."

Can you ever know if you really mean something like that? I don't know, but just saying it was something. I opened up Amy's butterfly wings and smoothed my hands over the soft, pink-tipped breasts inside. I coaxed my conductor into a waltz and she sang.

I dreamt the *Lacrymosa* that night. *Lacrymosa* means "tears" in Latin. It is the seventh movement of Mozart's Requiem, the last thing he wrote before he died, and the sound of it will make you cry only if you are human and alive. On the night of his death, Mozart beckoned three of his friends to his bedside to sing through the parts, but he couldn't go on. He dismissed them, then turned to the wall, never to write another note nor take another breath.

Making love to a butterfly in a cornfield with a song of death playing through your head. If you are not careful, there is something about this that will change you.

Chapter Fifteen

Sunday
Capriccio

Listen carefully. The land traversed by the water was filled with rolling hills and shallow valleys. But the two great bodies pressed against one another and lifted the hills into mountains. The water ran faster, cutting the valleys into canyons. The land fell from the sides of the canyons and exposed the rock underneath, great domes and walls of granite. The land grew chill, and glaciers came down from the north. The glaciers carved the sides of the canyon, splitting the great domes and turning the canyon walls into sheer cliffs festooned with hanging waterfalls.

I was living in the Santa Clara Valley. Nancy had left her husband's trailer and moved to a friend's cabin deep in the woods of the Santa Cruz Mountains. The point between us was Castle Rock State Park, a hilltop spread of dry chaparral, oak forest, and great clusters of exposed rock—and the logical meeting place for our final farewell. On weekends the place was peopled by squads of rock climbers, some scrambling freehand up the flatland boulders, others using ropes and pitons to rappel down the larger faces. Occasionally someone was hurt; every few years someone was killed, a wrong step on the rocks, one catch breath of misplaced balance, one finger's misfire along the rope.

Nancy and I met in the dirt lot just off Skyline Boulevard and started our hike downhill into the redwoods and ferns, knapsacks full of bread, cheese, and wine. We followed a shallow creekbed, then headed overhill to a field of winter-green grass, where we stopped to watch the birds and consume our lunches. The unseasonal warmth of the day met with a full bottle of zinfandel to dull our senses and make the afternoon sun two shades too bright. After a while we hiked on up into the scrub and oaks of the chaparral and stopped at a point just off the trail, a wedge of sandstone looking out on the dark tablespoon shovels of Big Basin Redwoods Park and on to the San Mateo shore.

I knew all along what she was going to tell me, and although the idea of seeing her no more carried some level of sadness, it appealed to me in another, less easily defined way. My story was this: with the help of Nancy, I had freed myself of Stacy, but I was not free of Nancy, so there was still a connection. Let me put it this way: are you truly cured of the disease if you are still taking the medication that keeps the disease away? It was time to cut my final string and get on with it; it was time to do it all by myself.

"I'm going to give him another chance," she said, brushing back her hair in the afternoon wind playing Indian scout over the layers of mountain and shore. "I've been with the poor bozo almost half my life. I can't just leave without giving him this one last try. He said he'd give up the marijuana. He said he'd go see a counselor with me."

"You're right," I said. "You should. You have to give him another chance, for your own sake. If you leave without giving him another chance, you'd have doubts for the rest of your life."

"You don't mind?" Nancy asked.

"It's not my place to mind," I said. "He's your husband. I'm just the guy you have great sex with."

She laughed and lay back like a lizard against the sun-warmed rock, picking up her eyes in that peculiar languid smile of hers.

"You've been great, Michael, just great. You've taken me all those places I wanted to go. Have I been good for you? Have I helped you forget her?"

I was distracted by a movement on the rock below me. A lizard crept forward, nudging his glove-leather snout into the sunshine, then bolting back into the shade when I spoke.

"I think I'm ready, Nancy. I think I'm really ready. I'll never forget our Christmas."

"I wouldn't think you would, you dirty so-and-so."

"Or that card you sent me. Or that three-legged cat of your roommate's."

We balanced a smile between us and cast our eyes at each other over the grain of the sandstone. The wine was having its effect.

"Come on," I said, leaping back onto the trail. "Let's see what else we have to see."

By the time we rounded the far hillside to the area with all the best climbing rocks, we were down to a snail's pace, stopping every three minutes to kiss each other, exploring for perhaps the last time. It took me back to our first date, how she had attacked my mouth, tongue extended, and how I stopped to teach her the magic of the lead-in, the tingling anticipation brought on by the moment when your lips are close but not yet touching. I call it the aura kiss, two pair of lips separated by the width of an eighth note, staying there until you are about to explode, until some southern wind brings them together. She's learned a lot, I thought, holding her atop a bare dirt hillside, kissing her ear as I lifted a hand to feel her breasts through her T-shirt.

We stumbled like embarrassed teenagers through a throng of mythic weekend adventurers straight from a beer commercial, dumping their tan sinewy muscles and neon clothing over the rocks into a vertical existence. They watched us as though we were aliens, two trivial lovers in a gritty world of head rush gut-sports. As we walked on out of earshot I told Nancy I could hold back no longer. I couldn't go to her place, and she couldn't go to mine (having promised her hubby an early return). We would just have to do it in the woods.

As all fantasies do, this one regressed from a great idea to a pleasurable possibility to an awkward quest to just have done with it. We kept spotting hideaways off the trail but always shied back, afraid someone with keen eyes would pass by and discover us. Finally I led her up a steep deer path to a clearing shaded by oaks. We left on our shirts and shoes but took off the rest, using our shorts to protect our private parts from the dirt and rocks beneath us.

Nancy was completely unsure by this time, stuck on the idea that this was not only silly but a betrayal of her pledge to her future ex-husband. I picked up on her anxieties and kicked things into high gear, laying her back and entering her quickly, hoping by now to just get the thing done. She was surprised by how fast I came, but it was no surprise to me. I had places to go.

I am driving along Highway 120 near Modesto, headed east to the shrine of the great Yosemite, because that's where this car is taking me. The Cowboy Junkies are on the portable tape deck next to me, singing my plight in their roadside whisper, a song called "Escape Is So Simple."

Escape is *not* so simple, but escape is what I am doing. I am heading up the streams of my impulses as only a natural man with an automobile can, working my personal history through the cow grates and line patterns of fleeing orchards, the hanging-pendant stoplights of small towns and the fruit stands with their minor-Picasso handpainted signs: *Peaches*

59¢/lb., Bing Cherries $2.99/basket, Sun-Roasted Peanuts and Pistachios.

How can I explain this? There is no excuse for my running, but there are reasons. We are all of us trapped by time and terror, the dawn-to-dusk constrictions of our daily lives, and just occasionally we have to burst from the net. I *am* the postapocalyptic man. I am tired of looking at my left wrist for no reason; the sun is up and by damn I am driving into those trees! I follow only my speedometer, and I watch the flagstaff of the temperature gauge flick between H and C. These are all I need, these and a general sense of non-direction.

Listen to me. I woke up this morning in a Silicon Valley cornfield, coated over by a dull headache and several bruises to my side and legs, and next to me, sheathed in the sequins of an Oklahoma butterfly, lay a beautiful, half-naked woman. I was half-naked myself, having passed out after doing with this woman, this Amy Fine, what I think I did.

She might as well have pushed me over Niagara Falls in a tin bucket. What demonic alchemy of party punch, enchantment, and classical music had driven me to this? I was not ready; no one had prepared me. I found my jacket hanging from a cornstalk, ripped along the sleeve and covered with dust. After fastening my belt buckle I took the jacket and covered up my lovely companion, then snuck as quietly as possible down the row and up the street to my car.

I dragged through the door of my studio in panic. Soon Amy Fine would wake up. Soon Amy Fine would call me, ask me what the hell did I think I was doing, or call someone else and ask them what the hell did they think Michael Moss was doing. Soon I would be a man possessed, some tender green part of me left behind in that lovely cocoon, a drying husk out in the cornfield. The only thing that could save me now was to change my location, for in another part of the country I would cease to be who I was. I would be ill-defined there, viewed by people who knew nothing or little of me. This was where I needed to go. But how?

I pulled my wallet out of my pants pocket and tossed it on

the dresser. The wallet hit the dark stained wood, clanked against my jewelry box and opened up, coughing up its shiny underside of photographs, driver's license, laminated finance company calendar, and the holographic image of an American Eagle at the center of a smooth, untested rectangle of plastic. There it was—my invitation. The eagle spoke to me, and when it opened its mighty beak the words spouted out bright and clear: Get Lost.

And so now I am covering the Big Valley, a remarkably flat scoop of earth they call the San Joaquin. The endless straight shots of farm country turn into the rolling, windy dodge lines of the Sierra foothills, still green from the spring rains, then it all escalates into mountains, snow-tipped almost into June, shooting up like cell doors, knocking down your horizons, pointing only upward with nothing on the other side save the plain brown wrapper of Nevada.

I pass the sign reading You Are Now Entering Yosemite National Park and begin scanning the roadsides. It is midafternoon now; it is time to find something, and I don't know what because knowing is not a part of this trip, only following. A brown sign with ranger yellow lettering rears up on the right—Merced Grove, only two letters from mercy—and this is the only sign I need. Hell-a-loo-yah, I have to start somewhere. The rough asphalt stews up into rough dirt, potholes chucking me up in my seat anytime I get settled. The land grows darker and darker as I ramble forward, climbing into the bottom spaces where the sequoias will shoot out of the earth, trees with skyscraper attitudes.

It was the tree I would go to when I needed to cry. In sixth grade I planted the tree at the corner of our yard and I watched it grow, weird and convoluted, branches winding around with no sense then shooting straight up like elevator shafts. The time I cannot talk about yet, I went to a tree and threw my tears on it, just like I used to on my childhood tree, felt the bark scratching the back of my scalp as I wallowed in sadness, lagoon waters left still to warm in the sun. And the headlights of neighbors flashing by on the road, wondering was that a ghost I just saw, or was that a young man crying against a silk oak?

The road ends at a gate—No Cars Beyond This Point, Merced Grove Trail, 1.2 miles. Do I have a choice? Certainly not. Impulse has brought me here; impulse will damn well cover my tracks if I go hiking into strange woods in pursuit of icons. I steal a paper bag from the back seat of my car and start out.

The trail breaks out of the woods for a half-mile and onto a hot field of grass. The sweat beads up on my forehead and drips into my eyes, blurring the vision behind my sunglasses until I have to take them off and hook them into the collar of my T-shirt. Just as I am about to return for fear of dehydration—I have brought no canteen, not even a soda—the woods come back, thrusting me into easy twilight. They grow thicker and thicker until I come upon the ferns that signal the great trees, and then they come like giants, ring upon ring of thick-barked gargantuans, upward-shooting flagpoles of high, straight branches, trunks more than five arm-widths around, their sides draped with huge gargoyle burls.

I have to drive myself in on the impulses, for this may be a key, this may be a piece of what I'm looking for. Bring it in, fold it up, put it in your pocket, read it through your fingers— what are you telling me, where do I go now?

Just then a Steller's jay squawks and buzzes over my head, almost brushing me. He lands on a low branch and glares at me like a fussy professor, emitting a raking sound at the top of his lungs like he will die on the spot from heartburn. He jumps back across the trail to another sequoia and looks back again, daring me to follow. I pick up my secret brown bag and head behind as he hops and flies back and forth across my vision, leading me deeper and deeper into the grove. Of course, I can't be sure if he is leading me or if I am chasing him.

I don't need to wonder much longer because there it is, bathed in crisscross shafts of sunlight, the sequoia tree of my dreams. The jay lets out one more sturdy screech and buzzes my head on its way back out of the grove, seeming to say

"You're on your own, kid." I settle down onto the dusty floor of the trail, struck by a sudden pain in my butt. I edge up a little to remove a small, sharp sequoia cone from the seat of my shorts. A crossing breeze delivers one or two notes to my ears, humming forth across the grove, hinting at a melody I can't quite deliver, a sustained high note flowing into some kind of drunken waltz, ragged, corny, cymbal crash on the third beat. I shake it out like a dirty blanket; time to stop wondering, time to make a ritual.

I stretch up to a standing position, already stiff from the drive and the unexpected hike and the uncomfortable position of the dirt. I reach into the secret brown bag at my side and pull out the plastic stained-glass rainbow of a dragon's tail, or rather a dragon kite's tail. Once I reach the end, reeling it out like a magician pulling scarves out of someone's mouth, I untie the string from the main body, latch it over a low stub on the sequoia's trunk, and circle a path around my wooden mecca, holding the tail high as I string it around. I have enough to go around twice and a little bit more, then I tie the end of the tail in a knot around an exposed root, away from the trail.

I pace backwards to look at my work, but something isn't right yet. I need that song, that waltz, think drunk, think baritone, think...

Pizza?

Wheeeen...the...moon hits your eye like a big pizza pie, that's amore!

The absurd chemistry of ancient tree, plastic kite and '50s novelty tune rode me along in an extended frenzy of skipping back to my car, but the feeling lasted not too long. Hopping over the gate with its little warning sign, I spotted a jet way up above the mountains, laying out an inverted snail's path of steam and smoke, and the judgment for round one hit me square and obvious: *This is not it.*

The anticipation driving into the great valley of the Yosemite is a killer, the sensation of nearness almost as unbearable as an aura kiss. You find yourself driving along the boulder-strewn Merced River, then you're off on a turnout eyeing the granite lighthouse of Half Dome, and before you can think about it much further you're standing in a meadow, straining your neck at the white waterlace of Bridalveil Falls and, just across the street, the great block of El Capitan shrugging its shoulder off to the lowering sun.

In late afternoon at the end of the weekend, the drive in is no sweat, but the tourists heading the other way are tailgating each other slowly back out in nature's own traffic jam, back to Placerville, back to Stockton, back to that air-conditioned apartment house in Fresno and that packing-house job in San Francisco, back seats peppered with excited kids who will soon evaporate into push face snoozers, losing the four hours between here and Gilroy like so much time travel.

But they have nothing to do with me, they are only cross-the-way scenery. I drive past the wide meadows and the gorgeous even curves of the Merced, watching spire after spire come and go on either side, into the strangely suburban theme park of Yosemite Village. The visitors center seems the smart place to go, and I park across the lot with the very idea of going there, but then the notion strikes me that this trip has nothing to do with official recommendations. I will do just the opposite; I will do whatever is ill-advised. I get back in the car and keep on driving.

A friend of mine who is a Yosemite buff—anal-retentive note taker, map collector, postcard sender—told me once that you have to make reservations at least a year in advance to get into the acclaimed Awahnee Hotel. So that is where I go. I cruise around the souvenir shops and grocery stores and continue on a road that appears to be headed straight into a granite cliff but veers off pleasurably into the cleanest parking lot in the valley. The famed Awahnee sits there like a scared but proud child at the bottom of a humongous pile of deathly granite, waiting for the right moment to be sledge-hammered back into its weak man-made history. We are things made of glaciers, speak the cliffs, titanic sheets of ice that would wipe you out in no more than a decade, a tick of the minute hand on your geographical watches. Shiver, little one, shiver! Enjoy your moment.

Enough already. I'm getting truly whacked out. So I take my day's growth of beard, sequoia dirt-stained white tennis shorts, and grubby Oakland Athletics T-shirt and parade them into the rustic yet elegant lobby of the esteemed Awahnee. After losing myself in all the soundly official hubbub, I gravitate to a friendly-looking young woman at what seems to be the registration desk.

"I'd like to stay tonight," I announce, as if I were Joseph with the wife outside in the Range Rover about to go into labor. Is there room at the exalted Awahnee?

The woman looks at me in consternation. Should I give him the party line first? Yes, I will give him the party line.

"You know, usually you should make a point of making your reservations at least a year in advance. The Awahnee is much in demand, and we wouldn't want you to get stuck here this late without a place to stay. The park gets congested sometimes with people who haven't planned ahead."

I cut her off. "So is there a room?"

She shrugs me off silently and turns to a drawer full of little index cards, flipping through them, looking at one, flipping past it, finding another, and pulling it out. She sets it on the counter and etches a little mark on the side with her pen

"Yes," she says. "We have one on the meadow side. But it's a suite with a queen-sized bed. Rather expensive, I'm afraid."

"How much?" I ask.

"Two hundred dollars," she answers, firmly, with that *listen dammit this is the legendary Awahnee, not the goddamn-Motel 6* tone.

I grip my wallet inside my pocket so as not to shriek. I am unaccustomed to such figures. This impulse buying takes some practice. But the power of the American Eagle on my little share of the world's magic plastic collection shines through to my fingers, calling out in braille: "Do it. You know you want it, why not buy it? I'm your friend, remember? I give you power." This must be the same flirtatious hiss that brought Eve so much trouble back in Genesis.

"I'll take it," I say, in my *I am after all an oil baron in disguise, don't mind the tacky major league baseball underwear, I am just trying to fit in with you lower lifestyle folks* voice.

Missus friendly desk clerk checks another mark on the index card, returns it to its file, takes my credit card, goes through all the necessary charging machinations, and sooner or later hands me my key on a large round of plastic.

"Your room is on the second floor, to the far side of the hotel. Dinner is served from six to nine in the main dining room."

"Thank you," I say.

"Enjoy your stay," she says, and smiles. Ah, I am accepted. I am one with the historic Awahnee. I will steal a towel and as much hotel stationery as I can lay my hands on.

I eat the largest piece of beef I have ever seen for dinner, and I work off the extra tonnage wandering back through the grove of rustic cottages behind the hotel. I circle around to the meadow side, past the lobby where some traveling opera singers are entertaining the remaining guests, ultra-rich folks who can afford to stay in this earthly paradise Sunday through Sunday through Sunday. Once I clear the other side, in the gloaming of the day, as I look up through the pines to the last stripe of butterscotch sunglow tipping the magnificent pile of a Half Dome sundae (that remarkable piece of stone, how it draws the eye till you're almost sick of it!), I hear a scurrying above me.

I raise my eyes to find something racing through the pines above me and toward the hotel, slithering not quite like a bird but something a little more disjointed, a little irascible. A bird with a bad reputation, maybe. A bat!

I crook up my neck a little more and see three of them, gridlining their lumpy little figures over the darkening frame of the sky. Then I remember something a friend told me. If you throw a pebble up into the flight paths of these little devils, they will attack them as if they were the insects they generally feed upon, because they use natural radar and can't tell the difference. You can play catch with bats! Glorious Mercy!

I scratch around below me and find a few little chunks of granite or some other stone, but what other stone exists here in the valley of Granite? and stand there waiting with the little chunks pocketed in my hand. I catch the path of one of the winged rats screaming by through the light from the lamppost outside the hotel. It is coming in at me nice and low, and before it hits ground zero I flick the rock up into the air, then watch the little flying squid veer on a dime; they're better than hummingbirds, I swear, the way they can change directions so fast. The rock vanishes from the sky and you can almost imagine the sound of the first bite—crunch! yuk! what the hell is this, f'godsake! fuckin' tourists!—then the pebble drops back to the ground at the base of a pine tree fifty feet away.

Then two more of them come screeching across my ceiling, coming in at slightly different angles, and here the game is getting better already. I roll two pebbles into my throwing hand and squirt them upwards, watching the bats veer at the same exact time and almost hit each other in their flurry to collect their food stamps. One of them misses, just by a foot, the other one catches it and deposits it elsewhere. Just over Glacier Point, next to the tall dark stranger of Sentinel Dome, a little more than half a moon peeks out at my nocturnal gaming. I let the light burn into my retina just a moment, then shake the sliver into a red line as I turn back and ready the bait for my next flying idiot.

Rocks. Bats. This fits, I thought. *This is a start.*

Chapter Sixteen

Monday
Andantino

I had breakfast in the bright log-laced cavern of the Awahnee dining room, seated at my lone table beside a horde of healthy-looking Irish redheads straight out of a Norman Rockwell—Flanagan, O'Reilly, McDevitt, or something—and they had to be eating potatoes, hash browns at least. The littlest girl, gangly eight-year-old, perked up in her private school monogrammed sweater and asked McDaddy if she could have some coffee.

"No, dear, coffee is only for grownups."

"Ah, Daddy! Can I have just a sip? Can I? It's all right, I won't turn into some sorta *monster* will I?"

McDaddy gave O'Mommy a look of consultation across the table. O'Mommy sent back that almost invisible yet

consummately clear nod, and McDaddy handed his mug
down to little Katie or Shannon or whatever.

"Now, drink it slow," he said. "It's hot, now."

"Mmm-hmmm, mm-hmmm," hummed Katie, already in
the act. She backed away from the table for a show-stopping
swallow, then grimaced as the bitterness of the forbidden
brown liquid attacked her taste buds.

"Ooooh! Yecchh! Augh! How can you *drink* that stuff?"

Before McDaddy could give any answer a carrot-topped
older brother butted in. "Daddy, are we seeing the falls
today?"

I tried to phase the little monsters out as I returned to the
last of my sunny-side-ups, folding up the whites in a stab and
inserting them into my mouth. I was making a pig of myself
on purpose; I was planning a long hike today, so I needed to
fuel up. You could never eat too much in the high country. The
waitress came by and gave me the once-over (is he done? is he
not done? do I take his plates yet?). I waved an arm toward my
dishes, giving her the okay, then downed the rest of my orange
juice and asked if I could get my check, please.

After breakfast I returned to my room and packed up what
little clothes I had brought with me. I would not stay here
another night. I knew I would not stay anywhere two nights in
a row, but especially not here at two hundred bucks a clip.
Even my plan to spend the day in Yosemite was beginning to
spook me. I was settling in one area; something might catch up
to me. It seemed my business was to drop pieces of myself out
the window along these roads, one at every mileage marker,
but if I stayed inert too long the pieces would come back,
hitching rides from bearded, sunburnt truck drivers named Al
and Mac, until the pieces would come along and Velcro
themselves back to my side while I was having a drink in the
lobby of the glorious Awahnee. No sir, not for me.

I drove back out the valley, the Cathedral Spires firing up
in triplets to my left, then headed south ten miles or so to
Glacier Point Road. I climbed back up the mountain for
nineteen miles, until I rounded the final curve to Glacier Point

itself, square atop the same Sentinel Dome that was hiding the moon from me the night before during my game of bat-baiting.

Even at midday, the point was fairly vacant, just a few well-detached hordes compared to the inseparable Disneyland mass of parents, kids, and soda pop on the weekends. Yosemite is the *femme fatale* of the Sierra Nevadas, and its beauty is either going to kill it or save it. I walked up to the vista point, listening to the sounds of the families as I passed: a tribe that sounded sort of Arkansas twangy over here around the water fountain, a mother, father, and daughter speaking German at the bottom of the steps, and a ganglet of sinfully tanned Central Valley white trashers lined up for the refreshment stand, Mom wearing overstuffed cutoff denims fit to be confiscated by the Aesthetics Police.

"Well, Daryl! If she *wants* the cotton candy so bad, maybe you oughta just buy it for her or she's gonna holler like that all day."

Dad takes off his trucker's cap and crumples it in his hand, pointing the whole sweaty wad at his wife and rebutting, "You wan' give in to her, you go ahead. For all I care she can rot her damn teeth out, but this shit's costin' me a fortune!"

That was enough for me. I wandered off like the veteran lost soul I was and hit the steps to the lookout. The sun straight overhead made me squint, but I wanted to see this thing as purely as possible, no sunglasses allowed. I hadn't been up here for twenty years or so, but I remember how awestruck I was when I was a kid, and about now a good dose of awe was just what the psychiatrist ordered. The first thing I spotted when I got to the railing was the Awahnee, small as a Tinker-toy cabin, down at the roots of the facing cliff, and all around it a landscape straight out of fairy tale castles and romantic-era woodcuts. No one could dream a place like this, anyway; if they told anyone about it, they'd be toted straight off to the rehab clinic.

Half Dome was standing right beside me now, straight off to the right and over a couple of small drop-offs, its face angled to the side instead of that famed frontal view that gives the valley such personality (its guest of honor). I stared at it a good fifteen minutes, letting it burn into the backs of my retinas so I could bring it back later when I closed my eyelids.

Funny, though. Here in the wonderland of nature's Mona Lisa were none of the pieces, not one. I guess these trophies from God's mantelpiece were just too obvious to be of any help. The people who had religious experiences looking at Half Dome were the same kind of potatoheads who annoyed you with born-again pamphlets on your way into the shopping mall, the ones who collected black felt portraits of Elvis and thought *Gone With the Wind* was the ultimate in literary achievement. When you have no imagination, you flock to the obvious. No, I had to find my pieces elsewhere. Maybe close. It *felt* close. I stopped off at the fountain to fill up my water bottle, got in my car and headed back down Glacier Point Road.

I was about five miles gone when I spotted a trio of backpackers off the road, loading up, shucking their lumpish packs against their shoulders. They ran a quick inspection on all their car doors, then fell in down the trail, hitting the steady 2/4 of an *allegro* march tempo, following the road, then splitting off into the murky brown dust of the woods. I pulled into the lot and checked the arrow pointing to where the packers had just headed: Mono Meadow Trail. Yeah, that's it. I grabbed my water bottle, checked my car doors, and tailed off after them, cutting through the dust still floating in their wake.

The trail is a straight, even shot through pine woods, then it heads further downhill and perpendicular to the road toward Mono Meadow. Most of the meadow trail is underwater, this being the middle of the spring melt. There are plenty of overwater boards and logs, though, so I don't get wet until about ten stinking feet to the end when I try to jump from a log to a dry piece of trail, take a weak step, and land with a splotch right into the muddy bank, pasting it like modeler's clay all along the sides of my tennis shoes.

Just outside the meadow are woods burnt out from what

looks to be a year-old fire. Small saplings and grasses are
starting to grow back, but most of the landscape is still covered
with charcoal black logs and spikes of branches arching
upwards in throes of hot death, Satan's idea of a picket fence.
Each step forward brings a cloud of ash from the trail, a lot of
it finding its way into my throat.

Two bends later the trail turns into chaparral, dry fields of
granite slabs and dwarf pines interspersed with low-lying
desert scrub. After a mile of this, the heat is starting to get to
me so I climb up on a boulder and sit down while I uncap my
water bottle and take a healthy swig. Peeking around the
corner I can see Half Dome again, or at least the tip of it, and
nearer, to my right, a high full dome I will later identify as
Mount Starr King. *That's the place to go*, I think, the biggest
rock around. I stand up on the stomach of the boulder and
immediately hear the rasp of plastic on rock, my water bottle
it turns out, sliding down the face of the rock and resting on the
dirt below, happily burbling out all of its contents. Shit! I hop
down and manage to save a couple swallows, but I know I have
to find water now. I have heard too many horror stories about
backpackers and dehydration to take this little accident lightly.
You have to be careful out here in all this slim oxygen and
midday heat.

I keep my sights on the big grey bald spot of Starr King,
two miles down a twisting trailbed of irritating chunks of
granite, pieces just big enough to rip a chunk out of your ankle
if you give them a chance. It starts getting steep enough for
steps when I first hear the rushing of water. *Deo Gratias!*

A few hundred more yards downhill I have my rock and
my water all at once, a wide, pure stream (Buena Vista Creek)
lorded over by Mr. Starr King himself, a shadowy presence
just across the way. I take off my shoes and wade into the icy
drink to let the river feed its contents into my water bottle, then
sit on the bank under a tree to enjoy the feel of the snow melt
on the back of my throat.

Twenty minutes in the shade, and I am completely rejuve-
nated, ready to go, but then it occurs to me: I still haven't found

whatever it is I am here for. I fill my water bottle back to the
brim and walk along beside the stream, hopping from rock to
rock in places, in others traversing long piles of smooth,
rounded river rocks, bejeweled with flecks of quartz, sparking
away in the sun.

"I don't think we can make it!"

The shout comes from the middle of the stream fifty yards
up. A tall, stout man stands in the water, wiping his bald head
with a bandanna, holding a long steel walking stick staked in
against the current. He holds a rope around his waist, on the far
end another packer, a thinner, shorter man twenty years his
junior, balancing himself awkwardly against the cold water
ripping around his legs.

"Let's try further down!" shouts the older, taller man,
straining to make himself heard over the roar of the stream.
"Back to the bank!"

I watch them as they leapfrog back to my side of the
stream, stringing themselves carefully along with the walking
stick and the rope, and then they hop up onto the trail and
disappear. I balance myself down the spine of a log lying in the
creek, then hop a couple good-sized rocks over to the point
where the packers have returned to land. The bank is piled
with river rocks, ovals, circles, rounded nodes of granite, all
ranges of grey monochrome, in seemingly random configuration but for three large rocks set in a triangle. I kneel at the
triangle and feel my hands along the rocks within, looking for
the right touch, some sense of warmth or energy, but get just
the opposite, a flat square piece at the very center, the only
polygon in the pile, cold with the stamp of the packers' river
soaked shoes. I pry the rectangle loose and look beneath to
find the piece I have been looking for.

It is as perfectly spherical as a natural rock can be, and
settles into the palm of my hand like it was born there. I wrap
my fingers up around its breadth, then spin it up into the air and
let it plop back down. It is a light granite, charcoal grey with
flecks of black and white, shiny with quartz crystals, but it
isn't the look so much as the feel, the perfect roundness, the

size of a baseball, the weight of a softball. I know right away; this *is* something. I have made my first real move, my first notable discovery. I balance the rock in one hand, my water bottle in the other, and hop back up onto the trail.

The hike uphill was cooler but more strenuous, and by the time I reached my car I knew I lacked the energy to drive too much further before I would want to bed down for the night. I couldn't go back to Yosemite Valley, though; something would catch up with me there. I took Glacier Point Road out onto Highway 41 and headed south past the Yosemite golf course, one of the oddest sights you'll ever see, manicured fairways and greens right out in the middle of all this high country forest.

The names began to make sense to me once I got ten miles out of the park, out into national forest territory. Just past a town called Fish Camp (so named for a stocked pond set out for lazy sportsmen), I found a dirt road that was really just a long series of tightly bound chuckholes, leading out to a national forest campsite called Big Sandy, along the river and through the trees. I parked up the bank a ways, far from the mosquitoes, and built a fire from gathered branches while I watched the pines shoot out their silhouettes against the final day's light. When the wood drew down to coals, I cleared out my back seat for a good long sleep, my newfound granite baseball nestled safely into the square of my beverage holder, behind the gear shift. Tomorrow I head north.

Chapter Seventeen

Tuesday
Divertimento

So today I am flying through forty-niner country, west on 120 out of Yosemite, fighting off the call of those deadly granite cliffs to take one more look, c'mon just one more look, one more ain't gonna hurt you, is it? catching a brief glimpse of Half Dome through a crack in the mountains, hoping I don't turn into a pillar of salt. Back into the hills, I start hitting all those great old gold rush names, you can almost hear the miners shouting them in the saloons with their hoarse riverside throats, east on 108 out of Chinese Camp, north on 49 into Angels Camp, then back up into the mountains through Murphys and Arnold, north on 89 through Markleeville (now there's a good one) and up to Lake Tahoe.

Ah, Lake Tahoe. Now here's a place where things could

happen. The lake is likely the most perfect mix of pristine nature and illicit humanity in the world. I crawled on over the border into Nevada, the Evil State, and drove down the strip of South Lake into a quickie memory, a pastiche of my favorite month-long fling: crazy Kansas girl, me in a fringed cherry red Roy Rogers leather jacket, breezing her up to the lounge at the top of the High Sierra on a freezing winter's night and dancing the fast ones, the slow ones, the in-betweeners without pause. I was perfectly in love with her long-waisted farm girl's body, the way she knew my every move, the way I could see *her* moves before they came and perch my body in just the right position to welcome her, spin or shake, shimmy or dip, whatever—the most physically psychic evening I've ever spent. And the one song, the slow pop-jazz tune with the dip in the third beat, the beat we made our own, drawn deep into the well by the fingers of a bass player.

But today, today I'm alone, as I should be, because me, with my tired body, my diminishing wardrobe and my three-day beard, all of us, we are ramblers and adventurers, working ourselves into a state of pure receiverdom, a satellite dish mentality. The next code word bleeping in on channel 32 is INCONGRUENCY, and it points me down the end of the strip to Caesar's, the world of the mighty Roman epicureans transplanted into a civilization of seventy-year-old social security queens attacking the nickel slots like they were taking Carthage. And the cocktail girls with those incredible one-sided tops exposing one shoulder and perpetually threatening more. (Sure, they never do, but anticipation is ninety percent of the law in this town; you might hit the progressive jackpot, you might get that ace, you never know, keep on gambling, keep on ogling. Hit me!)

No, the umpteen stories of Caesar's are not here to give me the pure, clean picture of a Yosemite or a sequoia bandaged in colored plastic. The building is here to mess me up, toss me around in its crockpot blender of sound and image, and generally screw up my whole idea of existence as it stands out here in the benign flats and stripes of the parking lot. I welcome the challenge. In fact, I welcome the screwing up, as the lions and tigers who brought me here urge me forward through the burning hoops of those broad glass doors.

It's like one of those car commercials where they show you the inside of a car looking out on a waterfall. The waterfall is eerily quiet, until the driver opens the door, and you are in the middle of a breathtaking whoosh of water and rock. I stand before the entryway, hyperventilating, an ambitious swimmer hoping to get there and back completely underwater. I glance sideways to check my karma on the snow-tipped peaks circling the cold, deep mirror of the lake, and then I am in, hanging ten with a band of Japanese tourists in perfect blue suits. A lawn of plush, royally colored carpet leads you over the lobby and up the stairs into a jungle of machines specifically designed to purloin the money of innocents, spitting out comic-strip balloons left and right: Whoosh! Whiz! Bang! chinkle chinkle chinkle jack! dingdingdingding gazam! Welcome. Would you like some change?

For ten minutes I simply wander from band to band, spotting some huge woman in a lime green jumpsuit running three slots at once, noting the guy in the western gambler's vest, eyes so red you expect them to bleed right out, poor guy must have been at blackjack all night, all week, all month. He no longer has a life *out there*; he's just hanging out inside till some mega-earthquake closes down this joint that never dies.

Let me spell it out for you. There are small silver bells hanging in the air that you cannot see, but you can feel them and touch them and wave a hand through them if you want. They are the bells of fortune. People will drift through these battlements today and lose everything they have, and others will walk out with enough payola to buy their own McDonald's franchise. But let there be no doubt—redistribution will take place! And the bells, the bells will ring, and if they toll for thee, thou art one lucky son of a bitch. But don't bet on it.

As for me, I am no addict. I keep a strict hand on these things. I have seen too many friends sink away their weekends on the sure hunch that this time the ball will settle on red 14.

I have a system, and my system, for some reason, has become part of the spider web of signals I am following.

I trundle up to the cash desk, looking like hell, I am sure, but confident that a smile will break the grunginess and find me some kind, compassionate service.

"Hi. I need to get a cash advance on my Visa."

The lady is blasé blonde, cash-advance weary, but ready to tie me a rope and walk me through the steps. She tosses me a blunt afternoon smile and I grab on.

"Sure. Here. Just fill out this form, and let me see your card."

I take out my buddy the lifetime pass and thrust its eagle wings across the counter. The cash lady catches it between two fingers and slides it through the approval meter all in one motion. I am watching a pro. I fill out the form in detail, home address, work number, expiration date, favorite position (shortstop), favorite color (blue), favorite West Coast convenience store, and various and sundry other tokens of my existence, my signature at the bottom coinciding with a beep from the meter and an upside-down Approval signal. Ah, I am approved, and all is right with the universe.

"Like that in twenties?" she asks.

"Yes," I answer. "Please."

She hands me five wallet-sized portraits of Andrew Jackson and I am off to the change area.

"Oh, sir," I hear, just behind my ears. I turn.

"You forgot something." She holds out my credit card.

"Geez," I say, slapping a palm against my forehead. "Guess I'm feeling generous."

"Oh, and sir," she says, handing me my card. "Next time you may want to go to our cash machines." She points to the hallway, between the restrooms, little slot machines without handles. "No forms. A lot quicker."

Now, why she didn't tell me this before she made me regurgitate my life's history is beyond me, but what the hell, I'm in a hurry. I've got money to lose.

"Uh, yeah, right. Okay, I will."

I swivel on over to the slots and hand three of my bills to the change man, a silent little grunt who reminds me of a mafioso in training. He mumbles politely, shifts my wad into his cash drawer, and hands me three rolls of round dollars.

"Thanks," I say, and thus my system begins.

The Michael Moss slot machine system is absolutely foolproof, in that its principal aim is to lose money. The system is based on the theory that these casinos would be doing a pretty sorry business if their customers *weren't* losing money, and therefore the best that you can hope for is a few hours of worthless recreation. The trick is, start out expecting to lose such-and-such amount and stop exactly when you've lost it. Don't let this black hole of a horizontal Christmas tree suck you into its needles. The only time the Michael Moss system didn't work is when I was on a choir tour in college and I hit a thirty-dollar jackpot five minutes before the bus left. Even Michael Moss cannot lose thirty bucks in quarters in five minutes.

Thanks to my friend from the holographic aviary, I am starting out my system on a higher level; I don't usually mess with silver dollars. I stand to with my jingling wad and confront the huge chromium android at the entrance to the slot area—one long arm, Bigfoot-sized handles—slip in the first subway token, and I'm off on the A train. A single jackpot on my first sweep, but it is not enough to keep me going. I should've known; I wasn't ready for the big time. I am down to twenty bucks before my elbow's even warm, down to rookie level: the quarter slots.

Back to the change mafioso, the guy giving me the side of his eyes like the back of his hand, wondering, Jesus, wasn't this putz just *here*? He hands me two big rolls, one small roll of quarters, and now it gets complicated.

I cross the casino floor and head into the field of slots. Today being Tuesday afternoon, the place is soaked with senior citizens, and I watch in fascination as Grey Panthers feed their machines like hospital patients, intravenous, can't get the money in fast enough. One lady hits a hundred-dollar jackpot and doesn't even stop to savor the crash of coins on metal, just keeps dishing alfalfa to the rest of the herd.

So what am I looking for? Stars and jackpots? Nah. Bonus bars, little black strips of thunder? Nah. Too plain. I need color, agriculture. Fruit! I round the corner and there she is, Mabel the slot machine, refugee from the long green fields of California with her oranges and olives and cherries (love them cherries!). I break a roll against her side and pull up a stool. Before I start, I sleight-of-hand a roundish river rock from my jacket pocket and place it in the bottom of my change cup, pouring quarters over the top like water over the heads of sinners.

Mabel is no country bumpkin; she has the mathematical capabilities of a calculus teacher. The little wonder takes in three quarters at a time and serves out jackpots in five different directions, three horizontal, two diagonal. Sometimes the quarters spill out of her, and it takes you five minutes to figure out exactly what it is you've done. And here I am different than the oldsters. Winning is not good enough. I must know *why*.

My playing goes pretty well. I am two hours gone and still feeding away, hitting just enough of those vitamin-packed triple oranges to keep the pot healthy, just enough bottom-line double cherries to keep treading water. At one point I am up to eighty dollars, near as I can figure it, but there are universal axioms at work here. Why the hell stop unless you win enough to purchase a small condominium? I am here to ring dem bells, and you either ring dem big or you keep on, keep on till your slot hand blisters and your elbow stiffens up and you won't be able to throw a softball for a month.

After my eighty-dollar siege I hit the big recession, sure as shit, and the downswing of the rollercoaster awaits me like the face of hell. In three sweeps of the pot, I am down to a measly handful of silver discs. I carry my pauper's cup to the change area, only this time it isn't the mafioso apprentice but a nice-looking Latino gent who smiles as he shovels my quarters into the change sorter and reads me my total.

"That's ten dollars and twenty-five cents," he announces.

"You say you want that in nickels?"

"Yeah," I say. "Give me ten dollars in nickels, plus the quarter."

Uh-oh. Signals coming in. *Tick tick tick...*

"And, um," I stop and go and stop, not sure how to put this. "Could you, uh...not touch the quarter?"

The nice-looking Latino guy turns up from his drawer, not sure he has heard me. *Come on,* I think. *Don't worry. This guy's heard everything.*

"Um, not touch the quarter?" he says.

"Uh, yeah," I say. Jesus, I hope this guy doesn't take this personally. A scene is all I need.

"Sure, yeah," he says, still a little unsure. He picks a napkin out of the drawer next to him, drops it underneath the coin feeder on his countertop, and plunks a quarter into the center. He places the napkin in my upturned palm and watches as I fold it up and slip it into my wallet.

"Virgin quarter," I say, hoping to explain. "Good luck."

"Hey," he smiles, throwing in my two rolls of nickels. "I've seen everything. I hope it works."

"Thanks," I say, and turn to find the bum slots.

Nickel slots are like expensive solitaire, pure waste of time—but waste of time is an art that sometimes must be pursued. Why not waste time? Some of our most productive work hours turn out to be waste-of-time hours dressed up to fool us. Take this job I used to have...

For my time-wasting efforts I pick on a little machine specializing in black "special" bars and miniature Liberty Bells. Not many jackpots, but when you hit 'em, you hit 'em big. On my second pull I hit the triple on three-bar specials, good for a score of two hundred, which is pretty darn impressive until you figure out that translates to ten bucks. I work myself up to a peak of fifteen bucks, but winning at this point is beside the point. Here you're just looking to finish the day. At one point I even break with policy and play two machines at once like the senior citizens. Not a bad way to ease those stuck-in-the-nickel-slots blues.

Finally I have this thing to the mat, wrapping up one last trip through the pile with three surviving nickels safely in my hand. By now it is getting dark in that world outside the casino, and I have to get going, so I toss my last three beans carelessly into the machine, pull his arm with a heave-ho and call him a son of a bitch. You don't swear at the machines, son, it don't pay off.

And it doesn't. I am free. The Michael Moss system has worked its magic once again, and I am down to my quarter-in-a-blanket. I pick up my change cup and dump my lucky baseball river rock back into my hands. What I don't expect is a lone nickel underneath, which spills out onto the carpet, takes a spiral and settles at my feet. Well, hello there. I whip the napkin out of my wallet, roll the virgin quarter out on top of the lone nickel, and pick them both back up, folding the corners around the two of them and inserting the package back into my wallet, right behind my credit card.

I take a hike down the street to the High Sierra for a cheap buffet dinner (turkey and mashed potatoes with gravy for $3.97), then shoot up to the cocktail lounge for a gin martini and ten minutes of reminiscing about tall Kansas farm girls, red leather Roy Rogers jackets, and psychic dancing. Walking back down the strip toward the Caesar's parking lot, following the lights as they dance impressively across the electron screens of South Lake, I avoid a large group of hop-stepping teenagers by walking almost directly into a parking meter. I stop there for a second, thankful I have not dented my groin and curious at the impulse coming in off the lake like a breeze. *Take it, run with it.*

I reach into my wallet and pull out the napkin, jangling it in my hands until I can grab the lone nickel without disturbing the virgin quarter. I feel for the slot in the center of the parking meter's glassy-eyed face and roll it in, turning the crank until the red flag takes cover inside its gears.

"Take comfort," I say, patting the meter's cold metal head. "You are expired no more."

I take the strip back to 89, out of the Evil State, then north up the west side of Tahoe, watching the lights skim over the lake like waterbugs. I pass the road signs for dormant ski areas, Squaw Valley, Alpine Meadows, then into Truckee, where I find an agreeable roadside motel named the EZ-Snooze and bed down for the night. After brushing my teeth, I empty the contents of a High Sierra matchbox and place the virgin quarter inside, snuggled away in its cocktail bed sheets.

Chapter Eighteen

Wednesday
Menuetto, adagio

For the sake of polite society I spent this morning at the EZ-Snooze performing the complete shave and shower thing—perhaps now I will look more human and not like some wild beast roaming the countryside hunting down innocent objects for strange Satanic rituals. I traveled up the road a ways before stopping for breakfast at a steel-skin trailer in Sierraville, featuring placemats of the world's great mountains, eating Denver omelet off Kilimanjaro, and now it is through the quiet backcountry I climb, threading the High North Sierras, one hundred miles up on Highway 89, past Lake Almanor and into Mount Lassen Volcanic National Park.

It was about noon when I got there, the sun bright and sharp over my southern shoulder. I spindled the looping roadways until I reached the trail leading to Lassen Peak. I had never been there before, but an uncle of mine had told me about it, how you can reach the top on an easy two-mile hike from the road. Fast-food adventure, and from the peak of the trail a masterful view of the mountains, including, on a clear day such as this, the ghost of Mount Shasta a hundred miles to the northwest.

There's not much I remember from the scenery, or the hike itself, Lassen being in all ways, other than blowing its top every few hundred years, a relatively mundane creature. But then I started hitting snow. Almost June, me sweating right through my T-shirt from the midday heat, and I'm sledding across icy-crust snow banks in my fair-weather tennies. Sometimes the crust will not support my weight, so my feet break through and sink into the slush, soaking my shoes. My shoes then pick up every available drift of trail dust until I have gen-yoo-wine mudboots, caked with brown and gaining density as I go. Nevertheless, this snow is fascinating to me, and signals are coming in right and left and topside, but I'm not translating them very well, because to the top is where I'm going, to the top I must go. Why? Because I'm stupid, that's why.

Snow or no snow, I start dehydrating halfway up from the lack of oxygen and the heat. I am ten thousand feet up, and the atmosphere is growing increasingly muggy thanks to a storm front blowing in from the west. I can see the clouds riding in like dark Apache horsemen. But the hell with it, because to the top I must go, and after swigging half the contents of my water bottle I kick myself off this hollow log where I am resting and get myself back on the job.

This being Wednesday, the trail is absolutely deserted, with two exceptions. This Arabic-looking couple comes wandering down toward me, younger twenties, gorgeous people really, deep exotic eyes, broad smiles, skin of milk chocolate. They smile at me but say nothing. I offer up a western howdy, cringing at the frogginess of my unpracticed voice. The sound comes out like a bark—*Arf! Howzitgoin? Bow-wow!*—and they pass by. I go on for a hundred yards then turn around slowly, trying not to look too obvious. The young man grabs the young woman around her waist and sinks his hand deeper, down to the firm flesh of her butt, and just as they're working around the corner, he is working his hand inside her pants. As for me, I'd rather not see such things right now, in fact I'd rather not consider the issue at all, so I turn my eyes forward and proceed. Besides, the peak is in sight, right around the corner...

Wow! You want snow, you've got it. Only this isn't snow precisely, this is a glacier, a long oval flapjack of white running down to the left of the peak. Up two hills and I'm right in the middle of it, thinking if you aimed your skis straight down from here it'd be one hell of a ride right before you hit the rocks and smashed yourself into little pieces. The glacier runs the length of two football fields, so steep you have to wonder why it doesn't slide off like ice cream down the side of a sundae glass. *There's something I must do with this*, I think, but I can't put a finger nor any other digit on it. All this snow in the middle of nowhere—on the *top* of nowhere—no one watching, this, my friend, is a rare opportunity. Come on, think! But nothing comes, so I follow my initial commands— on to the top, to the top I must go.

The peak is a crow's nest of sturdy lava boulders, but alas, you cannot see the gypsy soul of Shasta. It is hidden, sur- rounded by clouds. But there over the eastern side you can see green, green, nothing but green, spreading in a pineneedle blanket all the way to a brown strip of yuk along the horizon, what must be the border of Nevada, the Evil State. While I am panning clockwise to the southern lakes—the aforementioned Almanor and a sister, Mountain Meadows Reservoir, to its left—I take a candy bar from my pocket and am startled by a rustling sound from a nearby bristlecone pine. A chipmunk pops his black nose out from its branches and, sensing suckers in the vicinity, scurries through the dust right to my feet. No caution whatsoever, and I know I have seen this species before: *ferris panhandlis*. This guy, in other words, doesn't bother with bristlecone nuts but prefers to work the local tourists. I am likely his only sales lead on a slow day. He perches at my toes and puts his front paws together, a pretty fair impression of prayer.

Above his paws, though, this critter wears a stoic, expectant face, like I am his own little chipmunk vending machine, just press the right cuteness button and I'll make out with the goodies. Does this kind of behavior get into the genes? Would a human extinction leave these little guys with no survival skills? Yeah, but then what the hell do I care? In any case, I'm not one to get in the way of natural corruption, so I rip a chunk from my Butterfinger and toss it his way. He picks it up like a linebacker going for a fumble and carries it back to the shade of the bristlecone, setting to his work, nibbling like a high-speed drill over the breadth of the chocolate, and striking the orange gold beneath.

So there is life at the top. But no life along that glacier, maybe a little lichen or something, but that's not life as we think of it. Life to us is large-sized mammals who wear size 42 suits with long sleeves. *Tick tick tick...*

Brrrriiinnnggg!!

There it is, that's the signal, and that's all I need. I take a last bite of my candy bar and fly down the trail back to the middle of the glacier. I wander downhill a little bit, careful of my steps, and start scooping my bare hands into the hard snow, keeping an eye out for objects to represent eyes and nose and mouth. This may not have anything to do with anything, I think, but this is surely universal, children of northern habitats have done this and done this and done this with no urging, with no notion of the metaphorical depth of their actions. Someone will come here tomorrow to feed the chipmunks, and they will find this man built of frozen water, and they will know what I look like.

I remember I had a scoutmaster, Mr. Tompkins, insurance salesman by day, who told us that downhill hiking could do just as much damage to your legs as uphill hiking. We all knew he was full of shit then, and I still know it now, as the hour and a half up to the peak converts to twenty soaring minutes back down. I am back to my car before I know it, sitting with my legs out the door while I apply a handy stick to the envelope of dirt and mud around my shoes. The parking lot is barren; the sexy Arabic couple must have found somewhere more private for their groping (how I hate and envy them).

I proceed on 89 to the north and west, looking for Mount Shasta, but I cannot see Shasta anywhere—the clouds have arrived and are obscuring everything. I find its small companion, a spooky next-door cinder cone named Black Butte, but the clouds won't even let me see the top of the cone, much less any sign of its pale bigger sister. I took a hike up to the top of the butte two years ago. The trail is composed of a zillion skateboard-sized igneous rocks that wear at your ankles until you reach the top, an otherworldly nest where the clouds whip around either side of you and the valley below is *right there* in wide-screen color, right along your front porch as you cling to the rocks at the top.

This time through I take the opposite direction, following a turnoff reading Lake Siskiyou. The turnoff road cuts through some surprisingly flat farmlands, past an elegant Victorian farmhouse turned bed-and-breakfast, and then straight on up to the lake, a gentle slate of grey not much larger than a pond.

I park the car and step down a couple of wooden platforms to Earl's Bait Shop, Sandwiches and Cold Beer. An old man is asleep on a stool, his long slim legs perched precariously over the counter. I try to wake him slowly, but end up startling him anyway. I mean, who the hell would come to this place on a stormy Wednesday?

"Uh-umm?…Yeah. Yep. Yep, well! How you doin'?"

I stand there for a second clearing my throat, not willing to settle for the frog-voice I came up with back on Mount Lassen.

"Mmm-hummm! Just fine. How're you?" There, that's better.

"Little slow, little slow," he answers in a groggy chant. "Weather's lookin' pretty nasty, not much business." He stops and looks at me for a few awkward seconds. I guess he expects

me to request something, like bait, or sandwiches, or cold
beer. *I* certainly don't know; I am waiting for a clue myself.

"Want to rent a boat, do ya?" he said, hopping off his stool
and rubbing his hands together.

I don't answer, staring blankly at the prices for
nightcrawlers.

"Well do ya?" he asks.

"Oh, yeah." I say. "Yeah. I shore do. Um, rowboat?"

"Eight dollars an hour, plus a driver's license for dee-
posit."

"Fine," I answer. "That's good."

"Here's your life jacket. Pick a boat off the pier and have
at it. I'd be in pretty soon, though. It's gettin' dark and these
clouds are lookin' mighty ponderous. Fishin'?"

"Oh, uh, no."

"Reck-ree-ational, huh? Well, you take care. Really should
have a partner out there, but I suppose you'll be all right, strong
fella like you. Have a good pull."

"Thanks," I say. I take the life jacket and flip my license
onto the counter, then go to the dock and pick out this
aluminum model on the end, unlatch its chain, and hop in.

I row toward the center of the lake and begin to feel
something as universal as snowmen. The rhythm of my
muscles against the oarlocks, the evergreen mountains dotted
with out-of-season ski lifts, patches of snow knocked up
against the grey ceiling, the edges of the lake right up against
the slopes. I have been here before, but not precisely *here*.
Some ancestor oaring his way across the lochs of Scotland,
fishing in the wee hours of the morning, fetching trout flesh
from the cold deep, and pulling his boat along with the
muscles of his shoulder and back: stroke, wait, set, stroke,
wait, set, stroke, 6/8 measures, dotted quarter followed by an
eighth, a full quarter, then back to the dotted quarter stroke,
wait, set, stroke, wait, set, steady dark minuet across the slate
mirror of an icy lake. And where is my conductor, my Shasta,
great white arms sweeping across my horizon?

I awake the next morning in the back seat of my car, body

bent forward from the awkward position, shoulders sore from rowing, eyes pained with the stab of pure sunlight off a chiseled ivory monster, right on top of me like the hugest snowy thing you ever saw in the world. It must have been there all along.

Chapter Nineteen

Thursday
Lento

Look carefully. The molten rock could not be held, and it erupted from the earth, building up layer upon layer until it formed a great volcano. The volcano cooled and then burst forth in a catastrophic explosion, sending debris flying many miles away. The sides of the volcano cracked open, and lava raced over the valley floors. Soon the volcano's insides were emptied, and it fell in on itself, forming a great crater. The crater filled with water and became a deep lake.

With a force like Mount Shasta staring into your driver's side window like an expectant traffic cop, you don't sleep much. Besides, I underestimated the strength of the wind yesterday and nearly blew out my arms getting back to the dock. Halfway there it began raining and I had to hurry (visions of lightning-fried fishermen in my head). I got back fifteen minutes after my second hour, but the old guy at Earl's Bait Shop took pity on me and charged me for only two. I guess I looked pretty miserable. In any case, the combination of muscle strain and trying to sleep in the back seat of a compact had my body ready to stiffen up like cooling lava; it was best to move around before I had no strength to steer.

I dragged myself over to the camp restroom to use the facilities and splash water on my face, passing a couple in their early forties readying breakfast over a camp stove. The woman had fine brown hair going straight back all the way past her waist. She tossed it to the side as she set paper plates on the picnic table. I moved on.

Once I returned to the car, there was nothing to do but get in and start with the impulses once more, and the first was to get as near as possible to my great white uncle. I returned to Interstate 5 and got off at the most logical place, the town of Mount Shasta. The main road headed straight up toward the mountain, and I followed it until it dead-ended in a residential neighborhood of pretty old Victorians with neat, bright trims of pink and white and New England blue. I turned into a corner market and picked out a Mount Shasta postcard, then hiked across the street to the post office, stucco fifties national park look with big artificial stonework playing out of the walls. I had no change for the automatic stamp machine, so I waited in line behind two silver-haired, plaid-shirted retirees.

"Hi. I need a stamp for a postcard."

"Just one?" The clerk was friendly enough, but he looked like Charles Manson, Kentucky straggler beard and starving eyes.

"Um, yeah. Just one."

Tick tick…

"Say, you know how long this thing'd take to get to Pocatello?"

"Idaho?" he asked.

"Yeah," I said. "Pocatello."

"Hmmm…" He combed a hand beneath his beard, closing his eyes to help him calculate. "Here to the main office in Redding by tomorrow, probably a day or two to Idaho, maybe one day in the office there." He opened his eyes. "I'd say by Monday."

"Fine, fine," I said. "Aunt Jesse'll be mought pleased if this beats me there."

"What," the clerk laughed. "Don't she like you?"

"Hah!" I laughed back. "Oh yeah, she likes me, but she likes to think I'm still out there somewhere when the card comes. Makes it more exotic."

"I see, I see," he said.

"Well, you have a good one now."

"You too," said the clerk. His eyes were already past me to the next customer, a tall, mangy dude who looked like he could be Charlie's brother.

I strolled over to the counter where they had the ball point pens on chains and filled out the address:

Jesse Hempton
243 Fish Camp Drive
Pocatello, ID 74538

The address was purely fictional; so was Aunt Jesse. So what should I tell ol' Aunt Jesse anyway? I flashed on one of Mr. Stutz's favorite sayings and scrawled it in: *A stone is frozen music.*

I licked a postage stamp featuring some aeronautics pioneer in scarf and goggles and stuck it on the square, then kissed Mount Shasta straight on the peak and let 'er drop into the Out of Town slot. Time to hit the road.

I'd taken Interstate 5 up into Oregon so many times I couldn't possibly take it now. I shot up to Weed and turned onto 97 instead, north toward Klamath Falls, across straight flat farm country then up into the dry mountains of the Siskiyous. On the way back down I was welcomed into Oregon by the usual passel of nagging mother-in-law road signs: 55—Speed Strictly Enforced, Slow Traffic Stay to Right, Littering Punishable by Fines Up to $500, Speeding Californians Subject to Castration. Okay, I made that last one up, but you get the idea.

The sun was out and beaming today; in fact it was almost uncomfortably hot. I took a rest stop at the border to change into my shorts and T-shirt, then I followed 97 all the way around Upper Klamath Lake, a remarkably long drive around a remarkably flat, brown, boring lake. The road at the south end got so closed in between the lake and the hills you were afraid some big rig was going to come along and swipe you right into the water. Once I reached the more open roadways of the north end, I started spotting mileage signs for Crater Lake, and it was funny, because the impulses were not all that strong. I mean, we're talking about Crater Lake here, big alien pool of water, perched on top of a mountain like some Titan's backyard garden hose puddle. But nothing coming in on my radar screens. Fuck it, I thought, I'm going there anyway. I turned onto Highway 62 and headed northwest.

And I was wrong. Yeah, Crater Lake was beautiful and all, especially today when the wind was so calm and the sky so clear. You pull over that rim on the entrance road, and it hits you square in the eyes, the surface a perfect mirror sliding out of the crater walls, and the banks still coated with snow, and that water, a shade of blue that shouldn't be possible outside of a Disney cartoon. God's private wading pool, but nothing coming in on the evening news.

One interesting thing: I got to the east end of the Crater loop road and stopped at a little vista/picnic area to eat the rest of a store-bought sandwich, and I heard something. A scuffling sound behind a bristlecone pine, then a little black nose popped out, and I was back with my chipmunk friend from Mount Lassen. You could swear it was the same animal. Same attitude, too—picked up the scent on that ham and Swiss and darted right up to my feet, identical expression of determined expectation. *Come on, buddy—out with it.* So this breed was a national breed, I thought. No way this lot's going to die out.

I extended a lengthy piece of breadcrust in his direction, and he nabbed it from my hand with his stapler-gun teeth. Almost got the tip of my index finger as a bonus.

Crater Lake was just a painting, though, a painting and nothing more, and after a half-hour or so of hanging out, I knew I had to move on. Even Renoirs you can't stare at for too long before heading off to the abstract expressionists. I took one final snap with my eyes, closed/open, and scooted off down the other side of the hill.

To the north of Crater Lake lies a desolate volcanic landscape, spread out between the mountains; you almost expect to see dinosaurs stampeding from the far forest like some Mesozoic safari theme park. Keep that window closed. I hit 138 across and headed due east back to 97 for the drag north.

Eastern Oregon is a lot drier than one would expect. You'll hit some lush farmlands reminiscent of Medford and Ashland to the west and south, but mostly the place looks like scrub-brush Arizona—flatlands of steel-wool volcanic rock stretching out to the horizon, brown-shrouded mountains hiding out in the eastern distance. I drove up through Bend and Redmond in the hot midafternoon sun, jotting off the snowcapped volcanic mountains to my left: The Three Sisters, each over 10,000 feet high (and their close relative, The Husband, at 7,520), then the lone figure of Mount Jefferson, as high a contrast against its arid foreground as Mount Shasta against the scrub lands of Weed. I hitched toward the northwest on 26 into the Warm Springs Indian Reservation, where I found lava buttes and formidable river canyons the color and texture of fine sandpaper. I stopped off at the Deschutes River to soak my feet in its surprisingly frigid water, spying on a group of fishermen hip-wading up the bend, then saddled back up and journeyed the sides of a long canyon.

Soon afterwards, as the land flattened out and the sun started shooting low bullets into my side window, my eyes were called to the side of the road by a line of strange formations. At first glance they look like amorphous piles of rock and wood, but then you begin to notice each pile stands equidistant from the piles before and after and holds a striking similarity, the hand of man way out here in the middle of nothing. Fence posts.

I turn into the side of the road, watching the dust trail behind me, and get out, stretching my legs as I brace my hands on the top of the car. The land nearing the fences looks like something out of those pictures sent back from Mars: red landscape, tiny craters, large rocks dotting the field in endless scatters. For a moment I feel an air of forbidding, like I shouldn't have stopped here, like this was sacred ground or something.

But I have to follow the impulse; this is, after all, my only job. I walk to the nearest fence post and can begin to make out its form. A center pole of rough, wind-hewn wood driven into the ground, with two other poles extended diagonally from each side, forming a tall triangle. The poles support a shelf two feet from the top, upon which are stacked a dozen lava rocks. Below the shelf, at ground level, another twenty rocks are piled at its base.

The function behind the form begins to come clear in my head. Even though it is calm now, this flat open land is a place that can suffer strong winds, and regular fence posts can't be counted on to withstand their force. The ranchers have therefore taken the most plentiful material available and used it to anchor their fences, creating these tripled fence posts to better suit the task. To me they begin to look like altars. Altars of rocks. The radar blips grow stronger. *Tick tick tick...*

I return to the car and pull out my water bottle and the baseball-sized river rock I have taken from Yosemite. I pick out a fence post the general shape of an isosceles triangle and remove the top lava rock from its shelf, then replace it with the baseball rock and open my water bottle to pour it out over the pile, the last real gush of water my granite friend will see for a long time.

It is probably a foolhardy thing to do, using up my last bit of water there in the middle of the Eastern Oregon wastelands, but sometimes christenings are more important than precautions. When I look up and spot the vanilla tip of Mount Hood to the north, I know I have made the right move. Something is really clicking now.

White giant to white giant seems a logical progression for the day, so I jump in my car and head straight for Mount Hood. I climb into the evergreens and turn east at the mountain's face, taking 35 around and up to Hood River. The lights of Washington State wink at me across the Columbia River as I drive into town looking for a good hotel.

Chapter Twenty

Friday
Pasticcio, teneramente

Listen carefully. The molten rock flowed onto the surface and down to the sea, filling the riverbed and forcing its water to the north. The mountains pushed themselves higher, causing the river to flow faster and cut deeper into the earth until it formed a long gorge. Great floods and glaciers followed, cutting into the sides of the gorge and leaving high, graceful waterfalls.

I walked down from my hotel to the riverfront, across the train tracks to a little breakfast place next to a sailboarding shop. Yeah, a sailboarding shop. Seems someone decided to make Hood River the Pacific Northwest capital of the sport, as unlikely as that may seem, and this morning, even as the overcast poured down the Columbia River Gorge (as it always seems to be doing), they were out there, freezing in their high-tech wet suits, waiting for that first good blow to jet them across the river to Washington State. Personally, I think they're lunatics.

I entered the restaurant and took a table by the window, looking out over a long quay where the sailboarders gathered with heavy-coated fishermen to prepare for their respective hobbies. I spotted two dozen ducks, a few geese, and other assorted fowl on the lawn just outside. No Bachelor Ducks these; these had ducksons, duck daughters, duck nieces, Huey, Dewey, Louie, the whole shee-bang. I felt particularly out of my element, but nothing that a warmed-up cup of coffee wouldn't cure.

The Columbia River Gorge is where they got the word Gorge-ous. All the way down this ribbon of water I can see land rising up from nowhere, a full hallway of fairyland nodules, cliffs, and islands, such a big river but all of it pocketed away beneath monoliths for safekeeping. I am too close to the Oregon side behind me to know that Mount Hood looms over us like a pure white godfather, contours cut like diamonds, but am reassured by the waitress that Hood is there just the same. Just across the hall I see the south lands of Washington State, a high plateau upon which some benign soul has arranged long rows of fruit trees and sweeping alpine fields shipped in from Switzerland with no tariff. I have to go there, and I'm sure I will, because I cannot even consider taking a step backward. Forward, northward. If I get real crazy, and my credit holds out, I may go all the way to Alaska.

I didn't bother lugging many of my possessions into the Hamilton—this three-story hunk of turn-of-the-century brick that rented me pillows and mattresses last night. Just a bag of essentials, and this morning I threw on my three-day-worn jeans, ready to leave as soon as I filled my stomach. I must see waterfalls today, I know that, and so I will head west on 84 toward Portland.

The highway snuggles the Oregon side of the gorge like a baby against its mother's breast, closer even than the rail lines which venture out toward the water, held in place by piles of boulders on either side. The sky this morning looks like it is bent on staying moist and dull all day, even threatening perhaps a medium-sized rain. I flip on the wipers every now and then to sweep away the mist gathering on my windshield.

My first stop is a little turnout on the opposite side of the road, toward the south, where I spot a sign. Hiking Trails, Elowah Falls, it says, and it sounds like just what the man ordered. I churn fast into the gravelly turnout, making sure to avoid traffic from the opposite direction, and slip to a halt.

Three seconds into the trail—John Yeon State Park, they call it—I know I am in a much different world than the wheat-colored hills of California. This is green, greener than I have ever seen it, birches and fir trees and ferns everywhere. The color is all the more intensified by the moisture, which drips on my head in friendly little spats from above. I am wearing my green Oakland A's baseball jacket, which makes me feel a little closer to disappearing.

What's more, there is a smell here that I swear I have not smelled since I was a child. All I can think is it has to be the fir trees, something the fir trees do to the soil, because it is a smell of the earth but a clear, glassine smell all the same. This is not making sense, but smells never do. I sniff in with a deep inhale, but the smell is lost in too much air, then go back to my normal breathing and let it pour over me with the moisture.

The trail starts out nice and flat, dirt-smooth, but soon it is steep and strewn with rocks. Two miles up I am suddenly hedged between a cliffside of pure rock and a railing of three-inch pipe, with possibly two feet of walking space, ducking under an overhang of tons and tons of pure frozen-lava death, at the same time trying to dodge puddles with my extremely porous sneakers and trying not to look down where the bottom lands of the riverside look like shots from a weather satellite. This cliff side is Gulliver and I am in his shirt pocket. Yikes. Around the corner I am struck with the sight of a stream shooting out of a far cliff, and this must be Elowah Falls. This can't be something nature did, this looks too intentionally designed, too perfect, but there it is, and I soak myself in the rapture of roaring water suiciding itself down a stock grey face of lava. *Well this is nice, but this ain't it*, says my little interior weather clock, so instead of hiking the next mile and a half to get to the top of this sucker, I am content to soak it in for another three minutes, then slip back under Gulliver's chin and tromp back through the mystical green forest to my roadside stallion.

Five miles down I stop on the river side of the road just to check out a little park and information stand, brochures for a ferryboat service that starts in July and ends in September. The pictures look grand, packs of touristy types gathered on the deck, drinking beers and sodas and shooting down the river canyons in their red, white, and blue Americana paddle boat. Just dandy. But I continue.

Now it is really raining. Not a pouring type of rain, but it is no longer just heavy fog settling on my windshield. My next departure from the car will bring me dampness, but I have decided that water has something to do with this trip, and not in some small supporting role. The idea of baptism comes first to the mind, but there is more in this theme than some Judeo-Christian rite. It must be the idea of erosion, flows of water pouring like time over the hard rock and carving cracks, ditches, a gorge. Water and time means power, and so I will not mind getting soaked. Or eroded.

My next stop is obvious because there at the roadside is what looks like some sort of nature amusement park—Yosemite comes immediately to mind. Then I see a sign reading Multnomah Falls, and I remember it from the tourist map in my hotel room, the second highest waterfall on the North American continent, just behind, you guessed it, Yosemite Falls. The pattern is starting to add up on my television screen. Can the third highest falls be far off?

To get to Multnomah you have to leave your car in a lot on the north side of the highway, then follow a concrete footpath underneath the highway and some train tracks to the falls. At the moment I go under the rail line, there is a hundred-car freight train thundering by. I look up as I pass, watching the wheels pound out their primordial beat against the steel. The sound is a constant din that neither fades nor rises, sort of like the roar of a waterfall.

I stop off at the snack bar and gift shop, replete with the requisite tacky varnished hardwood cribbage boards, memo holders, souvenir spoons, and other such crap with their appliquéd images of Multnomah, local geographic celebrity. I will buy something simply temporal, a candy bar and a lemonade, for the day's hiking is starting to wear on me, and I know I'll need the energy. The lady takes my money, hands me my drink, and I retreat to a bench at the bottom of the main pathway.

My bench faces up toward the falls, a swath of white energy twice the width of Yosemite against green-grey boulders and cliffs. An old bridge cuts in front of the falls in a beautiful high archway of steel and concrete. In the gift shop I have already seen the impressive photographs you can take from this angle: ask your friends to stand on the bridge while you take a shot of the falls above, and you will see just how high this thing is (620 feet, two football fields straight up). This same kind of shot is the only way to get across the idea of a redwood tree to someone who has not seen one; taken by themselves they look pretty normal, but stand your Aunt Betsy at the bottom of one and she looks like a mosquito in sunglasses.

I am seeing other photographs, too. Two athletic-looking dudes in their midtwenties pace up the trail in pastel warm-ups; I picture taking the whole scene with a slow shutter speed, letting the clothes smear Crayola ghosts across the majestic background, meanwhile turning the falling water to cotton-soft ice cream frosting over the boulders.

Another object I noticed in the gift shop was a row of disposable cameras. It was temptation of a potent form, but I passed it up because on this trip I cannot stop the flow of time just like I cannot stop the flow of water. Stopping it would take away all the erosion, whatever erosion I am expecting. Don't freeze the music, please; let it keep walking by, clean, fair measures at a time.

In any case, I am fueled up by now, and so I head up the trail, which is paved over like a golf cart path because of the constant traffic. It isn't bad today, probably because of the weather, but I pass a few groups of lumbering beer belly types and families dragged slow by that weakest link, the little girl trailing behind and screaming about how her feet are sore and she is tired so tired, and aren't they almost to the top yet. Moss's Axiom: Bachelor Ducks move faster than papa ducks.

The trail disappears into the woods for a half-mile, and when finally it comes out, it comes out on a small river. The route is tricky, and it takes you a minute or two to realize that this is Multnomah Creek, doomed water that will soon hurtle itself over the edge and be forever canonized. I cross the creek on a footbridge and dawdle around on the other side, off the trail, dipping my hands in its icy shallows and soaking in the green which here has been deepened even more by curtains of cobweb mosses hanging from the trees. Green green green, can you possibly get enough of it?

I hop back over to the other side, watching my steps on the wet rocks, and almost bite the big one off a large boulder that jerks over when I pounce on it, waterborne skateboard just waiting to run me on down the stream to a painful but quick death. I wing both arms back up and manage to save my hide, unfortunately dipping one leg calf-deep into the freezing drink. Yikes.

The trail follows the stream down for a few hundred feet and finally comes out on a deck directly adjacent to the head of the falls. You pace onto the boards with a certain confident recklessness but are quickly brought back when you dip your head over the railing and see just how far down one can go if one does not watch one's step. The parking lot below is not even big enough for Barbie and her friends; the cars across the highway are barely discernible, and the rail line looks like strips of HO gauge on Christmas morning. I step back a couple feet to where I feel safe and watch the water pour off the cliff.

The movement of the waterfall becomes mesmerizing after a while; the flow shifts in such subtle shadings of movement that you're not even sure if you're seeing them. After ten minutes of this buzz, I start following certain swatches of water, trying to track them all the way over, but inevitably losing the line of descent about halfway down. I'm sure it all gets pretty well mixed, anyway. Doing this, though, begins to pique my curiosity and roil up my internal tracking system. Something is coming to mind, and I have perhaps two minutes more of water-watching until it shoots off my personal clifftop to a foamy head.

I sit down on the deck and look back from the falls to the yards of water skipping down a small preliminary cascade, little suspecting its next radical maneuver. Potential there. Much potential. Innocent, untapped water waiting to be thrust into hydrodynamic immortality. That's magic water, that is. I must have some. But only at the moment of becoming. Otherwise it wouldn't count. My gears begin to click hard, screaming for WD-40 Quaker State, or maybe Pennzoil, churning up all kinds of mental heat. *Tick tick tick...*

Then I have my idea, but right as my plot pecks its way through the eggshell, a trio of teenagers appear around the bend of the trail. *Damn them. Oughta chuck them right over.*

"Hey, check it out, eh!"

Oh Gawd. Canadian teenagers. I'd been warned of this phenomenon. Three shaggy blond Anglos, one female, the other two big obnoxious males, stomping down the path like they own the place, ignoring me in my odd position on the deck, and racing for the railing like they were gonna swan dive right on over.

"Whoa, eh, wouldn't want to end up oot there, eh!"

"No no, eh, long long long long *LONG* way down, eh!"

"Ohhh, it's beautiful," said the girl, peering between their big shoulders at the white strands cutting over the cliff. "Imagine all the water that goes down there every day."

"I *told* you she'd get like this, eh," said one obnoxon to the other obnoxon. "Missy Poetess the Queen, eh."

In close proximity now, every "eh" was accompanied by a thrust of the elbow into the ribs. I thought the big one might get too rowdy and jab the smaller one through the boards.

"Fuckin' boring, ya ask me. Let's go down and get some more chow, eh."

The two blond gorillas tromped back up the trail, leaving the girl behind. She gazed at the waterfall in clear-eyed amazement, until one of her behemoth friends turned and yelled at her.

"Ay! C'mon, eh! Let's get the fuck goin' willya?!"

"All right, all right!" she shouted, then noticed me at her feet and let out a little gasp.

"Oh," she said, smiling. "I'm sorry. You scared the livin' daylights outa me." She took an ironic look at her two compatriots. "Real Canuck assholes, ain't they?"

I said the only thing that occurred to me, and it seemed to crack her up. "You take what you can get."

"Hee!" she squeaked. "I guess you're right. Have a good one, eh?"

"Yeh, you too."

She runs up the trail to the first bend, where she catches up with her blond bombers. I wait until they round the corner, then scout around the deck for appropriate materials. I find a green branch stuck against the river bank, someone's idea of a walking stick, and hoist it up, checking it for the proper length then setting it down on the deck. I pull the water bottle from my belt and open it up, taking a swig for good measure, then pouring the rest out over the falls. *Become immortal*, I decree.

For the next step I remove my tennis shoe and pull out the shoelace, using it to tie the water bottle to the end of the walking stick. I sit down on the edge of the deck, facing out over the falls, seeking the conversion point, the spot where the water first spills over and strikes pure air. But I can't reach quite far enough. I brace myself mentally, swearing not to look down, and slip through the railings of the deck onto the bank, locking a sturdy elbow around the deck post and extending the stick with my free hand. I hit the point solid this time, right at the center of the stream, right where the bottom falls out, and capture it in my bottle. When the bottle is half-full, the stick begins to shake in my grasp, and I decide not to risk making it heavier. I swing it all the way back around, until I can fit the whole contraption underneath the railing, and balance the stick so the bottle lands right side up on the deck. Letting go of the stick should help my balance, but just then my unlaced right shoe slips against a moss-covered rock. I catch myself, hugging the deck railing like my dearest friend, but not before I break my promise and look straight down over the edge of the cliff. Holy shit. My heart starts to do the cha-cha, and I have to wait what seems like five minutes before I hoist myself back under the railing and on to the deck. Believe you me, after nearly immortalizing myself on the spot where the water escapes the land, I deserve a victory chug of that magic H2O, but my inner impulses tell me not to. Instead, I take one last look at the crest of Multnomah and jog back down the trail, stopping to cup some of the stream in my hands and pull it to my mouth.

I continued west on 84 to Portland, crossing over the Columbia on the Jackson Bridge, a high arching band of steel that hit all the bad parts of town before widening out into the countryside. Mount Hood was not going to make an appearance today, as I kept an eye on my rearview mirror and saw nothing but grey clouds behind the Portland skyline. A few more miles along, I met up with the Great Western Runway, Interstate 5, and took it up to Olympia, then along the east side of Puget Sound toward Tacoma.

Ten miles past the state capital, the overcast finally clearing the way for a lemony afternoon sun, I spotted three things at once: to my left, long stretches of blue water that must be the Sound itself; to my right yet one more white ghost, the gracious hulk of Mount Rainier; and above me, a hallucination straight out of postage stamps and Old West movies. I couldn't make it out at first, and it disappeared behind me as soon as I could name it, but the white head and the straight black wingspan and the milky smooth curve of its flight gave it away. A bald eagle. My first bald eagle. This had to be some kind of directional. Between the white heads of eagles and the white heads of mountains, I had a clear path through the afternoon. *Tick tick tick...*

Tacoma calls my name and I answer, pacing along 705 straight into downtown and Market Street. What better place to be looking for the things you need? I park on the street and walk up the block quickly, as though I know what I am doing. It is six in the evening now and the streets are pretty empty, this being the business district, just a few stragglers finishing up their shopping and small signs of activity over at the corner bar and deli. Halfway up the street I find a music shop, Lou's Music, and I stride in.

These signals are the strongest yet; I have no doubt whatsoever that the object of my search will jump off a shelf and into my lap like a pet-store puppy. Well, it almost does. Straight in the shaft of light coming in through the south-facing windows lies my Tacoma Grail: a ring of wood lacquered in black, skin of goathide stretched tight all around by a strip of leather affixed to the wood with brass nails. The goathide sports tufts of fur here and there, left there on purpose, one would think, to prove authenticity. I loft the drum and strike a finger to it; it emits a ringing low thud, bottoming out and warping back, powerful. I pick up the pamphlet underneath and read the title: *Bohdrán: Celtic Drum, Trinity College, Made in Thailand.*

Well, I guess you can't actually get a Celtic drum made in Ireland, but this is the item all right; what other reason for going to Tacoma? I will need this sometime. This goatskin beckons to my hands and arms in the same rhythms as the oarlocks of my Scottish rowboat. I have felt this skin before. I have braced the cross-sticks behind this round beacon, heard its hollow ring in my ears, maybe even danced to its bleatings.

"Need any help?" Salesman, agreeable-looking college kid, clean-cut, sweater vest and tie, name badge says, "Hi, I'm Norm."

"Yeah," I say. "How much for this little trinket?"

He helps me find the price tag inside the pamphlet—$60.95—and I say, "I'll take it." He is almost taken aback that I won't ask at least one more question before agreeing to the purchase—professional pride, I suppose—but he leads me to the counter and fills out all the annoying specialty-store address forms and takes my credit card. I watch my holographic eagle with new affection as it disappears under the receipt.

"Yeah, always wanted one of these," I lie. "My uncle plays in a band in Dublin, plays one o' these here bow-drans."

"That's boh-rawn," says Hi-I'm-Norm, grinning. "The *d* is silent."

"Oh, yeah, right," I say. "Just kidding."

"And this," he says, holding up a two-sided drumstick, "is your tippler. Make sure you don't lose it."

Norm squeezes the bohdrán into a just-so sized bag and advises me to keep my drum out of the sun or the skin will tighten up and stretch itself out.

"Yeah, thanks," I say, walking out the door. I squint my eyes at the sun, noting the fishy smell coming off the waterfront two blocks down, trying to remember where I parked my car. I hold my prize up against my ear and thud the goatskin through the paper. I will definitely need this. This I will definitely need.

I drove due north to Seattle, watching with wonder as the interstate flew upward between two great valleys filled with Boeing factories, airports, and houses. The sun was drifting down into a bank of clouds on the western ridge, the light cutting across the road at odd intervals.

The readings were coming quicker and stronger now, and I was tracked in on them like a fog-bound pilot. In baseball parlance, I was standing on second, in scoring position, with no outs. I was into the cities now, and Seattle, the rainswept crystal the people call Oz, had to bring me something. I wasted no time, but a lot of money, getting off midtown and heading straight for the biggest building I could find. It turned out to be the downtown Hilton, $120 a night. What the hell. What was I gonna do with this money in my next life, anyhow?

After checking into a small but plush room, studying the sanitation-wrapped glasses, the dwarf soap and tiny shampoo bottles, and all those other great hotel curiosities, I donned my best clothes (a permanent press shirt I had saved for the occasion, a pair of grey brushed-denim pants I had worn for only one day) and drew a vertical line to the rooftop lounge where some blues-looking black piano guy named Digger Johnson was pushing out classics for the rich white folks like "Girl from Ipanema," or some other such crap, and listening to the rich white folks get drunk and tell him how damned good he was and how you just couldn't find singers like him back in Texas, dammit, and why dontcha play "Stand By Your Man," that there's one uh my favorites. Digger just smiled; he wasn't paid to have opinions. When the bartender queried I asked for a Rainier beer; what the hell, if you can't climb the thing you may as well drink it. I chugged it down, listening to Digger slide through "Kansas City" and "Great Balls of Fire" (finally, some good stuff) and watching the rivulets of gathered fog run off the window all the way down to the street, stopping by the lobby to check out. Five minutes later I am on the elevator, following suit.

I pad down Sixth Avenue and am tempted to head over to the waterfront, to Pike Place Market, something every friend who's ever been to Seattle has told me about. But that isn't it; this thing is leading me straight down into the Seattle night, pure flint darkness of clean steel buildings and spooky Northwest fog, broken only by the spark of voices drifting out of restaurants. Soon the hills bottom out, and Sixth Avenue draws up nice and level. It is getting late and cold; the windbreaker I've brought with me is not enough, so I walk quickly to keep up the temperature.

I cut westward to Fourth Avenue and press on. The pace of my walk, originally meant just to keep me warm, intensifies. *Everything* intensifies. After a block or two my breath comes in vaporized puffs, and I am starting to sweat inside my windbreaker. Turning the corner of Pine Street, I find a shopping center facing a square, soaring angular panes of glass, elevators inside jumbling up to small shops and boutiques. I am standing on cobblestones in the middle of the square, Westlake Park, surrounded by glistening stores, low yellow lights peeking out their windows like the eyes of cats.

The road has become stones, and stones must have water. This is the place. I pull my water bottle from my belt, brace my feet at the center of the square, pull off the cap, and let the airborne liquid finish its flight into my mouth, chugging the whole half-quart at a shot.

But the water is too cold, and I am asking for trouble, that accursed frozen-mouth headache searing up my palate and through my sinuses, a flighty scorch right up into my brain cells. I hold my temple between my hands, I rub my tongue across the roof of my mouth, all the tricks the kids at school talked about over ice cream cones and Slurpees, but it will not work, the goddamn thing is taking its sweet time emptying out my skull. I will die of brain seizure right here in midtown Seattle.

The pain dies off after a brief eternity, but down the trail of my small agony the *tick tick tick* turns into a solid ringing thump, as if the hollow *brrummm* of the bohdrán has joined its beats together into a solid highway of sound. The sound heightens and begins to sing in curtains of brass, then individual notes stray down from the one sound and form a melody. After the last crumbs of the pain drift off, I know it isn't my head at all. I look back toward Fifth Avenue and there in front of Nordstrom's is an old grey-bearded black man with a saxophone, fine felt hat on top of his stool, ringing an old jazz tune out over the street, making the cobblestones shake for me in a radical new equation: water is thawed out, water becomes sound, sound becomes time, time becomes sound becomes music.

I hitch my now-empty water bottle back on my belt and walk over to the storefront where he stands, watching the way his cheeks purse back and forth under the grey grizzle of beard, studying his faded burgundy topcoat and his bright red-checked scarf. I stop in front of him, pull out my wallet, and let three dollar bills drift like leaves into his hat. He nods at me in appreciation, and I stay on for another bar before I drift around the corner back into darkness. But I stop before the first parking meter, letting the unsung words drift in.

"'Round Midnight." Thelonius Monk. I look at my watch. He is right on time. I reverse direction and come back into the light just as he is wrapping it up.

He flutters the tune to sleep like a mama bird on a low branch, then looks up at me and smiles, gold tooth and all. I pull a High Sierra matchbox out of my pocket, take out a Caesar's Tahoe cocktail napkin and let it unravel, dropping my virgin quarter into his hat. The cracks open wider.

Chapter Twenty-One

Saturday
Interlude, l'istesso tempo

My vow of solitude held water for another three weeks, until the softball team gathered for its only wintertime affair, the Super Bowl party. I really didn't want to see Stacy, but neither did I want the simple possibility of her presence to reign over my social schedule. No matter what, the softball team would remain our one necessary connection, and I would just have to start dealing with it.

And so I found myself on the west side of Santa Cruz, searching for a parking space along the dirt shoulders of funky beach houses, skirting coves, and high cliffs over the Pacific. It's a beautiful part of town, but so random with its roads—no regular curbs, just sort of indeterminate patches of dirt where your car may or may not be safe. I pulled smartly in under a shaggy dead oak tree and reached in the back seat for my six-pack of beer and twin rib-eyes.

"Mikey!" Ralph, the biggest guy on the team, and most of that is latitude, not longitude. Ralph pretends to play third base, but he is really out there just to force illicit substances on his teammates. "Hey, man, wanna smoke some before we head in? Got some great stuff."

"Sorry, Ralph," I answered, pointing to my neck. "Dries out my throat."

"That's okay, man. Who needs to talk? Ha!"

"Yeah," I said, reaching back into my car for a frisbee, brought along just in case these couch spuds managed to drag their carcasses down to the beach. I was dying for some exercise. Without that weekly softball game I had a hard time keeping up my regimen. It would only get worse during the next two months, as our televised inspirations would be ruled by the lesser sports of basketball and that thing they played with that little black sliding disc and all those men with missing teeth.

But today was Super Bowl Sunday, our last chance for winter entertainment, and I had one more connection to Stacy, besides; a week before our last breakup I had bet her a steak dinner on whoever might face her beloved New York Giants. I wound up with the Broncos, the ultimate choke artists, but I would stick to my bet, because, exiled or not, I still felt the need for small pieces of revenge. The Broncos would at least give me a chance.

The day was unusually sunny, and I walked straight around the house where I found her with Kenny, sunbathing on the back deck. With their sickly white East Coast bodies, they looked like they came from the same family, brother and sister. In fact, I had never noticed how much like siblings they looked. Stacy acted friendly and distant at the same time, in that unnaturally natural way of hers.

"Hi Michael! Didja bring some beer?"

"Yeah!" I responded. She would not catch me in a down mood, by damn. This was a face-off I was going to win. "Same

shit we drank all summer!" I held aloft the cheap American
piss-water we all craved after our softball games.

Kenny smiled, for a second, and that would be the high point
of his day. The rest of the day he glowered, some anvil of thought
pressing against his head. What did he want? He was out of his
cast now, slowly gaining back his legs, and he had a beautiful day
with all his best friends, out on the back deck in a rare corner of
the world not much more than spitting distance from the Pacific
Ocean. I just wanted to leave, but I couldn't. I had to see this thing
through, just to push the envelope, just to see if I could survive.
I leaned down onto the sun deck's raw redwood surface, popped
open a beer, and watched a troop of wrens squabbling over the top
of a bird feeder. Inside, the pregame show was starting, the
stadium filling up.

Sure enough, the choke-artist Broncos succeeded in what
they did best, and Stacy's beloved Giants won the Super Bowl
by a wide margin. As for me, I considered my gamble a double
loss, since the settlement of a steak dinner involved yet
another meeting. I had to make certain I wasn't drifting back
into old, masochistic habits, allowing tiny votive candles of
hope to blur my vision.

The early indications were not good at all. I showed up at
her condo the following Sunday with twin T-bones in hand,
only to find her gone. I sat on the bench opposite her door for
fifteen minutes, watching a storm front crawling in over the
coast, and was about to call it quits when Sharise, one of her
roomers, showed up.

"Well, she didn't say anything about any plans this weekend," she said. "But you might check the Nite Owl on
Seabright. She's been goin' there a lot lately."

I told Sharise thanks and headed for the Owl. If I was really
smart I'd have gone straight home, but I guess I was in the
mood for a confrontation. When I walked in she was playing
pool. She gave me a kiss and a pseudo-apology which served
to defuse every one of my prepared arguments. She was drunk.

"I'm finally getting through to her!" she whispered. Stacy

motioned to her opponent, a woman twenty years her senior, ratty grey hair, dirty yellow blouse in need of ironing, lining up a bank shot with a cigarette dangling from her lips. "Working for me a year, and I'm finally getting through to her!"

"Getting through to her or just getting her blitzed," I didn't say.

"So employee relations is more important than dates with lovers," I didn't say.

"Go to hell quickly," I didn't say.

The whole situation made me see the clear outline of what our relationship had been all along. It was all control, and I never had it. I was an inflatable punching clown, she the kid knocking me into a wobble every time I managed to straighten myself up. No, don't risk making Stacy angry, because say what you feel, and you'll lose her, Michael, but goddamn you, you should've known you'd lose her all along, anyway. But this time was different. I didn't have her now. I could do what I damn well pleased. I drank three beers I didn't want and walked out, found a pay phone in the rain, and called a friend. She was tired of hearing my stories but willing to listen.

"Michael, go home right now. I want you to go home right now and get some sleep and wait for *her* to call *you*. Better yet, don't wait at all."

"Yeh, you're right," I said for the fiftieth time. "I will. Thanks."

I sat in my car across the street from the Nite Owl, waiting for the strength to leave, staring at the numbers on my odometer. Then she tapped on my window. I could have timed it, the way she reeled me back three movements before an escape. The clown straightened up, ready for another shot.

Two weeks later I found the depth of my illness when my windshield wiper went out halfway over the mountains. It was night, and I was driving her back to Santa Cruz, and suddenly my field of vision fell to glaring flowers of light through the rain drops. The only way I could judge the road was by the cars coming the other direction. I could have pulled over, but no, I went on.

You see, the wiper on Stacy's side worked perfectly; she could see everything and *do* nothing, an equation that left me intoxicated with power. I took it slow, we made it into town, but she worked up a tremendous headache clenching her jaw, tensing at each curve in the road. If taking pleasure in someone else's pain is a sickness, I should have seen it right then.

I slept in till eleven o'clock and had a huge breakfast in the hotel restaurant. For the first time on this trip I feel secure, I am far ahead of my secret identity, and I am taking the time to indulge myself in whatever luxuries come my way. There is a pianist across the lobby, playing tunes from *The Wizard of Oz*, and me over here before my first-ever plate of eggs Benedict, thinking of strange and wondrous journeys.

Had a dream last night. I was lead vocalist and rhythm guitar for a cowboy trio lounge act, Buckaroo Slob and the Outriders, dressed in fringed red buckskin cowboy jacket, big hairy chaps, and a bolo tie. We were playing this Reno casino called the Virginia Wheelhouse, grand fake southern Greek Revival architecture all around.

So, we're playing along like most nights, not so exuberant that we might interfere in anyone's keno game, when I pull out something we've just added to our repertoire: "Cool Water." Sons of the Pioneers. Bob Nolan.

And all of a sudden the folks at the roulette wheels and the blackjack tables start listening to us real intently. It scares me. I almost lose track of the words. They're just standin' there, paying no attention whatsoever to their money lying there on the table in front of 'em, just licking their lips real thirsty-like and swaying to the gentle cowboy beat.

And now everything has stopped. The social security slot slingers sit stone still at their machines, the dealers pull up chairs and turn our way. Then we end the song with the requisite three-part coyote howl—*ow-ow-owooooh!*—and complete pandemonium breaks out. Every last soul in that casino rushes the bar, demanding bottles of Multnomah Spring Water, airborne water packaged fresh from the top of Oregon's finest falls.

Well, like I said before, it's just a dream. Don't make too much of it.

I spent a couple hours in a laundromat around the corner from the Seattle Hilton to clean what little clothing I had, then threw everything into the back seat and shot out for the interstate.

The day was overcast and a little bit rainy, no real Washington downpours, just the occasional light smattering across the glass. I drove north, still not ready to retrack any mileage, then headed toward Whidbey Island, 525 northwest to Mukilteo (love those Northwest names), and across on the ferry. I timed my crossing perfectly, paying the man at the booth and driving on board about a minute before departure. The rarity of being on a waterborne vessel—combined with the convenience of having your car and all traveling accouterments readily accessible—heightened the excitement of going to a place I once called home.

I don't talk much about my family. My folks are retired and living in Michigan. I make sure to see them once a year, but we are not close. Perhaps, in the middle of all this solitary living, they have been crossed off my list along with everything else. I'll probably go visit them over Christmas, check out the islands of the Great Lakes with my dad—he'd like that. But back to here, where I am crossing to other islands. Let me tell you about them.

My father was a navy pilot, and when I was just entering the second grade his orders took us to Whidbey Island, scant miles from the Canadian border, to the naval air station at Oak Harbor. Life was tough on the family, since Dad was on deployment in the Pacific for most of our six-month stay, but for a seven-year-old boy the island itself was right next door to paradise.

The memories come in ten-second flashes, as they always do. One of them is of a deep spread of pine trees up the hill from our house, where my brother and sisters and I would go exploring and tree-climbing and clothes-dirtying. Another is of a trip to the air base on the Fourth of July, my first recollection of fireworks, lying on a comforter with my mom while the sky exploded in colors and dropped sparks into the sound.

The ultimate memory was of my affection for snakes, and how Whidbey Island was just (excuse the expression) crawling with them. I used to tell my friends that when Saint Patrick drove the snakes out of Ireland, they all caught a navy cargo plane headed for Whidbey, because they were all over the place, garter snakes and red racers and king snakes and diamondbacks and, well, we came up with names for the rest of them as we caught them. In any case, the island was the ideal encouragement for my new hobby, and I became an expert trapper. Unfortunately, I could never keep them alive after I caught them, since snakes are not as suited to the domestic life as, say, your average labrador retriever, and I had no good notions of how to feed them.

The walk home from the classic brick schoolhouse of Oak Harbor Elementary took me across numerous wooden groves and vacant lots, and I made it my daily routine to check under hollow logs and pieces of scrap metal and plywood lying around. These were the places where snakes hung out; you had to be very quick or they would scatter, and you had no time to consider whether they were poisonous or not before you grabbed.

One fine Tuesday afternoon I hit my personal notion of a jackpot when I skipped into my richest gathering ground, a grass-covered lot behind the corner grocery store, hefted up a particularly large piece of plywood, and discovered a nest of eight or nine baby snakes, black with red stripes—what we took to calling red racers for their speed, agility, and coloring. Brave, stupid second-grade soul that I was, I picked up the whole wriggling lot of them in a swipe and deposited them in my Beatles' *Yellow Submarine* lunch box and continued on my merry way, content with the afternoon's harvest. Stupid, short-attention-span soul that I was, I completely forgot the contents of said lunch box upon returning home and absent-mindedly placed it on the kitchen counter.

My mother came by moments later to clean it out and…well, she was surprisingly calm, considering, but let's just say it didn't exactly make her afternoon.

The snake-loving second grade snotnose Michael Moss always loved the ferries, and in the twenty-minute run from Mukilteo to Whidbey Island, I am living the thrill all over again, watching the chalkboard green water run under the prow and skim to the sides, white triangular slash buried in our wake. A ferry heading the other direction makes a similar track back toward the mainland, and a couple of kids on the deck wave at it, hoping for a response across our highway of water.

Most of the wise adults are inside next to the heater, but not me; I am determined to take this trip with the heart of an old sailor, out on the foredeck with the rain and wind cutting into my face. The moment we sight Whidbey, the visual data starts flowing in, and I am engorged: coastline of old Victorian houses, mist-covered docks holding rowboats safe on their moorings, the little fishing town of Columbia Beach shrouded and mute in shoulders of grey. I soak it all in with these twenty-years-older eyes before I check back in and follow the bored natives down to the car deck. I sit in my driver's seat and imagine I am some sort of James Bond figure, cutting across the water with no visible assistance, just me and these specially designed hydrofoils that extend beneath my car at the press of a button.

The guys with the neon orange paddles escort us from the hold, and, except for the retired lawyer with the whale-sized Buick trying to pull backwards out onto the dock, we are on our way with ease, skipping through town and into the musty green of the pines before we have time to regain our land legs. Highway 525 winds up the island on a northwest bearing, turning into Highway 20 halfway up for no apparent reason other than to confuse drivers. The forests to the side of the road are incredibly lush, piled through with enough ferns and thick moss to make the Columbia River Gorge look like the Gobi Desert.

The drive is varied, though, leading as well through stretches of pasture land and idyllic farms, half of them it seems operating concurrently as bed-and-breakfasts. None of this strikes my memory, because I'm sure second graders don't get around half as much as they think they do, and besides, my family was only here for six months. Just when I am bent on remembering nothing else, I pass long fields of strawberries and am thrust backward into another ten-second video, the vision of our whole family (save Dad) picking-our-own on a Sunday afternoon, then the smell of strawberry preserves that would permeate the house for days, all the sweeter because our fingerprints were on each and every berry.

A few miles from the strawberry fields, I find myself on a pleasant downhill run into the town of Oak Harbor itself, and I slow down just to spot the familiar name on the entry sign. If I had a camera I'd take a picture of it. Where the road leads into town you can see the harbor, grey and dirty at low tide. But I am headed the other way, uphill into town, looking for bites of the past.

All I remember at first are foothills, because that is where I am sure we lived, and so I head wrongly to the southwest side of town and turn into some likely-looking residential areas. Seeing nothing familiar, I turn around and am ready to head even further in the wrong direction, when I look out over the town and spot the old brick building perched on a hill right in the middle of everything.

Being just off the air base, the town has always been a military town, and it shows some of the quirks of military thinking. The streets, for one, are numbered in an unusually anal-retentive fashion. To get to the schoolhouse I take 400 Avenue to 60 NW Street, then right on 600 Avenue to where it crosses Midway. These are not directions, these are coordinates. These bozos thought they were still at sea! In any case, I am soon on the grounds, parking at curbside and racing out in the rain to feast my memory banks.

The front of Oak Harbor Elementary is immediately

recognizable, a long rectangular hunk of brick and white trim straight out of your classic Lewis-and-Clark frontier architecture guidebook, mixed in with measured portions of the New England school, stirred by the rigid stick of military design. The front is still beautiful, lush green lawn bordered by a neat line of maples along the sidewalk.

I decide to hold off the full picture of the place by cutting behind a newly installed annex to the fields in back. Once around the corner I am hit by an immediate burst of vision: a field trip, one of those incredibly bright, fragrant Northwestern spring days, trekking out across the schoolyard, wondering where buttercups came from, and all around us, in every direction, white-capped peaks on the horizon, the Olympics, the Cascades, all of them proud distant relatives who never visited but always sent checks on birthdays to let us know they were well.

Back around the building I come out on the swing sets in their boxes of smooth dark gravel, and the one ten-second bite of Oak Harbor badness flies forth. On a day like this one, slate-grey, dull sky, threatening rain, I was entertaining myself next to the swings by trying to hit one of the far poles with a rock, the usual childhood target practice that would lead to the seventh game of the World Series and an eventual place in the Hall of Fame as the pitcher with the blazing fastball and the incredible control who started off by throwing rocks at playground poles. The playground monitor, who I seem to recall as a fat old hag with large warts, a piercing silver whistle hanging from her neck, and no sense of humor whatsoever (although here my memory may be somewhat affected by events) told me not to throw rocks, little boy, or she would take me to the principal's office.

Not having yet cultivated the style and dash of a true rebel child (who would have immediately wrestled the playground monitor to the ground and stuffed wet gravel down the back of her dress) I decided to at least stretch my luck a little. Instead of dropping my remaining handful of rocks benignly to the ground, I would at least *throw* them to the ground, thus expressing my displeasure at this out-and-out misreading of my recess activities. Nolan Ryan wasn't built in a day, lady.

The playground monitor had apparently not had a good day. She immediately grabbed me by the hand and took me straight up to the principal's office, and, before I knew it, my pants were around my ankles and a man with what I shall always remember as a sadistic grin on his face was approaching me with a wooden paddle, and we *weren't* going to play Ping-Pong. The rest is painful, much too painful for a generally well-behaved kid whose only sin was the propulsion of small rocks two feet vertically to the unharmable ground, putting nothing in danger but his own feet. So there!

Well, enough of the Freudian playback. The impulse that comes on the heels of my mental recounting is so natural it doesn't even come with the little *tick tick tick* I have been storing in my shirt pocket all week. I stand there in the rain looking up at the boarded-up window which was once the principal's office, reach down to grab an overflowing handful of pebbles, and thrust them upwards into the spilling grey sky, not even caring if one or two of them might strike my cranium on the way down. Take that, you assholes! Ruin my childhood, wouldja?!

After three or four throws, I figure I have gotten it all out, and I take one last handful and slip it away into the breast pocket of my jacket. Rocks, water, wet rocks—these are things I should save. The weight of them makes an odd damp chill just over my heart.

I followed Highway 20 all the way up the island, stopping at Deception Pass to watch the jade waters of the channel swirl down in dangerous fantail currents against the dark stone of the cliffs. The road flattened out, and I found a series of luminous silver-colored factories across the water, towers and tubes winking their lights at me as I pulled into Anacortes. I took the road through town to the ferry station, where I discovered there was only one real way to go: I had to catch the eight o'clock morning ferry through the San Juan Islands to British Columbia, drive south to Victoria, then catch another ferry across the Strait of Juan de Fuca to Port Angeles, Washington, up on the round head of the Olympic Peninsula. Heading south was something I wasn't entirely prepared for, but neither had I the gall nor resources to continue northward. It was just too much, and here I had to trust my impulses. Running back instead of running away, some bright thing must be waiting for me on the way home.

I returned to Anacortes, checking into a brightly painted motel along the main drag, and crossed the street under end-of-the-world skies to the town bowling alley. While consuming a titan-size slab of beef and a good quart of mashed potatoes and gravy in the dark laneside eatery, I discovered a temptation impossible to pass up—a Saturday night special, two hours' worth of bowling for eight bucks. Nine games later, I limped back to the motel, ready for sleep and nursing early symptoms of arthritis in the fingers of my right hand.

Chapter Twenty-Two

Sunday
Valzer, reprise

Look carefully. The two great plates fought against each other and forced the lands of the eastern plate upward, lifting a range of mountains to the sky. Another range rose to the west of the first range, leaving lowlands between them that filled with the waters of the ocean and created a great inland sea.

February came and I was free of everything. Nancy went back to her know-nothing husband. He had finally agreed to go through counseling, and Nancy, for her part, agreed to move back in with him while they tried to work it out one last time. He would eventually go back to all his old habits—come home, turn on the TV, smoke a joint, fall asleep—and she would file for divorce. The last I heard, she had moved to

Alaska to become editor of a small-town newspaper and move
in with her new boyfriend, a twentieth-century frontiersman
who owned some land up there.

I heard very little about Stacy, which was absolutely fine.
Back in the valley, with my new permanent job, things that
happened on the coast were out of my reach. The softball team
was the only thing we had in common, but I had at least a
month until our first spring practice. I heard vague hints that
she was dating some executive from the East Coast, and I
suspected that this was what she needed, anyway—an older
man, a man of power, a man with enough money to match her
own.

Even my new housemates had little time for me. Being
engaged, they spent most of their time fighting over one
political family maneuver or another, and so I faded gladly
into the furniture. It was during this idyllic state of solitude
that I began what you might call the program.

It went something like this. Each and every weekday I
came home from work, changed into my shorts, and walked
two blocks down to the local park. I carried three objects: a
footbag, a novel, and my house keys. These were my sacred
instruments.

A footbag is a small leather beanbag that you kick into the
air, used by off-season soccer players to refine the coordination of their feet, knees, chest, and head. I would begin by
warming up, kicking the bag into the air and practicing new
touches, the instep of the left foot, the outside of the right, a
bounce off the head and backward to the bottom of an
upturned heel (this last one worked about once every hundred
tries). Once I was safely warmed up, I would go for quantity.

The ritual began as a simple pursuit of record numbers, but
soon, as I reached a hundred, then two hundred, this goal
became too far out of reach to keep my constant interest. I
needed little baby steps along the way, so I created a personal
incentive plan. I gave myself five attempts to reach fifty
touches. If I didn't reach fifty touches by the fifth attempt I had
one more shot to save myself: I had to get a hundred touches

on the very next attempt. The punishment for *not* reaching these marks was the ending of the day's ritual (a punishment fueled mostly by pride). This system motivated me to keep playing with the footbag each day until I got so tired I could no longer keep up the numbers. Thus, as I slowly but inevitably improved, I pushed myself further and further into the evening.

But the real exercise, and the heart of the footbag's healing powers, came when I would find myself on runs of five and six hundred touches. By the time you reach five hundred touches the bag is an extension of your body; the rhythm is inexorable, automatic. You begin to focus in and lose track of the small annoyances, the sweat pouring from your forehead, the tiredness of your legs, the small kink in your left ankle. You are lost to the world, numb and yet more clear than ever, for other than this little blue and white package flying from your left foot, the screen is full of snow, no direct images, just a constant bright white fuzz. As we Californians like to say, there is something very Zen about this.

The real blowout to the whole routine was the ending: after your body gives out and you cannot manage to reach a hundred touches on your final attempt, you then have to reach a hundred touches one last time before you are allowed to quit and go home. This was a killer, especially when you'd be on eighty-five on your first try and get distracted by a gnat in your eyes and let the footbag slide to the ground off your shin. Later on I would further the masochism by adding one final requirement, a behind-the-back kick followed by ten regular touches, then kicking the bag at least twenty feet into the air for as long as you could.

After my ritual I would perform fifty sit-ups in search of that flatter stomach look, then stretch out on the grass for a cool-down and a short read. My need for grounding led me to the classics; my reading list consisted of *Pride and Prejudice, Jane Eyre, Don Quixote de la Mancha*, and a second memorable run through *The Great Gatsby* (in which I discovered that Fitzgerald had written not a novel, but a cleverly disguised hundred and seventy-nine-page prose poem).

Within weeks I was losing weight, gaining muscle, and, I think most importantly, learning the power of solitude. The valley cooperated with me by supplying a weatherless February—although only the stiffest of rains would've kept me from my appointed rounds.

My first venture back into the social life was the first installment of spring training, the second weekend of March. Though it was tempting to relegate Catch This to the expanding collection of my past life museum, the call of the little white ball was too strong, and as yet I had no other team.

Our first practice was both brief and violent. Dana, the team's premier victim of ballophobia, was for some reason pitching batting practice to her boyfriend Brian. Five strokes into his turn, Brian hit a searing line drive back up the middle that followed a string directly to Dana's nose. From the sound of the impact you might've expected imminent brain damage (believe me, softballs are not necessarily *soft*). She began screaming, and the team rushed to her side in a panic. Unlike Kenny's accident the year before, this one was not the least bit funny. We held her up on a picnic table while blood spurted from her face, and Johnny, who'd just spent a year as a tow-truck driver and was used to emergencies, held someone's T-shirt to her nose and began asking her questions to keep her out of shock.

"You're all right, Dana, you're all right. Now, what do you think, should we get an ambulance? Do you want one of us to drive you?"

Dana's eyes looked wild and frightened, and all she could say was the word, "Drive." We carried her to someone's van, and two or three of the guys took off with her to the hospital three miles away. The rest of us just stood there, not knowing exactly what to do except clean the blood off the pitcher's mound and call it a day. This was not the most opportune way to start a season.

Still, we were back the next week, up on the west side of

town at William Frawley Memorial, readying for a practice game with the Live Oak Goons, a team composed almost entirely of print shop workers. Dana was understandably absent, holed up at home with her freshly broken nose, and her boyfriend Brian was gone, too, still dealing with the vision of that softball shooting off like a laser beam from his bat to his girlfriend's head. Dana's spirit was with us, though. Ballophobia had stricken the whole team, even guys who had never been afraid of the ball in their lives, and by the time we hit the fifth inning we were facing a twelve-run deficit.

As for me, I was playing very well, which pleased me more than it usually would because Stacy was there, and her presence seemed to be having no effect. She was playing on the other team, which made it a little easier (we had switched a couple players to even out the male-to-female ratio). I hit a particularly nasty liner to her in the third inning, and she did me the usual courtesy of running up too far on it and letting it bounce off the top of her glove.

By the sixth inning, though, I began to notice something. In between the pitches of my at-bat I glanced out to center to see Stacy dropping her head, not paying the least attention to what was going on. I laced a single to left and stood on first watching her. She looked off toward the ocean, barely visible past the third base side and over the downward hills of town, and she was biting her lip, a danger sign I knew from one too many anxious evenings. Something was on her mind, and not just on it, but stomping its size thirteen cleats all over her karma. I guess this meant I had to talk to her. She furthered my suspicions after the game by wandering down the right field line, purposely marking out a private place to which I could follow.

I walked up behind her, and when she turned I lost dominion over all the words that were being readied in the speaking section of my brain. We just stood there in the right field corner, land of ground rule doubles, searching each other for clues.

"Hiyah," she said, finally.

"How are you?" I said, passing directly from salutation to interrogative. Her eyes were swollen and bloodshot, result of either partying or crying, or, in her case, a combination of the two.

She peered up at two snow white clouds sailing out to sea over home plate, studying them as if their exact dimensions would be a question on some future tax audit.

"I'm not…so good," she answered.

I didn't really feel like saying anything—I was afraid I might come off sounding vindictive—so I waited until she went on.

"Michael, could you meet me at the condo in a couple hours? I've got to meet a friend for lunch, but I really want to talk to you. Something's come up, but I don't want to tell you until we've got some time."

"Sure," I said. "I'll go grab a cup of coffee and do some reading, and meet you there at, oh, five okay?"

"Shuwah," she said. "Five's fine." She got nervous and dug the toe of her cleats into the foul line. I had to lighten things up.

"Hey," I said. "Give me a hug, wouldja?"

My newly honed feelers sensed some small river of urgency in her embrace, but I let the feeling pass. I had trained myself out of that old habit of overinterpretation. Some things you could just *let go*. I pointed my glove at her and said, "See you at five," then strolled back to my equipment bag, leaving her leaning against the right field fence.

She was a half-hour late, a habit of timing I'd come to expect. She apologized profusely and led me from the courtyard to her door. She offered me a cup of coffee, and we sat down on the couch. Just as she was settling down, relaxed against a big white cushion and blowing wisps of steam off the surface of her mug, she clicked her tongue and got that "I've got an idea" look.

"I've got an idea," she said. "Listen, I've got to pick up some wine from my wine-of-the-month club. Why don't we take it down to the beach and have a fire? Yeah, that's it, let's do it."

What could I say? I was only along for the ride, obviously. We threw some firewood and a bundle of newspapers into her car and were on our way. We took off into Soquel, to Bargetto's just off the river, and picked up two bottles of gewürztraminer, then headed to our beach through the random residential streets south of town.

An hour later the sun was fully gone and the fire at the final tips of its flaming before settling down to glowing orange coals. We were through our first bottle of wine, a sweet, high-alcohol variety, and were set to start on the second. Things were getting warm and fuzzy, and Stacy and I were getting warmer and closer. Finally in her natural state, she turned to me with languid, half-closed eyes and told me the news.

"Michael, my promotion finally came through. I'm going back to corporate headquarters in New Jersey, probably by June, and..."

She had to stop because she had surprised herself—her eyes were welling over with tears. She wiped them clean and went on.

"I guess what I'm trying to say to you is, the prospect of leaving this...lovely place...has made me realize that I've been wasting my time lately with a lot of jerks, and now, since I only have a little time left, I want to spend it with the people I really care about, and especially...with you."

I didn't say anything, I just leaned over to take her face in my hands and kiss her for a good long time. In the grand picture of things, this was exactly what I needed: a chance to continue our romance, no matter how limited by time and geography, but on my terms, knowing I no longer needed to fill up my self-portrait with borrowed paints.

That night, in bed, as soon as we had begun, I noticed a circle of bluish-purple on her breast. A hickey.

She saw where I was looking and tried to explain in sad, regretful tones. "He was a real jerk, Michael, a real arrogant...jerk." I ignored her bruises and returned to my pleasure. Redemption was in sight.

My finger hurts like a bitch this morning. I have sworn off bowling for the rest of the decade. I think I must have strained a tendon or something; I can't even button up my jeans. God, it's such an innocent-looking sport. I mean, you never hear about bowlers spending a year on injured reserve.

I woke up at the ungodly hour of six o'clock, showering quickly and hitting the road amid dark, dark mist, neon hotel signs flashing me directions through town and then left through neighborhoods of clean, beautiful old houses to the water and the ferry dock. I paid for my ticket and parked my car at the head of one of the half-dozen waiting lanes. In my anxiousness I was an hour early, but that was okay, because I had to make sure I made this ferry; it only ran once a day. I picked up a local newspaper from the stand outside, checked into the well-heated waiting room and bought some coffee in a poker-hand cup (full house, two kings) from a vending machine. The paper was nothing exciting, extremely local news about rising ferry tolls and the usual local-kid-makes-good who had just made the starting rotation of the Texas Rangers fresh out of the University of Washington. I closed my eyes for a second or two and woke up forty-five minutes later to the sound of loudspeakers calling out passengers for Sidney, British Columbia.

I rushed to my feet and let the blood well up to my brain before I staggered out to my car, discovering ten others waiting impatiently behind me. The flagman signaled me in to the left side of the hold (is that starboard?), and I waited a few minutes before I opened the door and crawled out into the narrow space between my car and the hull of the ship.

Up a couple flights of stairs I broke through the cabin doors and found something of a floating amusement park. It was Sunday, family excursion day, so I should have expected it, but after so many days of solo quietude, the color and noise of thirty to forty children, mixed with the vinegar shouts of two dozen parents trying to rein them in, really struck a match to my nerve endings.

"Mommy, Mommy, Mommy! I need more quarters for the

Monster Machine!" cried one little runt, pulling hard enough on the hem of his mother's skirt to rip.

"Now, Michael," she answered, "I'm not going to let you play anymore until we leave the dock. Go sit with your sister."

This one was remarkably well-behaved and meekly departed to play cards with his sister, but the rest of the menagerie was out for blood, running loop-de-loops around the table legs, hanging from the railings in the snack bar line, demanding in loud tones where the hell the bathroom was. I had to get out and get out quickly, so I paced outside to the foredeck. As soon as I opened the doors, the cold morning air hit my face and the boat shook, breaking slowly from the dock, heading out into the great pallid soup of Puget Sound.

If a spanking in the principal's office was my most vivid bad memory of Washington State, my most vivid good one is this, this same ferry trip, taken one spring day with my mother, two sisters, and brother to Victoria, the gem of British Columbia. The fog that lies low and dark today is the same as it is was twenty years ago—I couldn't ask for better reproduction—but I distinctly remember spotting patches of snow as we passed the San Juan Islands, something I am not likely to see today, here in the early part of June. I stand on one of the two prows pretending to be some kind of 18th century tar, braving cold and wind and bad complexion and just enjoying the snap of the wind in my face. We approached the evergreen pelt of a large island growing under the grey wet curtains, and just then a father with three yapping kids skipped out on the opposite prow, signaling my return to the belly of the beast.

I had to get myself two items now—food and a nap—so I lined up behind all the little brats charging their batteries on sugar-laden pastries and candy bars. I purchased an orange juice and a poppyseed muffin, which I sucked down with the verve of a true sailin' man. I found a bench at the starboard windows and, following the model of the man behind me, stretched out lengthwise and closed my eyes.

I didn't have much of a chance for actual sleep, what with the whirring racket of our on-board busybodies, but I did manage to waver in and out of consciousness a couple times, which seemed to do me some good. I finally gave up and scavenged a copy of the *Seattle Times*, which I stripped down to the page with the comics and the crossword puzzle. I carried my prize to the dozen rows of chairs on the indoor observation deck and whipped out a pen. The Fr. rivers and Lat. abbrs. warmed my brain bit by bit, and I fought not to notice the attractive woman sitting across from me, a redhead with well-defined, almost theatrical features, and large marquis-cut blue eyes. But this was a feeling I hadn't dealt with in a long, long time. This was...this was attraction, wasn't it? Kindly step-brother to lust. The naming of the feeling was a surprise, and though I couldn't figure its place on this odd journey of mine, I could turn it into a mental photograph: a flashing red beacon atop a buoy at night, straddling the U.S./Canada border, sending out heat. What makes this light flip on and off and catch my sailor's eye is the book she is holding, which turns out to be a musical score, Rachmaninoff's Piano Concerto No. 2. Her marquis eyes cut back and forth over the measures, calculating the right hand against the left, figuring the spread of the arpeggios.

This is music, this is water, this is attraction, and my signal to take the next logical step. It's not what you think. I fill in "weasel" on 56 Across ("Mouse-eating mammal") and stroll out into the cottontail fog along the foredeck. The deck is split into two prows, and I step all the way up the left side until I stand at the very fore of the ship, the rusty floor of the car deck on one side, the deep green of the Puget Sound on the other. We pass a camel's hump of an island rising from the water just a few hundred yards from a larger island with an inlet, and cruising by we are headed out to open water. The sky will not shed its clouds, but it brightens slightly as I look back into the morning sun, a disc of pale white through the overcast.

I reach into the zipper pocket of my jacket and pull out a handful of hate, the smooth dark pebbles of my playground revenge. I hold them there for a second, recording their deep colors against the pink of my palm, then cup them into a ball and thrust them over the side. They scatter in the air and chip a honeycomb of pockmarks against the smooth water. I dig in for a second handful and repeat the action, then pull out one last pebble and chuck it the long way over the edge of the car deck, watching it strike the churning water right before the boat runs it under.

Rocks, water, music. Rocks, water, music. I can only play the mental soundtrack of this burial at sea if I talk about music, and about silence. It's like this: When a singer is not singing, he is *not* doing nothing, for he is measuring silence, counting the beats of rest until his next entrance. When do the rest of us ever stop to measure silence? No, we are preoccupied with noise, the constant positive instead of the rare negative, when the only thing more powerful to our senses than a sudden sound is a sudden stoppage of sound.

My choir once sang in Grace Cathedral, an imposing Gothic edifice in the heart of San Francisco. One of the pieces we sang was a negro spiritual ending in the fashion negro spirituals often do, an extended fortissimo chord raising its volume over the track of five measures, then climbing its loudest peak a millisecond before it cuts off into nothing. Mr. Stutz would train us to dramatize the cutoff even further by removing the glottal stop. In other words, instead of cutting off the sound with a sudden constriction of the throat and mouth— resulting in a percussive *gluh!*—keep your instrument open as if you are going to sing this note all the way to Tuesday and simply discontinue the tone. In Grace Cathedral, we achieved the effect with perfection, freezing our audience in surprise as our disembodied chord coursed through the Andean stone vaults a full nine seconds.

This is how I am feeling right now. The rocks have completed their journey back to the water and I am left with overtones and echoes, weaving in and out of each other like strands of yarn in a scarf, leaving me as clear as this waveless green slate over the railing. I am Beethoven, scoring the Ninth Symphony, gone deaf already but crafting my sounds through memory and imagination, the only two forces I have left.

The rest of the day is a cafe wall full of photographs. The loons sitting low like black kayaks in the water. The line at the dock for customs, explaining to the Canadian officer that I would be in his country only four hours. The road signs so noticeably different than American signs, every message outlined in red or white borders, as if to say we are closer to the English and therefore need fringes on our markers. The clean Britannia checkerboard of blue, white and pink cottages, royal piping leading into the Londonesque city of Victoria, all brass and brick and rain-scoured streets with the sudden surprise kitsch-corners of Indian souvenir shops with their row upon row of miniature totem poles and carved wooden masks, razor sharp, bacon-colored edges tasseled in fur and rawhide. The mighty squat of the Empress Hotel reigning over Victoria Harbor and the resplendent ornamentation of the Parliament buildings, fronted by strict square rows of marigolds.

I had two hours between my arrival in Victoria and the departure of the ferry back to Washington State, and so I walked up through the crowded Sunday streets to a used bookstore, to a modest shopping mall with running fountains trailing you everywhere, and to a brass-lined, red-upholstered seafood bar and grill with the requisite photographs of old-time fishermen and ladies' fashions. I downed a Bass ale and an order of salmon (had to eat seafood, this was a harbor after all, this was the Pacific Northwest after all), made a steal of a payment thanks to the current exchange rates and my plastic eagle friend, and headed back to the docks, stopping along the way to help a lady from Kansas take a photograph of herself and her buddy from Bremerton.

I spent most of the trip south to Port Angeles just agog at the dark mastery of the Strait of Juan de Fuca: hordes of blackening rain clouds stretching down from the ocean, black dolphins jumping in friendly arcs to port and starboard, huge oil tankers and freighters passing us on the way to Victoria, the American flag flying behind us on a backdrop of Vancouver Island fading over the water. By the end of the trip, the rain kicked into spurts and starts until it was a steady sprinkle, and

I stood out on the deck with one other brave soul, a rancher from Texas, discussing the Southwest heat, his prize Appaloosa, and his son the flying doctor from Seattle.

It was almost night by the time we shuttled in around the long breakwater of Port Angeles, but I was newly energized and had to drive on. I looped through town and onto Interstate 101, heading west then south at the fringe of the Olympic Peninsula, knowing somewhere there were more large white mountains but knowing too I had no time to wait for them to appear. The rain stopped by the time I hit Olympic National Park, and the moon—a hair nigh on full—broke through two seas of cloud to guide me as the road circled Lake Crescent, the middle of it seemingly broken through with a huge slice of mountain. I pulled into a turnout to read the lake's Indian myth (the mountain slammed into place by some angry god who decided to break their lake in two as punishment) and stood there afterward reaching my eyes out over ten-P.M. waters, black as a grand piano, spotlight of moonglow cutting a path across its ebony varnish. I measured the silence in meters of waltzing, 3/4 and 6/8, coarsing along the shadows of the mountains.

I stopped in a town called Beaver for a serving of lasagna and root beer. The waitress, cute and thin with her dark hair feathered back in that appealing country fashion, looked me over as if she could tell I carried valuable information. I drove south and south and south, ignoring the salt-water call of the Pacific through breaks in the shoreline pines, blinking myself along as the road turned inland and shot away toward the moon. Thinking of my bohdrán, my Celtic drum still sitting unplayed on the seat next to me, I took Aberdeen as my finishing point, and somewhere around a half-hour after midnight checked into a trucker's motel on the south side of town. Before drifting to sleep amid white-breathed covers I found in my mind the odd quantity of a fantasy—myself and a blue-eyed pianist inside a cabin atop a mist-covered island, nestled together before a spice-fire offering of cedar logs. I balanced it there like a glass of waterfall and let it slide down my throat, silvercast overtones widening out and pulling back in my ears as the pianist turned into a conductor, waving her hands over the black water in a circle of three beats.

Chapter Twenty-Three

Monday
Contredanse

Feel carefully. The ocean met the land in hard places and in soft places, and the waves tore at the soft places until they were taken away. The water hollowed out the remaining stone into a natural arch, until the roof of the arch collapsed and left a tower of rock standing alone against the water.

I woke up in Aberdeen in a deep fuzz, my head wrapped all around by a turban of elephant-sized lint. I had looked at this day as the day of reckoning, the day of awakening, of discovery, of all those other inspiring nouns, and the first thing I did instead was spend five minutes attempting to remove the packaging from one of those miniature bars of soap. This was not good. The shower helped some, but right afterward I came

into the bedroom studying the cable guide, tempted to spend
the whole day hooked up to the television, and stubbed my toe
viciously against the steel rails of the bedpost. I jumped onto
the bed in pain, bending my leg upwards and finding the skin
on the side of my big toe scraped back and bleeding. The sight
of it made me shudder; I seriously contemplated an old-
fashioned fainting spell, but I hung on.

Through some small miracle I had grabbed a box of
bandages in my flight from my long-ago apartment, so I had
some chance of saving enough blood to get me to breakfast. I
wiped the toe off with a paper-thin motel towel (what will the
maids think?) and quickly wrapped the bandage around it,
careful not to overextend my still-sore bowling finger.

So now I was limping, and blinded by psycho-lint, and
wanting only to dive back into my mattress and waste the day
here in the center of the United States of Anonymity. I'd come
too far, that was it, too many miles of unfamiliar road had
messed me up for good. I was beginning to forget who I was,
which I guess was the whole point of the trip, but now it was
nothing but unsettling, tripping my stomach into gadfly nau-
sea, akin to the burbling after you eat too much junk food at the
county fair. Cotton candy dreams will shrivel to sugar lumps
as soon as they hit your mouth. What was I doing?

And so, naturally, I hit the road. It took me three trips back
to the room to make sure I'd packed everything, and even then
I discovered twenty miles south that I'd forgotten my box of
bandages. I made a silent vow to bleed no further during this
trip. To hell with it, I was on the road, I was heading home, and
the lint was spinning itself loose on the heat from my defogger.
I checked my watch and made another silent vow—to find
breakfast at the first roadside place I spotted after ten o'clock—
but I hadn't counted on the loneliness of the south Washington countryside, long stretches of lowlands and riversides
with few signs of civilization.

I coursed into a small town somewhere off Willapa Bay,
pretty farms and wide fields of grass surrounding old houses
seemingly cut off from the last fifty years of history. When I

found an actual intersection with an actual stoplight—albeit a flashing red stoplight—I pulled over at the corner, certain that here I would find nutrition.

Through the plate glass of the corner store I spied what looked like dinette tables, typed-out menus, primary-colored salt and pepper shakers, and artificial flower arrangements— all the telltale markings of cheap breakfast. I cruised on in, discovering a store that was half-diner, half-household appliance outlet. The young man at the counter and the young woman at the tables looked downright astonished to see me; I suppose Monday morning was no time for a man with the telltale neon sneakers and baggy shorts of El Turista to be sidling into town. I sat at a table for a few minutes, for some reason expecting service—you know, what with the absence of a midmorning rush and all—and too many minutes later the young woman approached.

"Vould you be vanting, ah, breakvast dis morning?"

Ah, that's why. Language barrier. I've obviously wandered into a little-known settlement of Pacific Northwest Amish. She had that frightened look of the immigrant passing through Ellis Island, not sure if the new land or the new customer would be patient and kindly or eat her alive with his ugly Americanismo. I attempted patience.

"Yes. I'd like two eggs, sunny-side up, ah, some bacon, a cup of decaf, and a large orange juice."

"Zunny-zide up?" she asked. Oh boy.

"Cooked on one side," I explained, holding out a level palm as my visual aid. "No flip." I turned my hand over to demonstrate. She smiled for a split second before going back into her repentant puppy act.

"Oh, yah. Okay, I zee. Vill be just a…minute."

Minute my ass. She returned to the kitchen, which was separated from the dining area by a flip-up counter. In other words, I could see everything she was doing, and what she was doing was not much. After a couple minutes of deep contemplation and banging things around and really not accomplishing anything, she went to confer with the man at the household appliance counter, whom I took to be her husband (this was looking more and more like a mom-and-pop operation). He came back to the kitchen with her and conducted a lengthy search until at last they discovered a tub of margarine at the far back corner of the refrigerator.

It became apparent that I would need something to keep myself occupied for a while, so I told my nervous hostess that I would be right back and stepped down the street to a squadron of newsstands in front of the laundromat. I found the Sunday edition of the Portland paper and scratched out enough ransom to free it from its metal box, then folded it under my arm and headed back. The sun was completely out of the overcast now, and I was enjoying the feel of it against my face.

As I reentered the diner, mein hostess cultivated an increasingly worried expression on her frau's-brow, finally coming over to tell me my coffee would be a few more minutes. "I make fresh pot; ve haff one pot zo I make new pot uff dekaff for you."

I forgot—in Washington State they don't drink decaf; they only keep it around for visiting Californians. I hoped I wasn't giving myself away. I nodded to her and sat back down, burying myself in the national news and discovering all I had missed during my dismissal from reality. In other words, nothing had really changed. The world somehow went on without me. I scanned the gossip page looking for news of world-famous conductor Amy Fine checking into a clinic after her abandonment in a cornfield by a one-hell-of-a-cad tenor. (But aren't they all in the end? See an opera sometime.)

The decaf came to me within five minutes and at least that was something, but the eggs took another ten (apparently they were using a propane camp stove), and finally my bacon, burned to a crisp, alongside an over-pulpy orange juice shake. I really had to tell all my friends about this place. I left without complaining, but I didn't have the Christian forgiveness to leave a tip. Some things should not be rewarded, even for someone new to the country. I did, however, buy a transistor radio from the household appliance section, a $9.95 bargain special. I left my newspaper for use by future victims and rolled along the road back inland.

I sat the radio on the seat next to me and tuned into some odd public radio station playing Irish folk music, sobbing ballads and hearty drinking songs and jumping reels from pipes and harps and fiddles that fit the riverside greenery to a T. The road curled up and back between inland and coastland, always along some river or delta or harbor (water, water everywhere), until finally it laid out a gunshot strip to the Oregon border.

The crossing at the wide mouth of the Columbia was just as interesting as I'd been told. I stopped at a memorial across from Cape Disappointment (now there's an inspiring name) where Lewis and Clark had made camp after finally reaching the Pacific. A carved wooden statue of the duo stands there perhaps ten feet tall, noble and rugged except for the absence of Clark's telescope, making it look like he's making a tube of his hands just for fun. Lewis stands next to him with his rifle at his side, not amused whatsoever. I walked to the end of the turnout and found an old church, perfect white cross at the steeple, perfect white gull using it for a posing post. Alas, I had no camera. The sides of the church were strips of barren wood, turned grey from the salt air and ocean wind. I tried to peek inside through the stained glass, but it was too dark.

The crossing to Astoria is a long flat span encased by steel trusses, rising steeply at the Oregon side to allow for ships coming through into Portland. I took the rise to a trio of bawdy Irish drinking songs, then boarded the exit heading back onto 101 in a sharp curl.

The weather couldn't make up its mind. The minute I hit the top of the hill and the flatter parts of Astoria, the clouds moved in and threw drops onto my windshield. It was then that I realized one of my wiper blades was loose, so I crossed a double ribbon of railroad tracks and pulled into a gravel lot at the side of the road. I hopped out and circled to the passenger side, stretching one end of the rubber blade until it reached the metal clasp at the tip, then set it back down against the glass. Then I saw the field.

It was just on the other side of the tracks, a pig's paradise of a baseball diamond. The infield was all dirt, not a spot of grass. The rains from this morning (and from the sight of it, all week) had turned the dirt to a quagmire of mud, slopped up in waves and dollops as if twenty seals had been turned loose on its surface. Under the grey clouds it could look no more desperate, no more pitiful, except for the pitcher's mound, peaked by a toothpaste strip of rubber cleaned by the rain. As for home plate, you couldn't even see it; it lay underneath a puddle of brown water penned in by the backstop.

Enough with it. I hadn't received a signal all day, and I wasn't going to get one looking at a shithole diamond out in the rain. Surely by now my visions should carry grander designs than this; I am almost to the end, after all. I got back in the car and drove on, listening to the wiper blade squeak a few times until it adjusted itself and quieted to a dull slap at the corners of the glass. I floored it out to the Oregon coast and began the long, long drive southward.

Granted, some of it was beautiful, hilly farmlands of golf-course hues, dairy farms with cows in black and white formals instead of the tans and browns of their California brethren. And, just once in a while, a crescent of ocean between the hills, blue reminder of the macrogeography. But I had gone out of range of my satellites. I kept waiting for the *tick tick tick,* but it wouldn't tune in. I stopped at Bay City for a lunch of snapper and salad. I paused a few miles further at a roadside golf resort to whack a few balls at the driving range. But these were just hobbies, just the usual distractions to keep you alert on the road, to keep your body from stiffening up under the ordeal of restless sitting that we call driving. I began to switch my feet on the gas pedal, letting my left foot do the work for a while so I could rest the aching heel of my right.

At the onset of evening I was beginning to give up, thinking this just wasn't the day of reckoning after all. I began the drive down the Oregon Dunes, which was, if not inspiring, at least a geography of a different stripe. I stopped off at a vista point, eyeing the miles of sand baking in the now-orange sun low over the ocean, pedestrian-journal footsteps along the ridges and valleys, the occasional sand graffito, names and lovers dug into grain piles for sport. But nothing, nothing of consequence. Speak to me, dammit! I retreated to the bathroom and drank from the water fountain and kept going, hoping I might run out of coastline and get somewhere that mattered.

Since the day held nothing for me, I looked forward to the night. The sunset seemed a natural marker and so, armed with my Celtic drum, my bohdrán, I raced to the top of a hill south of the Umpqua lighthouse to catch an orange ball half sunk by the horizon. *The perfect time, the perfect time*, I thought, creeping as far forward as I could to a grassy knoll fringed by thorn bushes, pulling my tippler out of my pocket as the sun disappeared into the salt air and...

And nothing. I struck the drum but could not *play* the drum, receiving nothing for my effort but sound without rhythm. The stroke of my Shasta oars, the dark waltz of Washington's lakes, the reels from the Irish radio station, all had left me. It was a pleasant sunset, but my anticipation was a mistake. I felt like the cymbal player at the end of the march, embarrassing the rest of the orchestra by striking my weapons a half second before my cue. I didn't even wait for the afterglow to set in, but ran back to my car and pushed on with a new sense of urgency.

I ripped through the lights and hills of Coos Bay and proceeded southward another hour before I stopped at a cute little railroad theme steak house in Bandon. Seized with a sudden hunger, I consumed a steak with fried clams, a salad, and mashed potatoes with thick, fat gravy, then followed it up with an apple pie à la mode. Ah, this was country eating. I ate it all up in half an hour, then waddled out to the car and kept on going, kept on going, now up the steep slopes into the evergreens, looking over the low coastal mountains into lightless pitch.

Here's what I figured: I figured the drum had something to do with tonight, and I figured some other Celtic thing would come into play. I had woken up in Aberdeen, after all, I spent the morning crying my heart out to tragic Irish ballads, and all day, all this trip, I had seen nothing but green, green, green. Something had to add up here, and I had to make the first step before I hit the California line into old New Spain.

Just past the mouth of the Rogue River and through a town called Gold Beach, the road tailed up between two cliffs, one up from the road, one down. I drove carefully, measuring the distance to the sprays of fuzzy white down, down, down on the beachheads, then turned to find a candle glow over the cliffs above me, to the left. Outside of town the same cliff grew a cap of silver, and half a mile further I realized it was the moon, a full moon. The road rose to a bend that looked like a far corner of the world, and at the reach of the bend was a large, wide turnout, and this was it. I knew this was it. As I turned into the spread of gravel and dirt, my bohdrán fell from the seat next to me, slipping down to the floor of the car.

I cut the headlights and race around to the other side of the car, reaching in to rescue the drum from its awkward position, snatch the tippler from the seat and pace right out to the clifftop, one step from the edge, worn sandy dirt scoping down in the darkness to a cold, thundering ocean. I hold the drum back toward the moon, goatskin shining silvery white, then raise the tippler and skip it down over the surface.

The sound is more hollow than a bohdrán should be, eliciting more of a *buh-wuhm* sound, something you might expect from an untuned kettle drum; in ideal situations, you were supposed to heat the bohdrán next to a fire before playing it to tighten the skin. But I have the rhythm now, no doubt, my wrist relaxed and supple and quick, my fingers holding the tippler's slender center like chopsticks and letting the weight of the double ends knock themselves back and forth from the trampoline of the goatskin, holding the cross of wood with my other hand and ringing the sound out over the ocean.

The reel from this morning is fresh in my ears, circling me about with the sour spit of the Uilleann pipes at the lead, double fiddles holding the beat dead-on and fast, opening up the sound to let the bohdrán in, thundering the undertone with a circle of rolls, tracking a primary pattern each few measures, but switching it slowly around like an aural mirage, letting it fade around to something new without 'fessing up to the change, a tick, a double-tick on the edge of the drum just to let them know you're there and not stupid or slow or somethin', but then back around to the middle of the skin, hurling balls of resonance out over the fiddles and the squeeze-pulse of the pipes and around and around and around like the drumhead, back into a slowing coda with a final, long, rumbling roll, and just when you can't stanit nuhmore a final quelling thump…let it fade, let the ocean take it into the rocks, let the moonlight varnish it up and send it back to you in a package saying yes, this is the start of something. This is your beat for the rest of the night and inside the beat the tippler says *tick, tick-tick, tick, tick-tick, thump!*

I look behind at the lights of the bridge over the River Rogue and walk reluctantly back to the car, holding the bohdrán naturally now, not like some goddamn hang-it-on-a-wall piece of folk art but as an *instrument*, a maker of sound, something to be played and fingered and thumped upon at regular intervals until the skin glosses over from wear and loses its bounce. The road is finally alive, and from here on out the signals will come in circular beats and rowdy jigs.

I cross a dazzling high bridge bracketing a canyon just off the coastline and turn out at the other side, walking back to the road sign and reading the story of its construction, named after a cop killed in the line of duty and supposedly the highest bridge in the state. I peer over the chain link fence to find long steel beams curving down and away to the far side and am fairly impressed. Slipping back into my car, I turn on the radio to find a country station all the way from Reno. I have to laugh at the title: "I've Never Lost in Love (Not Counting You)."

The gas gauge hits empty going through Brookings, the last real town before California, and I pull in at a gas station. The guy at the cash register is a real entertainer, and we chat in fat friendly tones.

"Yeah, can't wait to get back to California," I say. "Don't ever know how much I miss it until I have to leave for a while."

"Zat so," he says, ringing me up for eight-ninety-five. "Been up north a ways?"

"Yeah, up to Canada, actually, though not far in, just through Victoria and back on the ferries."

"Ah, those ferries, they're great. Took one all the way up into Vancouver last year with the wife. Sunshine all the way up."

"Sunshine, eh?"

"Yeah. What, you didn't do so well, huh?"

"No," I answer. "'Fraid not, but it was okay. Same kind of weather as when I first took the trip, twenty years back in second grade. Just how I wanted it."

He tugs at his full grey beard and laughs quietly. "Ah, nothing like reliving memories just the right way. You take care now, don't go driving too late."

"No problem," I say, pocketing my change. "Take care yourself, don't get too cold out here."

Ever since nightbreak the sky has been pure and untouched, nothing but cloudless, silver-plated blue, but the second I rise into the skyline arboretum of Redwood National Park, the fog packs my screen in wet white cotton, and I discover I have blown a headlight. I bear down on the road, creeping the narrow, wet asphalt and watching out for campers pulling tight curves from the other direction. I pass a roadside attraction featuring giant redwood carvings of Paul Bunyan and Babe, familiar items from my previous trips northward, but now vested with a ghostly frame, blurred just enough to make it seem like they will come alive any second, grab themselves a redwood-sized surfboard, and hit the beach.

The trees loom over the road like Titans, the mist enveloping their skyward branches like great pale sweaters. I try to pick a clue off their growth rings, some with a thousand, some with three thousand, interior circles brimming out like waves from a pebble, history marked down in cellulose. I strike a clearing flat out on some sort of meadow, the fog cowering thick at the ground and thinning out as it rises, and then the idea hits me. A sacrifice.

I have to sacrifice something. It is the next logical step, and I know now what I am looking for: an ending, a closure. I have already gone about the business of forgetting who I am; now it is time to find out who I will become, and to do it I have to give a precious object to the beat of the forest and the ocean and the moon.

Flowers. It has to be flowers, it's always flowers. Right? You've seen it in the movies. Some poor slob dies at sea and his widow comes to the ocean once a year and throws a dozen posies or roses or carnations or whatever the guy's favorite blossoms were, and the bouquet drifts in and out on the waves as the closing credits come in and the music comes up and the theater lights turn on. But this late at night? Where the hell am I?

A sign. At roadside, lit up by jerry-rigged spotlights: 24-Hour Mart, Food, Gas, 1 Mile. Well, if that isn't a signal, gollyshucks, what the hell else could be? The fog is letting up. Things are beginning to clear.

I step into the store, probably looking like I am going to rob the place and dash into the redwoods. I mean, you know the feeling, you're wired after umpteen zillion hours of tracking them dashed white lines, and you figure to everyone you meet you must look like hell warmed over, vagrant desperado just waiting till they turn their innocent little backs before you pistol-whip them and take all their cash as well as their five-year-old child sitting at the back of the store playing video games. This store is full of wood—wooden walls, wooden shelves, pile of firewood next to the furnace, redwood souvenirs. A short, Eskimo-looking lady walks out from the back and gives me the expected once-over.

I periscope up and down the aisles as if I am searching for some sort of normal thing, until she can tell I am lost and asks me if I need help.

"Yeah, um. You wouldn't happen to have any…flowers? You know, roses or something?"

"Oh, no," she says. "No flowers today. We'll have some in the morning, maybe."

I look around some more, like I don't believe her or something. Hey, I'm desperate; I am so sure that this impulse is right and I have to find some way to follow it through or I will burst. I think of asking her if she has any flowers growing out back in a garden or something, but I chicken out.

"Well," I laugh, covering up my pseudo-mystical intentions. "I can always tell her I tried, I suppose. Heh-heh."

The Eskimo lady looks at me with an understanding but wary eye.

"Bye," I say.

"Good night," she says.

Well that isn't it, I guess. I keep an eye out to the side of the road just in case I pass any country homes with rose bushes along the fence. I can just see getting shotgunned stealing marigolds from some ranger's front yard. There's an ending if you want one. It is during this roadside scan that I spot my next sign: Patrick's Point, 10 miles. There it is, my Celtic place. Scotland to Ireland, Washington to California, Aberdeen to Patrick's Point, all under a moon the general shape and disposition of a bohdrán.

I turn off at the final Patrick's Point indicator and down a dark, tree-shrouded road into the ranger station. There is no one there. I stop and read the sign about self-registering and leaving the money in the little cash box on the post and ignore it, looking around once then driving on through, feeling slightly wicked. No camping here, Mr. Ranger, no day use, no dog on a leash, just a midnight visit from a friendly warlock, and that's not on the menu, bud. One act of rebellion can't do but help my mission. In order to sacrifice, you have to sacrifice.

So, enough rationalization. I have been to Patrick's Point, on a camping trip three years ago, so I know the roads pretty well. The main road pulls in around a field crisscrossed by hiking trails. To the right you will find the dark stripe of Agate Beach, mile after mile of tiny rounded quartz pieces impossible to hike along but fun to sift through your fingers.

I drive on to the main lookout and sit in the car, still unsure of what it is I am supposed to kill off. I think about the last few days and try to line up the keys in a logical fashion, hoping the formula will lead to something I have right here in the car, something that will represent the old things and yet open the door to the new things. My rituals so far have been all about objects and elements, rocks and water, always the meeting of objects and rocks and water. Well, here in front of me I have the rocks and the water. What is the object? Something human, perhaps, something man-made that can be thrown to the rocks and the water and bring back the rhythm and unfreeze the stone, the stone that is me, the stone, the rock, the river rock from Yosemite—my first clue—the rock that was shaped like a...

Eureka! I shoot out of the car and open my trunk, find my navy blue sports bag and dig inside, there underneath the smell of dirt and leather and the old sod of cleats and vinegar sweat of kneepads and batting gloves—a solid white moon-shaped sphere, held in by stitches, scarred here and there by the loving stroke of bats and the scrape of pebbles and just waiting to meet up with the Pacific Ocean.

The moon stands behind me like a spotlight, making me all the more cautious as it stretches my shadow to the height of a major lurker. I am pointed in the direction of the namesake seastack of Patrick's Point when a sign on the trail catches my eye: Wedding Rock, a turn to the right. It is perfect.

Two turns later I find a line of orange traffic cones around a warning sign: Trail Closed for Repairs: Do Not Use. Fuck that. Rebellious act number two coming up. God and the moon are on my side, after all. This baby has to be delivered to her mother.

Wedding Rock shoots up, chalk white in the newly clear moonlight, ridges threading off her dangerous sides like the lines of Mount Shasta. She is a chunk of hard rock standing out against the Pacific alongside her big Irish brother; the waves coming in between them fairly explode from the bottleneck.

I seem to remember she is named Wedding because the park's first ranger was married there. I watch my steps carefully, knowing the usual stairs of wooden slabs might not be in their places, and zig-zag my way up the brush-covered hill until it comes out on her slippery rock terrace.

I literally watch every step now; the terrace has none of its railings but many crevices and bumps just waiting to send me into the surf. It would be embarrassing, after all, to have people think I committed suicide. And in such an unimaginative fashion.

Firmly atop the level ground, I gather myself and take a look around: to the south side, between here and Patrick, a gallery of jagged sculptures along the cliffs, rocks fitted neatly into their places, nailed down hard by the violent, constant waves. I look to the north, to the spot off Agate Beach where I spotted my first blue whale, a nautical block beyond the surfers on a summery autumn morning, a spout of water, a crescent of blue flesh and gone, back to its mile-long scuba dives on the southward road to winter.

Then one more direction, back to land: my car a dull box in the parking lot, and the moon, trailing a glowline straight toward me over trees and rocks and shoreline bluffs. I let the hum of the bohdrán circle against my growth rings until the rhythm is right, and I turn to face the black ocean.

I feel the seams of the ball thick against my fingers, ragged at the stitches from one too many batting practices. I inch forward to the edge of the cliff, calculating the space I will need to complete my sacrifice. I breathe in, then out, in a trail of vapor, reach my arm long straight and back and, planting my left foot against a rift in the rock, thrust it all forward, feeling the pitch in my heart and my breath as I loose the ball to the sky.

The trip is more silent than possible, the whiteness of my missile drawing a sinking arc into the blue blackness then dropping below the line of the cliff's edge right at the moment it will strike the Pacific. In the rush of the water and the rush of my body I can see or hear nothing after it falls. It is simply gone, gone without a sound. And she is gone. And this has been it all along. Amen.

I pray to the person who finds a waterlogged softball along Agate Beach, the one that reads "Catch This" in scrawled light orange Magic Marker: make use of this poor creature. He has been through a lot of things which were not his fault and would like very much to retire to some nice dry plain where he can tease shortstops into the outfield only to disappear in the morning sun. Heading back out on the road to Eureka (yes, Eureka), I have a sudden thought, and hold up my wrist to the moonlight shooting in through my side window. It is four minutes after twelve, right around midnight.

Chapter Twenty-Four

Tuesday
Etude

I don't really remember how I got home. Technically speaking, I took 101 down through Ukiah, through Marin County, a crawl through the stoplights of oceanside San Francisco, and then south on Interstate 280 to San Jose. Metaphorically speaking, I surfed the skyline and could not have counted the hours if they flashed digital readouts from the clouds.

I remember only two clear images. The first was an archetype of postcard shops everywhere: the north end of the Golden Gate bridge as I hopped on its back, the evening delivery of fog layering itself through the orange stanchions like icing on a cake. The second is an image of music, one you cannot freeze, an image that lives in the boundaries of time and counts upon its passage for meaning. I am sledding down the San Mateo hills along the slow-arching swings of 280, pondering the cartoonish roadside sculpture of Junipero Serra wagging a finger in the general direction of Half Moon Bay. I raise the following hillside and look left to civilization's necklace, an army of lights ringing the bay, the San Mateo Bridge sinking gracefully into the water, battalions of airliners invading San Francisco International (these things may not even be within sight of each other; to me it is all one sweep of motion). And now I am staring into the evergreen face of the Santa Cruz Mountains, masking the ocean view that must be on the other side, and then I look at one spot in the sky as if I am expecting it (the moon not yet risen, a blackboard waiting for equations), and there she is, a meteorite, running a time exposure flash across my vision, chalk dust over the blue-black ceiling, homing in on Crystal Springs Reservoir with a burst and a hisssss…

And I know how they talk of shooting stars. If you don't know the rules, you never were a child: when you see one, you must wish immediately and wish only once, before the grain of the streak vanishes from your corneas, else you will not get your wish. And why? I have my notions. The superstition is not there just so you can get your wish; wishes are lemon drops that melt away once they touch your mouth. The superstition is there so you will know what you really want in the first place. No time to think, only to wish, and to know your most immediate desires.

As for me, I see the flash too directly, and it burns reverse colors across my eyes. The picture comes out pink, lips of pink marble. I make my wish for Amy Fine and nothing else. I have to get home now.

Chapter Twenty-Five

Wednesday
Allegro, colla voce

Somehow it got to be the next day, that is the day following, and I awoke, only it wasn't day yet, and yet, I was wide awake. Is this making sense? This hour when I awoke was an early hour, an hour not meant to be experienced by emotionally unstable persons. This used to happen to me on Christmas when I was a kid. I stumbled to my dresser in fuzzy grey light seeping through the blinds and groped for a notepad. Some zombie elf from the night before had looked up Amy Fine's address on the roster of the Westfield College Choir and scribbled the information there on the top sheet; the handwriting looked oddly familiar. I pulled the page from its thread moorings and tucked it into my wallet before I headed to the bathroom for a shower.

She lives in the Rose Garden neighborhood of San Jose, a settlement of elegantly aging homes along wide tree-lined lanes, elms and maples drooping their branches over the sidewalks in a protective hunch. I pull off the main drag and into a garden curlicue of courts and lanes, then make the final right at a brown adobe castle, and there she is, 529 Calle Vista.

Hers is an adorable little English-style cottage, high-pitched roof, square front of clean white stucco, little clay red path winding up through low hedges to a semicircle porch. I park across the street and make my way along the sidewalk like a prowler, hesitant to cross to the other side lest she feel my presence too soon. Is she up? Does it matter? I am too far gone now. I must proceed.

A wiry Vietnamese paperboy rolls by on his big-tread mountain bike and tosses his cargo halfway up her path. A small Siamese cat crosses the yard to sniff at the paper, then jumps back behind the hedges as I approach. I pick up the paper and walk carefully to the porch, carrying the headlines across my heart like a shield. Three, four seconds more and the deed is done, the finger presses the doorbell, and I am fully committed.

I am ready for rejection, but not for how quickly it comes. In the faint morning light I can't be sure, but I believe it is the disheveled face of Amy Fine that appears through the crack of the doorway one half-second before the door slams back, sending out shock waves that stagger me five feet away.

Oh well, if I am going to be stupid, I may as well go full-bozo. I march right up to the wood, thin coat of peeling red paint, and knock assertively. Nothing happens. I try again, only this time I call out, "Amy? Amy, are you there? It's me, Michael."

Nothing. So now I bang hard, three times, madman-loud, and I shout: "Amy! It's Michael! I just want to talk!"

The sound that comes through the door then is like something from a horror film, so firm and low it sends shivers through my heart.

"Go home," she says. "Go...the hell...home."

"Amy, I just want to talk. I know it's early, I know I…Can we just talk?"

Now her voice shoots up three octaves, and she shrieks at me. "What the fuck do you want?! Just go away and leave me alone!" I hear a thump and the door ticks forward. She is leaning against it. She is upset. But she is right past this door. The image of my meteorite is four inches of wood away from me, and I am stuck.

I continue to talk, feeding her reasons, apologies, entreaties, whatever I can dream up short of threatening suicide, but now she is not even answering. Ten minutes later I am ready to give up. I turn my back to her door and sit on the porch, wondering what can I possibly do next? Three states I've crossed, three states back and forth, and now I come up four inches short. The Siamese paces back up the path and sits at my feet, looking for affection. I reach out to scratch him behind the ears, and he gets that squinty-eyed, crunched forehead look, cat ecstasy. If only things were that simple.

I can't keep up my massage for long, though. My hands are worn out from my nine-game bowling injury and a week and a half on the steering wheel. I pull my fingers from his head and squeeze them together for therapy. My cat friend senses this is the end of his fun so he retreats back to the hedges, playing make-believe chase games with a large brown maple leaf.

It is then that I notice the narrowness of Amy's street. I am close enough to the pink Victorian across the way to be in their front yard. Through a crack in the white lace curtains I spot a pair of elderly eyes, checking me out for signs of trouble, domestic disputes, or other possibilities. A minute later a middle-aged Mexicano next door to me starts loading his pickup with landscaping equipment, finishing each thrust over the tailgate with an inquisitive look in my direction. Hmmm, nosy neighbors, narrow street, quiet block. *Great raw material here*, I think. Just the right conditions for making a scene. But how to start? I tuck Amy's newspaper under my arm and pace back and forth along the sidewalk. A song is teasing my mind but not quite coming in, like I am driving through a tunnel and the FM station is fading in and out: *When the...When the...*

Yes! I fling the newspaper to the ground in victory and shoot out both arms, aiming my chest straight at Amy's front door.

"Wheeeeeen thuuuuuuuuuh...moon hits your eye like a big pizza pie, that's amore!"

More volume!

"When the world seems to shine like you've had too much wine, that's amore!!"

Too sweet! Belt it, baby!

"Bells'll ring, tingalingaling, tingalingaling, and you'll sing Vi...ta Bella!"

Yes!

"Hearts'll play, tippy tippy tay, tippy tippy tay, like a gay tarantella!"

I circle as I sing to watch Amy's neighborhood come alive. The Mexicano next door freezes in his tracks, grunting under the weight of a large lawnmower, unable to let it down or load it up from the shock of some crazy white boy singing in his neighbor's yard at six in the morning. The old lady across the street has abandoned her window watch and is now on her porch in the universal stance of indignation, legs shoulder-width, hands firmly on hips, nose straight out like a good bird dog, ready to rush in and call the cops on me in a New York minute.

"Wheeeen thuuuuh...stars make you drool just like pasta fazul, that's amore!"

Two white-faced mutts point their snouts over the fence across the street and start whimpering, then barking, then howling, which rouses every canine within a half-mile radius and brings three more neighbors out their front doors.

"When you dance down the street with a cloud at your feet, you're in love!"

Now with purpose! Grind this sucker up, boys!

"*WHEEEEEN YOOOOOUUUUU WALK IN A DREAM*

BUT YOU KNOW YOU'RE NOT DREAMING, SIGNORE! SCUZA ME, BUT YOU SEE, BACK IN OLD NAPOLI, THAT'S AMORE!!!"

I stop. Every dog in the neighborhood has signed on for backing vocals; a ragged chorus of yips and howls rings itself merrily around the block. Everything else is silence, especially the line of neighbors who stand atop their welcome mats in bathrobes and sweat pants, stunned. The only one who seems to understand is my Mexicano friend next door, who drops his lawn mower with a crash and begins to applaud and hoot. I spin in dizzy elation to check Amy's door.

Nothing. Closed tight. This one's tough, she is. *Well what the fuck*, I think. I yell, "One! More! Time!" and drop to my knees on her lawn:

"WHEEEEN THUUUUH…MOON HITS YOUR EYE LIKE A BIG PIZZA PIE, THAT'S AMORE! WHEN THE WORLD SEEMS TO SHINE, LIKE YOU'VE HAD…"

"Stop! Shut up, for Christ's sake!"

Ah. There she is now. The magic red door swings open, and there stands Amy Fine, frowning under shower-wet hair as she waves me into the house with frantic motions, shouting at me in urgent, foul-mouthed whispers. "For God's sake you lunatic, get in here, fucking Jesus Christ shit, get the hell in this fucking house before you wake up the whole goddamn neighborhood!"

I scoop up Amy's newspaper and run to the door, victorious, past Amy in her blue terry cloth robe and into the house. Amy slams the door behind me and immediately spins around to drop me with a right hook. Some blurry seconds later I find myself eyeball-to-eyeball with the mottled grey carpet of her living room floor, fighting to reattach myself to the steady passing of seconds, rubbing a hand over what feels like a marble casting of someone else's jaw. This is not going to be as easy as I had hoped.

I peer up by and by and find a brass clock over the mantel, and I watch it until I can distinguish the hour hand from the minute hand. My vision slowly clears and I pull myself to a sitting position against the couch. Amy is facing away from me, framed in the light from the kitchen, legs shoulder-width apart, arms stretched down and tight, holding her fists knuckle-white like she is fighting off the urge to choke some small animal. Like me.

She is in on me close-up before I have a chance to catch my breath.

"Just what the fuck do you think you're doing, Michael? What the FUCK…do you THINK…you're DOING?!"

I don't dare to lift an eyebrow, much less speak. I sit there like a sponge, ready to absorb. Her voice is revving up on the letter Y.

"Y…Y…You leave me in a fuckin' cornfield for Christ's sake, you little piss ant mother fucker in a fuckin' CORN-FIELD like fuckin' OKLAHOMA or some shit and you fuckin' LEAVE, leave me with nothin' but your fuckin' tuxedo jacket, *which* by now you should know looks as though it went through several paper shredders. You disappear into the fuckin' *mist* for a week and then you come back *here* and sing me some goddamn DEAN MARTIN tune and wake up every one of my neighbors and…and…and everything's supposed to be just ALL RIGHT!? Is that it, Michael?!

"I've lived in this neighborhood for a long fuckin' time, you know, and I happen to LIKE it here, and they used to think highly of me, but now, now they think I'm some halfway house for lunatic tunesmiths I suppose and just, just, just…"

She is right on top of me now, spitting in my face every time she hits a good consonant, and even though I have no control over my facial functions, I try to move my mouth to form a response. Apparently this pisses her off even further. She grabs a good hunk of hair on the back of my head and gives it a twist as she stands there up against my face, breathing hard, looking like hell's hostess. And she whispers the end of her thought in a growl.

"Just what…is so goddamned…URGENT…that you had to get inside my house just now. *Teeeeeeell* me."

She takes my hair and thrusts my head to the side, pulling

out a few strands as she goes. I am in shock. After my face rebounds off the couch, I sit there, holding my jaw in one hand, my head in the other, hoping she hasn't broken anything. Amy seems to tire. She breathes heavily before falling back into an easy chair, legs and arms flopped over the sides, hair scattered all around her face, hazel eyes still burning a hole right through me.

I have no control over time now, I am adrift in it, I couldn't tell you a minute from a 3/4 measure and we just sit there for what seems like hours, symphonies, staring at each other. When my voice finally squeezes its way out of my lungs and through my mouth, it is someone else's, some collapsed refugee speaking through a chicken-wire screen at a rage-drugged audience.

"I have to tell you a story…" I say, feeling the pins of my jaw warming back into their places. "I have to tell you where I've been, what's happened to me, what I found out…"

Amy continues to stare at me, arms folded across her chest like armor. Any miscue on my part could lead to further beatings, so I pick my words carefully and speak slowly.

"I started out that morning…after I left you…and I didn't know where I was going, but I knew I had to get somewhere, because…I went to Yosemite, I just sort of ended up there…and I found a rock at the river, and the rock meant something. I didn't know what…"

Something clicks. One, two, three, one, two, three *tick tick tick…*

Tick.

"I didn't know what to think. She wanted to take me on a vacation with her, to Hawaii, to make up for everything. She was getting a big tax refund, and she wanted to take me to Hawaii…"

It was going to be me and Stacy alone in a beach front condo on Kauai. She talked about it all the time, every morning over coffee, yeah, it'll just be you and me, won't it be wonderful, Michael? Oh, I love you…

She talked also of Kenny, about how Kenny was getting

drunk almost every night and having fits and continually pushing her to go beyond the borders of their friendship, and it was such a sad thing, she said, because she would do anything to help him but they had such a strong friendship, they were like sister and brother really, and she wouldn't risk that for all the world, but it seemed like she was going to lose him either way.

Two weeks later she told me she needed to cover some unexpected bills, so the vacation wouldn't be to Hawaii, after all, but how would it be if we went up the coast to Mendocino—there's some real nice bed-and-breakfast places up there—oh, wouldn't it be beautiful? I'm sorry we couldn't go to Hawaii, Michael, but there's all those moving expenses to look forward to this June, and I really have to wipe my slate clean before I head off, and times are so tight right now.

And now the softball season had begun, and her friends looked at me the way you look at rotten peaches in the supermarket; this is the young undeserving one and he has entranced one of ours, and he doesn't need her as badly as Kenny does—Kenny is in pain. They were my friends on the field, but elsewhere I knew I was on the wrong side of this.

And then the vacation. My vacation, dammit, I had earned it, after all. Then the vacation kept being pushed back and pushed back. It hasn't gotten here yet, Michael, I don't know what's taking them so long, but I really have to wait until the check comes. Let's go out for dinner tonight, okay? And then we can go watch Joe sing. Maybe he'll let you go up and sing something, wouldn't that be nice? Don't worry. Right after Easter, I promise.

And finally, the weekend before Easter, and I drive over the hill and find out she isn't there, and maybe I knew she wouldn't be there for the game but maybe I thought she would be home afterwards and maybe we could do something, go wine tasting, build a fire at the beach, make love afterwards and hold on tight so the housemates don't hear. And my teammates looking at me as if they knew some deep, terrible secret, and all they would tell me was that Stacy and Kenny had gone away to Monterey for a camping trip, they always went on trips together, no big deal, and they probably just got held up, you know how much she loves shopping in Carmel. And I played along because I didn't want to know the truth, either. And I sat in the quad outside her condo until sunset, and I thought, well, yeah, this really sucks but I'm sure she's got a good reason. She'll call me tomorrow and explain, and I'll drive over the hill for dinner, and I'll bring her roses, and I will have my three months of pleasure, by damn, that is what she owes me, that is what *life* owes me, that is what belongs to me. I am in control now and I have earned these three months.

And her voice on the phone that night, quaking, pregnant with trouble.

"I'm sorry, Michael. I'm sorry I couldn't be around today, but…Michael, I have something to tell you. Kenny and me, well, we camped out at the beach last night, and we had a little too much to drink, and one thing just sort of led to another and things…just…happened."

Tick tick tick tick…

The world stopped. The ticking began in my head and the world just stopped, like God had strung a blanket of fermatas over all the clocks and the whole of my world was waiting for the arms of a conductor to wave everything forward, but the church was closed now and there was no conductor, no Mr. Stutz, no Amy Fine, no late-night public television Leonard Bernstein to save my life from inertia, and my only reaction long frozen minutes later was to ask, How *could one human being do this to another human being?* How did this work? The whole thing smelled of conspiracy, and how could you blame me for thinking some international spy network had hired this odd, attractive devil of a woman to weave me in and out like a yo-yo, catch me, release me, catch me, release me, cut the string and let me sink into the marsh, stunned into powerlessness only minutes after control had returned my finger to the road map?

I tried to call a friend. He wasn't home. It was late. I left the house to take a walk. My housemate saw me heading out the door, saw my glazed, reddening eyes, and asked me if I was okay. She told me not to do anything foolish. Her voice carried a note of genuine worry that only made me feel smaller and more pitiful.

I stumbled to the park, counting my steps over the sidewalks and curbs. The waves of my sobbing reached into my legs and made it hard to walk, but I kept on. My eyes filled with warmth, my nose with moisture, my face swelled against the chill night air. The world in front of me grew more and more distant, and I thought to myself, *I must remember this. I will need this later. I must remember this.* When I reached the park I slumped past the tennis courts and the barbecue pits, up the low mounds of grass to the field, where I found my favorite tree, a rough-barked silk oak I would lean against while I read my novels in the early evenings. I knelt beside it and hung my arms around its torso, letting the sweet roughness of its bark scratch against my cheek. Take careful note of these tears, I thought. I will remember where the salt settles across my face, where it burns the skin, and the tears falling into roots and wine-smelling soil and hoping to God I wouldn't use up all the water in my body.

When I finish the story I begin to cry for the first time since, and this is the feeling I remember, buried in the cornrow threads of a terry cloth robe, the world smelling of Amy Fine's hair and her sweet shower soap dampness. But the tears will not cut into my skin this time, nor sap the moisture from my body. They will only break through the stone, open up the cracks, and ready the land for rain.

Chapter Twenty-Six

Six Months Later
Coda

I hold a sweet vision from my days of ritual. I am shooting hoops at the Catholic schoolyard, sweating through my clothes, and I have set myself a difficult task before I can go home. The sun is a half-hour gone. Storm clouds have come in on the night, and the only light remaining is a peach pie slice of afterglow under the front, over the mountains.

I am standing on the out-of-bounds line thirty feet away, setting the hoop in the center of that sepia light, and telling myself I must sink this shot before I go. It is the only thing left. I shoot one off the front rim. I shoot one off the back rim. I shoot one in-and-out. I shoot one that misses the backboard completely and bounces off the metal poles behind. Ten shots more, and I am exhausted and fed up and willing to try anything, so I scoop the basketball up in one hand, reach back like a baseball pitcher, and hurl it high into the air. The ball disappears into the darkening clouds. The only thing I can see is my slice of light past the hoop, and so it is there that I look. The basketball drops from the sky and bullets straight in, hitting the bottom of the net so hard that it jumps back up a notch before falling peacefully through. I smile to myself and pull one fist back toward the other. It's time to go home.

I was happily unemployed for a month after I returned, watching the interest pile up on my very expensive vacation through the Pacific Northwest. Don't believe the promises of plastic eagles. Roxy Cater called and tried to patch things up, but there was no reason left for me to let my brains rot out in the halls of National Auto Credit. I told her no thanks but wished her well, and I hope she knows I meant it. A month later, Sasha Novesceu got promoted to managing editor of the *Eagle*, and I took the position of arts editor. I'm really scratching now, and I may have to give up my apartment as the rent continues to rise, but my mind is happy and full with a diet of plays, concerts, operas, and nightclubs.

Spring training will be here in another few weeks, and I am missing it badly, feeling like I must be part labrador, longing to chase balls through the dewy March grass and fetch them back to the pitcher. And always, looking for that karmic moment. I will rejoin Catch This, but it will be a much-changed team from years past. The days of free love and beerball are dying out as my teammates enter their forties and learn how to spell C-H-O-L-E-S-T-E-R-O-L.

Amy Fine and I shared some wonderful times. She was my key back to the river, and now I am in it up to my neck, running upstream with both arms pumping. She and I didn't last long, but we managed to concoct a romance with all the charm and spice of a Mozart sonata. Perhaps just a little bit too much trauma and violence in the beginning, but of course most of that was my fault. Oh, I know, it seemed like Amy and I would find that elusive storybook ending, but great sex and noble conflict is no guarantor of eternal bliss. This is the real world, and sometimes things just don't last. In any case, she pushed me back into life, and for this I am grateful beyond description.

And that's not all. Amy taught me enough about conducting that I became the tenor section leader of the Westfield College Choir. Imagine that. This spring we perform Mozart's Requiem with the San Jose Symphony, and I look forward with especial fondness to relearning the mysteries of the *Lacrymosa* with the eyes and arms of a teacher. Amy has given me Mozart twice now; to ask much more would be greedy and foolish. Sometimes I can barely believe all the things that I'm doing.

In Alex Blanche I have found my long-lost best friend. We've dropped the bit with the mister this and sir that, but we've kept the mutual respect and the *adagio* conversations. He's worked out his spousal troubles just fine, fixing his schedule so he's able to spend more time with his wife. I met her, and now I know why he was always so lonesome without her. She's wonderful. They're both wonderful. We're going over tomorrow to watch the Super Bowl with them.

We? Oh yes. I'm going out with Brownie now. Oh, I know, her real name is Sheila, but she likes it when I call her Brownie. You see, a couple months after I broke up with Amy, one of Brownie's letters was delivered to my mailbox by mistake. I was not about to let lightning strike twice with no result. Remind me to tip my mail carrier.

Tonight I am taking Brownie to an old Fred Astaire flick at the Varsity. It's the one with that great song: "Three A.M., no one in the place, just you and me…" I forget the title, but you know it. Brownie's no singer—what's that old joke? she couldn't carry a tune if it had a handle on it—but that's okay. Fred and I can supply all the vocals we need, and maybe later I'll dance her through the kitchen.